SURVIVING JOY

SURVIVING
JOY

A NOVEL

JP MILLER

DONALD I. FINE, INC.
New York

Library of Congress Catalogue Card Number: 94-061911
ISBN: 1-55611-448-6

Manufactured in the United States of America

10 9 8 7 6 5 4 3 2 1

Designed by Irving Perkins Associates, Inc.

For Ingo and Kate

ONE

EVERY NIGHT AROUND nine or nine-fifteen I started listening for
the rusted-through muffler of Dad's pickup truck. He'd leave
the job around four-thirty and drive straight to Steve's Place
over on East Eleventh Street and put in the next four hours more or
less drinking beer and shooting the breeze and playing bar games and
whatever people do in honkytonks, and then he would head for
home. You couldn't set your watch by his routine, but he didn't vary
by more than fifteen or twenty minutes. He knew just how drunk he
could get and still drive, and how late he could go to bed and still get
up at five feeling like a day's work. His coming home was an excuse
for me to quit trying to concentrate on my books for a few minutes,
until he sailed through the living room and into the middle bedroom,
throwing me a jovial and blurry "How y'doin', Cowboy?" on his way.
He usually needed about one minute to undress, stretch out on the
single bed, and start to snore, but on this night, by nine-thirty, he still
hadn't come home, and his lateness made it even harder for me to
keep my mind on what I needed to keep it on. There was something
missing from my life, something I couldn't talk about with Mom or
anybody else, except my friend Chester. It interfered with my studying. Sometimes before an exam I couldn't focus on the subject, and
later I couldn't sleep. I'd go to class exhausted, do poorly on the
exam, come home depressed and wanting a nap but needing to hit
the books again. Tonight was one of those nights. I got so tired of
staring at the page and not seeing anything I closed my eyes and let
my mind go where it had been trying to go all evening.

1

"You're not asleep, are you, honey?"

I almost jumped out of my skin. It was Mom, three feet in front of me. She had this light way of floating silently over a floor and seeming to materialize out of the air. Her voice was light, too. It belonged to hidden sadness. "You've been studying so hard, honey. I thought a nice cup of tea might perk you up." She was carrying a tray with two cups of green tea and some oatmeal cookies. She had read my thoughts, no doubt about it. It was only nine-thirty. Her habit was to come out of her room around ten-thirty with her *Science and Health with Key to the Scriptures* folded over a finger, lean down, smelling of spring flowers, kiss me goodnight, sniff to see if I'd been smoking, say "Goodnight, honey, don't stay up too late," and go back to her room and close the door. But tonight she was a full hour ahead of one of her most dependable schedules. She'd said to me a thousand times, "We're creatures of habit, Dubby." So why would she do this strange thing if she hadn't heard my thoughts?

She sat beside me on the creaky wicker sofa. She was one of those people, like Abraham Lincoln, who could look beautiful and homely at the same time. She was only in her mid-forties, but she already had a full set of false teeth. They had been made for her at the School of Dentistry for a greatly reduced fee, and they hurt her mouth. Still, in the yellow light of my one study lamp, with her Scottish fair skin and blue eyes, and her sculpted Cherokee face, she seemed ineffably beautiful. Maybe this was because of the deep compassion she felt for other people's woes.

"You've been pretty troubled the last few days, Dubby," she said.

I thought I'd kept up my normal breezy attitude, including singing bits of arias off-key and improvising on the upper end of "Chopsticks" with Jenny. But Mom had antennae that were at times almost supernatural. She attributed this to her large dose of aboriginal blood. I knew there was no point in saying she was wrong, so I said she was right: It was this stupid trigonometry. "Howsomever, Mom," I said, with a little verbal swagger, "I've got my loop on 'er, she's down, and by the time the brandin' iron's hot, I'll have her hocks wrapped tight."

Mom's eyes got shiny. I was her scholar, with all the nobility, spirituality, sensitivity, and intellect she had prayed for in her son. "I know you will, honey." she whispered. We were keeping our voices down because little Jenny was sleeping with her dolly in the front bedroom just a few feet away. We drank our tea and nibbled on cookies. She didn't seem concerned about Dad's lateness. She had something else on her mind. "You know, honey, I noticed last Saturday night you got home real early from your date with Betty, much earlier than usual."

"Yes, ma'am. Well, Betty's mom's one of the readers at their church now, so—"

"A reader! Oh, my, she must be a wonderful woman. It's an honor to be chosen a reader."

"Yes'm. So she kind of wants Betty to come home earlier now, and come to church on Sundays."

"Well, I can understand that, absolutely. So that's it. Betty must be a wonderful girl. I've always let you sleep on Sundays, honey, because you were out with Betty, and youth must be served, like they say, but since you'll be coming home earlier now, maybe you could come with me to our church this Sunday."

"Yes'm. Well, I could, if you want, but if I get home early on Saturday, sometimes I like to study awhile, and anyhow, Sunday's still the only day I get to sleep late."

"I know. I understand. Absolutely. You and Betty like each other, though, don't you—a lot?"

"Well, yes'm. I mean, you know, we're not in love or anything, but—"

"I understand, honey." She read me a short poem about taking your troubles to the Lord in prayer. Poems about the Lord always made me squirm. While she read I stared at the safety pin that was holding her robe together on the side. This robe was a miracle of mends and patches. It was the kind of thing the Salvation Army would not have accepted.

After the poem she expressed her opinions on some of the important events in the news. I was not expected to comment, just to listen and learn. I didn't mind this because I hadn't acquired a comprehensive view of world affairs, and I was sure that almost everybody knew more about them than I did. She touched on Japanese aggression in China ("Those people are always fighting"), the continuing search for Amelia Earhart ("She's alive, absolutely. She knows her onions, that gal"), and of course the Nazis ("Roosevelt will find a way to get us into that war, mark my words, absolutely"). Mom believed that FDR had a hand in just about everything that was wrong in the world. By the time she had kissed me and told me not to stay up too late and gone back to her room I was almost convinced that she was waiting for my friend Chester to call, so she could get an idea of what we talked about. But naturally if he had called while she was there we wouldn't've talked about what we always talked about.

As I watched her disappear I thought, Mom, I honor you and love you, but my platonic personal life has got to be revised. If I can get a little of what I'm always thinking about, I'll be able to put it in its proper place in an ordered existence and concentrate on passing trig.

This was not going to be as easy for me as it seemed to be for most people. First of all, even though I was already seventeen, I was practically a virgin except for having been seduced when I was twelve by Mrs. Sandusky, who used to live across the road from us down in Matagorda County. Mrs. Sandusky was a mother, and I had been taught to respect mothers, so when she started playing with me, and I got hard as a hammer handle even though I didn't want to be, and she kissed it and almost swallowed it, and told me I was already as big as a full-grown man, I started practically having a nervous breakdown on the spot, and I shook for a couple of weeks afterward like I had the palsy.

This lady was about the nerviest individual I ever bumped into. She would come across the road and chat with my mother and have a cup of tea with her and then ask if I could come over to her house and fix the back screen door and my mother always said yes. I would hang back because I was afraid if I did it again I would either have a heart attack or Mr. Sandusky would come home while I was in the short rows and shoot me, or both. Mom thought it was because I was lazy and didn't want to patch the screen. Mrs. Sandusky even showed Mom, right in front of me, where a mosquito had bit her on the top of her leg pretty far above her knee, on account of that hole in her screen. She flashed me a little bit when she did this, and I had to walk away with my hand in my pocket, but all this was lost on Mom, who was a good neighbor and wouldn't think of letting Mrs. Sandusky get bitten by bugs on account of her boy being too lazy to help. Besides, Mrs. Sandusky always gave me a quarter for taking care of her problem, and I gave the quarter to Mom for groceries, and that made it a good deal.

I loved and admired my mother and contended that she was a

4

brainy lady, but where sizing up people was concerned she was like a customer in a three-card monte game.

This project with Mrs. Sandusky ended all of a sudden when they moved away. A neighbor from down the bay road told my mother that Mr. Sandusky found out that Mrs. Sandusky had been showing her mosquito bites to the pastor of the church, but my mother said she would not believe that if somebody tied her hand and foot and drug her behind a horse all the way to Palacios, absolutely. Nobody asked me my opinion, because I was twelve.

Anyhow, that was the end of my sex life, at least with other people, right up to and including this night of trigonometric futility. I just didn't know how to go about getting it going. I kept waiting for some lady to fondle me and stick her tongue in my ear like Mrs. Sandusky did, but none of my mother's other women friends seemed to be into anything but poetry and reading and recipes and discussing *Science and Health with Key to the Scriptures.*

So I was glad when Chester called me, no matter how late it was or how much I didn't know about what I was being quizzed on at Rice Institute the next day, because what I was learning from Chester was life, Life, a subject I was failing in, a subject my mother wanted me to keep failing in.

We had moved to Houston so I could graduate from a city high school and be close to Rice, which didn't charge tuition, and to get my mother close to my father, geographically at least, so that they could move back under one roof—a financial decision rather than an amorous one, this being the sixth year of the Great Depression. If they hadn't done this, I wouldn't've been able to go to college, even a free one like Rice. I'd've had to hook up with another construction gang, pushing a wheelbarrow or being water boy or shoveling rocks into a concrete mixer for twenty-five cents an hour, like I was doing the summer I met Chester. There weren't any real jobs around, and the only reason I was able to get the donkey-work was that my father was a job boss for a construction company. Twenty-five cents an hour might not sound like much, but it beat hell out of a dollar a day, which is what they were paying down in Matagorda County for working shrimp nets or stretching barbed wire or cowboying.

When I quit the construction gang to start college, my father didn't say anything, but I could tell he thought it was kind of putting on airs for a poor boy to quit a paying job in the middle of a Depression, for any reason whatsoever.

Chester came right out with it. He called me a dumb-ass. "Where you gonna git cigarette money? Where you gonna git the money to git girls drunk and take 'em to motels? Ever think about that? You are too downright pitiful dumb to think ahead!"

I was pretty worried about Chester's opinion, because he was several years older than I was, and knew a lot more about Life than I did. He used to show up on the job just about every day with his eyes looking like dead cockroaches and his mouth tasting, he said, like a wrestler's jockstrap, and a whole herd of buffalo stampeding through his head but with a story of conquest to tell that made it all seem like a cheap price to pay. He'd describe the girl's parts, public and private, how she moved, what she said, even the noises she made when all of a sudden she commenced to spasm like a bigmouth bass trying to shake the hook. One day while we were having our sandwiches in the shade of a trailer he got so carried away imitating the way this girl gasped when his drill bit struck oil that he got a piece of baloney stuck in his throat and came pretty close to choking to death till an old Mexican concrete puddler punched him in the solar plexus and made him throw it up.

I couldn't let Chester tell me all this stuff without giving something in return, so I lied a lot about what was going on in my life. I told him I was going out steady with a really fine girl, which I was, and that I was humping her ears off, which I wasn't. I described all the places we did it, including my mother's gray Dodge, and Heights Cliffs in broad daylight, and even King Courts on South Main when we had the money. Everything Mrs. Sandusky did to me down in Matagorda County I ascribed to Betty, and I have to say that Chester was impressed that a girl could be considered by her mother and my mother and the whole community as being a nice girl and still get away with doing all those interesting tricks. I hated to lie like that about Betty, but I knew that Chester would never meet her, and I told him the wrong name anyhow, just in case.

For some reason Chester called earlier than usual on this Thursday night, right after Mom went back to her room. He had a girl he wanted me to meet. She was the first cousin of his latest discovery, the untamed critter, he said, who had reminded him that humping was like butchering a hog—everything was usable. He didn't think

6

he was going to have the time or the strength to tackle this cousin hisself, and he didn't want her to go to waste.

"Well, thanks, Chester, but—" I turned my back to the part of the house where my mother's bedroom was, and kept my voice down low. "I don't have the dinero for going out on a date right now."

"Tol' ye, ditten I? Pinbrain son of a bitch. Shuttena quit yer job!"

"And anyhow, I've got this trigonometry exam—"

We arranged for me to meet Hilda that Friday afternoon after I had my exam. Chester would take us riding in his car (He had made carpenter's apprentice and was getting forty cents an hour now), and he would pay for the Cokes and cheeseburgers and bring a bottle of Southern Comfort and we could park out at Heights Cliffs. "You can fuck Hilda in the back seat," he said, "while I fuck Susie in the front." He and Susie usually used the back seat because there was more room, but since I was his guest and his buddy, and it was me and Hilda's first time, he wanted it to be his treat.

He and Susie went to motels a lot now, he said, since he was making forty cents, and he knew the night manager at King Courts, so "Mr. and Mrs. Johnny Jones" signing in one night and "Mr. and Mrs. David Copperfield" another night and so on didn't get anybody in trouble. It was against the law to check into a public inn with a person other than your legal spouse. The manager was even supposed to write down the license numbers of the cars that came to King Courts, and Chester's buddy did, but he always got his number wrong on purpose. Chester said he wished he could afford to rent a two-bedroomer so we could have a hell of a party and play switch with Susie and Hilda, but two couples checking in together got the attention of the vice squad sometimes, and they'd come and knock on the door and ask to see your marriage license, and if you didn't have some proof of matrimony they'd run you in unless you had a ten-dollar bill to use as an argument against it.

As soon as we hung up I knew I wasn't going to get my mind back on inverse hyperbolic sines again this night, not that it had been. It was only about ten-fifteen, and I could still hear the crowd in the park, watching the fights. I slipped on my cowboy boots and my beat-up Stetson and went to Mom's room and told her I was going out for a walk. She was propped up in bed studying her "lesson," which consisted of reading *Science and Health* and referring to the Bible according to a plan in the Christian Science Quarterly. I knew the thrill

7

of her life would be for me to say "Mom, I've finished my trigonometry; can we study the lesson together?" But I couldn't make my tongue form the words. It would never happen. I'd probably get interested in trig first. She was aware that I was going to smoke while I was out walking, and probably even look at those loose girls that hung around the park, but she didn't say anything. Her way of handling these dangerous inharmonies was to "know the truth." She offered me a nickel for ice cream, which I accepted, and told me to have a nice walk.

At that exact moment we heard the special sound of Dad's muffler coming toward the house. He was later, and therefore probably drunker, than usual. Not that he ever came home staggering or mean; the only difference was that he was more garrulous, sometimes, which was embarrassing in its foolishness, at least to me. We heard his pickup truck skid in its usual way as it swung into our driveway. Drunk or sober, Dad drove like he was bulldogging a steer, so Mom and I deemed everything to be normal. It was not until we heard the other car, following close behind him, that we realized something different was going on. A troubled shadow passed across Mom's face. No matter how tanked up he got after work, Dad would never be so unwise as to bring one of his honkytonk buddies home with him and risk the polar ice cap Mom could create without raising her voice. The pickup slid to a violent stop in front of the garage. We heard the car behind it, too, heavy and solid and richly humming, as it stopped without skidding. Mom looked out the side window. She took a deep breath, and muttered "It's Dixie" in the same voice she would have used to say "smallpox."

I joined Mom at the window and put my hand on her back. She was rigid as a post. The sight—sometimes even the thought—of Aunt Dixie always made her stomach knot. She would never admit that she hated Aunt Dixie, because her religion told her not to hate, but the presence of the woman often made her physically ill; sometimes she had to go throw up as quietly as possible before she could manage anything else. It was apparent that Aunt Dixie had come to sleep over; she had driven the one hundred and twenty miles up from Espada, no doubt by prearrangement with Dad, though nobody had bothered to tell Mom she was coming. This was standard practice for Aunt Dixie and Uncle Boo. When they came to Houston they didn't ask to stay with us or wait to be invited, and no notification was considered necessary. They treated our house as their house and Mom as the woman responsible for doing the cooking and cleaning and making them comfortable. When Dad first brought Mom home to Espada as his bride, according to Mom, all the family gathered to meet her, having been apprised of her bloodlines, which were very important to most people in that part of the world. The first thing Aunt Dixie said to her was, "Well, I swan, you sure don't like like a Indian!"

Mom was blue-eyed and blond, but in profile she looked like the sister of the man on the buffalo nickel. Dad said, "Well, Dixie, she's half Cherokee, but she has always lived white."

"Well, as far as I can see, if you're half Indian you're Indian, just like if you're half nigger you're a nigger. But that's fine with me, Billy. You're my big brother, and she's your wife, and I'm gonna treat her like family."

Mom told me that the worst part about it was that the rest of the family didn't seem to be embarrassed about Dixie's bad manners, so she was probably speaking for all of them, and later on when they were all at table eating chicken and dumplings cooked up by Grandmother Johnson, Dixie suddenly burst out with "Well, I'll be hornswoggled! You coulda knocked me over with a feather, Billy, when Mama told me you done gone went and married a squaw!" Mom said that at that moment, even though Dad protected her with a gallantry he'd never shown since, telling Aunt Dixie not to ever talk like that to his wife again, she had never been able to feel happy around the Johnson family. Something shriveled up inside her, and whenever Aunt Dixie was around, Mom could hardly hold her shoulders up straight and look people in the eye. She had been branded a squaw, with the pejorative meaning of the time: tepee dweller, government ward; she knew she was a person, a free citizen, but somehow she could never quite rise to her full height around Aunt Dixie. Once, when we lived in Matagorda County, at a time when my father was not there, Mom had got a fat envelope full of documents from somewhere in Oklahoma. Everything looked very official. She had sat down at the kitchen table and studied these papers for hours by the light of a kerosene lamp. Then she had gone to the fireplace and put them in the fire, one by one, watching with squinted eye and tight mouth till every scrap was burned. Then she had explained to me that we could have shared a big piece of oil land if we'd gone to live on a reservation. I didn't understand. Did she mean we'd be rich?

"No. We'd've had a lot of money, but we wouldn't've been rich. We'd've been reservation Indians. I don't want to be an Indian. I want to be a citizen. And that's what I want for you too, honey. Don't ever give that up for anything. That's the best thing there is."

Still, when she was around Aunt Dixie, there was a little bit of reservation Indian, she told me, a little bit of squaw in her. She did not quite have the strength to rise above it. She hoped she would, one day.

And now here was Aunt Dixie, tacky in a pair of green slacks and a pink blouse, her fingernails and her lipstick red as fresh blood, half drunk, standing in the headlights between her Chrysler and Dad's pickup, talking in a low voice with him, urgently and conspiratorially, settling something they had to get settled before coming into the house.

"Dubby, honey, if you're going to take a walk, you'd better ske-daddle out the front door," Mom said, clicking her teeth together between every two or three words, gearing up to face the devil with a serene face.

"Yes, ma'am. Thanks, Mom." I was glad to escape. My being there wasn't going to make the situation any better for her.

Heights Park only took up part of a block, and it wasn't much of a park as parks go, with a few swings, seesaws, benches, a couple of tables where old men played checkers, and a grassy area where on most Thursday nights a makeshift ring was set up for the amateur boxing matches. There was nothing official about the fights or the equipment. The ring measurements were guessed at, and a cord was stretched between stakes driven in the ground. If a fighter fell against the cord, the stakes fell over and the fight was halted till the ring was repaired. There were no managers, no seconds, and no ringside physician. The fighters were mostly daredevil high school and college boys, or local toughs who loved to hit people, legally or otherwise. The spectators were the fighters' sweethearts or pals, sometimes their proud fathers, boys like me who were more interested in watching the girlfriends than the fights, and a few locals with nothing better to do than watch two unskilled young males throw wild haymakers at each other. The combat usually lasted less than the scheduled three rounds. If a warrior got knocked down, he often stayed down, being winded and grateful for the excuse, especially if he was wounded. Frequently a sweetheart or a brother or a father would jump in the ring and stop the action when eyes threatened to puff shut or lips were split. There was no big ignominy in this, no championship at stake, and—usually—no money. The fights seldom turned vicious unless two fathers bet on their sons against each other, or two local rowdies got in the ring to settle a grudge.

The minute I joined the little crowd near the ring, Roscoe Baill collared me. "Tex," he said, "I was hopin' you'd show. We got important biness together."

Roscoe had a nine-to-five job as a laborer in a mill that squeezed oil out of cottonseed. He always had that heavy, sweet smell of cottonseed oil on him. If he was within ten feet of you and you had your eyes closed, you'd say to yourself, "Oh, Roscoe's here." I'm sure he took plenty of baths, and washed his clothes once in a while too, probably, but when you crush a cottonseed you get an odor that won't quit. I often wondered why Roscoe worked so hard organizing the fights. He didn't do any of the fighting, but he spent hours on the phone convincing people to take part and to show up to watch. Maybe he just liked to watch fights. Or maybe he had dreams of discovering a Jack Dempsey, or a white Joe Louis, and getting rich. There was no chance of him discovering a black Joe Louis, because this was a white neighborhood, and if a young black man showed up for any reason except to cut grass or shine shoes, or if he showed up for any reason at all after dark, the local toughs would gleefully punch him and kick him into unconsciousness. Then some merchant would call a black ambulance from a black hospital and tell them to come get him, just to get him off the street to keep the neighborhood looking nice. The ambulance would come and take him away to the hospital or the morgue, and that would be the end of it.

There were a lot of white people in the Heights who believed this was a deplorable social situation, and some people even spoke out publicly against it. They were called nigger lovers and considered by the majority of churchgoing citizens to be traitors to their community.

The good of the community was what Roscoe wanted to talk to me about. There was a lull in the fighting as the next two contestants stripped off their shirts and stepped into the ring and stood while their gloves were laced on, and their friends shouted encouragement to them:

"That sissy cutten squash a fly, Charlie!"

"Bust 'im a good 'n on that beak he calls a nose, Cal!"

Roscoe had me by the arm. "Tex," he said, confidentially, "somethin' big's goin' on." He had a mouth like a slit in a wide piece of meat, and when he spoke confidentially, leaning close, his lips squirmed like a couple of parallel fishing worms. "We gonna commence to have intramural fight nights with other Houston parks. It's big. Citywide. Community pride. Foller me? You gotta help me, Tex. The first team of fighters is comin' here next week from—guess where? River Oaks. RiverfuckinOaks! Them's them rich sonsabitches. They got shorts with their names on 'em, boxin' shoes, cups —even mouthpieces! And they got everything from flyweight to heavyweight. You know where we're weak? Middleweight. I got Spooky Harnett willin' to go, but he cain't fight his way through a cobweb. We got to win this one, Tex. We cain't let them rich bastards beat us, not us, Heights Park. You got to fight middleweight for me. You cain't let me down. You cain't let the neighborhood down. This here is us agin them. We got to win it. I know you can fight, Tex. I seen you throw a baseball. Anybody that can throw a baseball like that has got to have a good overhand right. And you got a good left, too. You're fast. You got the reach. You keep that left out there, pop pop pop pop pop pop pop, then when you got the guy droppin' his left to try to cover up, you come over with that overhand right. Outta here! Eat grass! Ten and out! Best set of punches in the world. That kraut Schmeling whupped Joe Louis with that overhand right. Bam. And you got it. Don't let me down, Tex. We need you. Heights Park needs you. Whattaya say?"

My mind whizzed through every possible escape plan without coming up with one that wouldn't leave me looking chicken. Roscoe took my hesitation to mean I was too modest to consider myself worthy of a place on his team. I gave him this notion by muttering "Aw, hell, Roscoe, you're bound to know plenty of guys that can handle themselves better in the ring than me."

"I got good boys, no question, Tex. But I ain't got no middleweight. You had the gloves on a few times, ain't you?"

"I had a few bare-knuckle encounters, like everybody else, but fighting in the ring, hell, Roscoe, I don't know beans."

"There ain't nothin' to know! You're fast. I seen that lightnin' fast glove o' yours snag line drives on the pitcher's mound woulda went right past ninety-nine out of a hunnert pitchers into center field. I seen you whistle that fast ball past them boys, ffft! What's to know? Put on gloves, pop that left in the guy's face, popopop, throw that overhand up side his ear, lights out. You got a kayo punch, Tex. Don't let it go to waste. Heights Park needs you, boy."

The fighters were ready. Both wore the long pants they'd worn all day. One was barefoot, and the other wore the hightop workshoes with cleated soles he'd worked in through his eight-hour shift on a road gang. They wore real, regulation boxing gloves, but there was no thought of protective cups, jockstraps, taped hands, or mouthpieces. These were considered sissy frills by park fighters. Only boxers from places like River Oaks would wear such unmanly contraptions. Of course, professionals wore them, but they were forced to, it was said, by Boxing Commission rules. It was generally believed they would've preferred to fight it out with no gloves and no rules, back-alley style. This was the image most of them created with their talk before a fight.

Roscoe was the announcer, timekeeper, referee, and sole judge. He said, "Hang around, Tex, and I'll give you some more pointers. We got to win this deal."

"I'm studying for an exam. I just came out for a walk, Roscoe." I started to add that I wasn't a middleweight, anyhow, only coming in at 145 pounds soaking wet, but I figured if I said that he'd want me to fight as a welter. Most people guessed my weight wrong on account of my height and my high-heeled boots and tall hat, and the loose shirt I wore and the way I hunched my shoulders forward to make them look broader. I knew it was fakey to try to look bigger than I was, but I couldn't seem to break myself of the habit.

"Jes stay put fer a minute," Roscoe said. "This'll maybe go one round, tops."

He hurried into the ring, being careful not to touch the cord and knock over the stakes. "You boys all set?" he asked. They nodded. Roscoe went into his announcer's act. "Folks," he raised his voice, although there weren't more than thirty people at ringside, "folks, this ought to be a doozy. In this corner is Mad Dog Murphy, one hunnert an' thirty-two pounds. Mad Dog comes from West Fifteenth Street. A couple of months ago Mad Dog went three rounds to a decision over Wily Willy Polk from Heights Boulevard. In this here corner we got Carl "Kayo" Burke, one hunnert an' twenny-eight pounds. Kayo hails from over Studewood way."

Both boys looked to be about my age and at least as scared as I would've been in their place. Roscoe called them to the center of the ring and said: "Awright, boys, le's have a good clean fight now, and when I say break, break and don't hit below the belt, and may the best man win. Go back to your corners and come out fighting when I say go."

There were no stools in the corners. Roscoe had a watch with a sweep second hand. He stared at it, raised his right hand, and barked, "Go!"

Both boys sprang forward, swinging roundhouse rights. Both missed. They lost their balance, fell into a clinch, and wrestled each other to the grass.

"Awright! Slip! No knockdown! Git up and git to a neutral corner! Gotta wipe yer gloves."

The two boys, both panting as though they had fought ten rounds, untangled themselves, jumped up and went to the same neutral corner, discovered their mistake, and both tried to go to the other neutral corner at the same time. The small crowd laughed. Roscoe jumped in between them.

"Hold it, hold it, Kayo. You there, and you there, Mad Dog." He looked for his towel to wipe off the gloves. It had been hanging on the cord that defined the ring but had fallen to the grass. He went to pick it up. The two boys jogged in place and glared at their feet.

I backed out of the crowd and went home.

TWO

I F IT HADN'T BEEN after eleven o'clock I'd've come down the alley and through the back gate to save half a block, but I didn't want to set off the dogs in the backyard of the Clancy house behind us. Once they got started they kept up a three-hound chorus for an hour. So I came home along Seventeenth Street, to the front of the house. Dad and Aunt Dixie were in the front bedroom. I could see them— Aunt Dixie piled up in Jenny's bed and Dad in a straight chair beside her—discussing something serious, pondering with stupid, beery looks on their faces, leaning close together to keep their voices down. I walked silently down the driveway past Aunt Dixie's big shiny Chrysler; I could smell the newness of it. I wanted to get in it and start it and listen to that big jungle cat purring under the hood; but I was repelled by it too, because it belonged to Aunt Dixie and Uncle Boo, and that meant that elegant as it was, it had been smeared with an invisible film of meanness that could never be polished away or painted over. I sneaked into the house through the back door and saw that Mom's light was still on, the dim bedside lamp, so I tapped once and opened her door and tiptoed in to kiss her goodnight. She was just sitting in a straight chair, looking bleak, not reading, staring off into the emptiness. Her shoulders were down. I wanted to say something to cheer her up, but I couldn't think of anything, and besides, little Jenny was asleep on a pallet on the floor with her face turned away from the light. Mom turned it off as soon as I came into the room. She had left it on only so I would know she was waiting up for me. I kissed her and went out and went to bed in the middle bedroom in the twin bed next to the window. I knew that Dad would finish talking with his sister after a while and come in and lie down on the other bed and start to snore in fifteen seconds after his head hit the pillow. In spite of their beer they kept their voices down. I could only catch a stray word now and then. Finally I heard Dad say, "Well, you handle it, Dix, and good luck. My alarm goes off at five." Then he came into the middle bedroom and shut the door behind him. I acted like I was asleep.

The next morning I heard the breakfront open in the dining room, and the subdued clink of plates and silverware. Dad was long gone, and Mom was setting the table with her good china, which wasn't very good, and her best silverplate for Aunt Dixie. I could smell bacon and cornbread. Mom was trying to be a good hostess to her husband's sister and to prove to herself she didn't hate her, and probably to overcome the squawness she was feeling. I went in the bathroom and washed up. Then while I was dressing for school I heard Aunt Dixie come out of the front bedroom and exclaim, "My goodness, Letty, I coulda ate in the kitchen!"

From the low volume and brevity of Mom's response I could tell that her shoulders were still down. When I got into the dining room, which was only big enough for the breakfront and the six straight chairs that went with the table and a path barely wide enough to walk all the way around it, there was Aunt Dixie sitting at the head, and Mom serving her a big fluffy cheese and tomato omelette with bacon and hot buttered toast. I could smell that it was real butter, so Mom must've gone next door and borrowed it from Mrs. Glaros, who was always up early getting her husband off to his job driving the ice delivery truck. "Goodness gracious sakes alive, Letty!" Aunt Dixie said. "You remembered my favorite kinda omelette!" Then she beamed at me with her mouth full and said, "Good morning, Dubby!" with that phony exuberance that always put me on my guard and made me wonder more than ever why she had driven all the way up from Espada to spend the night at our house. The one thing I remembered most about Aunt Dixie was that she didn't wash up in the morning and didn't brush her teeth, and her breath would knock a mule down at fifteen paces. That part had not changed. "Letty, this is my kind of coffee—hot and strong!" She was drinking it black, which might help her breath in time. She was dressed in the same shamrock green slacks and loud pink blouse she had on last night. She took drags of her Camel while she had her mouth full of food. It would've done me a world of good to hear Mom say she hated her, because I hated her, Mom's religion not having got a hold on me yet and, though I would never have said it out loud, not having much chance of ever doing so.

Then I realized that there was another reason Mom was serving—and always had served—Aunt Dixie in the dining room instead of the kitchen—a reason Mom might not even be aware of herself: the kitchen was where she fed the people she loved, and she didn't want Aunt Dixie to contaminate it.

I ate fast because I had to leave for school and also because I didn't like being at the table with Aunt Dixie, and I didn't want to hang around and find out what she had on her mind.

She noticed I was rushing. "What time do you have to be in class, Dubby?"

"In about forty-five minutes."

"You got plenty time. I'm going right there. I'll drop you."

Mom had not sat down with us, but she was hearing everything from the kitchen. She came to the door. "Oh, we don't want to be any trouble to you, Dixie. Take your time. He'll get the bus."

"No, Letty, I want 'im here. I got to talk to y'all two. Why don't you come on and set down with us?"

"Well, I'm giving Jenny her breakfast." Jenny had automatically stayed in the kitchen to eat. She didn't like Aunt Dixie either. Good for her.

"She's big enough to git her own grub, Letty. Don't spoil your kids." Aunt Dixie didn't have children, so she knew all about how to raise them. "This won't take long. Come on, set down, Letty."

I could see Mom struggling against the squawness that Aunt Dixie's cruelty had inoculated her with such a long time ago; she hesitated for several seconds, her eyes darting, her lips pressed together; then she lost her battle and slipped into a seat across from Aunt Dixie.

"Letty," Aunt Dixie said, lighting a fresh Camel, "my brother is a very smart man, a engineer. And he is wasting his life working for contractors that use his brains and lay 'im off when they feel like it, an' hire 'im back when they feel like it, which ought not to be, with a man of his brains. By the way, remind me, Letty, I got some stuff in the car, couple dresses and stuff my cousin Val's kids grew out of, it'll fit Jenny, and it's hardly wore atall, plenty good still. Le's git to the point. I got to git back to Espada. Boo's there all by hisself, with nobody to take care of the pastry counter, so I'll make this short and sweet. Me and Boo want to put Billy in bidness. He can be rich. There's a new thing, and we want to git in on the ground floor. It's gonna be big. Prefabricated houses. Prefabs, they call 'em. Maybe you read about 'em." Mom nodded, looking straight ahead. "My brother can build anything. Anything atall, and better'n most builders. Boo and me want to make 'im rich. You never expected to be rich, did you, I mean, all things considered. Well, you're gonna be. Billy and me talked it over a long time. He wants to do it. There's one little catch. It's a family bidness, got to start small. He can't do it all by hisself, and he can't go paying out high wages to some lazy damn stranger. He's gonna need family help. Dubby, you are a smart boy. Smart bookwise, but dumb otherwise. I will never forget as long as I live you seeing that rat in the bakery and instead of closing the door to the front and then trying to catch 'im, you chased 'im right out front in the pastry shop and give Miz Petty a conniption fit and her dropping Skunky's tenth-birthday cake and then slipping in it trying to run from that rat. People still laugh about that, but Boo and me don't laugh. It cut down our bidness in the bakery for quite a while. And then the time you had a break from delivering bread, and you set out front reading a book, and Miz Sanders says, 'What you readin', Dubby?' and you says *The Origin of Species.*' Her and me didn't even know what the damn thing was, till I looked at who wrote it and realized it was that fella Darwin that claimed the Bible was all hooey and there wasn't no Adam and Eve and our forefathers was all apes! Now, that was a blasphemous book that was not allowed on the shelves of the Espada Public Library, but here you were, a twelve-year-old boy, a-setting up there reading that thing as big as you please! And you got it from Miz Iannaccone! Now, Letty, most mothers down in Espada wouldn't let their kids go within a hunderd yards of that woman's house, her livin' there all by herself in that big house on the bay, and that house full of visitors, mysterious visitors come by boat, every weekend, partypartyparty. No church in that female's life, just visitors from out of town! And yet when she needed somebody to trim her palm trees, Letty, you let this boy go over there and come under her influence, and come away with the loan of that devil-book! If he was sposed to be trimmin' palm trees, what was he doin' in the house? What kind of a conversation did that woman have with a boy, to be givin' him that trash to read? Miz Sanders told the story all around town and people started comin' into the store and sayin' stuff like, 'What kind of a nephew you got there, Dixie, anyhow?' and I'm sayin' to them, to put the best face on it I can, 'He's just a boy tryin' to impress people, boys jump over the traces every way they can, he'll grow out of it.' Well, you didn't, did you, Dubby, not yet. But you don't live in Espada anymore, so the folks down there don't know it, so I don't have that embarrassment to put up with. Anyhow, here you are seventeen, and your daddy says you're not into anythin' practical yet, still into all kinda weird books and poems and other countries' languages, and God only knows what-all. And your mama encouragin' you, the way your dad tells it. Right, Letty?"

I looked at Mom. She had turned the color of dried cornshucks. Her eyes were slitted. She was looking straight out the window, taking long, slow breaths. She didn't answer, but Aunt Dixie answered for her.

"The answer is yes, and your daddy, smart as he is, don't know how—or I hate to say it but it's probably true, don't have the guts—to stop it, to say it oughta stop, even. Well, I do. I'm here to tell you, as family, as family ready to risk a lot of hard-earned cash on your future, for your good, the time has come to come into the real world. You got to quit college, all that hoitytoy crap, and help your daddy get rich. You can be a rich boy, a boy with a car, a partner in the newest, growin'est bidness in the universe, Dubby, and the time is now. There, I said it, like I told your daddy I was goin' to." She mashed out her Camel in what was left of her omelette in Mom's best plate, in spite of the fact that Mom had put out an ashtray for her, and she just looked at first Mom and then me, waiting for us to react. I was so scared I could hardly breathe, not for me but because of Mom, who seemed turned to gray stone, just sitting there in silence. Then something started to happen to her body. First she leaned forward and pushed her behind very slowly against the back of the straight chair, then she slowly sat up, and up and up, until her back was straighter than I'd ever seen it, and then she slowly turned toward Aunt Dixie till she was looking her square in the face, and her eyes were just little specks of blue fire flashing out through cracks in her squinted skin. It seemed like a minute before I heard her say in a steady whisper:

19

"That will never happen."

"What did you say?"

"You heard me, Dixie."

"Repeat what you just said."

"I said that will never happen."

"You are a crazy woman. You are draggin' my brother down. He's not goin' to go on like this. He's goin' to leave you."

"Goodbye, Dixie."

"I said he's goin' to leave you. What'll you do then, Letty?"

Mom's voice was not excited. Her mouth didn't tremble. Her breathing was regular. She seemed more relaxed, just sending out freezing blue rays from her eyes into Aunt Dixie's. Finally she said, lighter than before, "Goodbye, Dixie."

Dixie got chalk white with fury, pushed her chair back with a loud scraping noise, stood up and marched toward the front door. Under her breath, but loud enough to be sure we heard her, she said, "Squaw!" Then she went out the door and slammed it.

I think I was in shock. What had just happened could not be real. Then Mom gave me a sweet smile, and said, "Take my car, honey. I don't want you to be late for class."

"Thanks, Mom." I heard Aunt Dixie's new Chrysler start and back out of the driveway. I went to pick up my books from the living room. When I turned back to Mom she was humming something that sounded like a spiritual or a hymn, and clearing the table. I went through the dining room toward the back door. She stopped me.

"Dubby—"

"Yes'm."

"Be proud of your Cherokee blood."

My throat closed up, but I managed to push through, "I am, Mom." Then I nodded, because I wasn't sure she could hear the words.

She took something out of her pocket. "Here's a dollar for gas, honey."

When she placed it in my palm, her fingers closed around my hand and held it for a few seconds while we grinned at each other. Then I ran out the back door.

THREE

NOW THAT MOM had turned down two chances to be rich—the first time to be sure I grew up a free citizen instead of a reservation Indian, and the second time to be sure I stayed in college—I felt a lot of pressure to do well in class. I flunked my trig exam and went into a cold sweat. I started imagining those shoals of life Mom talked about. My face was still feeling clammy when Chester's old green Pontiac pulled up beside me where I was waiting on the esplanade outside the main gate of Rice. Chester and Susie and Hilda were in the front seat, but as soon as the car stopped Hilda jumped out and opened the back door and jumped in, leaving the door open for me to join her. She scooted across to the other side with one knee up on the seat, and I ducked my head to get in, and the first thing I saw was no panties. The second thing I saw was Hilda's wide mouth and heavy bright pink-painted lips separated by a line of small, even teeth. I still had my head full of quadrants and radii, spinning around each other in a blur the way they'd done while I'd been staring at my exam paper. Hilda must've thought I was some kind of a drip, because instead of looking her in the eye and saying howdy or something I sat down and faced forward and tried to compose myself. I heard Chester say "This here is my buddy W. W. Johnson, the college genius, known to millions of grateful females as Dub the Stud." I heard the girls giggle as he continued: "Dub, this here is Susie, and beside you, you lucky houndog, is her sweet little cousin Hilda. If you play your cards right, she might let you shake hands with her on the third date." Both of the girls went into near-hysterics at Chester's introduction. All I could think of was that Hilda's mouth looked like Mrs. Sandusky's labia majora with teeth.

It didn't take me more than thirty seconds to get into my gun-slinger act. This was the character I learned from reading Wild West Weekly. I had practiced it till I could seem—when it worked—as cool as any two-gun waddie with his back to the bar daring the quick-draw artist with the big rep to make his move. I'd start the process by controlling my voice and my diction so that I drawled out something dry like, "Third date, huh? Does that mean I might get a kiss after about a year?"

Susie and Hilda thought this was about the funniest thing they ever heard anybody say. Hilda was leaning against the side of the car, with her right knee on the seat and her foot hooked under her left knee. As she laughed and bounced around in the seat she kept wink-ing at me with her unpantied crotch.

Contrary to my fantasies, this did not ignite me. It scared me. I think it was because I had heard so many stories about loose women and disease, or maybe because I had been a little bit worried ever since Chester had told me he was going to do me a big favor and let me and Hilda do it in the back seat while he and Susie did it in the front. I had been so desperate to get ready for my trig exam that I'd been able to put this out of my mind part of the time, but now I had to face the fact that the idea of doing it with a total stranger while somebody else was watching from a couple of feet away made me extremely nervous. What if I started to shake like I did when Mrs. Sandusky pulled my pants down? The idea of that was so scary that if I hadn't got pretty well into my gunslinger act I'd've started shaking right then and there.

"My God," Hilda said, staring at me up and down, "Chet didn't tell me you was so *big!*"

I stuck with my gunslinger role. "Lady," I drawled, "you ain't seen nothin' yet."

Susie and Hilda went off into gales of laughter. It was then I real-ized I smelled alcohol. It had taken me a few seconds to believe my nose, because it was only a little after four in the afternoon.

"Ole Dubby is six foot two and he ain't full growed yet," Chester said. "He'd'a been six foot five already if the good Lord hadn't turned so much of 'im under fer feet."

More gales. Susie was lighting a cigarette with difficulty. She passed the pack of Camels back to Hilda, who flipped one up for me. I shook my head and took out my Bull Durham, which I had swiped from my father's humidor just before leaving for my exam.

"Well, Hil, you know what they say about big feet, you lucky gal," Susie said.

Hilda laughed so hard she blew out the match while she was trying to light her cigarette.

"We done sampled the Southern Comfort," Chester said. "Wanta snort?"

I told him I'd wait awhile, till my lunch settled. Hilda watched me roll my Bull Durham. She was full of admiration for my skill. She wanted to know if I'd teach her how.

"Well, sugah, I don't rightly know. How old are you? I don't want to be messin' around with no jail bait."

When Susie and Hilda got finished laughing, Hilda told me she was twenty-one. For the first time, I looked at her really close, and I could see that she was all of that, if not more. Her teeth between those ever-moving bright pink lips were perfect, except for a few black spots that looked like rot between some of them on the side, and her long black hair was a little on the greasy side, pulled straight back above her ears and held in place by a couple of tortoise-shell combs. Besides the thick lipstick, which she kept licking to keep wet, she had on mascara and some kind of green stuff on her eyelids. I could just see that pink lipstick all over my shirt and collar.

Hilda was staring right back at me, sucking on her Camel, smiling like she liked what she saw. I smiled back like I liked what I saw too, but I didn't. When she raised up her hand to take a drag of her cigarette, I could see that her fingers were stained nicotine yellow and there was dirt under her fingernails, visible in spite of the white polish she had on them, which was chipped in a few places around the tips. I knew right then without any flicker of doubt that I did not want to really know this woman, even to mow her yard, much less in the biblical sense.

Chester was driving out Memorial Drive toward the north part of town. I guessed, knowing him, that it being too early to eat, he was figuring to head for Heights Cliffs so we could park and knock off a quick one before we went to a drive-in for dinner. It was going to be daylight for some time yet, but at Heights Cliffs, according to Chester, you parked at any time, day or night, and went about your business, and nobody ever bothered you, except to stare once in a while, on account of they were too busy theirselves, pounding on that doorway to paradise.

I didn't have much time to figure out a believable, gentlemanly way to escape. I didn't want to insult Hilda or my buddy Chester, but at the same time I didn't want any part of this paradise. I had always thought I was pretty ingenious, but as Heights Cliffs drew closer and closer, I started to think I was just as dumb in personal relationships as I was in trigonometry.

Susie tipped up the Southern Comfort and took a big slug and turned around and offered it to me. "Better have some of this chicken likker, Dub."

"I'll wait a little bit. I still got heartburn from my lunch."

"What did you have?" Hilda asked.

"I had huevos rancheros at Billy's Chili Pot, with a whole bunch of Tabasco."

"Oooh, hot sauce is sexy," Hilda said.

"Yeah, but to tell you the truth, I don't think you ought to ever eat huevos rancheros in a greasy spoon like Billy's. They can give you rotten eggs, and cover up the taste with pepper, and I wouldn't be too surprised if they did that to me."

Chester glanced back at me. "Belly actin' up on you, Dub?"

"Kinda."

Hilda took a big swig of Southern Comfort and shoved it at me. "This is good for what ails you, honey."

"No, thanks," I stammered. I knew I had my problem solved.

"You know why they call it chicken likker, don't you, Dub?" Chester said.

I did but I said I didn't. It's not polite to not let people finish jokes.

"One drink and you lay!" Susie finished for him.

Although they had heard this line a hundred times, they all laughed. I didn't. I had my plan.

"Chester, would you mind pulling over on the shoulder for a minute?"

"What's up, Dub?"

"Well," I kind of groaned, still in my gunslinger mode, but a little groggy-like, "nothing's up, yet. But I think my lunch is about to be."

24

"Oh, my God," Hilda said, moving as far from me as possible. "Pull over, Chet, quick. He's gonna woof his cookies."

Before the car came to a complete stop I hit the shoulder running, and started throwing up. I could always throw up whenever I wanted to. I don't know where I acquired this talent. It was just God-given, I guess. I hadn't done it for quite a while because there's not that much demand for it, but right there on the shoulder I proved I hadn't lost the knack.

When I crawled back into the back seat like a kicked puppy, Hilda offered me a mint. I took it.

"We'll get you a Coca-Cola, honey," she said. "Ice-cold. That'll fix your stomach. Always does."

I could see she had a lot of mother in her.

Susie was helpful, too. "Hil'll take good care of you, Dubby, won't you, Hil?"

Hilda pursed her shiny pink lips and aimed a kiss in the general direction of my abdomen. She cooed in baby talk: "Hilly gonna make him tummy all better."

"I don't think I better go," I whispered. "I feel another problem coming on. Y'all better drop me off at a filling station where they got a restroom. And I'll catch a bus." I had to go back to Rice for Mom's car.

Nothing will make people more willing to dispense with the pleasure of your company than diarrhea, real or imagined. I felt fine, but there was no way in the world I was going to kiss—much less anything else—a woman who was willing to kiss a person who had just puked. A woman like that, in my opinion, probably didn't lift up her hair and scrub the back of her neck.

They let me out at a Gulf station. Hilda was pouting. There wasn't much said in the way of polite goodbyes. Chester did promise to call me, and that was about it. As they drove off I heard Hilda say, "Well, shit, Chet, le's go on out to the Cliffs anyhow!"

And Susie giggled. "Yeah, lover! We'll figger out somethin'!"

The first words out of Mom's mouth when I walked in the front door were exactly what I knew they would be: "How'd you do on your exam?"

"I think I did okay. Trig's not my best subject, Mom." I wanted to say "Waterloo," and get it off my chest, but on the rare occasions when I flunked an exam, she went into mourning. This consisted of weeping, lamentation, doom-saying, and finally coming down with a sick headache that sometimes lasted three days. We could be broke, we could be without Dad for months at a time, we could be evicted, we could be making dinner out of day-old bread bought for a nickel, we could even get a visit from Aunt Dixie and Uncle Boo—any oppressive boot of fortune on our necks—and Mom would be the first to bounce back, happy-go-lucky, optimistic, picking us up with her zeal for the future; but the slightest sign of scholastic ineptitude in me was a dagger in her heart. So, though my answer wasn't what she'd hoped, it left room for hope. It put the bad news on the back burner. Instead of two crises, one now and one when the grades came, we'd only have the later one. A worthwhile lie, mathematically, and I could always explain that I'd misjudged how badly I'd done and lie out of the lie.

I congratulated myself on not having taken even one sip of Chester's Southern Comfort. If I had, I'd've had to wait several hours to come home, because Mom could smell alcohol from a mile away, the way a puma smells a faun. She always kissed me the minute I walked in, not just for the kiss but to sniff my breath. I could tell she'd caught a whiff of the Bull Durham, in spite of the mint Hilda had given me, but she chose not to react, except with a quick accusatory glance as she turned away. My enslavement to nicotine would be handled through the Divine Mind. She was also against drinking, gluttony, sex out of wedlock, revealing apparel, all appetites of the flesh, plus lying and profanity. She also didn't have much use for Catholicism, Judaism, and Franklin Delano Roosevelt. That was the short list. She had a lot of disapproval about a lot of things, but to be fair, somehow she usually came off as a fine and lovable person. Her disapprovals were more intellectual than personal. She took in strays, both animal and human, no matter what their faults, and treated them with genuine compassion. Down in the flatlands of Matagorda County, when we lived across the road from Mrs. Sandusky during the deepest pit of the Depression, Mom kept a big pot of red beans and fatback on the kerosene stove for the many haunted-eyed dispossessed who wandered along the highway, hungry and hopeless, heading from Somewhere to Nowhere, dreaming of miracles. The federal government was as helpless as they. It had nothing for them. Their miracle was Mom.

"Y'all set right here on the steps," she'd say, to a lone dusty hobo or a hunger-stunned family, "and take the weight off o' your feet, and let's see what we got. Dubby, how 'bout a pitcher of water for the folks?" I'd bring a pitcher of cool water from the water barrel (hauled by sledge from the artesian well a quarter-mile away), and she'd bring out cold homemade cornbread and plates of red beans and mugs of buttermilk, and if there were children she could sometimes rustle up a few squares of fudge with pecans in it. This menu was dictated by the fact that you could buy a one-pound bag of dried red beans for a nickel, the fatback came from our own hogs, the buttermilk from our cows, the corn for the cornbread from our own cornfield, and the pecans from our pecan trees. Well, not *our* pecan trees. It was a rented place, without running water, electricity, plumbing, or a telephone. Sometimes Mom couldn't pay the fifteen dollars a month rent (Dad had followed the scent of something to Houston by this time, and wasn't much help), but the owner, Mr. Gottlieb, who lived in Bay City, never turned a feather when Mom told him she couldn't pay on time. She could pay when she got it, he said. He'd rather have us living in the place than for it to be standing vacant. His kindness didn't change Mom's opinion of Jews in general. She always referred to Mr. Gottlieb as "a good Jew."

In the summer of 1936, after we joined my father in Houston, in another rented house, this one with electricity and plumbing, Mom still gave wayfarers part of whatever we had and helped sick neighbors and relatives by caring for their kids and "knowing the truth." That's the way everything was treated, from broken ribs to the sniffles. There wasn't even an aspirin in our house. When she got one of her sick headaches she just rode it out in the dark bedroom, with a Christian Science practitioner treating her from afar, and me reading passages from Mary Baker Eddy's works to her for a few minutes every day. She knew other women who got this same kind of claim, she said—meaning ailment—and had doctors and nurses coming in all day, and dosed themselves up with materia medica, and they spent more time in Satan's claws than she did. In my observation this was true, though I considered myself too impure to rely on "knowing the truth" to take away the blinding headaches I sometimes got when I smoked and drank too much on a weekend away from home.

On these rare occasions I would sneak a couple of aspirins and feel better right away. I figured I'd have to study *Science and Health* for several years to get the same result.

Even the whiff of tobacco she'd caught on my breath and my ambiguous report on my trig exam couldn't dampen Mom's spirits after I told her I was staying home this Friday night instead of cruising around with Chester. She'd never met him, but she'd answered the phone several times when he called, and she didn't like his sneaky-sounding voice or his bad grammar. She wondered aloud why he, an unambitious, long-winded ignoramus, was always calling a young college boy at eleven at night and keeping him on the phone for an hour at a time, just listening to God only knows what. It's true that my contributions to the conversations consisted of "You're joshin' me, Chester," and "She sounds like a goin' Jessie!" or "And you could still make it out to the job in the morning?" Mom, as pure as she was, and always looking to be closer to God, was not above standing close enough to her bedroom door to monitor my end of the conversation on the phone in the living room, which was the only phone we had. If we'd had one that she could listen in on and hear her innocent boy's spirituality being polluted by sex and obscenity, the effect on her health, in my estimation, would've been approximately the equivalent of my failing three final exams.

But fortunately she didn't seem capable of suspecting Chester—or me, for that matter—of the true depths to which we could fall, any more than she'd suspected Mrs. Sandusky.

To celebrate my spending Friday night—Mom's worst night of every week—at home with her and my little sister Jenny, she decided to make a pineapple upside-down cake. This was one of her specialties, along with red beans and chocolate pecan fudge. So right away I was sent to Mr. Schultz's store to get the canned pineapple and the brown sugar and other things she needed for the cake. Jenny went with me. She was eight, and she tagged along with me a lot. She'd've followed me to Rice in the mornings if I had let her. She thought I was the greatest thing since peanut butter, and I felt the same way about her. I guess I took the place of a father for her, in a way. Although we had our father technically living with us, he was there only during the week for a few hours, to sleep and to take an occasional late supper alone. When he was there he didn't have much to say. On Friday mornings when he left for the job he ostentatiously took his fishing gear with him, and we didn't see him again until Monday night. I knew the only reason he came home at all was out of a sense of duty, to make it possible for us to have a roof over our heads while I went to college and Jenny went to grammar school. How much longer would he continue to do this? He had left us twice before, once for more than a year, so he could do it again. He had sent money during these absences but not much. He didn't have much, but he had tried to share what he had. It was himself he had trouble sharing. Maybe Aunt Dixie knew his plans. I could tell that Mom had this in her mind, too. Maybe this Monday night he wouldn't come home at all, even late and all tanked up. He and Mom had no physical contact and so little to say to each other that you had to wonder how they got together in the first place. This was a mystery I knew I'd never solve, as separately, in the rare moments they talked to me about anything personal, each professed to love the other. They just couldn't stand each other's ways. He liked to drink and joke and raise all kinds of hell and be with people, and she detested his drinking and smoking. The only way beer could get into our house was in his belly. She could tell the difference between the odor of beer and the odor of hard liquor on a person's breath. When she smelled hard liquor it meant to her that he probably had some stashed in his pickup or in the garage, because you couldn't buy it by the drink and he probably hadn't drunk the whole bottle, and he certainly wasn't going to throw the rest of it away, money being as tight as it was. So she'd go out and search the car and the garage after he went to sleep, and when she found the bottle she'd pour the contents on the ground and put the empty bottle back where she found it. The message was that he wasn't to bring liquor to her house, and he was to dispose of the bottle elsewhere, as she didn't want the neighbors to see it in her garbage.

While I was grateful to him for the personal sacrifice he was making for us, I could never understand how a man could make the living and support a family—even badly—and let the woman tell him who he could and could not bring into her house—the "her" stuck in my craw—and which of his friends were welcome. The result was that he didn't bring friends home and spent as little time there as possible himself.

He had a lady friend. Mom knew it and I knew it, but Mom didn't know I knew it. The whole charade was being played out for the benefit of little Jenny and me so we could believe our Mom and Dad were cleaving ever and only to each other, like the preachers say. I'm sure Dad wouldn't've cared if we knew, but Mom always tried to protect us kids from what she called ugliness.

On our way to Mr. Schultz's store Jenny hung onto me tight, her cool, tender little hand squeezing my fingers. I knew what pride a father must feel to have somebody so vulnerable trusting and loving him so much and depending on him. I was sure Dad must've felt that, some time or other, but he'd never let it show except for an occasional glimpse, which you had to be watching for to catch. Maybe he was afraid of his own emotions, coming from a scuff-knuckle clan of working people where boys don't cry. Or maybe he was so resentful of Mom's long list of disapprovals that he couldn't feel truly a part of the family. I didn't dwell on this much. This was the only family I knew about from the inside, and for all I knew they were all pretty much alike, seeming one thing on the outside and being something else on the inside.

Jenny was clutching a penny for BB Bats in her free hand, and the closer we got to the store the faster she wanted to go. She was like a thirsty horse heading for a water hole, hard to hold back. By the time we got to the front door, she had me almost on the run. But then I saw something coming toward us out of the store that made me skid to a stop, almost yanking Jenny off her feet.

It was the kind of vision I'd conjured up many a night after one of those marathon hot wrestling matches with Betty in the front seat of Mom's Dodge that always ended with that Great Referee in the sky blowing his whistle for time limit before I put her shoulders to the mat, leaving me ready to run barefooted through a field of cockleburrs to chase down and violate a jackrabbit.

The light was behind her, which made her form stand out in detail. As she got close to us I could see she was maybe sixteen or seventeen, with long hair the color of baby cornsilk, no makeup, and bare feet. She was slender without looking bony, and she had a way of walking I'd never seen before, a lazy, unself-conscious way of swinging one bare foot in front of the other with a kind of twisty, swaying motion that made her look as though with each step she was going to lose her balance. She was sucking a red Popsicle. She wore a faded yellow cotton dress that came to just above her knees. As she brushed past us in the door she looked up at me and I imagined she smiled a little, though most of her mouth was on the Popsicle at the time. And then she was gone, or going, her yellow hair swinging behind her as she snakewalked away in the opposite direction from our house. Jenny was tugging at my hand, but I was frozen in place, staring at first one perfect part, then another.

"Dubb*eee!* Come *on!*"

Jenny yanked hard at my arm. I almost snapped at her, my sweet little sister, to shut up. There was no chance I was going to take my eyes off this living embodiment of all my carnal fantasies until she was out of sight. If it hadn't been for Jenny I'd've followed her to find out where she lived. It wouldn't've been the first time. I had the impulse to tell Jenny to wait in the store and I'd be right back, but my sense of responsibility—of *something*—took over, and I just stood there, ignoring Jenny till the vision turned the next corner to the right. I even had the impression that she glanced back at us before she disappeared, but it was dusk and I couldn't be sure.

These few moments shook my little sister's sense of oneness with her brother; we both felt it. Still, she clung to my hand all the way home, but in silence. As soon as we got there I went in the room I shared with Dad and got out my notebook and wrote, "Lust is stronger than brotherly love."

FOUR

OM PLAYED PIANO by ear. That Friday night she and I and Jenny sang corny songs like "The Isle of Capri." There's nothing like pineapple upside-down cake and a glass of cold milk to make people sing and forget their troubles. Add to that some hot margarined popcorn and Mom's graceful hands pounding on the old upright, and somehow joy comes out of nowhere and surrounds you. Mom loved the sentimental love songs, sung in the traditional way. If anybody jazzed them up it infuriated her. "Major Bowes' Original Amateur Hour" was her favorite radio show. If a performer she liked got the gong, she cried. If a performer she liked won the prize, she cried even harder. These events were more important to her than Hitler occupying the Rhineland, or Mussolini annexing Ethiopia, or the Spanish Civil War, or even Joe Louis knocking out James J. Braddock to become heavyweight champion of the world. They were not more important than truly great tragedies such as Franklin D. Roosevelt being elected for a second term, but they helped her forget.

When Chester called that night I told him I couldn't talk because we had company, which we didn't. I had to whisper this into the phone, because Mom was against lying for any kind of purpose, and she was in earshot at the time. I just didn't want to hear about Chester's adventures with Susie and Hilda at Heights Cliffs. I had come to one of my instantaneous conclusions, that I was not going to live my sex life vicariously through Chester's vivid reportage, and I was not going to rub bellies with his kind of females any more than I was

32

going to sit down on the public toilets at Herrman Park Zoo. I was going to spend all my houndog time from now on looking for and trying to make out with the Girl in the Yellow Dress.

Early the next morning I told Mom that my trig exam had taken so much out of me I was going to cut my Saturday classes. I'd already cinched ones in both of them, and I needed a day off. She didn't question me. I put on my battle-scarred cowboy boots and the beat-up ten-gallon hat I used to wear when I was cowboying for the Circle J Ranch down in Matagorda County in summers gone by, and sauntered over past Mr. Schultz's grocery store to the next corner and turned right. I spent the whole day in my gunslinger mode, walking the neighborhood, hoping for a glimpse of the Girl. I saw several others that weren't bad, but none of them measured up. I knew the one I was after, and I was a stubborn cuss, especially in my hat and boots.

That night I had my regular date with Betty, with the usual result —a sore mouth from two hours of nonstop kissing, and the standard frustration. I tried to take stock of myself. Why was I going out with her when all I got out of it was being unable to walk upright without sharp pains in the groin for hours afterwards? And if I had to be impolite and give a direct answer to the question "Is Betty a prickteaser?" wouldn't I have to say yes? Why did I always stop when she said stop? Did she mean it? Why didn't I push a little harder and find out? I had to answer myself that it was all for unworthy reasons that I did these things or allowed them to be done to me. I went out with her not because I loved her but because Mom approved of her, even without knowing her, because her mother, whom Mom also didn't know, was a Christian Scientist. The result of this was Mom's encouraging me to have dates with her. By encouraging I mean financing. I couldn't really go out with anybody without financial assistance. I worked around the house, but that was because there was grass to mow and dishes to wash and garbage to be put out, not because I got paid for it, the way some kids did. An allowance? The word was unknown in our family. So on Saturday nights, because I was going out with a young lady who was being brought up in Christian Science, Mom lent me her car and gave me enough for movies and hamburgers, and I took it, like a Corn Indian hanging around a mission. Sunday mornings, after a date with Betty, I always felt like a failure. I always knew in my soul that I was afraid to push for more

for fear she'd tell her mom and her mom would tell my mom and I'd
be disgraced. And worse, I wouldn't even be able to go out on Saturday nights anymore. I got another maxim out of all this pondering:
Pennilessness is powerlessness.

The next morning, much as I hated to do it, I went to church with
Mom. It was a form of pre-expiation of guilts I was hoping to have. As
much as I respected my mother's religion, sitting in church through
the whole service gave me the willies. I had let a girl inveigle me into
going to her Baptist church one time, down in Matagorda County,
and the preacher had ranted and raved and pounded on a Bible and
made a fool of himself, and it had been kind of fun. And another time
I had walked into a Catholic church just to see what it was that my
mother was so against, and here were these gentlemen in fancy robes,
one of them swinging a silver pot that gave off smoke, and beautiful
music, and a lot of colorful statuary. I'd found it kind of dramatic and
mystical, and even a little bit scary. But in the Christian Science
Church everything seemed to be carefully arranged to keep you from
having any emotion. I guess that's the influence of the word *science*.
Two people, a man and a woman, both sort of self-contained and
businesslike, stood before us on a bare platform and read alternately
from the Bible and *Science and Health*. The atmosphere was hushed
and pious and formal and, at least for me, intimidating. I was sure it
was my fault. I just wasn't up to that hard a search for the truth that
would make me free. Since we were always late we always sat in the
back, and this gave me a good view of the congregation, so instead of
listening to the readers I stared at all the people in front of me that I
could see just by moving my eyes but not my head. As far as Mom
could tell I had my eyes on the readers at all times, although I was
actually trying to analyze the people, one by one, making up their
lives, their habits, what they liked to eat, even how they talked.
Sometimes when I met them I was amazed at how close I had come,
other times I was completely off. But it was more fun than piety. I
was usually surprised when the service was over.

On this particular Sunday, when the service ended, three people
popped up in the front row and headed for the side exit. One of them
was, even from the back, magnetic. When I thought about it later, as
I did off and on all Sunday afternoon, I realized I had not seen the
other two at all, except to note that the one who opened the side door
was a man, the next was a woman, and the third was hardly more than

a silhouette I could only describe as angelic. She glowed in the sudden sunlight for a moment and was gone. I only saw her for three seconds or less, not her but a vision of her, the upper part of her, blurred by changing light and interposed forms, with the outstanding feature being dark hair knotted at the back of a small head that flashed in profile for a split-second only and then vanished, an old-fashioned memory out of a picture book or a gallery. In my mind, because of her perceived perfection, and her evanescence, she became the Angel. There was none of the goatish obsession that had possessed me on my first sight of the Girl in the Yellow Dress; no, not a hint of it. There was only enchantment, momentary belief in— what? Something beyond the real, something—I didn't want to think it, but I had to accept the thought—something that had to do with God. Was it because I was in church? No. I put it out of my mind as much as I could. It was a girl. I was a boy. The rest was a trick of nature. Still, I wanted to run down the aisle and out the side door and get a good look at her, but it would have been impossible against the traffic. I thought I would hurry out the front door and around to the side of the building, but no, Mom had a grip on my arm. I had to walk out sedately with her and stand out front in the sunlight and say hello to her friends and make polite conversation. That was part of going to church with Mom. I made up my mind on the spot that all this would be worth suffering through next Sunday, to get a good look at the Angel. No doubt she had been a product of my lonely imagination, and a close stare at her in the glare of day would send her crashing into reality. In the meantime, I had done a good deed; Mom needed church, and she needed to show off her son, her college boy, and to socialize with her friends of like religious persuasion. It made me restless, made me clench my teeth, but it smoothed Mom out every time. For the rest of Sunday she always seemed to have risen above the ugliness of her lawful wedded husband being down on the Texas Colorado in an old house trailer drinking beer with another woman.

That afternoon I got into my hat and boots and went out to track down the Girl again. Common sense told me she wouldn't've turned right at the corner if she didn't live on that street, and she didn't live too far up that street, either, or she'd've got her red Popsicle at a store on Nineteenth Street instead of Mr. Schultz's. I wandered the neighborhood till sundown like a lost dog, with no luck.

On Monday I got a shock at Rice. At the end of trigonometry class Mr. Rickul handed back all the test papers except mine. He asked me to stay so he could talk to me. He was a non-threatening type of person, mild-mannered and soft-spoken, and I already knew I had failed, so with my gunslinger stoicism I waited for whatever extra verbal punishment I was to receive. When we were alone he handed me my paper. Miraculously, it had a four-minus marked on it, the lowest non-failing grade possible.

"I know you're doing fine work in some of your other subjects, Woodrow," he said, looking around to see if there was a spy nearby to overhear his confession of unprofessorial softheartedness. "I saw your exam paper that Mr. Battista posted on the bulletin board with a one-plus in Spanish. He told me it was the only one-plus he ever gave. And I saw your poem in the *Thresher* last week. I know you're a serious person, so I bent over backwards not to ruin your scholastic record. If you flunked out of Rice, could you afford to go to a place where they charge tuition?"

"No, sir."

"Well, for now you haven't failed. For now."

"Thank you, Mr. Rickul. I'll try to justify your kindness." If I hadn't been in my gunslinger mode, I might've cried, in spite of my lifelong indoctrination against it.

That day, after classes, instead of going to Autry House for a couple of hours of ping-pong, I caught a bus home and hit the books with fervor so I could have the evening free to roam the neighborhood again. I put in an extra hour on trigonometry, in honor of Mr. Rickul, solving, with the help of my textbook, all the problems I'd left unsolved on the exam. I waited until I had a lot of work done so I could say something upbeat when I went in to see Mom. She had been in her room with her door closed when I got home and hadn't come out, so I feared that she had come down with one of her sick headaches. Outside her door, even before I tapped, I got a whiff of the sour smell of vomit, but I had trained myself to act like I hadn't noticed, so I tapped, waited for her to say "Come in, honey," and entered. She was in bed, propped up, with a damp cloth on her forehead, reading from *Science and Health*. She had her teeth out, which made her look old. Usually she'd take a bullet in the heart to avoid being seen without her teeth; she was vain about her looks and her size nine quadruple-A shoe encasing what she called her "patrician" foot. Her maternal grandfather, after all, had been a chief. But this late afternoon of the day that would tell us, at least temporarily, if Aunt Dixie's bitter words were true, she had succumbed to doubts, to the pains of memory, to an almost desperate search for words from Mary Baker Eddy or the Bible that would tell her no, he's not going to leave you again, he'll be home tonight as every Monday night, and you will still have for a while longer what little you have left. She smiled at me, pretending everything was the same, but her face was drawn and pale and her eyes, peering over her half-glasses, seemed not to be really seeing me. My first thought was, she isn't even aware that her teeth are not in her mouth. I faked great triumph; I had finished working out all the trig problems I missed on my exam. I expected to do well from now on. "That's wonderful, honey. I know you will," she said, holding out her arms to hug me. She had gone to great lengths to disguise her breath, as she always did; she smelled of Listerine. I told her I was going out for a little walk. She told me she was going to study for a while, and then we were going to have macaroni and cheese and red beans with fatback for dinner, along with homemade coleslaw. I told her that sounded good to me, better than good, great, as long as we had plenty of iced tea with fresh mint out of the backyard. I bounced out of there, both of us grinning and miming that it was going to be a beautiful evening.

I went to Mr. Schultz's store at exactly the same time Jenny and I had gone there on Friday, except that this time I didn't have Jenny in tow. After I hung around Mr. Schultz's for a while I left and went around the corner to the right and walked my usual search pattern, with no result. In the middle of the second block there was a lady undressing in her front bedroom with the shade up. I stopped to watch that for a few minutes, so it wasn't a total loss.

When I got home Mom was in the kitchen with her raggedy robe on and a kerchief tied around her head and her teeth in but pale and rheumy-eyed and unsteady-looking. She was putting on the water for the tea. The beans had been cooking all day, and they—or Mom's special spices and the fatback—filled the kitchen with their seductive aroma. Jenny was kneeling in a chair making cookie dough at the table. "Mom said I could make oatmeal cookies all by myself," she piped. "An' put 'em in the oven and take 'em out all by myself, too, and I'm big enough to not burn myself either, Mom said, didn't you, Mom?"

37

"I sure did, honey, and we're going to set the table in the dining room and treat ourselves like company!" Turning away from the stove, she suddenly stiffened, then cocked her head. "Shh! Listen!"

Jenny and I listened. Jenny said, "I don't hear any—"

Mom gestured violently. *"Shhh!"*

We still didn't hear anything. Then Mom bolted out of the room, ripping the kerchief off her head. Jenny looked at me, her eyes wide at this strange behavior. She took a breath to speak. Then I heard it: the muffler. His muffler. There was no other muffler like it. And it was headed our way. Mom had heard it from a long way off. Her ears were tuned to it. It was only six-thirty on an overcast night, a night that had gone from dusk to darkness in a few minutes. He hadn't been off work more than two hours, and the new school he was building in Pasadena was an hour and a half away, through quitting-time traffic. Was he sick? Had he been laid off again? Was he coming home to pick up his possessions? Was that it? Was he leaving us tonight, moving out? Jenny watched me for a clue, her tiny hands covered with cookie dough. I said, "Hey, better get those cookies in the oven. Looks like Dad's home for dinner."

"Yeaay!" She went to work on her cookies, more than willing to believe everything was fine. I heard the pickup skid on the gravel as Dad swerved it into the driveway with even more exuberance than usual and then skidded to a stop in front of the garage without slowing first. Maybe he'd got off at noon—maybe it was raining in Pasadena—maybe he'd been drinking all afternoon and was three sheets to the wind. Was Mom going to come back and finish cooking dinner? It wasn't like her to run. Then Dad walked in the back door, cold sober, his arms full of grocery bags, a big grin on his face.

"Hiya, Cowboy. Hey, Jen." He wasn't the hugging and kissing kind, nor, unless he was well-oiled, the talking kind either. He put the bags on the table. Jenny was sniffing them.

"Barbecue!" she squealed.

"Ice cream, too. Better put it in the icebox." His voice was matter-of-fact. "I'm gonna take a bath." He was about to go out when Mom came in from her bedroom. She had put on a dress, and brushed her hair, and put just a little color in her cheeks. She and Dad looked at each other in silence for a couple of seconds. They were not inimical, not cordial; they were wary and formal, almost as though they were strangers, which I guess they had become again—physically, at least.

"Well," Mom said, as though it were a complete sentence.

"He brung barbecue and ice cream and potato chips and onion rings!" Jenny yelled.

"I'm gonna wash up," Dad said, not looking anybody in the eye as he went out.

"I just put some fresh towels in the linen closet," Mom said to the empty door. Then she finished her thought to Jenny and me, "There was sun this morning. They dried nice. Smell sweet."

It was a strange but pleasant dinner. Dad came out dressed in fresh khakis. He told us, in a reserved way, like a guest who wasn't sure of himself, about a couple of funny things that happened on the job that day. This was his way, I figured, of apologizing for leaving it to Mom to turn down Aunt Dixie's proposition, and letting us know without saying so that he was proud of Mom for sticking to her guns, and maybe even proud of me for not wanting to be in the prefab business. He didn't mention Aunt Dixie, and neither did Mom, and you couldn't tell from the conversation she had even come to visit. It was a good couple of hours, and then Dad said he had to go talk to Joe Brodus about the concrete pour tomorrow. Joe Brodus was one of his beer buddies, no doubt waiting for him at Steve's Place, ready to help him catch up on his brews, brews that Dad would tell him sure would've gone good with that barbecue.

It was comforting, in a funny way, to hear Dad come skidding into the driveway about eleven-thirty that night and to know his routine was back on track. I was on the phone with Chester, telling him I couldn't talk because I had a big exam in the morning. This was a lie. I didn't want to get sucked into his crowd again. I was going to concentrate on finding the Girl.

Dad came sailing in, flipped a salute at me, muttered, "Howdy, Cowboy," and disappeared into the hall. He went into the bathroom and pretty soon I heard him in the middle bedroom stretch out on his bed, groan contentedly, and break wind. In about a minute he started to snore, so I closed my books and went to bed, too. His snoring didn't bother me. I was used to it.

The next day after classes I caught the first bus back to the Heights, because I realized that the Girl, if she had moved to our neighborhood and wasn't just a visitor, had to be going to John H. Reagan High. So when the final bell sounded there and the kids came pouring out, I was standing on the corner where she would have to pass if she was going to walk from the school to our neighbor-hood. She never came.

I studied hard till dinnertime. Mom was impressed with my seri-ousness. I intended to study some more after dinner, but I got rest-less. I needed to roam, to have a smoke, to check out that show-off with her shade up one street over, maybe even get lucky and find the Girl.

As soon as I got out of sight of our house, I started rolling a Bull Durham. Real cowboys, one of which I considered myself to be, can roll a Bull Durham cigarette with one hand on horseback at a dead run, or on top of a boxcar rolling along at fifty miles an hour. I never tried the latter, but I have done the former, it being sort of an initia-tion ritual for the summer cowhands at the Circle J. So now, to keep in practice, I rolled my smoke in the dark while strolling along. Up ahead I noticed there was a light on in the third house, a shabby little place that had stood vacant for months, with its yard unmowed. As I drew abreast of it, I became aware of a squeaking sound coming from the dark front porch. In the shadows there I made out two forms in the swing, the chains squeaking as they swung back and forth. As I reached for a match to light my Bull, I realized both the forms were female, and one of them was almost certainly the Girl. Instead of bringing the kitchen match out of my pocket, I pulled out an empty hand and patted all my pockets.

"Excuse me, ladies. I hate to bother you, but could I maybe trou-ble y'all for a match?"

There was a short delay in response. The swing went creak, squeak, creak, squeak.

Then the older woman said, sort of grudgingly: "Joy, go get 'im a match."

The younger female got up and went dutifully into the house, not hurrying. Dark as it was, there was no mistaking the swinging yellow hair and the snaky gait: Joy was the Girl.

I sauntered up the cracked sidewalk. The grass was fresh-cut. I could smell it. Pretty soon after I got up on the porch, Joy came out of the house with a box of kitchen matches. She was wearing a faded green dress this time, one of those cotton things that get thinner and lighter the more you wash them. She handed me the box, staring at me, unsmiling.

"I appreciate it." I lit my cigarette and handed her back the box. "Thanks. Y'all just moved in, huh?"

"Friday," the woman said, in a way that was intended to discourage conversation. But Joy was still looking at me, with the sides of her mouth crinkled, not at all disapprovingly, so I was encouraged.

"Well, welcome to the neighborhood. My name's Dub. Dub Johnson. I'm from around there on Seventeenth Street, in case y'all need anything."

"Okay, Doug," the woman said.

This time I'd've had to be a fence post to not know I was being dismissed. "Well, good evening to you, and thanks again, ladies." I retreated down the steps with the same nonchalance as if I'd been treated politely.

"Did you say Doug?" Joy asked.

"Dub. Dub Johnson." I said it back over my shoulder, knowing her mom wanted me to keep going.

"You go to Reagan?"

I heard her mom mutter warningly: "Joy."

I stopped about halfway out to the street. If Joy could buck her mom's bad nature, who was I to chicken out? "I did last year. I graduated."

Joy sounded disappointed. "Oh. Well, I'm going to be going there."

"Joy, let the boy go. All he wanted was a match. Cain't you see he's got someplace to be?"

Joy huffed impatiently at her mother, and sat down beside her in the swing and started it swinging again. Creak, squeak, creak, squeak.

"Well, good luck over there at Reagan, Joy." I tried not to sound lame, but I was sure I did. It always took some of the starch out of me to be treated mean. How could such a perfect girl have such a tacky mother? I sized the woman up as a high school dropout from a home with no books. She looked like the type that would pick up a rattlesnake with her bare hands and bite his nose off.

I remembered to turn right when I got to the end of their walk, so as not to give the impression I had gone out for a walk just to find them and borrow a match. My houndoggery was in full bloom, but I was scared too. I was almost sure she was underage, and considering my dishonorable intentions, I was in an awkward situation. I was

41

underage too, but nobody cared about statutory rape of boys. A lot of people didn't care about the legal age for girls either, as long as they were big enough, but I was sure Joy's mother wasn't one of those. She would have Joy's age down to the year, month, day, and hour she came into this world. I already knew, just from her bringing me the box of kitchen matches and watching me light my smoke, that I wasn't going to fall in love with her, but I wasn't going to be able to stay away from her either. It was pure lust. You don't marry girls that walk like Joy. I walked faster, in a hurry to get home. I already had a maxim I wanted to put in my notebook.

FIVE

MOM CALLED ME from the kitchen as soon as I walked in the door. I told her I'd be there in a minute; I had to write something down before I forgot it. She thought I was hurrying to go to the bathroom and gargle with Listerine so she wouldn't be able to smell smoke on my breath, which I was, but the most important thing, even more important than not getting caught smoking, was to get the thought in my notebook. Mom was proud of this, proud of my respect for thoughts, my fascination with maxims and epigrams. "He got that from me," she always said. And she was right, but if she'd known the true story she wouldn't've been proud. I just never had the heart to tell her that it was her monotonous repetition of the old saws that drove me to start looking for some fresh ones. She would say, "You can't teach an old dog new tricks" or "Don't change horses in the middle of a stream" under such predictable circumstances that I could've beat her to the punch most of the time if I'd wanted to be impolite. But I never had much respect for people who made their mothers feel bad on purpose. We all hurt our mother's feelings often enough just by being imperfect, so why try for it? Anyhow, let's say that a convicted murderer out on parole gets into a fight in a honky-tonk and kills a man. Mom's reaction was, "A leopard doesn't change his spots." Or I'd come home from the store with the wrong brand of something, when the other brand was two cents cheaper. "A penny saved is a penny earned," she'd say. Or trying to convince me to put a quarter a week in a savings account, "Great oaks from little acorns grow." These words sometimes—even when I was twelve—made me feel like Strangler Lewis had me in a headlock. That is when I started reading books like *Poor Richard's Almanack*, and the *Maxims* of La Rochefoucauld. Right away I noticed that even these gentlemen said the same things over and over again in different ways, but at least they were less boring than the same old tune on the same old fiddle. So I started collecting them, and every once in a while, before Mom could come out with "You can't make a silk purse out of a sow's ear," I'd say, "There never was a good knife made out of bad steel, Mom." By the time I was fifteen I'd memorized a lot of this wisdom for no other reason than self-defense. The next thing I knew, I was making up my own. Mom was aware of my lined notebook with "THE MAXIMS OF W. W. JOHNSON" printed in green Crayola on the cover. I kept it hidden in the bottom of a drawer under my baseball cards. She was too honest to ever sneak a look, but she was tortured by curiosity, so sometimes when I dreamed one up that I thought was pretty remarkable, I'd tell it to her. She never failed to be dumbfounded by my brilliance. Later on I'd usually discover the philosophical equivalent of it in Ben Franklin or La Rochefoucauld or Martial or Pope, or all four, but I wouldn't let on. After all, Mom's pride in me was one of the few pleasures she could afford.

I also noticed that the old fellows wrote down their advice for other people but didn't use it much themselves. And neither did I. Every time I went into my collection I saw recipes for being successful, for living without mistakes, for improving my moral character—all of which I was ignoring in my daily life. I resolved to do better. But first I wrote down this observation: Houndogs never wait for love.

If my instincts kept insisting that Joy was rapids and the roar of the falls was just around the next bend, why not go ashore now, like any sensible person would do? If I didn't pursue her, nothing would happen. So that night, lying awake listening to my dad snore, I resolved that the chase was off.

The next morning I waited for the bus as usual at the corner of West Seventeenth Street and Heights Boulevard. It was a long trip all the way from the north side of Houston to the south side, with a change of buses halfway there. My bus came and I let it go by. I realized I was watching the next corner where Joy would pass as she was walking to school. I called myself a lot of uncomplimentary names. I took *Chief Modern Poets of England and America* out of the books in my arms and flopped it open and ran my fingers over the first line I saw—" 'Is there anybody there?' said the Traveler"—to remind myself of the pleasures of Mr. Williams' English class. Full of resolve, I slammed the volume shut and clutched it like a prayer book, hoping it would give me strength. The bus came. I started to get on it. I put my foot on the first step and then acted as though I'd forgotten something and stepped back. I walked to the next corner, the street she'd have to use to get to school, and there was her mother walking toward me. I was so full of guilty thoughts I was afraid to meet her. I acted as though I hadn't seen her and kept right on walking along the boulevard. Now I was going to be late to Mr. Williams' class. I got out in the street and started trying to thumb a ride. Joy's mother waited on the corner for the bus. Did that mean Joy was home all by herself? I thought of waiting till her mother got on the bus and disappeared and then going back and knocking on her door. What would I say? What would happen if one of the neighbors saw me? They all knew me. How would I explain myself?

My thumb worked well. A Fuller Brush man picked me up. As it happened, he was going all the way across town and out South Main, headed for Sugarland, and he could drop me off right at Rice Institute. He talked my ear off, but I hardly heard him. When he let me out at the main gate he said, "Boy, stick to the books and you won't have to knock on doors for rent money."

"Yessir. Thanks for the ride, sir."

Mr. Williams forgave me for being late. He was a gentle philosopher, a benign nurturer of young dreams. Unfortunately, his class and all my other classes were blank space in my brain that day. I was obsessed with my own weakness one minute, and with my cowardice the next. I was weak to let three buses pass while hoping to get a glimpse of a person I'd sworn to avoid. Then I was a coward for not going around the block and down the alley and up to the back door and knocking, on the chance she was there. I could've explained that I was soliciting for my friend who delivered the Houston *Post*, if anybody'd asked. What if she'd been there, hoping I'd do that? She'd've invited me in, said she was eighteen and not a virgin, and we'd've hooked up like a couple of wildcats all day. Those things happen. Why was I so chicken? And why was I so dumb? Why didn't I ride all the way to Sugarland with that salesman, and then catch another ride to Blessing, where Mrs. Sandusky lived now, and knock on her door and say, "Lady, your long grinder is back in town"?

In French class, I relived every moment of my hours with Mrs. Sandusky, starting with walking into her house after she hollered, "Come on in, Dubby," and wandering through empty rooms to an open bathroom door and seeing her standing in the bathtub in her birthday suit, and jumping back out of the line of sight, and her giggling and saying, "What's the matter, Dubby, you scared?" and me saying "No, ma'am," although I was practically petrified with terror, and her sashaying out of the bathroom without a stitch on, calm as if she was dressed for church. She was sort of on the hefty side, not your average September Morn, but you'd think she just had won a beauty contest, the way she was so proud of what she had. "Don't tell me you never have saw a nekkid lady before, Dubby!" I told her sure I had, plenty of times, but I was sort of taken by surprise because my mother had sent me over like she asked her to, to kill a snake in the cellar and close up the hole where it got in. While I was telling her this she had started fooling around with me, and smiling at me, and the next thing I knew she had it out and was starting my education. I had heard of boys getting their education like that from older ladies. It was kind of the accepted way, down there in Matagorda County. I guess it was actually sexual abuse of a minor, but I didn't realize it at the time, not that I'd've known what to do about it if I had.

Mr. Bourgeois' voice came at me from a long distance, but I finally recognized it. "Woodrow," he said, "is vere somefing wrong?"

I told him no, I was fine, just daydreaming about what would happen if an American playwright wrote like Molière. This pleased him; he forgave my inattention.

After classes, instead of hanging around Autry House for a couple of hours playing ping-pong and watching girls walk, I hurried straight home and wrote in my notebook, "A good lie at the right time is just as important as the truth." While I was at it, I changed "Lust is stronger than brotherly love" to "Lust is stronger than anything else." Then I changed into my khaki work clothes and tennis shoes and got the lawn mower out of the garage and oiled it and pushed it nine blocks to Mr. and Mrs. Potter's house.

According to Mom the Potters were Jewish but had Americanized their name to be like regular people, and as far as she was concerned they were, because, she said, they didn't act Jewish, which was the important thing. She and Dad had bought our house from them, and Mom said she thought it was a bargain. Mr. Potter held the mortgage, and he was easygoing about Mom not making the payments on time, which happened more often than not. I was left to understand that little things like these were what she meant about him not acting Jewish. This was pretty much the way she had evaluated Mr. Gottlieb down in Matagorda County when we rented from him, and since I had never had any major financial dealings with anybody, Jewish or otherwise, I didn't feel like I was qualified to have an opinion of my own. But I remembered that my bag had been short-weighted when I picked cotton for Mr. Dupree in Matagorda County, and I'd been cheated by Mr. Burk when I milked for him at his dairy farm, and by my own Aunt Dixie when I trotted all over Espada with a bushel basket on my shoulder delivering fresh bread from Uncle Boo's bakery, and by a few other people too (admittedly I was easy to cheat), and I knew none of them were Jewish, so I put the whole subject in a category of needing further investigation.

It was a little soon to mow the Potters' lawn, and when I got there Mrs. Potter told me so, but now that I was there, she said, I might as well go ahead. I felt kind of ashamed because I knew she was right but I was using the grass as an excuse to bring up the subject of the house on Sixteenth Street, and the new tenants.

Mr. Potter had some kind of a problem with his heart, and he spent a lot of time in bed. When he was at home he wore a skullcap and walked very slowly and stooped over, not picking up his feet but sliding them along in his house slippers, but when he was out in the world, taking care of his rental properties, he dressed just like everybody else, except maybe a little neater, and he had a quiet, courteous, friendly manner about him. When I cut the grass, even when he wasn't well he always came out and spent a few minutes asking how I was getting along in school and how my family was, even when Mom was behind in the mortgage. But on this day it was Mrs. Potter who came out. She told me Mr. Potter wasn't feeling well. She brought me a Dr. Pepper, ice-cold, and a couple of homemade cookies when I was about halfway through the mowing. She said I should've waited till a cooler day to push that heavy thing around, and I said when it got hot and humid like this there was probably a storm coming, and I thought if a lot of rain got dumped on the grass the way it was now, it might be too wet to mow, and the grass could definitely get away from us, and the yard wouldn't look too good, and besides I didn't mind the heat. She was an educated woman, very small, with a sweet face and an even more gentle voice than Mr. Potter, if possible. We sat on the steps because she said she thought I needed a breather. I congratulated her on Mr. Potter's having rented the house on Sixteenth Street, and she said yes, it was a good thing, because that house was always a problem, it wasn't very nice, and it was hard to keep good tenants in it. And I said I'd walked by there and noticed there was a lady and a girl out on the porch, and she said yes, they were the only ones that were going to be living there, and she hoped they would be comfortable and happy. Then she looked at me, appraised me with a thoughtful, sad expression, and said, "I do hope they'll be good neighbors."

"Oh, I'm sure they will be," I said. "I don't know 'em, but I did have a brief conversation with them and they seem like nice people."

She nodded, not looking at me. I got the impression she was worried about something, something she didn't want to talk about. Then she turned her head and looked up at me. Sitting side by side with this little white-haired lady—I took her to be about sixty—looking into my face searching for something made me very uncomfortable. I knew that she had a university degree from somewhere, and I'd heard she read Sanskrit, and a couple of other offbeat languages, and was a real thinker; when you tangle with a real thinker it's always scary. I tried to act like the situation didn't exist.

"These are really fine cookies," I blurted out. Not being ready to speak, having my mouth full of cookie, I spewed out a few dry crumbs, which made me feel like a lamebrain. Mrs. Potter didn't seem to notice, though. Whatever it was she had on her mind superseded temporal things like cookie crumbs.

"Dub, may I ask you a personal question?"

"Personal? Oh, sure, yes, ma'am."

"Do you have a sweetheart?"

"A sweetheart? Yes, ma'am. Well, sweetheart—maybe that's a little on the strong side, for an expression of it, by definition. I have a girlfriend I go out with, you know, on Saturday nights mostly."

This was the first time I had ever had a serious conversation with Mrs. Potter or, for that matter, any lady resembling Mrs. Potter in age and learning and, well, dignity is not the word for it, maybe intellectual or moral substance would be closer to the thing I felt coming at me out of her face.

"Good," she said. Then, "Is she a nice girl?"

"Oh, yes, ma'am!" We weren't doing it, Betty and I, so she was a nice girl. That's all it took to be a nice girl, but I had the feeling that Mrs. Potter meant more than that, although she didn't pursue the matter. Instead, she pondered some more.

"That's good to hear," she said, finally. "This world is full of other kinds. Dub, Mr. Potter tells me you're a fine student with a good intellectual future."

"Thank you. I hope so."

"Your mother is very proud of you. I'm going to trust you with something that is very confidential, something that, if it got out into the world in the form of gossip and did any harm to the person I'm going to speak about, would make me ashamed of myself, but I'm going to tell you this for your sake. You know, Mr. Potter and I are very particular about who rents our houses.

"Yes, ma'am, I know."

"One reason the Sixteenth Street property stayed vacant so long is that the people who can only afford a little house like that—it's just a crackerbox, and we know that, but for the right people it's a home—most people that poor, well, let's say many of them, not most—many of them are people of less than desirable character. That doesn't mean they shouldn't have a place to live, no, but what it does mean is that people like Mr. Potter and me, who depend on our properties for a living, have to be careful to get renters of good moral character, people who will pay their rent and keep the property in good condition. I'm sure you understand that."

"Yes, ma'am."

"So we go through a process when we're looking for a renter; we check out references, and inquire around. Mr. Potter checked up on the lady who moved into Sixteenth Street. I don't recall her name, I usually stay out of those things, but she turned out to be a wonderful person, a poor woman who works hard to raise her children. She told Mr. Potter her husband left her for a divorcee. Her son is married, and her daughter, whatever her name is—"

I almost said "Joy" but held my tongue.

"—will be living with her. Mr. Potter got some disturbing informa-

49

tion about the young lady, so disturbing he almost decided against accepting her mother as a tenant. He accepted her only because she works for a religious organization and got such excellent character references that Mr. Potter decided to take a chance. I tell you these things, Dub, because I believe you're mature enough to honor the confidentiality I spoke about, but perhaps not mature enough to—to, shall we say, resist all the temptations that appear in the paths of young men. Well, no one is, no one is supposed to be; the world wasn't designed that way, was it?"

"No, ma'am, I guess not." She was making me very nervous.

"So here's what I have to say, Dub. This is between you and me and no one else. It may be gossip. That's the danger. Or it may not be gossip. That's a worse danger. The girl, we are told—or Mr. Potter was told, by a couple of their former neighbors—is rather strange."

"Strange?"

"Different. Unusual. Mr. Potter got stories of her threatening to kill her mother. Of running away. Of skipping school. Of sleeping in the cemetery and refusing to come home."

"Sleeping? In the *cemetery?"*

"She was drunk and had passed out, they said. She was about twelve or thirteen at the time."

"Holy—" I was so struck with these details that I didn't have time to give a calculated reaction. I just managed to cut off the impulsive one.

"Yes. Please remember, Dub, the girl may have been going through a period of hormonal imbalance because of her age and some emotional pressures we have no way of knowing about, and she may be perfectly all right now, and I don't want—I don't want to damage her—I'd hate myself if I did—but you deserve to be forewarned. You have your future to protect. I know you won't let this go any further than these steps, will you?"

"No, ma'am, I won't. I don't know the girl, and I sure wouldn't want to cause her any trouble."

"I know that. Here." She took a fifty-cent piece out of her apron pocket and put it in my hand. "I'll pay you now, so I won't have to come back out when you're finished. You always do a nice job, Dub. Give our regards to your mother."

We both got up. I gave her my empty glass. "Thanks for the cold drink, Miz Potter." She smiled and went into the house. I don't know how long it took me to finish the lawn. My mind was spinning with those tales about Joy. I was glad Mrs. Potter hadn't told all that stuff to Mom. She'd've said, "Forewarned is forearmed."

SIX

I T WAS FRIDAY evening again, that sundown time that seemed to put our house in a state of suspended emotional animation, of silence, of going through the motions of being alive with no goal but to survive the paralysis of the hour and come out the other side of it with the will to go on. This was Mom's condition every Friday night, and it infected me and even little Jenny, who didn't understand it but felt it and let it carry her along, sensing it would be over sooner or later, as it always was. I didn't understand either, of course, but I knew what caused it: My father had left the house as usual before dawn with hardly a word and tonight he wouldn't be coming home, even at ten or eleven, even all beered up, to be a presence in the house. Sundown on Friday was the time that brought this home to Mom with the most force. It was a time she had to work through with her *Science and Health*, a reminder that she had failed to hold her man, a hardworking man who now gave part of what he earned to her to honor some period of the past, now dead, that they once shared. These Friday sundowns had a slow doombeat that I could almost hear as I watched her with her books, forcing her way through the emptiness she knew would stretch out before her as long as she lived, while somewhere out there in the night a woman she had never met had found a way to make him happy and keep him with her.

This painful time was usually my time to escape, but tonight would be different. I'd taken a sacred oath to be a better person, to conquer trig, to be a comfort to my mother, and especially—taking into account the bizarre information that Mrs. Potter had entrusted to me—to avoid all contact with Joy. I would submerge my houndog-gery, keep my mind on a high plane, banish the black mist of melancholy that enveloped the house, and make Mom feel loved and appreciated and not alone.

"Dubby, how come you don't never take me with you to the store no more?" Jenny crawled up on my lap and hugged me in that soft, sweet-smelling way of hers. I was sitting on the wicker sofa, trying to figure out the best way to bring the house back to life, and Jenny came at exactly the right time.

"Well, 'cause you're too little, too mean, too ugly, too—"

"Du-uh-*bbee!* Be nice." She put her hand over my mouth to stop me, then took it away.

"Too—"

She covered my mouth again, and held it there while I made noises like a burglary victim with a tape over his mouth trying to call for help.

"You promise not to be mean, I let your mouth go?"

I nodded. "Mmmhmm." She took her hand away. "How would you like to help me make a cake, a chocolate one?"

She squeaked. "You and me? A cake? With icing? Chocolate icing? Can I lick the pan?" She jumped off my lap and ran around the room, out of control like a colt on a frosty morning.

"We have to find out if Mom has money for all the stuff first. Let's play 'Chopsticks' and maybe she'll come in here and we'll tell her what we want to do."

Jenny and I could play "Chopsticks" like one person with four hands. She played the left and I played the right. We'd been practicing since she was five. Playing this piece always made us laugh. Sure enough, as soon as we got up to speed, Mom came to the door, holding her finger in *Science and Health* to mark her place. She was startled by the sudden joy. She was accustomed to us being paralyzed by the gloom at this time on Friday, like she was.

"Mom," I asked, still racing my fingers up and down the keyboard, "have you got enough money for the makins of a chocolate cake?"

"Me and Dubby gonna make one!" Jenny squealed, not missing a beat. "And I get to lick the pan!"

Mom stood there kind of misty-eyed, looking at us for a couple of seconds, then she smiled. "I think I can scare up a couple of quarters."

53

Jenny and I skipped out the door, across the street, past Cooley Elementary School—which took up half the block—and on to Mr. Schultz's, holding hands and swinging our arms. The only things we needed to buy were chocolate and shortening. Mom had all the rest. We went straight to where the baking chocolate was, and there was Joy. She was staring hard at the prices on two bags of sugar and didn't see us at first. Then she put one bag back on the shelf and turned to go and almost bumped into us. She and I stared at each other for a full three seconds, like statues.

Jenny tugged at my arm. "Dub*eee*."

Joy said, "Hi, Dub." Her voice the night I borrowed the match had been just a nice, soft, sort of careful sound, but now that her mama wasn't with her it made me think of the hot sorghum syrup mixed with bacon grease we used to pour over our pancakes Sunday mornings down in Matagorda County. It was a voice you could smell and taste. She was barefooted again, and wearing the same little washed-thin cotton dress she had on that night, faded to a green so pale it almost wasn't there.

"Oh. Hey. How's every little thing, Joy?"

"Pretty fine. What y'all doin'?"

"Nothin'. Hangin' aroun' the house."

"Me, too." She moved to leave. "Well . . ."

"This is my little sister, Jenny."

"Hi, Jenny."

Jenny didn't like this stranger talking to her brother in that tone of voice, and she was too young to fake it. She didn't acknowledge the introduction. "Dub*eeee!* Come *on!*"

"Well, y'all have a nice evenin'." Joy moved away, something slender and boneless magically standing upright, defying gravity, somehow managing to ripple forward without collapsing upon itself. I watched transfixed till she was out of sight and even after, undeterred by Jenny's tugging and protesting, struggling to regain the straight and narrow, my resolve, the dream I had of being a good person instead of a spineless houndog. In my mind I said: There's nothing wrong with this girl. She is just a friendly girl, friendly and lonely. But I'll still be good. I will be worthy. I will have the courage of my convictions. Get thee behind me, Satan. I will be courageous. I am courageous. I am.

I said aloud: "Captains Courageous!"

Jenny was sure I was crazy. *"What?"*

"Captains Courageous! It's at the Heights Theater! It's got Freddie Bartholomew, and Mickey Rooney, and—"

"Freddie Bartholomew! Mickey Rooney!"

Her eyes got wide. She jumped up and down. I thought she was going to do her wild colt gallop around the store, knocking things over, but I grabbed her and held her back.

"Oh, heck, I ought not to've mentioned it. We can't go."

"Oh, Dubby, how come?"

"Well, honey, this is the last night, and we don't have any money. Once we buy this stuff, Mom said we wouldn't have any money till Monday night when Dad comes home."

"Aw, darn, Dubby. *Freddie Bartholomew!"*

"I know. But we might as well forget it. Unless—"

"Unless what? What, Dubby? What?"

"Aw, you wouldn't want to do that."

"What? Do what?"

"Well, if we didn't buy the chocolate and didn't buy the shortening, there'd be enough for the movies."

"Aw, Dubby. Then I wouldn't get to lick the pan."

"Well, wait, now. There might be enough for a nice Popsicle, and the movies, too. If—"

"Oh, Dubby! Yeah!"

I got her a red Popsicle, just like the one Joy was sucking on the night I first saw her, and we skipped home to ask Mom if the substitution was all right with her.

Jenny ran into the house yelling about going to see Freddie Bartholomew. By the time I got in the house it was all settled. Mom just had to wipe the red Popsicle juice off of Jenny's mouth and chin. That's when I demonstrated that I was just as brilliant as Mom thought I was, though in a way different from anything she imagined or desired. I told her I had already seen *Captains Courageous* (a lie) on a date with Betty, and it was such an inspirational movie I wanted Jenny to see it. What I suggested was that Mom and Jenny go, and I'd stay home and try to get some studying done. She didn't want me to make this sacrifice, but I told her about how Spencer Tracy played this old Portuguese fisherman (this was according to Betty, who had seen it), and Freddie Bartholomew was a spoiled English kid, and this old fisherman taught him the value of honesty and being obedient. A very inspirational movie, and Lionel Barrymore was in it too, and Mickey Rooney. Mom was worried about getting by, moneywise, till Monday night, but I told her I was going to cancel my date with Betty for Saturday night, and that would save some money and the gas I would use on that trip all the way across town and back. Mom loved my unselfishness and consideration. She and Jenny hurried off to be sure and get a good seat.

Woodrow Wilson Johnson, your mother, a spiritual person, an idealist, named you for a great president who was also an idealist, who envisioned all nations joining together to bring permanent peace to this earth. Never in the history of namesakes has there been a bigger defiler of a noble name than you, W. W., with the possible exception of that drifter named Jesus who stabbed a whole family to death on their farm up east and then drove off in their new Ford. But was even he, this murderer, any more devious with his own mother than you, W. W.?

As soon as Mom and Jenny turned the corner and headed for Heights Theater, I washed my face, combed my hair, brushed my teeth, gargled some Listerine, put on my hat and boots, put a sack of Dad's Bull Durham in my shirt pocket with the little tag hanging out, and headed for West Sixteenth Street.

The second I turned the corner by Mr. Schultz's store I heard the squeaky chain. I could see her dimly, all by herself, with her legs crossed, rocking the swing impatiently by jiggling her bare foot. She saw me and waved. I waved back but kept on sauntering as though it would take more than a mere female to make me shift into high gear. I was in my lone gunslinger mode. The gunslingers in Wild West Weekly always rode slower when they sensed they were about to be drygulched. They didn't turn their heads, but just cut their ice-blue eyes toward the gulch and let their hand hover over their hawgleg ready for a lightning draw.

I could see Joy's mom through the window in the lighted living room, sitting by the radio. I didn't say anything to Joy as I came up the walk, hoping not to attract her mother's attention. Joy was humming the tune to "It's De-lovely" very softly, and smiling, and she had quit jiggling her foot, uncrossed her legs, and was swinging ever so gently. We didn't say anything. She patted a place beside her in the swing and I sat down, and she kept the chain squeaking just enough to let her mom know that everything was about the same as ever. For some reason I was replaying in my head everything Mrs. Potter had told me, and I was looking for any signs of craziness. I could hear the radio through the window, male voices, black male voices, and Joy's mama laughing. "Amos 'n' Andy."

Joy put her hand on my leg over my left pocket in a friendly way and smiled at me. This took me by surprise, because if you don't know if a girl is innocent, or kind of forward for necking but still pure, or downright crazy, or a roundheels, or more than likely—considering the mama she had—a hardshell Bible-thumper, you don't know how to react to a thing like that. I thought I had a decision to make but it was made for me: if I didn't move her hand right away something was going to rise up and bump against her sweet young fingers. So I picked her hand up and held it tight between both my hands. I was glad it was dark, so I wouldn't be embarrassed by the Intruder. I was trying to keep my breathing steady, and she was smiling at me. There was a lot of confidence in her smile, as though she owned me, or was my boss, or knew something I didn't know. She pulled my hands holding her hand up to her face and put my left thumb in her mouth and started sucking it.

I never would've believed that anything could shock me and scare me and paralyze me again after what Mrs. Sandusky did, but this was so unexpected I thought for a couple of seconds I was going to pass out. At least Mrs. Sandusky kind of worked up to things. Joy just went for it, like a baby going for a nipple.

Don't ever let anybody tell you your thumb is not a sex organ. I guess anything would be, with Joy's tongue wrapped around it. The Intruder sprang up like he heard an alarm bell. She reached down and took hold of him; she knew he was there. How old could she be anyhow?

She took my thumb out of her mouth and whispered: "I wish I didn't have my panties on."

"What?"

"Mama's listening to 'Amos 'n' Andy.' She won't even go to the bathroom while they're on." She was unbuttoning my fly.

"But—"

She wiggled out of her panties. She pulled out the upright Intruder and gave him a big wet kiss and got astraddle me in the swing.

"She'll hear us."

She ignored me. She guided him in and started scrubbing hard.

She stuck her mouth on mine and our tongues started twirling around each other and her hips did the fastest and most complicated set of bumps, twists, and waggles I ever heard about, even from Chester, who claimed to have had everything. He hadn't had this. If he had, he'd've described it to me or tried to. It was like one long spasm going in three directions at once. I started coming immediately, but after that first one—and if Mrs. Sandusky hadn't made so much out of it I'd've thought it was just a regular everyday thing—the old Intruder settled down to some long grinding. Which, right now, hearing that chain squeak and having my back to the window so I couldn't tell where Joy's mom was, I didn't want. The way Joy was shaking and quaking maybe she wouldn't last long. Not as long as "Amos 'n' Andy," anyhow. Not fifteen minutes. Compared to what Joy was doing, Mrs. Sandusky's movements, especially when she just sort of lay back and closed her eyes and whispered, "Slower, baby. That's nice. Real slow, now," were about the speed of a taffy pull. "Easy, easy, make it last." The whole time, except for the very end, Mrs. Sandusky always kept glancing out the window through that little slit she left when she pulled the shades down, watching the highway for any sign of Mr. Sandusky's car. Of course after thirty or forty minutes, with her eyes all shiny and damp and sweat beaded up around her hairline, she'd pant, "Okay, baby, turnin' the corner now. Le's get ready—ready to head fer home, baby. Headin' fer home, now. Here we go. *Now*, baby, *go! Go! Go!*" And I would go, slamming away as fast as I could, but it wasn't in the same league with this conniption fit Joy's crotch was having in the swing.

Then all of a sudden Joy began to shudder and quiver and whimper, and then she was still. She jumped off. She had her panties in her hand.

"You better go. I gotta go warsh, 'fore Mama smells me." She bent over and gave the Intruder another kiss, very affectionately, as though she liked him better than me. "Mama leaves for work at eight in the morning. Can you come over?" She went into the house, not waiting for my answer. She was too smart to need it. Or too crazy. Was she crazy? Or just reckless? How reckless do you have to get before you're classified as crazy?

I eased out of the swing so as not to make it squeak a different tune, and stayed hunched over to be as small as possible, and flitted off of the porch, silent as a ghost. Joy's mama would never know I'd been there. I realized I didn't even know their last name. Just Joy and Joy's mama. Joy's mama was either a divorcee or a widow, I decided. Either way, in my opinion, the man was lucky.

I went straight home and washed my underwear and the front of my khaki pants with soap and water and ironed them almost dry and hung them on the back of the straight chair in my room. Then I took a quick bath and put on some clean underwear to sleep in. When you're dealing with a lady who can tell the difference between beer breath and whiskey breath from across the room, you don't take any chances.

Roscoe Baill called. He was doleful. "Bad news, Tex. River Oaks whupped my boys, five to four, las' night. You know who the swing match was? Spooky Harnett, middleweight, TKO, first round. You coulda saved us, Tex. I cain't believe you don't care no more 'bout yer neighborhood than that, Tex, honest to God. Made me sick to watch them River Oakers strut. That great left-right combo o' yours woulda took out that fuckin' middleweight o' theirs in no time flat. Listen, Tex, can we talk tomorrow? Heights Park needs you, boy."

I begged off. Big study load. Exams. Maybe at a future date.

I didn't mention it to Roscoe, but I wondered: if his boys were fighting for the neighborhood, how come the neighborhood didn't turn out to watch? Anyhow, the idea of letting some stranger pound on my brain to amuse a few other strangers didn't thrill me.

What great left-right combo? I never threw a left-right combo in my life.

By the time Mom and Jenny got home, I was propped up in bed, studying. I don't know how I managed it, but I not only looked virtuous, I felt virtuous. Mom and Jenny loved *Captains Courageous*, and Mom was convinced that if any mother ever had a noble son, she was that mother.

SEVEN

SATURDAY MORNING I didn't put on my big hat and chaparral-scarred cowpoke boots because I wanted to dress like a boy on his way to Reagan High School to take part in a baseball game. We didn't have uniforms. All we needed was tennis shoes and a glove. My glove was a Pepper Martin model, cracked and worn through in a couple of places, and resewn. It was heavy with neat's-foot oil.

I had traded a rickety shoat for it at a Barter Day down in Espada not long after Mrs. Sandusky moved away.

Mom made me a thick peanut butter and raisin sandwich on whole wheat bread, and put it in a paper bag with a perfect red apple and a piece of homemade pecan fudge, since I was going to be gone all day, what with playing ball and then going with some of my buddies to watch the ball games at some of the other schools. I was out of the house by seven-forty-five, walking fast to get to Heights Boulevard and Seventeenth Street in time to watch Joy's mama get on the bus a block away.

I was ashamed of myself for not being ashamed of the way I was deceiving Mom. She believed without hesitation, without so much as the upflick of a brow, that my two Saturday classes had been canceled because of midterm exams. If she wondered why midterms lasted so long, she didn't say so. I knew her gullibility was an element of her innocence, of her determination to blot out inharmonious thoughts, so I was even more ashamed that one of the feelings that made up the mixture boiling up in me was pride, perverse pride, in how devious I was, how skillfully I had created a whole day in Mom's imagination that had nothing to do with the day I was planning to have.

Another feeling, gloom, intruded on my pride. I knew where that came from: I loved my literature and language classes. I cherished the explosion of white clarity in my brain, the physical jolt of ecstasy when suddenly a new idea—new to me, at least—or a special human dimension flared into being before me. I was going to miss that today. I had traded it for a day of lust. I told myself that a red-blooded ex-cowpoke like me was entitled to dalliances of the flesh. Were these not part of being a man? Still, it seemed strange to be feeling guilt instead of elation.

I walked across Heights Boulevard and sat on the bench near Mr. Moreno's homemade hot tamale cart. From there I had a clear view of the corner of Sixteenth Street where Joy's mom would be catching the bus. She showed up about five minutes after I got there. I ducked my head so the bill of my Houston Buffs baseball cap hid part of my face, and she just stood there without a suspicion in the world that somebody was watching her, much less that somebody was so excited watching her get on the bus that he was pulling in big gulps of air like he had just run a mile full speed. The bus pulled out and I sat there, waiting for it to get out of sight, on the theory that she might have forgotten something and decided to get off and go back home.

"You playeen baseball gane today?" Mr. Moreno practiced his English on me, and I practiced my Spanish on him.

"*Si. Juego a la pelota. Adios. Buena suerte.*" I left him, walking in the direction of Reagan, which was not the way to go to Joy's house. My theory was that it was better to go a little out of my way, on the off chance that Mom would choose this time to drive somewhere and see me walking along Heights Boulevard long after she expected me to have disappeared in the direction of Reagan High. So I went one block down toward the school, and then turned right and went two blocks over to Fifteenth Street to be sure nobody saw me walking up Sixteenth Street, which I would be hard pressed to explain, even with my lightning mind for lies. Also, if I went up Sixteenth, I would walk right past Mr. Schultz's store, and I didn't want to take a chance on Mom choosing this time to walk over there to do some Saturday morning shopping. Mr. Schultz was very nice about "writing it down" if Mom had a cash problem.

My plan was to go up Fifteenth Street an extra block, turn right, cross over, and double back down Sixteenth to Joy's house. I was a little self-conscious in my baseball cap and carrying my glove and lunch bag, heading in a direction where there was no baseball diamond within a mile. But my explanation in case some housewife jumped out at me and said, "Why are you going in that direction to play ball?" would be that I was going to meet a friend of mine. I would just keep walking to avoid rude prying.

When I got to Sixteenth Street and turned toward Joy's house I started getting cold feet. If one of the neighbors saw me go into that house, a half hour after they'd seen Joy's mother leave for work, and me carrying a baseball glove and a brown bag, wouldn't they think that was suspicious behavior? We had only lived in the neighborhood a little more than a year, so we didn't know all of the neighbors, but they had seen me around, and they would surely wonder what I was doing there after the lady of the house had gone off to work. When I got about three houses from Joy's, Mrs. Salibo, a very nice lady who lived at the end of the block I had just left, came out of Mr. Schultz's store and headed for home with a bag of groceries and with her pretty five-year-old daughter holding her hand. There was no way to avoid her. We met right in front of Joy's house.

"Going to play ball, Dub?"

"Yes, ma'am."

"Well, hit a home run for me, huh?"

"I'll try, ma'am."

This took place as we were passing Joy's house going in opposite directions. Mrs. Salibo knew Mom. They had both worked on the same committee to collect funds for victims of the New London School disaster. As I went past Joy's house I heard her tapping on the window. She was motioning at me to come on in. I waited till I was sure Mrs. Salibo wouldn't see, and then held up two fingers, hoping Joy would know I meant two minutes. By the time I turned left at Mr. Schultz's store I was so nervous my skin was too tight for my bones and my knee joints were trying to lock. I was only half a block from my house. I had walked seven and a half blocks and was almost back where I started. I looked behind me, ahead of me, and all around me, and then I ducked into the alley behind Cooley School and ran stooped over to Joy's backyard and up to her back door and started knocking. The shades were all down. I didn't see Joy or hear her coming, but pretty soon she pulled open the back door and just stared at me. Then she unlatched the screen and shoved it open and jerked her head to indicate that I should enter. As soon as I got in the kitchen she latched the screen door and shut the wooden door and turned the bolt. Then she pulled her dress over her head and was naked.

I must've sounded like a creature from another planet when I said, "Where can I put this stuff?"

"What is it?"

"My baseball glove and my lunch."

She squinted at me for about three seconds. Then she turned her back and walked toward the front bedroom. I thought what she mumbled was, "You're nuts," but I couldn't be sure.

Her bedroom was small, with nothing much but a bed and a chest of drawers. She threw her dress in the corner and fell over on her back on the bed. I put my cap and glove and lunch on the floor by her dress, and then I had an attack of self-consciousness. I had never undressed in front of a girl before. Mrs. Sandusky had undressed me every time, and somehow her physical imperfections had made me comfortable with my own. But with this girl, this beautiful, green-eyed, self-confident, pastel person lying there glorying in her own naked perfection, I was suddenly stricken with the awareness that my legs were a source of mirth to all who knew me, especially my father. Humor about my legs was a staple of his. "You got a lot of guts, Cowboy, to walk around on stilts like that." Or to a friend: "This boy of mine went wadin' in the Gulf one day in his bathin' suit, and a whoopin' crane come up and started flirtin' with 'im." The truth was that I was almost six feet three and weighed only 144, and my legs weren't much bigger around than some people's arms.

I must've hesitated a long time, because I heard Joy say, "You gonna do it with your clothes on?"

Maybe she was so anxious to do it she wouldn't laugh. I was so nervous the old Intruder, usually the first one up in the morning, hadn't twitched. I took off my shirt and threw it on top of her dress, and then my high-top tennis shoes and socks, and then I sat down on the bed and started to slip out of my Levis on the theory that my legs looked fatter when they pressed down on the mattress. Joy jumped up and grabbed the bottoms of my pantlegs and yanked them off, and then got hold of my drawers, and pulled them down, and dropped to her knees and took the poor shriveled Intruder in the softest, warmest, and wettest mouth a boy could invent in his sweetest dreams.

The next several hours pretty much consisted of constant repetitions of the standard sex act. There wasn't nearly as much variety as with Mrs. Sandusky, but then we liked what we were doing so much we didn't want to change. Mrs. Sandusky had let me know in no uncertain terms that I had a rare talent of being able to keep on going even after my weapon had fired a round or two. I didn't know till now that she wasn't just flattering me to make me feel good. As soon as Joy found out that I wasn't going to be one of those famous Minutemen, she started lavishing affection and praise on me and going wild over a toy that her experience had taught her was undependable and temporary at best. I got to wondering about her experience even while I was still adding to it, the way people's minds start drifting when they're doing the same thing over and over again and they don't have to concentrate on it anymore, so when I finally got winded and told her I had to have some time off, I asked her flat out how old she was.

"Sixteen."

I wasn't surprised. I summoned up a pale imitation of my gun-slinger cool. I said, "Jailbait."

"Scared?"

"No way."

"I knew you wouldn' be. You're strong. You're brave. My fighter was chicken."

"Your fighter?"

"Uh-huh. Eddie Suggs."

Eddie Suggs was a local pug at least thirty years old, with more losses than wins and a reputation that placed him one rung below a mangy coyote. Naturally I had to hope I was making an incorrect assumption. "Eddie Suggs? You mean you—and him—?"

She giggled. "I called 'im Eddie Sucks, cuz of what he liked to do to me." She giggled again, thinking about it. "You ever do that?"

"Do what?"

"Eat at the Y. That's what Eddie calls it."

It took me a couple of seconds to realize what she meant. "Can't say I have." I thought the only men who actually did that were those oily-haired Frenchmen on those postcards.

"Wanta learn?"

"You mean—now?"

"Uh-huh."

"Well, not right now, I don't. I'll try it later, you know, some other time, but right now, to tell you the truth, I'd rather eat my peanut butter sandwich."

She jumped up and stuck her head through the door into her mother's bedroom, and then came back and stretched out on top of me. "It's already after two o'clock, if you can believe it."

"What time does your mom come home?"

" 'Bout six, quarter of sometime."

We split my sandwich and my apple and my square of fudge. Joy got two Cokes out of the icebox. While we were eating propped up in bed I found out her last name was Hurt, her mother worked in the office of a Protestant church alliance that corresponded with Christian missionaries all over the world, and her twenty-five-year-old married brother Roy worked in the kitchen of the Swingatorium, a nightclub that specialized in that new dance, the Swing.

Joy worked there too, on Saturday nights, as a bus girl. Her mama would've never let her do it, except that her brother was there to chaperone her and bring her home when the place closed. That made it kind of hard to get up for church on Sunday morning, Joy said, but her mama was strict about church. In fact she was strict about everything. "She won't let me wear lipstick, or any makeup atall," Joy said. For a moment she looked like a little girl about to cry; then she shook her head angrily, making her hair swing. "Sometimes on Saturday nights when the kitchen is closed the guys ask me to dance, but my brother has orders not to let me, because Mama says when a girl jitterbugs everybody sees her panties. An' dancin's immoral anyhow, she says. She says I'm going to grow up to be a God-fearin' virgin or else."

"Does she still think that?"

"Oh, sure," she said seriously. "Mama's deaf, dumb, and blind."

A strange transformation took place in her eyes. They opened wide and filled with tears. She compressed her lips and took deep breaths, gone off in her mind someplace I couldn't follow, where she didn't want me or maybe where I didn't exist, a place I had nothing to do with. Then suddenly she bolted up out of the bed and darted out of the room, her body all tensed up and bent over like she was going to

65

throw up or lose her balance and fall forward. After a half a minute or so I got out of bed and peeked out in the living room and saw her stalking back and forth like a thing made of sticks, stiff and cold and lost, not human, with no clothes on but like an animal that has no concept of nakedness, not naked. I didn't know whether to speak to her or go and put my arms around her or jump into my clothes and sneak out of the house. I got the image of a baby abandoned, a baby that had never sucked at her mama's breast, never got the hugs babies want, a little savage thing looking for something missing and not knowing what it was. I was scared and wanted to run, but instead I went to her, two people closing in on each other in some kind of misery, and put my arms around her from behind. She stopped and just stood there shaking, not crying but seeming to suffer excruciating pain. A strange thing about human beings is (and even then I made a note to write this down) that when another person gets in this kind of shape, the only thing you can think of to say is their name. I said, "Joy . . ."

She shuddered and turned her face halfway around and looked up at me like she was surprised to see me there and disappointed it was me. Then she started to keen, and finally she said, "I want my daddy . . ." Then she was sobbing so hard she was just a bundle of bonelessness and tears. If I hadn't been holding her she'd've been down on the floor. I helped her back to the bed and lifted her into it and went in the bathroom and got some toilet paper and wiped her face and gave her some to blow her nose on. She kept on staring at me like she couldn't figure out what I was doing there.

I tried to be adult and comforting. I said, "Maybe someday he'll come back."

She echoed the last two words incredulously, in a whisper: "Come back?"

"Well, guys do, sometimes."

"Come back?"

From the sound of her voice I could've just told her the sun rose this morning in the west.

"Do you ever hear from him?"

"Hear from 'im?" Her voice seemed to be coming from a long way off.

I had the feeling I was going through a supernatural moment, but I refused to believe it. I said, "Well, if he just ran off with another lady, he—"

"He's dead," she whispered. "He's dead. He killed hisself."

"But—your mother told Mr. Potter—"

"I know." She seemed very tired all of a sudden. "I know." She was all cried out, all everythinged out, dead-voiced. "That's what she tells people, that he run off with a floozy. He cut his throat with a piece of broke windowpane. They found 'im in a flophouse out by the ship channel. They tried to fix 'im up in the funeral home so's he'd look okay at the viewing. Mama said there had to be a viewing. That's the way to do stuff like that, the right way, she said. When I looked down in his coffin he had on a new suit. First time I ever saw 'im in a suit in my life. Uncle Phil paid for it, so's he could look nice in his coffin. And he had a neat haircut, too. And if you didn't know what happened you prob'ly wouldn't see the long mark under all the makeup on his throat up close to the top. But I saw it. I was twelve."

I thought, twelve. That's when Mrs. Sandusky happened to me. We can't help having thoughts we're ashamed of, unworthy thoughts. At least I never could.

"While I was looking at the mark, Mama and her brother, Uncle Phil, come up to me real close, and they both put their arms around me, and Mama said, 'Well, Phil, you're gonna have to be her substitute daddy now. You're the one gonna have to walk 'er down the aisle when she gets to be a bride.' "

Her voice wasn't dead, like it had been; it was alive with hatred.

"And all I could think of was, after what you done to my daddy, you bitch, I will never give you the satisfaction of walking down some aisle for you to brag about me being a bride. If I ever get married you sure as hell ain't gonna be there. No way."

It was one of those times you feel like you ought to just nod understanding and keep your mouth shut, but I never have been able to do that. So after a few seconds, I said, "Your dad must've been a real nice guy for you to love 'im so much."

"He was the nicest person God ever put on this earth, bar none," she said. "Wanta see a picture of 'im?" She scooted out of the bed and got her purse and took out his picture. She was beginning to feel better, or more with me, at least. Before, when she was pacing in the living room, she hadn't looked naked, but now she did.

Her father was a handsome young man in a white sailor suit, with a sailor hat cocked on the side of his head and an impish smile. It was a boyish face, maybe even a little bit weak-looking, but I didn't think it was up to me to judge that.

"He was a ship's cook," Joy was saying, her voice full of love as she looked at the picture. "When he was home he cooked the greatest food you ever tasted in your life. He made Mama's cooking look like sawdust. And he'd tell me stories about all kinds of places he'd been to, like London, and Sydney, Australia, and New York, and Cape Town, and you name it. And when he come home from a trip he always brought me nice presents, and beautiful things for Mama and for Roy, too. But Roy didn't like 'im."

"His own son didn't like 'im?"

"Roy's like Mama. They disapprove of everything that don't go like the church says it oughta. They called Daddy a bum. He liked to drink whiskey. He got awful drunk sometimes. I mean he couldn't help it. There are people like that. I mean, they drink and then it gets to 'em, you know? They don't do it on purpose, that don't make sense. I mean, does it make sense that a man would deliberately spend all his money on getting so drunk he fell down in the street and wet his pants and had to be took care of like a baby for a week? I mean, no human would do that to hisself on purpose. Nobody's that dumb. It just gets to 'em before they know it, before they can stop it, you know? But Mama always treated 'im like a bum. He'd get back from a trip and get drunk when he got offa the boat and then he'd show up at one o'clock in the morning in a taxi and no money to pay for it, and the driver would knock on the door and wake Mama up and she'd have to pay the taxi and the man would drag Daddy up on the porch and drop 'im like a tow sack full o' garbage and me and Mama'd have to haul 'im in—Roy wouldn't touch 'im!—and undress 'im and warsh all the shit and piss and puke and blood—seems like somebody always decided to beat 'im up just because he was drunk! —warsh that stuff off of 'im, and put 'im to bed like some great big ole helpless baby. And the whole time Mama never stopped hollering at 'im what a no-good, rotten bum he was, even when he was so passed out he didn't hear a word she was saying. And she'd git mad at me because I'd talk nice to 'im and try to make 'im feel better, because he was so sick, and when somebody you love is sick all that crap and corruption don't bother you so much, at least not me, it didn't, not like it did Roy and Mama. But Roy didn't love 'im. He agreed with Mama that he was a hopeless sinner and a bum. But he wasn't. He wasn't. Whenever he was sick, you know, drunksick, Mama wouldn't even cook anything for 'im to eat the next morning. She'd say, 'Well, you sot, you ginhead, you made your bed, now lay in it,' and she wouldn't let me get 'im even a glass of water, and she'd send us off to school and then she'd leave him there in the house all by hisself, sick as a dog. And I'd double back and go home and give him some Bromo-Seltzer, and make him some soft-scrambled eggs and toast and coffee, and take it in to 'im. And when Mama found out she'd switch hell out of me. But it was worth it. And when he got well, even kinda well, oh, he was something! He taught me to cook all kinds of pastries and cakes, and how to fix a ham by punching little holes in it and shoving cloves of garlic in, and how to sew stuffing in a goose, and he could play the mandolin and sing like an angel. He had a voice on 'im that wouldn't quit! He coulda gone on the radio, a lot of people said it! And he knew some of the funniest songs you ever heard."

She started singing and jumped off the bed again.

> *Oh, I'm Captain Jinks of the Horse Marines!*
> *I feed me horse on corn and beans!*
> *I often go beyond me means*
> *To cut a swell in the army!*

She was a funny sight, prancing like a horse, bareass, and singing that silly song with tears on her cheeks. Then she put her daddy's picture back in her little imitation leather wallet and into her purse, and crawled up beside me in the bed again, and got real close like a person looking for affection and security, not sex, and just held onto me for about a minute, without saying anything. Then she said, "One night when a taxi come and the driver come up and knocked on the door, Mama said, 'Keep 'im! Here! Here's enough to pay you for taking 'im back where you got 'im!' And she give the guy some money and the guy drove off with my daddy in the middle of the night, and me screaming like a pig gittin' butchered and Mama and Roy both pounding on me and telling me to shut up, I was waking up the neighbors. That was the last time I ever saw my daddy till I saw 'im in his coffin."

"Well," I said, "no wonder."

"No wonder what?"

I guess I was thinking something like no wonder you've got a loco streak, or no wonder your life is like it is. I wasn't sure. It was something I couldn't tell her. I said, "No wonder you're upset."

"Oh, I'm over it, just about. I mean mostly. Once in a while it gets to me, but I can hannel it, missing my Daddy, I mean. The only thing I'm not over is hating Mama. I dream about killing her in different ways. Sometimes I think about putting rat poison in her Coke, or pouring kerosene on 'er and setting 'er on fire, or stabbin' 'er with a icepick and leavin' the back door open with muddy footprints so's it'd look like somebody come in and did it from outside. One time down at Grammaw Beggs's place I saw Mama gettin' a bucket of water from the well and I thought about shovin' 'er in and I got the picture of her down at the bottom of that well hollerin' to get out and Grammaw Beggs deaf as a doorknob and Mama down there hollerin' for about a month till she passed out and drowned and I commenced to laughin' so hard I couldn't stop and I peed my pants and Grammaw said what was so funny and I said I ain't tellin' and she said I was crazy as a bedbug and she wished Grampaw Beggs was still alive he'd give me a switchin' I never would forgit, but I still couldn't stop laughin', because thinkin' of Grampaw Beggs bein' dead tickled me even more, because he was the meanest and ugliest ole sonofabitch I ever come across in all my born days, bar none. He was as ugly as a mud fence and mean as a stepped-on rattlesnake! Sometimes when Daddy was at sea and we didn't have money to pay rent we'd stay with them on their place over in East Texas, ugliest, scruffiest place you ever saw, no paint on the house, no screens on the windows, no wallpaper, weeds ass-high in the yard, no neighbors, yard full o' chickens and hogs, no radio, no lights just lamps, no nothin'! And Grampaw Beggs hated kids, so every time I opened my mouth he said shut up, and every time I moved he said set still, and every time I asked for somethin' he said no, and I couldn't go anywhere or talk to anybody, and he figgered out some reason I needed a switchin' two or three times a day! He'd pull my panties off and bend me over his knee and whale the livin' daylights outa my bare little butt with a sweetgum switch till I couldn't hardly set down. I can still smell that sweetgum! The switch'd break and that gum was all over my butt, sticky as hell, hard to warsh off, and I'd smell it all the rest of the day. Then I'd have to go to church and set on a hard bench with my butt all striped with switchmarks, and if I squirmed even a little bit Grampaw would lean down and whisper to me that if I didn't stop movin' around he was gonna switch me the minute we got home. So when he died I was glad, and I had trouble actin' like I was sorry. I kept thinkin' I wished it had been Mama. Sometimes when I look at Mama when she's mad she looks just like Grampaw Beggs, just as mean and ugly, like daughter, like father. And right now when I think about Mama down in the bottom of that well hollerin' help help help help till she chokes to death on water I feel like I'm gonna start to giggle again! Wanta see what my daddy brought me from Holland?"

I knew right then that the smart thing for me to do was to get out of there and hide someplace where she would never find me, but I knew I couldn't be smart about what she had. I was like that boogie-woogie piano player down on Congress Avenue that they said made a keyboard throw off sparks and sound like nothing in creation. Everybody said he ought to be in the big time making them holler beat me daddy eight to the bar in the hottest joints in Harlem if he didn't mainline heroin and pass out on the keyboard in the middle of a gig, and his answer was that he knew it was going to kill him but he couldn't stop. And it did. So right then and there, with Joy rustling in the closet for something she wanted to show me, I knew what the piano man was talking about, and it scared me.

She brought out a pair of wooden shoes. She was proud of them. "They fit me when Daddy brought 'em home, but they weren't too comfortable. I was really little when I was twelve. I kinda sprouted up when I was fourteen. He brought me some Meskin jumpin' beans once. They were cute. Did you ever see any jumpin' beans?"

"I was down in Mexico once, uh-huh. I saw some then."

"Mine quit jumpin' after a while. Uncle Phil was real sweet to me after Daddy died."

Her mind was jumping around worse than a jumping bean.

"Sometimes I wish I had a bottle of gin and I could drink it and pass out like Daddy. I did it one time, and it was just a long pretty dream that went on and on and nothin' hurt, you know? It was right after we buried my daddy, and I was hatin' Mama like she was a dead rat in the soup kettle, like I still do, but then it had ahold of me like you wouldn't believe, and I run away from home that night and wandered around out there by the ship channel where Daddy died, and I found a ole guy to buy me a bottle of gin, for my daddy, I said, and he did it and told me good luck, and I had a drink right out of the bottle, and then I hid the bottle in my purse and took a bus out to the cemetery where my daddy was buried, and I had to tell the driver I didn't have any money and he let me ride anyhow, and he asked me why I was gettin' off at the cemetery at night and I said I wasn't, that I was going to cross the field on the other side to my house. And when I got to my daddy's grave the ground was still mounded up on top of him, and I set down there on the dirt and started drinkin' gin and talkin' to Daddy. I told 'im I loved 'im and I missed 'im, and I even poured 'im a drink of gin on the dirt over where his head was, and then I got sleepy and laid down on that dirt, and I swear to God that dirt was warm! It was warmer than the ground around it and warmer than the grass! It was warm! And I fell asleep on my daddy, with his heat coming up from his grave, and I slept like you cain't believe—like a dead pig in the sunshine! And when I woke up it was daylight, and I saw some people comin' toward me, and I run into the woods with the rest of my gin, and that night I went and laid down on my daddy again, and drunk the rest of the gin because I was so hungry, and the next thing I knew I woke up and my Uncle Phil had me in his arms and was carryin' me out of the cemetery. Then I got sick and puked all over his uniform. He took me home and Mama said I was crazy, flat-out crazy, and if I didn't git my screws tightened up pretty quick she was gonna have 'em throw me in the booby hatch or in the reform school, one or the other. She said I was just like my daddy, and if I didn't watch it I was gonna turn out a ginhead just like 'im. About a week later Uncle Phil come by and took me and Roy to a Houston Buffs baseball game. Even though I had just lost my daddy I got excited and screamed and yelled and had fun. Roy just set there like a bump on a log. I forget who was the pitcher for the Buffs, but he was handsome. Uncle Phil said the greatest pitcher he ever saw was Dizzy Dean. He pitched for the Buffs before he went up to the Saint Louis Cardinals. You know about him?"

"Ole Diz won thirty games for the Cards in nineteen thirty-four."

"Is that a lot?"

"Yeah, that's a whole bunch."

"Anyhow, Uncle Phil didn't like Roy, and he didn't invite 'im anymore. Roy was nine years older 'n me, twenty-one, and already sort of sniffin' at everything and everybody to see if they were up to

snuff in his estimation. He was just as—whatchamacallit—as Mama
—you know, looking people over and decidin' if they were good
Christians, and everythin'—there's a word for it—"

"Judgmental?"

"Yeah, that's it, judgmental. So he give Uncle Phil the creeps. One
day Uncle Phil drove me out the highway to a stock auction where he
knew some cowboys. We stopped on the way and got ice cream cones
to lick on, and when we headed out the highway in his patrol car he
turned on the sireen and it made my scalp tickle. I told 'im I'd give
anything if he'd teach me to drive, so he turned off on a country road,
an old dirt road winding across the prairie, and said for me to set on
his lap and he'd let me steer. So I set on his lap and he floorboarded
that thing and we really took off, sireen screaming like a banshee,
and a big cloud of dust flying up behind us. I got so excited I peed all
over both of us. He stopped the car and got out and looked at the
front of his pants and they were soaked! We laughed till we just
about fell down. He said, 'Hell, Joy, I cain't go back to the squad
room and let them boys think I done wet on myself!' So we laughed
some more. And he knew of a creek where we could go swimmin', so
we drove over there, and he made me look the other way while he
took off his pants and drawers and hung 'em up on a limb to dry, and
then he took off all his other stuff and left it in the car, and then he
jumped in the water, and he looked the other way till I got my
clothes off and then I jumped in, and he was a perfect gentleman,
and it wasn't embarrassin' at all. 'Course I didn't have any titties atall,
and no hair on my pussy, and I was built more or less like a boy. So
we had a good time and his pants and underdrawers and my panties
and my skirt dried out, and we looked the other way till each other
got dressed and then we got in the patrol car and took off. After that
he give me regular drivin' lessons, setting on his lap, and one day I
felt somethin' hard pokin' me underneath and I knew what it was but
I didn't say anythin' because I didn't want to embarrass 'im. I mean,
I knew all about hard-ons because growin' up with a brother in the
house, even if he is kind of a sanctimonious drip, you see 'im with a
boner every now and then, and we girls talk about that stuff as much
as you guys do. Then, when I got thirteen Uncle Phil says to me what
did I want for my birthday? And I said I wanted him to take me out
to our private swimmin' hole and let me drive all by myself after we
got on the back road. So that's what we did, and I brought a picnic,

and we got undressed and went swimmin', and somehow we didn't turn our backs anymore, we were kind of used to seeing each other nekkid, and then we sat on the bank with our feet hangin' down and ate our sandwiches and drank our Cokes and I looked down and Uncle Phil had this big boner pointin' right up at me, you couldn't believe it, and he was trying to act like it wasn't there. It was the prettiest thing I ever saw, prettier than a doll any day. I couldn't help myself, I just reached over and took ahold of it, and Uncle Phil said, 'Joy, you ought not to do that. That's not nice.' But the thing was like squirmin' in my hand, you know, and I couldn't let go of it, and the next thing you know he pulled me closer to him and started foolin' around with me and rubbin' my little button. He knew right where it was! I rubbed it every night and I didn't tell anybody I had it and I thought it was a secret, but his big ole finger went right to it! I was really flabbergasted, but I was happy too, 'cause I had this magic little bump and nobody but me and my uncle knew about it! Boy, was I dumb, huh? Anyhow, one thing led to another, and the next thing you know, me and Uncle Phil were lovers, and I stayed so hot for 'im I couldn't think of anythin' else, and the first time I sucked 'im off I liked it so much I wanted to do it every time we happened to be in a place where nobody could see us for a minute or two, like even in the room across the hall with the door open while the whole family was having Thanksgivin' dinner in the dinin' room. Oh, it's so nice to do, you know, and see the guy so happy. It just makes me feel like I'm the most important person in the whole wide world, you know, to be doing something so nice for somebody. Oh, I love screwin' too, but that takes more time. When did you start?"

I had her there, without even lying. "I was twelve." I didn't tell her I not only started then but stopped too, till now.

"Oh, you were lucky. That's why you're so good, you had a lot of practice. My fighter was almost as good as you, but not quite."

I felt queasy. I wouldn't've knowingly shared a cigarette with Eddie Suggs, much less anything else.

"At first I used to dream about marrying 'im. He lived next door to us last year out in Park Place. Those houses are even closer together than here. He used to train in his backyard. He had a punching bag in his garage. I'd hear it in my bedroom in the morning when I was getting ready for school. He made it go real fast. Then he'd come outside and do all kinds of exercises on the grass in those little shorts, you know? He had the cutest butt! Sometimes he'd spar with a friend out there. That really made me hot. I'd watch out the window and think about him doing it to me, think about being married to 'im, a famous fighter, and watching all his fights and cheering for 'im, and 'im being champ of the world and stuff, and his name in the papers all the time, and 'im doing it to me every morning and every night, and me cooking him these great meals and helping 'im stay in shape to be the champ, you know, and having kids, and being a perfect mama that hugs 'em all day and never yells at 'em, and not even let my mama come near 'em to make 'em wish they was dead, like she done me. And Eddie 'n me'd have this cute little house in the country, and when he went off to fight I'd always go with 'im and we'd be true to each other and always be in love! Can you believe how dumb I was! Dreaming up all that junk before I even got to know 'im! One morning I stayed home from school sick and I just walked over to 'im in the yard and asked 'im if I could watch 'im punch the bag. We went in the garage and I asked 'im if he was the only one home, and when he said yes I kissed 'im and he shut the front door of the garage and we did it on the floor. It was a dirt floor with oily black dirt and we got really covered from head to foot with it. As soon as he finished he slid back a ways and started licking me. It was really nice. I thought, well, that's something he does real different from my Uncle Phil. Uncle Phil, he don't just lick, he gets down there like a hog in a trough. I don't even know how he breathes."

Her voice had dropped almost to a whisper, and her breath was shaky, and her eyes were closed, and she was slowly rubbing herself, like she was all alone.

Woodrow Wilson Johnson, scholar, person dreaming of glory, ambitious to be a finer human being, this girl is crazy. She is going to bring you down. Get up and get out of here. What is keeping you here but lack of willpower? When you do get courage to rise, fool, walk away and don't look back. You have more chance of surviving an unarmed encounter with a rabid grizzly.

She was talking again, low and fluttery: "We went in Eddie's house and took a shower together and washed each other off. He asked me how old I was and I said eighteen, and he got down on his knees in the shower and licked me again. It sure did feel nice. He said he was on the fight card that coming Friday night. He give me two tickets and told me to bring a friend. I couldn't stay home from school anymore, so I ran home at lunch and did it with him every day on a clean mat he put down in his garage. Then Friday my brother took me to the fight. Eddie lost, but I got so hot watching them two guys punching each other, I come close to making a pass at my brother on the way home."

She is trouble. Run. Run for your life.

"Like I told you, my brother is very religious. The next day he made it a point to take me with him to see Eddie. He told Eddie we enjoyed the fight and we were sorry he lost, and he was going to get married soon and move across town with his bride, and he hoped Eddie would let him give him complimentary tickets for an evening at Swingatorium. Eddie was real nice with Roy. He had one eye puffed all the way closed, and one of his cheeks was blue, and his lip was split, and he was a mess. He kept looking at me the whole time, and I wanted to do something to make him feel better, but I couldn't on account of my brother being there. And then—" She suddenly sobbed and couldn't go on. She just sat there, gritting her teeth and trying not to cry. I got the impression she had done this a lot in her life. Finally she looked at me sort of pitifully, more like a ten-year-old than a veteran participant in cunnilingus and fellatio and probably other arts I hadn't heard about yet. "Why do brothers have to be so mean?" she whimpered. "He told Eddie that going to a real prizefight and meeting one of the fighters had been a thrill that his fifteen-year-old sister would never forget! You ought to have seen the way Eddie stared at me! And that afternoon when I went over to see him he wouldn't open the door! And he said, 'You lying bitch! Don't you ever come near me again!' I just about cried my eyes out the rest of that day."

The only thing I could think of to say was, "I'm sorry."

"Well, I don't care about losing Eddie, 'cause I got you now, and you're better. I just don't like for people to call me bad names, is all."

She started to kiss me again, but I got up and moved away. "We better not forget what time it is."

"Oh, heckiolies! I have got so much to do. Come on, le's take a bath."

They didn't have a shower, just a big old tub with four iron lion's paws holding it up. We got in together and she was like a carefree little girl again, splashing and giggling. I tried to act that way myself, but I had only one thing in mind—escape. Get out while the getting was good.

She dried me off so carefully and gently and lovingly that I almost forgot she was crazy. When we were both clean and dry she said, "I wish you'd do what Eddie did."

"I don't like to do things in a hurry. I want to learn to do it right, and then make you happy."

"Even a little bit is nice."

"Joy, honey, I don't want to get all het up again. We might forget what time it is, and be crammin' an' jammin' when your mama comes strollin' in."

She giggled. "We would, too! Oh, you are so level-headed! Thank God! And you're not chicken, like Eddie. You don't care how old I am. And you're not one of those nincompoops that uses rubbers. I hate rubbers! Don't you?"

Rubbers. They hadn't even occurred to me. I had owned one once but never got to use it. "Hate 'em?" I said. "Hey, do I take a bath with my socks on?"

She said we had a little straightening up to do to be sure to keep her mama in the dark. "This is my mama's sheet," she said, yanking it off of the bed where we'd spent most of the day. "Mama told me to take it off of the bed and put it to soak, but she didn't say we couldn't use it for a while first. See here, I got a nice clean sheet for my bed, right here." She had folded her own sheet neatly and put it on top of her chest of drawers. We put it on her bed. It looked fit for a God-fearing virgin. Then she shaved off some thin pieces of yellow lye soap her mama had bought instead of laundry flakes to save money, and we threw those in the bathtub half full of warm water and shoved her mama's dirty sheet down in there and sloshed it up and down real hard so as to make suds, and left it to soak.

I was wishing I could take a nap, but even if I'd had time I wouldn't've done it there, because I was sure she'd come after me again, even though she said her legs were trembly and she was start-ing to feel sore.

I was anxious to get out of there. I kissed her at the back door with about as much passion as a husband going off to work. She didn't want to let me go. She said, "Lotsa kids no older 'n us get married. They run off and lie about how old they are and the justice of the peace marries 'em. I bet you'd make a nice husband. I'd be a nice wife like you wouldn't believe. I never would let my husband be miserable like my daddy was. I'd make 'im happy night and day. I'd brag on 'im and feed 'im good and pet 'im and make 'im feel like a king, and no other man would git within a country mile of his private stock, which would be all his to do what he wanted to with any time he pleased. But you're a college boy. You gonna be somebody someday, but I can dream, can't I?" Then she kissed me in a different way, not passionately but softly, sweetly, even kind of sadly, and backed away from the door.

EIGHT

W HEN I ARRIVED at our kitchen door Mom took one look at me and burst out laughing. "Dubby Johnson! Look at you! I do declare! Absolutely! Don't take another step! Get out of those clothes and let me put 'em in the machine! How in the world—?" She left the question unfinished, knowing that I had spent the day playing baseball and had slid into bases and flown through the air with my glove extended as far in front of me as possible to snag a fly ball, landing on my belly and skidding several feet afterwards. She was proud to have a son who did things like that—went all out for the sheer joy of achievement.

My achievement in this case had been the result of running and sliding on my side, back, and belly over and over again for ten minutes in Joy's side yard between the house and the hedge while she watched through the window, languidly sucking her forefinger, apparently considering my activities perfectly logical and unremarkable. I even found a little gravelly area and managed to skin my elbow. Then, the perfect image of a boy whose day has been spent in spirited competition on the baseball diamond, I waved to her and jogged into the alley, pretending not to see her crooking her wet finger to coax me back into the house.

As I undressed on the little enclosed platform behind our kitchen where the washing machine sat, I had trouble answering Mom's questions about my day, not because my powers of invention were diminished by fatigue but because I had created an illusion of reality for her so perfect that I felt a sharp sting of fear about my true character: did I have a criminal mind?

This question haunted me as I stripped to my underwear and threw everything but my tennis shoes in the washing machine. Mom was very proud of this machine. She was one of the few women who had one. Dad had found it abandoned on a vacant piece of land he and his work crew were clearing for a construction project. A compulsive fixer, he had loaded it in his pickup truck, brought it home, repaired the motor, and set it up on the perpetually damp and moldy-smelling porch that he had built outside the kitchen door for storing tubs and other things that took up too much space in the house. It was a monstrosity, just a big heavy washtub on legs, with a motor-driven agitator in the middle to take the place of the scrubwoman. It sounded like a two-ton dump truck straining upgrade, and it shook the whole house. It had to be filled by a hose connected to a hydrant outside by the back steps and emptied through a hose from the bottom of the tub that ran down through a hole in the floor. All we had to do was open a valve and the washwater flowed out and splashed on the ground under the house. There was one big precaution we had to take: the second we started the motor, we had to dart into the kitchen and shut the door, because the porch was a breeding ground for flying cockroaches, and when the machine started to groan and whine and shudder as the agitator bumped left, right, left, right, sloshing the clothes in the soapy water, the roaches came up like a fighter squadron, crashing at full speed into everything and everybody who had not escaped into the kitchen or outside.

It was primitive, but I never heard Mom complain about it. She had spent too many hundreds of hours bent over a scrub board.

For consistent behavior I had to take another bath, as though the one at Joy's had never happened. After that I took a nap. As I was falling asleep I noticed I was smiling.

I dreamed that I was in class and Mr. Williams asked me to talk about the symbolism in Christina Rossetti's "Goblin Market," and my analysis made him and the entire class gasp at its depth and percipience. "This is the first time I've ever understood that poem," Mr. Williams said. When I woke up I remembered the dream perfectly, except for my keys to the symbolism. Then I realized I was only half awake and my dream had combined my regret at having missed Mr. Williams' class and my fear of a recently discovered bas-

ket overflowing with poison fruit. Any fool could understand the
symbolism of girls withering prematurely after sucking the juice from
toxic peaches.

I took out my notebook, sure that a thought worth keeping was
about to move my pencil, but nothing happened. Not only that, but
the other thoughts on the page seemed trite to me. I knew I'd
learned something that can't be learned in books, but how was I to
write it down? I finally wrote, "Some things can't be learned; they
can only be discovered. They can't be got from books any more than
they can be put into books." When I read this over it sounded so
obvious, I erased it.

My two-hour siesta had left me feeling triumphant. I knew that I
was changed. The corny thought came to me that I was no longer a
boy but a man. I wondered if my voice would be different. I dressed
in clean clothes and combed my hair and went into the kitchen and
started a conversation with Mom. My voice was deeper, but I knew
right away it was because I was thinking of it. It would be my same
old voice as soon as I forgot about it. Still, I was different. I was
confident now I was going to be able to study without thinking of sex
all the time, and if the sex started to intrude, well, it was there,
available on short notice, as much of it as a man could need.

Mom told me Betty's mother had called while I was asleep. She
just wondered what had happened between me and Betty for me to
cancel our regular Saturday night date. Mom and Betty's mom didn't
know each other, but they had a lot to talk about on the phone since
they were both Christian Scientists. Betty's mom knew me because
I'd come there to pick up Betty, but my mom didn't know Betty,
except from all the nice things I'd said about her. That, and the fact
that Betty "had been brought up in Christian Science," was enough
to prove to Mom that she was an exceptional girl, chaste, and honest
and good-natured, and probably smart to boot. So my cooling off on
her was a blow to Mom's dreams. "Confide in me, honey," she said.
"What happened?"

I had the urge to say, "Nothing happened. And that's why I'm fed
up with the little prickteaser, Mom." But instead I said, "Mom, it's
not anything that happened. It's just, you know, I like Betty a lot, but
she's kind of interfering with my thought processes when I study.
And besides, I'd be better off if I had a girlfriend on this side of town,
somebody I could take for a walk or to the movies or something

without spending so much money on gas and wear and tear on your car."

Jenny walked in, bouncing her red jacks ball. "Dubby, can you play jacks with me?"

Mom held up her hand to stop the interruption. Then she said gravely: "Dubby, most girls out there looking for a fine young man like you do not come from Christian Science families. That is why I prefer to think of this as a simple pause in your relationship. Absence makes the heart grow fonder. After a while your eyes will turn away from the dross and back to the gold. The course of true love never runs smooth, honey."

"Dubby talked to a girl last night," Jenny piped up.

"Well," Mom said, smiling at me to remind me that little sisters are their brother's keepers, "I'm sure she was a nice girl."

"She ditten look nice to me," Jenny said. "And he called her by her name, too. It's Joy."

"Oh, Mrs. Hurt's daughter," Mom said. "They just moved in, over on Sixteenth. Did you meet her, Dubby?"

"Well, sort of. Like, hi, you know, at Mr. Schultz's."

"I'm sure she's a very nice young lady," Mom said. "Her mother—"

Jenny persisted. "She ditten look nice to me."

"Jenny," Mom said, warningly. "If you can't say anything nice, don't say anything." Then she turned to me. "I met Mrs. Hurt the first day they moved in. I'm on the Committee, you know, to disseminate our literature, so I was there before the van left. I gave her a sample of the *Monitor*, which she promised to read. I think she was a little bit afraid of me when she found out I was a Scientist. She expected me to act like a witch doctor or go into a trance or something, absolutely. So I did some good, just dropping in on her and letting her know Scientists are Christians too, and we have a lot in common. We had a nice chat. Her husband left her for a floozy. Her son is married and lives out on the South Side somewhere. She is a very religious woman, very strict. I think she said she was Baptist, but she may have said Methodist. I'm not sure. But whatever it is, she's raising her daughter in a strict Christian tradition. So Jenny, honey, judge not that ye be not judged."

Jenny was not convinced, but she was tired of the subject. I went out on the front porch with her and played jacks. Jenny was impressed with the speed of my hands. Every time she saw a fly, she wanted me to grab it. I didn't swat them; I snatched them on the wing. Sometimes, if they were crawling, I grabbed them between my thumb and forefinger. I recognized the slow ones that I could catch this way—they were larger and fuzzier and blacker and had a glint of blue-green on their backs. One of these landed on Jenny's bare knee. She was sitting spraddle-legged, watching me throw jacks. I said, "Don't move." She held still. The fly crawled toward a skinned place on her knee. He was reckless. I'd heard they got drunk on fermented garbage, and that's the way this one acted. Jenny couldn't wait. She slapped at it and it buzzed up and circled. "He'll come back," I said. "Let me get 'im." He landed again in the same place. I plucked him off her knee with my index finger and thumb, slammed him hard to the floor to stun him, and stepped on him.

"How you do that, Dubby? How you do that?"

"I have to go wash my hands." Since the polio epidemic, when the doctors announced the discovery that the disease was being spread by flies, everybody washed their hands with soap after touching a fly, or touching anything that was fly-crawled. Even hungry people would throw away perfectly good food if a fly walked on it. Mom had given me a penny for every five flies I killed, payable in cash as soon as I produced the corpses. Our house was virtually fly-free in no time. Most people got rid of them by spraying with Gulfspray, in a sprayer that had to be pumped by hand, like a bicycle pump. But Mom couldn't afford Gulfspray, and my method was more of a sport and kept the money in the family.

Jenny followed me to the bathroom to watch me wash my hands. She yelled at Mom: "Dubby grabbed another fly!"

"That's nice. Be sure and wash your hands, Dubby."

Jenny ran into the kitchen. "He jus' grabbed 'im—hup!—like that! How he do that, Mom?"

"I don't know, honey. Practice, I guess. I can't do it, I know that. I even miss with the flyswatter sometimes, absolutely."

I came into the kitchen. Jenny started pulling on my arm, my shirt, insisting on an answer. "Dubby! Tell me! How you do that? Now, come *on*, Dubby!"

"Well, honey, I don't reach for 'em. If you reach for 'em, they're gone. What I do is, I *think* my fingers to 'em."

"Come *on*, *Dubbeee!*"

Mom shook her head. "Don't tease your sister, Dubby."

"I'm not teasing. That's what I do. If my hand is here, and the fly is there, I just say to my hand 'Be there.' Not 'Go there.' 'Be there.' And my hand is there. That's about all I can tell you."

Jenny spent about half an hour trying to think her hands to different places. Finally she gave up.

We had a great Saturday evening. Red beans and fatback, with chile peppers and whatever Mom put in to give it the flavor nobody else could achieve, cooked on a low fire all day, till each bean was a special treat to bite down on, and cornbread and iced tea. Then we made fudge, and Mom played the piano and we sang some of our old-timey favorites, the sentimental ones for Mom and the funny ones for Jenny and me.

Every now and then I thought about Joy. I wondered if her legs were still shaky and her knees weak and if they interfered with her clearing tables at the Swingatorium. It was comforting that her brother worked there to watch over her and to bring her home after the Swingatorium closed at two o'clock in the morning. It was strange that her mother treated me like a skunk-squirted stray dog when I introduced myself that night on the porch and never mentioned that she had met my mother. Maybe Mom hadn't impressed her with the normalcy and harmlessness of Christian Scientists, after all.

The angelic vision I had seen—or invented—in church the previous Sunday had recurred to me with decreasing frequency and diminishing intensity during the week, so that on Saturday, my busy Saturday, I had not experienced it at all, not consciously, at least. But when I woke up on Sunday morning it was in my mind, as clear as it had been that first brief moment. I tried to put it out, to negate it, dismiss it. I preferred to lie in bed and forget church and relive my long Saturday of unadulterated lust, but the vision suffused me, beckoned me. It held the promise of love. I got up and helped Mom make breakfast, and announced that I was looking forward to church, but I wanted to sit closer to the front, if it was okay with her, because last Sunday the people in front of me rustling about had made me miss some of the text. This was a gift to Mom, a moment to cherish and nourish. She promised we'd get there early enough to sit down front. I dressed in my thirty-five-dollar suit that Mom had bought for my graduation from Reagan the year before and was still paying for on easy terms, and I managed to guide us down to a row near the side exit on the right. I waited with controlled breath as the church filled up, but the vision did not appear. We had to rise a couple of times for people to get past us. Mom took this opportunity to show me off to her friends. "You know my boy Woodrow, don't you?"

"My goodness, Woodrow, is that you? You sure have sprouted up!"

While I was standing on these brief occasions, I managed to twist around and scan the back rows, and the people still coming in. There was that dumpy Margaret that Mom had talked me into escorting to a piano recital last summer. She waved, but I acted like I didn't see her. Nowhere in the church was there anything even remotely akin to an angel. The service, when it finally started, was so dull it stupefied me, though the people around me, whose faces I studied out of the corner of my eye, seemed engrossed in it. When it was over I shot to my feet hoping I could lead Mom out the side door and avoid all the small talk and sanctimony of walking one small step at a time up the aisle shoulder to shoulder and rump to belly with all those perfumed and soul-cleansed people, but it was not to be. Mom had my arm, and we were going to proceed up the aisle in an orderly, unhurried way and participate in the social ritual of standing around in the sunshine in front of the church and beaming at each other. I turned to face the long walk, and it was there, the vision, the Angel, flashing past my sight for a split second, a lightning flash only, nothing but a pert little head on a curved ivory neck, dark hair knotted severely in back, passing from the indoor light to the sunlight, then gone.

"Oh, my God."

"What, honey?"

I realized the words had come from me. As usual, instead of an honest response, instead of saying something like "Mom, can we hurry? I just saw a girl I have to meet," I said, "I just remembered I didn't bring a book home that I need for my exam on Monday."

"Maybe you can borrow it from somebody, honey."

"Let's hurry. I'll call around when we get home." Mom did hurry with me up the aisle, as much as one can hurry in such a situation. When at last we arrived on the front lawn, there was not a sign anywhere of an angelic presence. She had vanished. I hid my anguish, the ridiculous anguish I felt at such an unreal loss, and strove to be mature and take my time and give myself over to chatting politely with Mom's friends, an essential part of going to church.

That afternoon my maturity started wearing off and the sap started rising in me. I studied for a couple of hours and then went out for a walk while Mom took Jenny to Herrman Park Zoo. I walked past Joy's house and saw that the shades were all down and there was no sign of life. That would be normal: up late Saturday night, early to church on Sunday, siesta all Sunday afternoon. But those drawn shades made me realize my original complacency about Joy being a handy deep well I could go to whenever I felt dry was misplaced. There was such a thing as limited access. There was her mom, who was going to look on me as the son of a woman who wouldn't take an aspirin even if she had a headache. Mrs. Hurt was sure to ask herself if a woman who called a "practitioner" instead of a doctor when somebody in her family was sick, and believed this practitioner off somewhere else could "know the truth" and cure what ailed her without any medicine, could possibly have a son who wasn't a little bit loco. And then there was the place, the private place to achieve our conjunction, not to mention the time required for our "climb," as I wrote in my notebook, "to that fine frenesi which, once known, makes every other state of being only an unremarkable way station."

That description stayed in my notebook about five minutes, about the time it took for me to picture Jenny rummaging in my drawer and finding it and bringing it to Mom and asking her what it meant.

I erased it, then, not sure the erasure couldn't be deciphered, I tore out the page, ripped it into small pieces, and watched it spin around the toilet bowl and disappear.

NINE

ONDAY EVENING I walked over to Joy's house. There was no one on the porch. My gunslinger persona was easier to assume than ever, now that I knew for a fact that I was a lover and not just a tumescent boy for Mrs. Sandusky to have fun with.

I knocked. Pretty soon Mrs. Hurt opened the door. I took off my big hat.

"Good evening, Miz Hurt. I just come by to bring you regards from my mother, whom I believe you know, and to ask—"

She listened that far with a scowl which asked clearly but silently what in God's name this boy was doing knocking on her door. Then she interrupted with: "Joy's doin' her homework." She started to close the door.

"Oh, I wouldn't want to interfere in her studies. I was just wondering if sometime I might have the privilege of escorting her to a movie over on Nineteenth Street, ma'am."

"Joy's doin' bad in school. She's not goin' anywhere for anything till she quits failin' Spanish." Her face disappeared as she was saying this and I saw the heavy front door coming toward me. My boot heels stuck to the porch, and the door banged shut eight inches from my nose, which would've been an effective discouragement if she hadn't said the word *Spanish*. I took a couple of deep breaths. My boots didn't slide back even an inch. I knocked again and waited. Mrs. Hurt finally yanked open the door and glared at me. "Are you deaf?"

"No, ma'am. I speak Spanish, and I thought maybe I could have the privilege of helping your daughter with her lessons. Tutoring her. Free. For nothing, I mean."

She looked at me sideways. "I'll say one thing for you, boy. You got the nerve of a brass monkey. How do I know you know how to talk Spanish?"

"Well, you could trust me, ma'am, unless you speak Spanish enough to test me out. I was born in San Antonio, and I went to a school where all the kids spoke Spanish instead of English, so I grew up speaking it. I got a one-plus on my last Spanish exam at Rice."

"You sure do strut your stuff, don't you? Well, come on in, and let's see what you can do. But I'm not paying you. And this doesn't mean you're taking her to the movies or anywhere else. I'm very particular about the boys that make the acquaintance of my daughter."

"Yes, ma'am. I don't blame you, ma'am. My mother said you were a good Christian lady and you were bringing up your daughter to be a good Christian, too. She said you were very strict. That's why she approved of me asking permission to take her out."

"You won't git permission to take her out," she said quickly, "if that means going riding in a car. Joy is not allowed to go with boys in a car. I know what goes on, and it's not going to go on with my daughter. If you help her with her lessons and if you meet with my approval, I just might give you permission maybe to walk her to the movies. That remains to be seen."

"Yes, ma'am."

This all took place just inside the front door. I could see through to the kitchen, where Joy was watching us out of the corner of her eye while pretending to be looking at her book. Mrs. Hurt led me back to the kitchen, indicated a chair across the table from Joy, and introduced us: "You remember this boy that come up on the porch and borrowed a match?"

Joy looked at me with a straight face and said: "Kinda."

"His name's Bud. Her name's Joy."

"Excuse me, ma'am. It's Dub."

"Dub? Is that a real name?"

"It's a nickname, ma'am. From my initials, W. W."

"Dub's a dumb name."

"Yes, ma'am."

"W. W. claims he talks Spanish and he can help you learn it better."

"Well, Mama, I sure do hope he can. 'Cause this stuff makes me want to climb up on top of the Esperson Building and jump off."

I told Joy the way to learn a language was to say the words out loud over and over again so your mouth learned them and your tongue learned them. I had her repeating *"mi madre," "mi casa," "la cocina," "la mesa," "el perro,"* over and over again and enjoying it. I particularly complimented her on the way she pronounced a word that is always difficult for Anglo-Saxons to say—*perro*—meaning dog. But she learned to say it perfectly in no time, rolling her double *r* like a Mexican native.

"Look, Mama, I say it like a Meskin," Joy said. "See how quick my tongue learns?" She and I both kept a straight face at this, and Mrs. Hurt agreed that Joy's tongue was a fast learner.

After two hours I had Joy saying whole sentences over and over again, like a parrot, and laughing and thinking Spanish was fun. Mrs. Hurt didn't leave the kitchen the whole time and didn't crack a smile, either. She just puttered around, wiping the drainboard several times, snapping some beans, ironing a blouse, hardly ever turning her back for a second, as though I might commit some obscene act from my chair with the kitchen table between us. Finally she sat down next to Joy and did some knitting, glancing at the clock. After a while she said that would be enough for tonight; she wanted Joy to get to bed early. She didn't thank me, but Joy said brightly, *"Muchas gracias, Señor* Johnson." Then she asked her mom if I could teach her some more tomorrow night, because she thought she could learn so much from me. Mrs. Hurt didn't look at either of us. She turned the corners of her mouth down. Finally she said, "I'll think about it." Joy had deported herself the entire evening like a Christian virgin, and I had acted very tutorial. We felt we deserved her mother's trust.

Mrs. Hurt saw me to the door, leaving Joy in the kitchen. Joy called out *"Buenas noches, Señor* Johnson," as I was leaving, and I said *"Hasta mañana, señorita."*

Tuesday I stayed late at Rice, doing my homework in the basement library to avoid the temptation of sneaking over to Joy's house before her mother came home at five-thirty. Joy got home from school at about four-thirty so there was a one-hour red zone there where doing a Speedy Gonzales would be like crossing the double line to pass on a curve.

When I got home about six Mom told me Joy had called at four-thirty to thank me for my tutoring and to say that her teacher had already noticed a big improvement in her Spanish, and she was looking forward to her next lesson. "I know people," Mom said, "and that girl is a nice girl. She has the voice of a devout young lady."

I called and Mrs. Hurt answered, and I asked her if it would be all right if I helped Joy with her Spanish again. I made sure that on the phone I had the voice of a young gentleman.

Mrs. Hurt said she guessed it would be okay.

I tutored Joy Tuesday and Wednesday evening and on Thursday she got the first *A* on a Spanish quiz she had ever gotten. She called my mother at four-thirty and told her so. When I got home at six I called right away and got Mrs. Hurt and told her that *Mr. Deeds Goes to Town* was playing at Heights Theater, and I had heard it was a very inspirational movie, and I would take it as an honor to be allowed to walk her daughter over to Nineteenth Street to see it and walk her safely home again.

Mrs. Hurt said she guessed it would be okay, so long as we came straight home after. She didn't mention the *A* Joy had got on account of me.

Joy wasn't quite ready when I got there, and I was left standing in the living room. I heard her and her mother arguing in her bedroom. They were trying to keep their voices down, because in their dinky little frame house you could hear everything that went on. I could tell Joy was exasperated; I heard her exclaim "Mama!" Then, after a few more seconds, she flounced into the living room, mad as a wet hen but ready to leave.

It was an overcast night, a quarter of eight, and it was already dark. We went around the corner past Mr. Schultz's. When we got to the entrance to the alley, Joy was still steaming. Suddenly she stepped into the shadows, hiked up her dress, and wiggled out of her panties. She stuffed them in her purse. "She makes me wear these white ugly things ever' time I go out! An' then, when I git home, she inspects them! Bitch!" After that she quit pouting, and we hurried so as not to be late to the movie.

By the time we got to Nineteenth Street, we could hear excited yelling from the park about a block away.

"What's all that yelling?" Joy asked. She was wearing her light green cotton dress, and no part of it was still for a second.

"Oh, that's the fights."

90

"*Fights?*" She got very intense. "What kind of fights?"

"You know. Guys boxing. They have 'em on Thursday nights."

Joy made a little squeaking sound, and a ripple went through her whole body. "Oh! I wanta see it!" She panted with her mouth open, like a sheepdog on a hot day.

I thought her reaction was a joke, but then I saw that she was actually having shortness of breath, and squirming like she was going to wet her pants.

I tried one more time to stay out of trouble. "It's a terrific movie."

"I don't *care!*"

"I saw it. It's really—"

"Then you can tell me the story! So I can tell Mama! *Come on!*"

She had me by the hand, and her voice was little-girlish, almost like Jenny's as she yanked me in the direction of the fights. She trotted, leaning forward, pulling me along, making eager-puppy squeaks. When we got to the back of the crowd—about fifty people —there was a fight on in the ring, apparently a rouser for a change. Joy pushed her way through, dragging me behind her, people making way without wanting to take their eyes off the action. I was self-conscious about pushing forward, being tall enough to see from the rear, so I nodded apologies to everyone we passed and remained stooped over so they could see over me. When we got to the very front, close to the ring, we dropped to our knees. Joy still clung to my hand. She was scratching my palm with her fingernail and bumping her haunch against mine, and continuing to pant as though she couldn't get her breath.

In the ring were two lightweights I'd never seen before, both wearing real boxing trunks, both with enough experience to be ripping at each other in a controlled, semi-skilled way instead of the usual wild roundhouse rights and falling-down clinches. Unlike most of Roscoe's contestants, these two relished the fight, seemed to want to take each other's head off. Both had bloody faces. They were standing toe to toe, neither willing to give an inch.

On her knees beside me, Joy turned toward me, put one arm across her lap to hide her other hand, which disappeared up her dress, frantically strumming some special spot. Her eyes rolled up, her lids fluttered, she shuddered, and right there, with fifty people screaming at the fighters and almost falling over us in their excitement, she had an orgasm. She grabbed me and pulled me to her and kissed me

91

deeply. I accepted it, but it just wasn't in my nature to be that reckless. I was aware that the round was over, that Roscoe was shoving them apart and yelling *"Stop!"* For some reason Roscoe had never bothered getting a bell for these events, I suppose because then he'd have to depend on somebody to ring it, which would take some of the control away from him. Roscoe had to physically push the two boys toward neutral corners. They still wanted blood. The crowd clapped and yelled and whistled. Since this was a tournament with a visiting park there were two volunteer judges from neutral neighborhoods. Roscoe stepped over and got their scorecards, and pulled a card and a stub pencil out of his own pocket. He studied the cards for a few seconds. Then he called the two boys to the center of the ring. They were still glowering at each other.

"Folks," Roscoe shouted, as though talking to a thousand fans, "was that a doozy, or was that a doozy?" The crowd clapped louder and whistled and yelled the fighters' names, about evenly split between "Wildcat" and "Nightmare."

Joy leaned close to me and whispered, "I like the one with the tattoo." Then she stuck her tongue in my ear.

The tattoo was a snarling blue wildcat on the fighter's left forearm.

Roscoe shouted, "Here's the decision, folks! Judge Harry Keene from Norhill has it one round for Wildcat Hames, one round for Nightmare Mullens, and one even!" Boos and cheers. "Judge Danny Diamond from Beaumont Road scores it two rounds for Wildcat and one for Nightmare." Boos, catcalls, cheers.

Joy screamed, "Yeaaaay, Wildcat!" Wildcat looked at her and waved a glove. Roscoe looked our way too, and saw me, and motioned that he wanted to talk to me.

"And the referee's card has it two rounds for Nightmare and one for Wildcat!" Roscoe shouted. "The decision—a draw!" He held up both fighters' hands.

The crowd booed. Half of them yelled, "Wildcat!" The other half chanted, "Nightmare!" Wildcat reached across Roscoe and slammed his glove into Nightmare's face. They both broke loose from Roscoe and started fighting again.

"No! No! Knock it off!" Roscoe yelled. He grabbed Wildcat, which gave Nightmare a chance to slug him. Nightmare's second shot landed on the back of Roscoe's head.

The crowd laughed and egged the two boys on. One of the judges jumped in the ring and helped Roscoe separate and hold them.

"I whupped yo' ass six ways from Sunday!" Wildcat screamed at Nightmare.

"Yeaaaay!" Joy yelled. She was jumping up and down, clutching both her breasts.

"Gimme them gloves, you two jackasses!" Roscoe said. "We got more fights comin' up!" The helpful judge started taking the gloves off of Nightmare.

Nightmare spat at Wildcat. "We'll settle this 'thout gloves, you little fairy!"

As soon as their laces were loosened, both boys jerked their hands out of the gloves and jumped out of the ring and ran to a dark clearing. Most of the crowd followed.

Joy was trying to yank my arm out of its socket. "Let's watch! Come on, Dub!"

Roscoe yelled: "Hold on, folks! We got some more good match-ups!"

Only about a third of the crowd, the older men, remained at ringside. I let Joy drag me toward the bare-knuckles contest fifty feet away. We got there just in time to see a big woman grab Nightmare from behind and hold him long enough for Wildcat to land a right flush on his chin. The big woman, who had a red, yellow, and blue tattoo on top of one breast ballooning over the top of her blouse, let Nightmare drop to the grass, reached for Wildcat's hand, and said, "Come on, sugah, le's haul ass."

She hustled the bloody Wildcat away from the crowd. Nobody seemed to care about Nightmare. Disappointed at the sudden ending, they wandered back toward the ring. I knelt beside Nightmare, who was sitting up shaking his head. He was bleeding from the mouth, nose, and ear. Joy was not concerned with him. She was pulling at my hand. "We're gonna miss the next fight, Dub!"

Nightmare looked at me with crossed eyes. I said, "Hey. You okay?"

"Fuck you," said Nightmare.

Joy and I headed back toward the ring only to find Roscoe blocking our way. "Tex, don't let me down now. We need you. Our middle-weight didn't show. If we win tonight, we gonna win the city championship. This is the only team comes close to us, 'cepin River Oaks.

We cain't lose the middleweight on a forfeit, boy! Look, he's a little shitbird, pardon my French, Miss—hey, Tex, this here one's prettier'n a two-hunnerd-dollar mule!"

Joy was tickling my palm with her fingernail. She smiled at Roscoe and said, "Thank you."

"This boy can fight! Did you know that, honey? He gonna win one fer yore pretty yella hair! He gonna go in there with that straight left —pop pop pop pop pop—and that overhand right like that Kraut whupped the nigger—*Boom!*—Goodnight, Sweetheart, put out the cat and lock the door. Ole Tex here he gonna win the middleweight fer you, no sweat!"

Joy had been staring at me with shimmering eyes, biting her lower lip. Suddenly she screamed at the top of her voice, *"Yes!"*

All I could think of was: He's crazy and she's crazier.

"You're on next, Tex. He won't last thirty seconds. He won't land a shot. Jus' keep thinkin' move move move popopopopopop*boom!* You got the reach, you got the speed. Move stab *boom.*"

Joy grabbed me with both arms and exhaled a huge *"Yessss!"*

"I can't move with these boots, man," I drawled. No ten-notch gunfighter ever spoke with icier calm.

"They're offa there!" Roscoe said. "Honey, pull them boots. Git yore boy ready for combat! Come on, Tex, seddown rat chere. You have got the prettiest second in the hist'ry."

He put his hand on my shoulder and pushed down hard. I did not have enough gumption to resist. I sank to the ground like a gutless wonder. Joy dropped to her knees and started tugging at my boots. "Oh, Dub, honey, sweetie, oh, I cain't wait, I cain't stand it, I cain't wait to watch you kill 'im, kill im, just kill 'im, kill 'im for me, honey."

She's nuts. She is flat-out loco. She doesn't even know who I'm fighting. She doesn't even know who she wants me to kill.

TEN

NOTHING SEEMED REAL. Nothing had logic. It was going to be a prizefight, not the kind of a prizefight we saw in the movie theater a couple of weeks after it happened in New York, with two skilled professionals battling for a huge sum of money. Here the prize would be winning, or surviving with all your teeth, or with your brain more or less intact.

Why was I doing it?

If I was strong enough to fight, why wasn't I strong enough not to fight?

Everything was in slow motion, and I knew why: when I got scared, everything around me slowed down. I was going to write in my notebook, "Fear is the great awakener."

I was in the ring. A man I had never seen before was lacing on my gloves. They were damp inside, the same gloves that Wildcat or Nightmare had been wearing. No tape on my hands. That was for pros. No shoes. No trunks, just my dungarees. No protective cup. Joy was holding my boots, my socks, my shirt.

I hadn't looked across the ring at my opponent. Now I forced myself to think about him. I looked. He was short, maybe five-five, and a little pudgy, and baby-faced, and he looked to be as scared as I was. He had shiny red hair like brush bristles, freckles, and a large turned-up nose. He wore real boxer's trunks and boxer's shoes. And his mouth looked funny. His lips were misshapen. He had a mouthpiece! A mouthpiece. My God, without a mouthpiece, if he landed one on my buckteeth . . .

95

A fly was buzzing around my face, bumping into my nose, my eye, drunk from the lights and the abandoned Coca-Cola bottles and candy wrappers on the grass. If I didn't have these gloves on, I'd grab the bastard.

Roscoe was announcing us. "In this corner, from West Seventeenth Street—"

The crowd was laughing. Roscoe stopped his spiel and came over to me. "Tex, you ain't fixin' to do battle with that ten-gallon Stetson on, are ye? The crowd laughed and jeered. "Well," Roscoe shouted, "you folks don't have no trouble figgerin' out which one is Tex, now, do ye?" More laughter.

I went dead cold. Draw, podner. "I was aiming to keep it on," I drawled, "but if it's against the rules . . ." Somehow I managed to grab the brim in spite of my padded glove and sail it in a perfect looping parabolic arc into the arms of Joy.

She jumped up and down, hugging her armload of my possessions. "Kill 'im, baby!" she yelled.

"Okay, folks, Tex Johnson in this corner, weighing one hunderd and fifty-eight pounds, from West Seventeenth Street, and over here in this corner, weighing one hunderd and sixty pounds, from Beaumont Highway, Battlin' Billy Batchelder!"

Neither I nor Battling Billy got much of a hand. Only Joy let out a loyal yelp when my name was announced, and Battling Billy's name drew chuckles except from a plump lady in a canvas chair near his corner, puffing on a dark cigarillo. She growled in a hoarse voice, "Bust 'im in two, Billy!" I knew she had to be Billy's mother. She had the same big turned-up nose and the same copper-red hair.

Roscoe motioned us to the center of the ring and told us not to hit below the belt, and to break when he said break, and to shake hands and come out fighting. Battling Billy was shorter than I by almost a foot. He stared up into my face the whole time, chewing on his mouthpiece, pounding his gloves together, but I didn't meet his eyes. I was embarrassed. It all seemed pretty silly.

"Go!" Roscoe yelled.

Battling Billy took me by surprise. He charged at me with his head low, and swung so hard at my ribs that, when I skipped back and he missed, he turned all the way around with his back to me. I felt a breeze on my belly as his fist went by.

Hey, this son of a bitch is trying to cripple me. Why is he so serious?

He came back standing straight up and hooking with both hands. I backpedaled. He missed, and missed and missed. I was so busy getting out of his way I forgot to punch. When I finally remembered I was supposed to "popopop" him, he bobbed and weaved and brushed off my feeble jabs.

It was pretty obvious I had to do something to deter him before he put a permanent crimp in my backbone.

Think it there. Think it there.

He was getting winded. He stopped charging for a second and took a deep breath. Then he swung that right-handed spine-snapper again with all he had, but he got only air, turning himself half around again with the force of his swing. Then he righted himself and came back with those left and right hooks, all whistling past my skinny ribs. I remembered Schmeling's "I zee zompting" before his first fight with Joe Louis, and I remembered what he saw—Louis vulnerable to an overhand right when he threw that left hook.

I saw something, too.

I imagined a fly on Battling Billy's nose. The next time he threw that sweeping right . . .

Think it there. Think it there.

He threw it and spun half around. I saw a fly on his nose and told my right hand: Be there.

It landed. He flew backwards, blood spurting from both nostrils. The single rope gave way and he landed in the lap of the plump freckled lady in the canvas chair. The chair collapsed, and Battling Billy and the lady landed on the grass, the lady screaming and Battling Billy twitching, trying to get his bearings.

I had landed the only punch in the fight.

Joy was in the ring, screaming and hugging me.

I was glad she was holding me so tight because I might've collapsed if she hadn't. I was shaking harder than when Mrs. Sandusky pulled my pants down.

The crowd was silent, and a long way off.

I couldn't hear what anybody was saying. Joy and I walked out of the ring. The rope was on the ground, the ring stakes flattened. I looked back and saw that Battling Billy was on his feet. His face was a red smear, and his mother was trying to wipe the blood off with her skirt. Her legs were white as bread dough.

Joy and I kept walking. She was ecstatic. She grabbed my crotch. Then she jumped and rammed her tongue in my ear.

Roscoe caught up with us. "Hey, Tex! Tol' ye, ditten I? What a shot! But don't run off with the gloves, boy!"

I stood there while he unlaced the gloves and took them off my hands. I was trying to remember what I was going to write in my notebook.

One of the judges from the Wildcat-Nightmare fight came up and grabbed my hand and pumped it. "You have got a special talent, young man," he pronounced, like a preacher about to start a sermon. "Speed and power. How'd you like to make ten dollars?"

"Ten dollars?" Joy said, hardly trusting her ears. "Yes!"

The fight had lasted less than a minute, and I'd only thrown one punch, but I was out of breath. I wanted to get my Bull Durham out of my shirt pocket and roll one before I answered this sanctimonious-sounding man, but my hands were trembling, even though I was holding on tight to Joy. So instead of stalling, I drawled: "Doing what?"

He was a small, stoop-shouldered man with wispy graying hair. He had dandruff on the shoulders of his dark jacket. His red tie was greasy-looking at the knot.

He introduced himself as Mr. Daniel Diamond, manager and trainer of boxers, and asked if we could speak confidentially and—he smiled avuncularly at Joy—in private for only a few moments.

"Well," I said, giving Joy a hug, "this young lady is a special friend of mine, so can we speak confidentially? Yes. But in private? I'm afraid not, not at this time. Anything you wish to say to me can be said in front of her."

"Doing what?" Joy asked.

"I beg your pardon?" Mr. Diamond said, having decided it was important to have Joy on his side.

"What does he have to do to get the ten dollars?"

We had got away from the crowd at ringside. Behind us, Roscoe was announcing another fight, and two boys were having the damp gloves laced on. Joy had set my hat back on my head, but I was still barefoot and bare-chested, and her arms were full of my shirt and

socks and boots. Mr. Diamond took several more steps before he
made a careful answer: "We shall come to that in due course, Miss."

"My name's Joy."

"Miss Joy, your friend Mr. Johnson is a talented man. Professional
fighters in Texas, to get a license, must be of a certain age. Based
on—"

"I don't want to be a professional fighter," I said.

"Of course you don't," Mr. Diamond said. "But you, in the present economical atmospherics of our republic, would not be adverse to
collecting an easy ten dollars in cash, I imagine."

"He wants the ten dollars," Joy said. "But for doin' what?"

"We'll arrive at that, Miss Joy. Mr. Johnson, based on what I saw in
that ring tonight, you are a mature human, capable of independent
thought. I'm sure you are of the proper age to epitomize yourself into
the sporting event to which I am about to allude. I assume your age. I
don't insult you by asking you to prove it. Gentlemen have to operate
on trust. Now, a friend of mine owns a ranch out toward Beaumont.
He's a person who's very indulgent in sports. You know, in baseball
they have their minor leagues. The boxing game has a verisimilitudi-
nous concept, except that it is not so well known. The ten dollars
don't go toward making a man a professional fighter. The ten dollars
is just a token of depreciation from my friend for the precipitation of
talented young men in the entertainment of the afternoon. There's
not anything to sign, no licenses to worry about, nothing like that.
Just the enjoyment of precipitation in a sporting event. My job—not
a job, just a friendly jester to my friend—is to notice talent such as
you possess and to invite you to come out to the ranch of a Saturday
afternoon and join in the fun—and, of course, come away richer by
ten dollars."

"I git it," Joy breathed excitely. "All he's got to do is what he did
tonight, and we got ten dollars!" She twisted around and kissed me
on the left nipple of my bare chest, and then put her lips up to mine
and kissed me again with several little wet pecks, and then whispered loud enough to make Mr. Diamond smile: "Dubby! Ten dollars!"

"Three three-minute rounds, against an opponent of lesser ability.
If it goes the distance that's better than a dollar a minute. However,
misfortunately for the chaps who challenge you, such as that young
man tonight, the encounter is more likely to last a minute or less,

which brings your pay—well, not pay, reward is the word—your reward to ten dollars a minute."

Joy jumped up and down like Jenny always did when she saw an ice cream cone, and she covered my naked chest with kisses, all the time stammering and stuttering "Dubby! We're we're ri-rich! Te-ten dol-dollars! *MMMM*mmm*MMM*mmm!"

She has gone plain loony and he is a snake-oil salesman and I am standing here without a shirt on listening to them decide my life. I do not have any backbone, any willpower, any identity of my own. I am as suggestible and controllable as one of Dr. Pavlov's dogs.

"Of course, you mustn't say anything about this to anyone, because if the word should get out, I would have so many volunteers from young men so gratitudinous in these days and times for the opportunity to replenish their family coffins, that the reward would probably go down to five dollars or less."

"Don't you worry, Mr. Diamond, Dub and me know a good thing when we see it. We won't breathe a word."

"Don't they call you Tex?" Mr. Diamond asked.

"Everybody but me," Joy assured him. "Dub's my pet name for 'im, because we're pretty—you might say—close."

Mr. Diamond smiled in a very special way at Joy, his eyes lingering on some area below her eyes. Then he reached out and patted her several times on the shoulder. "I assimilate your meaning, Miss Joy. He's a lucky young man to have such a warm friend. Tex—if I may call you that instead of Mr. Johnson—"

"Tex is a fine name!" Joy said. "Don't you agree, Dub?"

I nodded. I was trying to think of a word.

"And you can call me Danny instead of Mr. Diamond, now that we're friends."

The word came to me: *unctuous.*

"Do you folks know where Ben Hugo's gym is, out on North Main?"

"I do," Joy said. "I was there once."

Her fighter.

"That's right fortunate, Miss Joy. Tex, do you think you and Miss Joy could come to Ben Hugo's sometime tomorrow, so's I can check you out in some of the rudimentaries of the sweet science of fisticuffs? When would be a good time? I want you to get that first ten-dollar bill this Saturday."

"Well, I got classes on Saturday—"

"Classes?"

"Yessir."

"Tex goes to college!" Joy piped up.

"College!" Danny exclaimed with great surprise and admiration. "A college boy—man. College man. I'm honored, Tex."

"He's a genius!" Joy said. "He even speaks Spanish."

"Speaks Spanish, too! Well, Tex, in our profession we don't make the acquaintanceship of many people of an intellectual susceptibility. I myself never had the beneficiary of a college education, although folks who know me always find that hard to believe. I got my education in the school of hard knocks, but the main thing I did was, I listened. When educated people talked, I listened, I heard the words, and I affiliated 'em unto myself."

One reason he spoke so carefully was that his false teeth were loose. I knew they were false because they were perfect, just like Mom's.

"What time of day are your Saturday classes finished, Tex?"

"Noon."

"That's perfect, Tex. You finish your obligatory curriculum, and meet me out front there by the main gate, and I'll pick you and Miss Joy up—I do hope Miss Joy will be able to honor us with her attendance—"

"Oh, shoot!" Joy said. "Wild horses couldn't keep me away!"

"Good. I'll pick you two up in my Buick Roadmaster at twelve-thirty on Saturday, and we'll have a wonderful afternoon."

Joy said: "You have a Buick Roadmaster?"

"I sure do, Miss Joy, and there's room for you in the front seat, between Tex and me. So what time can I expect the two of you at Ben Hugo's tomorrow?"

"I can be there by two," Joy said. "I'll leave school at noon and never look back. Oh, this is so deeee-lovely!"

"I'll meet you there at two, then," Danny said. "Remember, not a word about this to anybody. If word of these ten-dollar bills gets around, I fear an avalanche of young fellas will submerge on me, looking for the same fortunality as you have acquired." He grabbed my hand and shook it. "A pleasure and a privilege to meet you and Miss Joy, Tex. See you *mañana*. I talk a little Meskin myself."

He walked back toward the fights. I looked around for someplace to sit down and put on my boots, but the benches were all occupied. Joy watched Danny walk away. She seemed to be suffering from terminal elation.

"A Buick Roadmaster! And Dubby—ten smackeroos!"

"I got to put my boots on."

"Le's go to the garden at Heights Hospital. We can warsh your feet in the goldfish pond. Ten dollars, for nothing! Just a little fight. And we get to ride out there in a Buick Roadmaster! I think I died and went to heaven, Dubby!"

She grabbed my thumb and sucked it all the way across the park and down Twentieth Street to Heights Hospital, doing little skips and wiggles and squeals, and bumping her hip against mine.

I thought how happy I could make Mom if I came home and handed her a ten-dollar bill. But then she would ask me where I got it, and I'd have to lie. The idea of me being in a boxing match would put her in bed with a sick headache.

Maybe I could just keep the ten dollars and hide it and bring it out when we had another of our cash emergencies. I could tell her I found it under the stands at the football game and squirreled it away for a rainy day.

"You know what we can do with ten bucks?" Joy asked. We had arrived at the bench by the goldfish pool in the little garden behind Heights Hospital, and she had taken my thumb out of her mouth and sat me down and put both my feet in the pool, and was kneeling there washing them. "We can rent a room at the Main Motel, and get some beer, and stay there all afternoon and drink beer and do it. Beer makes me want to pee, and I come better when I need to pee. And then after I git you wore down to a nub and ready to holler uncle, I can catch the bus to the Swingatorium for my job. Oh, Dubby!"

She lifted both my feet up in the air and sat on the bench beside me and took one of my feet in both hands and started sucking my big toe. I almost went into shock with the shivers it sent all over me. She stopped just long enough to say, "You like it? Ain't it nice? My Uncle Phil taught me this one, too." Then she put my foot back in her mouth, nibbling and sucking all my toes and running her tongue in and out between them. Then suddenly she stopped and opened her purse and pulled out a white handkerchief and handed it to me. "Brought you a present," she whispered. "Look." She stuck her finger through a slit in the middle. "It's like a little bib. My Uncle Phil taught me this'n too!"

Then she unbuttoned me and let the wild Intruder out of his cage and put the bib in place and jumped on my lap and did the same number she did in the swing the first night, fast and furious and quick, so as to be sure to finish before we got caught. I looked up and sure enough, there was an old man standing in the window on the third floor, looking down at us. I didn't know how clearly he could see, but he saw enough to keep him watching instead of running off to tattle.

Joy knew what time the movie let out. She had called that afternoon before her mama came home. Neither one of us had a watch, but there was a clock in the window of the drugstore, so we knew how much time we had. We did it again on the back steps of a vacant house, and once more, fast, in the cab of a dump truck parked at a construction site.

Then Joy said, "Le's go to a Guff Station. The Guff stations always have the nicest ladies' rooms, and plenty of paper towels."

I washed my bib in the men's room at the Gulf station and squeezed it pretty dry between paper towels, then went out front and waited for Joy. She was in there a long time, but when she came out she was smiling. She said, "You gotta tell me the story of the movie on the way home." As soon as we started walking she stopped and squirmed and squeezed my hand, then pushed up against me and whispered, "Ooooh! Them rolled-up paper towels feel so gooood! I cain't wait for Mama to inspect my clean white panties, so I can tell 'er how insulted I am!"

ELEVEN

B EN HUGO'S GYM was on the second floor over a furniture uphol-
stery store in a ratty part of North Main. I got there at a quarter
to two, fifteen minutes early, so I waited downstairs for Joy. I'd
forgotten my bag with my peanut butter and raisin sandwich and my
apple on the kitchen table when I left home, so I was getting pretty
hungry. I was tempted to get a hot dog with my bus fare, but I
decided to wait till Joy got there and we met with Mr. Diamond.

I was not equipped for going to a gym. Mom's—and my—credo
was that I should try never to look scruffy at Rice, so I wore leather
lace-up shoes and creased trousers and an ironed shirt. Mom didn't
want me to look any different from the rich boys, but I did; some of
them looked scruffy on purpose, and the neat ones had expensive
neat clothes.

It was tacitly understood that bookbags were tacky. Unless you
were a drip you carried your books in your arms, loose, no matter how
many there were. On this day I carried my favorite, *Chief Modern Poets
of England and America*, plus a thin volume called *Nociones de la liter-
atura castellana*, and Rambaud's *Civilization Française*, along with my
tattered and stained loose-leaf notebook. They made an awkward
armload. While I was shifting them from one aching arm to the other,
an old black man with one leg and a crutch and a shoeshine kit
paused in front of me and lifted the kit and was about to ask if I
wanted a shine but saw in a split second that I was a non-customer
and kept going without a word.

I stepped back to the edge of the sidewalk and looked up at the second-floor windows, which had probably never been washed. On one pane was the word GYM, formed in block letters with time-yellowed adhesive tape.

At ten after two Joy was still not there so I decided to go upstairs, out of respect for Mr. Diamond. I had already spotted him for a four-flusher, but I reasoned that anybody with a fake-preacher personality like his needed to be liked, even if he was trying to catch you in a yawn so he could steal the gold out of your teeth. Besides, he was old, at least fifty, and Mom had taught me respect for age. She had more than taught it; she had sandblasted it into my brain with end-less repetition: "Miss not the discourse of the elders." This one came on usually when I argued with her about something, however briefly, or questioned established dogma. On such occasions her voice would rise: her son was treading on dangerous ground. The infallibility of biblical teachings as interpreted by Mary Baker Eddy was a given. Mom's answers to any question of religion, morality, or ethics were quotations from—to her—unchallengeable doctrine. My only de-fense was to withdraw quickly, with my own opinion intact. Some-times, in a stubborn mood, I'd say, "Well, Mom, you think you're right, and I think I'm—" That was usually as far as I got. She would cut me off with, "Honey, I don't *think* I'm right, I *know* I'm right." In the case of the discourse of the elders, I looked in vain for it in the Bible, and finally discovered she had somehow got hold of a quota-tion from the sacred literature of the Alexandrian Jews, which never made it to the King James Version. This would've stopped her from ever mentioning the discourse of the elders again, but I didn't have the heart to tell her. Where Mom was concerned, I always harked back to the reason for everything she did—love. And I always re-membered coming home one day from servicing Mrs. Sandusky and finding Mom in the kitchen in a cloud of steam, standing on one leg with her other foot—red and swollen to twice its normal size from a snakebite—up on a chair in a pan of ice water. There's no medication in her religion, only "knowing the truth," and she was in obvious agony, and crying, but she was canning the precious tomatoes be-cause they had to be canned. You don't want to cause a person like that any more hurt than you have to.

As I mounted the dark stairs toward Hugo's gym I realized why I'd waited so long for Joy without considering that she knew the place, knew how to get there and might already be up there: I was scared.

Why do I do things I don't want to do? Why do I find my feet moving toward something as though an unseen force is behind me with a big cloven hoof in the small of my back propelling me forward in spite of the unwillingness in my mind? Am I spineless, mindless, so lacking in selfhood I can't oppose other wills?

Halfway up the unswept steps the odor hit me. The door to the gym was open, and the smell drifting out of that space was something that I was sure could never be duplicated. It was made up of sweat, and urine, and unwashed feet, and damp leather, and dust, and bad teeth, and beer, and vomit, and cigarette smoke, and wet snuff, and chewed cigar butts, and fecal matter, and possibly a dead rat in the wall, and decaying garbage. I thought, God, I've got my mother's Cherokee olfactory nerves. Another scent: wet, termite-riddled wood.

I heard the machine-gun rattle of the light bag. I heard the bump of feet on canvas-covered wood, and grunts.

As I hit the landing I finally understood why I had come: adventure, excitement, exploration, Joy. And the ten dollars.

Also fear. To prove to myself that I could overcome fear. Maybe that was the biggest reason.

The door was open. I stopped for a moment. I could see two plodding heavyweights in the ring, mechanically throwing punches at gear-protected heads and flabby bellies. A small black man was having his gloves laced by a man in a knitted black cap. A bulky person invisible in a heavy sweatsuit and hood was rattling the light bag.

I stepped through the door just in time for a broomful of dust, candy wrappers, and butts to land on my foot. The sweeper had a flat nose, a bumpy face, ears that looked like tree fungi, a drooling open mouth, and blank eyes. Coming from the side so that we couldn't've seen each other, he was still embarrassed and contrite.

"Oh! 'Scuse meh!" He sounded like he was talking through a comb covered with tissue paper.

"That's okay, okay," I assured him. "My fault. I ought not to be putting my big foot in front of your broom."

He half bowed and scuttled sideways, thoroughly intimidated by the accident. "Oh, thang you, I'm sorry, sorry." He was trying to get the broom aimed properly again. I saw that he couldn't control his arms or his legs except within a general pattern. His jaw muscles didn't keep one side of his mouth shut.

I got a chill. I thought I recognized him from somewhere.

106

Joy wasn't there. I didn't see Mr. Diamond either at first, but he saw me. He came to meet me with an openmouthed, panting-puppy smile so big I thought his upper plate was going to fall out. And sure enough, before he got to me, he had to clamp his two rows of teeth together to keep them in.

"You're a man of your word, Tex, I'm happy to see." He offered me a bony hand, which I shook briefly. "But don't tell me we're going to suffer the dispossession of the accompaniment of Miss Joy."

"Well, she said she'd be here. I guess she got delayed." I closed my hearing to his words. Listening to him was like being forced to eat twelve cream puffs without anything to wash them down or time to rest in between. I put my mind on other things, letting it distill what he was saying: I could put my books in the office. Didn't I have any other shoes? I should come and meet Mr. Hugo, then Barney would tape my hands.

Barney was the man in the knitted black cap. Mr. Diamond introduced us as we went by on our way to the office. "Barney, meet my good friend Tex. He'll be with you in a minute." Barney nodded.

Mr. Hugo was built like a small barrel with a round head on top and arms and legs sticking out of either end. He had no neck. He wore a wide colorful tie knotted forward of his chin on his almost horizontal chest. He sat behind a desk that was so cluttered there were probably papers from ten years ago on the bottom of some of the stacks. The walls were covered with fight posters, some old, some new, overlapping, the corners curling out as though trying to find their way to the floor. He had been doing some record-keeping with a chewed-up pencil when we came in. He didn't look up when Mr. Diamond introduced us. He made a few more marks with his pencil, then said:

"Where you been fightin'?"

"Oh. I, uh—"

"I witnessed him performing a one-punch overwhelmishment of a tough competitor on an amateur card," Mr. Diamond said. "By my appraisment he's a prospect."

Mr. Hugo kept his head down and took a couple of breaths that clearly expressed a negative attitude. "Weight?"

Mr. Diamond said a hundred and fifty-eight at the same time I said a hundred and forty-four. Then Mr. Diamond followed up emphatically with, "He's a middleweight."

"The boy says one forty-four. He ain't hardly a full welter."

"He fights middle. He likes it that way. He moves light, punches heavy."

Mr. Hugo took a deep whistling breath. "Put on yer gear."

"He didn't bring his gear. He come straight from school."

"School?" Mr. Hugo could've been reacting to a flat tire or a bounced check, from the sound of his voice.

"College," Mr. Diamond said, as though that would make me more acceptable.

"Shit," Mr. Hugo said. "Call me when yer ready."

Mr. Diamond tugged my arm to get me out of the office. I said, "Nice meeting you, Mr. Hugo." He didn't answer. I stopped and said, "May I leave my books in your office?"

"Put 'em in a locker."

The first locker I opened had no hooks, but the second one did, so I hung my shirt in it. I was going to have to wear it at least one more day. I stacked my books in the bottom and went to see Barney. Barney talked in pantomime. He motioned for my right hand, wrapped it with stretchy cloth, secured it with tape, flexed it, then did the left equally fast. He handed me the padded contraption meant to protect my head while sparring. My mouth and my nose stuck out of it like targets.

Mr. Diamond brought me three old mouthpieces. They looked like a puppy had been teething on them. I picked out one that seemed like a possible fit, but I gagged at putting it in my mouth. "I gotta take a leak," I drawled, trying to summon my gunslinger, who seemed to have failed to return from Dodge City. I went to the half-open door of the toilet marked White, next to the one marked Colored. The stench was enough to make a sewer worker think he'd been trapped in a cave-in.

Jesus H. Christ! They passed a *law* to keep colored people *out* of this place? I wonder if it's against the law for me to use the Coloreds'? Could theirs be worse? Separate filth for white and colored, but they fight in the same ring, punch and butt and hit low and eye-gouge and taste each other's blood and hump each other's ladies . . .

I held my breath and avoided touching the sink while I rinsed the mouthpiece off and put it in my mouth. It didn't fit but it was better than nothing.

Barney handed me a protective cup with elastic loops. I put it on over my trousers, and Barney laced it tight behind my back. Mr. Diamond was fidgety. "Tex," he said, "since you didn't manage to bring your approved boxing shoes—" Here his little yellow-brown eyes, one of which was slightly cocked, bored into me, making it clear that listeners were supposed to believe that I owned official boxing shoes—"your *official* boxing shoes, from your home on the other side of the city from the university, I think you oughta work barefooted. Choopy here is going to go a couple minutes with you."

Choopy was the light-skinned black that Barney had been lacing when I came in. He couldn't've been more than five feet five or weighed more than 135, but he was impressive in his professional trunks, high-top leather shoes, and the easy way he seemed to fit into the headgear and the gloves and the general spirit of the place. He said, "Hey, Tex," and flipped a glove at me.

The padded canvas ring was about three feet above the main floor, with sturdy ringposts and four ropes, wrapped to prevent rope burns. As soon as I climbed into the ring, Choopy squared off, grinning. Mr. Diamond said, "Hold it, boys," and called toward the office, "All set, Ben." Choopy danced and skipped and shadowboxed and wind-milled his arms while we waited for Mr. Hugo. He was unmarked, graceful and quick, at home in the ring, joyful in motion. I was suddenly aware of my boniness, my meatless ribs, my gawkiness, and my status: in the world of fisticuffs I was lower than a greenhorn, lower than an ignoramus, lower even than a yellowbelly. I was naked on Main Street at noon. I just stood there like a totem, watching Choopy.

"Tex. Tex. Hey, Tex." Mr. Diamond was trying to get my attention. I hadn't recognized my own name. When I turned toward his voice, there was the Sweeper, the Drooler, standing right behind me, leaning on his broom, grinning at me. Several of his upper front teeth were missing. "Goo' luck," he said, with what seemed to be great affection.

Mr. Diamond tried to push him aside. "Lemme palaver with my boy, Truck."

Truck. Truck. Truck Ganney. Oh, God. Nineteen twenty-seven. Before the Crash. Dad riding high. Big builder, owns two homes, takes me to fights, downtown auditorium. Ganney fights Joe Howard for a crack at the great John Henry Lewis for the crown. Me, seven.

"Watch ole Truck there, Dubby, and you'll know what makes a winner. Never takes a backward step. Never been off his feet. Takes a punch like a tow sack full of sand. Land your best shot, he don't even blink, keeps coming, throwing leather. Know how he got the name Truck? They carried a fella out once that fought 'im. Fella at ringside said, 'Shit, sumbitch looks like he was hit by a truck.' Newspaper fella writing it up hears 'im say it, and he says, 'He was—Truck Ganney.' And he put it in the paper, and that's how Truck Ganney got his name. Before that he was Danny Ganney, and his name made people laugh. See 'im keep comin'? See 'im? See 'im shake off that shot? Coming in, throwing punches! *Yeah! See that, Dubby? You got 'im, Truck!*" Dad on his feet yelling, me hating to look, Howard going down, staying down, Truck bouncing around the ring like a wild man on springs, the next light heavyweight champion of the—

Truck didn't hear Mr. Diamond. "Goo' luck," he said again.

Mr. Diamond went around him, got close when I bent down. "Move and stick, Tex. Show 'im your speed. Roscoe Baill says you got a left like a piston. Keep it in his face. But don't throw that right, huh? Not the one I seen. This boy's a main eventer—valuable. Don't wanta hurt 'im. Show your right but pull it. Hand speed, huh? Foot speed. Moves."

Like a piston? I have?

Mr. Hugo appeared at ringside. Looking down at him, I couldn't see his legs. "Show me," he said.

"Okay, boys," Mr. Diamond said, and Choopy moved to the center of the ring, shadowboxing like an invitation to dance. I had no idea what was expected of me. How hard was I supposed to hit him? How hard was too hard?

Choopy darted in and hit me square on the chin with a left and a right, so close together they seemed almost simultaneous blows, setting me back on my heels. In spite of his jolly attitude, this seemed unfriendly. I finally put my feet in motion and skated backwards so that his next two efforts barely grazed the padding at my cheek. My left jab, which Roscoe had told me I had, existed only in his mind, but now it was in my mind, and I pictured it as being something like what Tunney did in Movietone News. Think it there. Think it there. And I started popopopopopping it in accordance with the picture in my mind. It landed. And landed and landed and landed. Choopy, outreached by six inches, his head bouncing back, punched air. I kept it going. I at least knew how hard wasn't too hard, at least to Choopy. Then something mysterious happened. He stepped back, danced sideways, feinted a couple of rights and lefts, ducked low and leapt forward and hit me a hard right-hand shot to the belly. It doubled me over for a second, but he didn't follow up. After all, he wasn't in there to kill me, I guess. So I staggered back, sucking air while he waited for me to straighten up. In a few seconds I moved forward, jabbing harder to hold him off. When he tried the same feint, I loped backwards, out of range. Then when he saw it wasn't going to work the second time, he didn't lunge, just laughed and waved a glove, like—nice move. Then he covered his face with his gloves to blunt my jab and moved in, weaving back and forth to cut off the ring, got me in a corner, and sprang off the canvas with an uppercut that caught me square on the chin and just about took my head off. I felt my neck get longer. I saw a constellation of pinpoint lights. The blow had turned me sideways. I grabbed for the ropes. The first clear thing I saw was Truck grinning up at me affectionately. I heard laughter. The two heavyweights I'd seen sparring when I came in, and the light bag puncher, and Barney—everybody in the place had drifted to ringside to watch my amateurish performance, and they were all laughing. I finally focused on Choopy again. He was doing a little tap dance in the middle of the ring. When he saw that I had him in my sights again he held up both gloves, palms facing me, to say he was sorry. I nodded it was okay, but I was steaming. Nothing ever made my temper flare like being made a fool of. I moved back toward him, working my jab again, right in his face no matter which way he moved, forward or back, or how he dodged and weaved. I knew how mad I was because anger made me faster, just like fear. Think it there. Think it there.

He did some stutter steps, tried to move in and out. My left stayed right there in his eyes. I picked out a spot on the left side of his headguard about halfway up the padding, and imagined a fly there. I saw the fly clearly, a big hairy thing, loaded with polio germs. Think it there. Think it there. Be there!

And suddenly my right hit the fly on Choopy's headgear and Choopy flew halfway across the ring, going down, his head ending up between the second and the third ropes, the third one catching his shoulder and shooting him like a bowstring back into the ring on his back.

He wasn't out, but he was stunned, and his first try at getting up failed. I held my gloves up with the palms facing him to apologize, but he didn't see me.

Mr. Hugo was furious. He said, "Shit! Don't you know how to spar, you fuckin' college fairy!"

I had my headgear off. "I'm sorry, Mr. Hugo." I went straight to Choopy, who had his back to me, and put my arm around him. "You all right?" Choopy dug his elbow into my belly so hard I almost threw up.

" 'Scuse me, white boy. Didn' see you."

He said it without looking at me. He hopped down to floor level and went to the light bag and started playing it like a drum, as though nothing had happened.

Mr. Hugo turned his attention to Mr. Diamond and me. "Danny, why are you wasting my time with boys that don't know shit from wild honey? You figger to fight 'im at the ranch? How much you payin' 'im?"

"Ten."

"Too much. He don't know shit."

"I promised 'im ten."

"Well, then, you gotta give 'im ten. But who you gonna put 'im in with? Where you gonna find somebody else green as him?"

I felt an arm go around my waist. Truck was giving me a hug and grinning happily at me, his chin wet with slobber. "Thawaguh," he said. "Thawaguh."

Mr. Hugo took a dollar bill out of his pocket and gave it to Truck. "Here ya go, Truck. Go on home, now. See you tomorrow."

"Thang you," Truck said, stuffing the bill in his pocket. Then he turned to me again and repeated, "Thawaguh."

"Thanks—Truck," I said. I had finally figured out he was saying "That was good."

Truck ambled away, walking like a sailor just come ashore, throwing short right and left hooks at the air.

Mr. Hugo made as if to go back to his office. Mr. Diamond stopped him. "Uh, Ben, I thought maybe you'd be willing to give 'im a couple tips."

Mr. Hugo stared at me, like he was sizing up a steer at the stock show. I just stood there being looked at, like somebody had a rope around my neck and had led me in front of the judge. My neck still felt stretched by Choopy's uppercut. A few more shots like that one, and I'd have a neck like those Burmese ladies in the National Geographic, supported by a whole bunch of brass rings.

"I'll give both of you tips," Mr. Hugo said. "Tex, you take yer schoolbooks and go home; and Danny, quit promising ten dollars to boys that don't know shit an' never will." He walked away. Mr. Diamond pulled me by the arm and hurried to catch up with him. "Ben—Ben—" he said. "Wait. Talk to 'im, Tex. Tell 'im you wanta learn."

I was feeling ashamed for taking advantage of Mr. Diamond. "I'm sorry," I said, and somehow my gunslinger persona showed up just in time to help me, "I don't want Mr. Diamond to feel like he's obligated. I guess the idea of the ten dollars kinda made me lose my judgment."

Mr. Diamond had got very tense and was shaking his head and waving his hands while I was talking. "No, no, no, I stand by my deals. We got a handshake deal and with me that's incontroversial. If Mr. Hugo will just give you a few pointers you'll be fine. I don't want you to lose out on that ten-dollar bill on my account. I'll scare up boys for your first couple fights you can handle easy, and after that, with your quick comprehensiveness—"

"Danny, can you shut yer face a minute? I got limited time here. Listen, boy, don't cross yer feet. When you move forward, keep yer left foot out front and your right one back. Don't cross your right one over or you'll end up on your ass. Only Joe Louis can get away with crossing his feet, and even he lands on his ass sometimes. That left jab o' yours is fast but pitiful, all arm. Don't hurt nobody. Move forward and turn your shoulders when you jab, get your weight behind it, and keep it up in his eyes. And for God's sake, keep the top o' yer left hand up when you jab, elbow out, like this, otherwise you gonna break yer hand or yer wrist. And slip punches toward where they come from, see a right coming, slip left, and if you get tagged, don't drop yer hands and look for ropes to hang onto—you'll get killed. Cover up and fall on the guy and grab him and hang on till your head clears, no matter what the ref says. And as for that sucker right of yours, you'll probably never land it in a fight. Throw it like that, you're open, good boy'll take yer head off. So that's a couple things to maybe keep you from gittin' killed. Best tip I can give you is don't show up."

He walked away. I thought Mr. Diamond was going to have a hemorrhage. He kind of choked and gurgled, "Aw, come on, Ben!" Then he put his arm around me and got very confidential. "He's sore at you because you dropped his main eventer."

For some reason, nothing Mr. Hugo had said made any sense to me. It all sounded like trigonometry. I was glad Joy wasn't there. Where was she, anyhow? She couldn't've got lost. She knew the place. Maybe she'd met her fighter, whatsisname, Eddie Suggs, downstairs and—she wouldn't do that. Yes, she would. She's crazy. She's the one who got me into this in the first place, and now I seemed to be in it all by myself.

I had a terrible headache. I thanked Mr. Hugo for his tips, and promised Mr. Diamond I'm meet him at 12:30 the next day, Saturday, in front of the main gate at Rice. Then I took the bus to Heights Library.

There were no boxing manuals in the card catalogue, but Mrs. Hicks remembered something in the youth section and helped me find it. It was a thin book called *The Manly Art of Self-Defense*, with a new binding recently put on by the library staff to protect its tattered, thumb-smudged pages. A thousand boys must've studied this book to give themselves a secret advantage in those scuffles that broke out in the schoolyard. I'd got a loose tooth and a split lip from one a year ago at John H. Reagan High, and yet it had never occurred to me till now that the boy who gave them to me might've read a book on how to do it. This one had pictures of the proper way to jab, hook, clinch, slip punches, throw right crosses, and move your feet for balance and leverage, all with simple explanations. I had found a buried treasure. I wanted to kick myself for not finding it before I went to Mr. Hugo's gym.

And yet my mind was only half on the book. Hampered by my headache, I had been trying to figure out just exactly how Mr. Diamond related to Mr. Hugo. I kept going over what had happened, what was said, how it was said, what their gestures and looks had meant, and finally it all seemed to start coming clear.

Mr. Hugo trained and managed fighters, so the more good ones he had the more money he made. That was pretty sure to be a fact. Choopy was one of his good fighters, a main eventer, a money-making property. That's why, when I dropped a bomb on him, Mr. Hugo had got so mad. Hurt Choopy, put him out of action even temporarily, and I'd hurt Mr. Hugo's business, cost him money.

Mr. Diamond was a scout. That was pretty sure to be a dependable fact. For bringing talent to Mr. Hugo he got a slice of the pie. If he brought somebody Mr. Hugo thought had possibilities as a pro, he'd take him under his wing, train him, and let him get some experience fighting "at the ranch," against other novices, till he was good enough to turn pro and go into some of the local prelims. At least this was the story I constructed in my throbbing head.

Building on these probable facts, I postulated that Mr. Hugo knew I wasn't a prospect (which I knew, too—I just wanted to make ten dollars), and didn't want me to waste his time or my time by getting into the ring at all, and that he even had a little streak of niceness concealed under his hard exterior and wanted to spare me further humiliation and bruises and possible real damage but gave me some tips anyhow because he didn't want to cut his cohort Mr. Diamond out of whatever he was going to make out of me fighting at the ranch. Mr. Diamond, with Joy helping to dull my instincts for self-preservation, and with Mr. Hugo's halfhearted compliance, had managed to bamboozle me. Mr. Hugo had even said that the best tip he could give me was not to show up. So if I didn't heed that advice, he could, with a clear conscience, join Mr. Diamond in concluding that anybody dumb enough to fight was dumb enough to be had and deserved whatever he got.

Having completed this line of reasoning, I asked myself what had taken me so long. My answer was: my mother's influence. I'd refused to accept the existence of evil. Get thee behind me, Satan. God is love. God is truth. Only love and truth have reality. If there is only harmony in your soul no disharmony can enter.

But all this presupposed my living in harmony with God. It was never going to work with devious, cowardly, opportunistic, lustful houndogs like me. I had to accept that.

However, in spite of being saddled, probably permanently, with these serious defects, I was convinced that I was stupid only sporadically. So I made an oath to withdraw from the equation that would lead to a wrong result and make Mr. Diamond and Mr. Hugo understand, *a posteriori*, that they had completely misread young and stupid-seeming Mr. W. W. Johnson.

When I got home Mom said Joy had called. It was about four-thirty. Mom had saved my peanut butter and raisin sandwich and my apple in the icebox, and I ate them, hoping hunger was the reason for my headache. Then I went to lie down for a while. I wanted to wait to call Joy till I was sure Mrs. Hurt was home from work so Joy couldn't try to talk me into coming over.

Mom had been watching me. She came in the bedroom and asked me if I was okay. I told her about my headache. She put her cool hand on my forehead and said, "Honey, close your eyes and let the Divine Mind enter you." Then she went out. I tried to do what she said, but never had I envied the world's vast, unenlightened horde of aspirin-takers more. I knew Mom was already knowing the truth for me, but a couple of aspirins might've speeded things up. I wondered if she was aware that I'd minimized my pain, and that my headache was more like a skullquake, about a seven on the Richter scale.

I fell asleep. When I woke up an hour later, my headache was almost gone. When I told Mom, she only smiled a knowing smile. I called Joy, and Mrs. Hurt answered. She growled, "Come over here. I got a crow to pick with you," and hung up.

I said, "Mom, I have to go over to Joy's. I almost forgot I had to tutor her in Spanish today. But I'll be back early. I'm staying home tonight."

She brightened. "Oh, wait'll I tell Jenny. She's playing dolls with Rosey at her house. I bought a coconut. I'm going to make a fresh coconut cake." She hugged me. "I'm glad you're helping Joy with her Spanish. They're nice people. It's not easy in this world for a woman with no husband."

TWELVE

I COULDN'T GET the unfriendly sound of Mrs. Hurt's voice out of my head, so as I headed up the steps to Joy's front porch I was as spooky as a posse-pursued pistoleer on a lame cayuse in a blind canyon. Joy was watching for me. She tapped on the window of the front bedroom. She had a white, panicky look on her face, and her eyes were wide and flashing wet, and she was shaking her head and waving her right hand wildly from side to side. As soon as she realized I'd seen her *no* signal, she disappeared.

She couldn't've meant *don't come in*, because there was no way I was going to be unwise enough to disobey Mrs. Hurt's summons and risk her calling my mother. So the only other meaning I could figure was that she hadn't confessed to anything.

Mrs. Hurt answered the door and said, "Git in here, boy." I obeyed. "Come on back here to the kitchen and set down, and don't try lying to me, you hear? You hear me?" She had about the coldest, harshest voice I'd ever heard come out of a woman.

"Yes, ma'am."

"You have already cut your foot with me, so don't make it worse by trying to lie, you hear? You hear me?"

"Yes, ma'am."

"Where was she going to meet you?"

"Meet me?"

"You heard me. Where was she going to meet you?"

"Who, ma'am?"

"Don't lie to me! Don't play innocent with me!"

117

I was glad I hadn't worn my hat and boots, which were kind of cocky. This situation required more of a harmless attitude. I looked at her helplessly for a couple of seconds, and then stammered, "I'm sorry, ma'am, I didn't mean to offend you, but I'm not quite up on what this is all about."

This didn't disarm her, but it set her back a little. Then she charged again. "I told you, boy, don't try to play innocent with me! I'm onto you! That young lady in there confessed everything! So don't try to weasel out! Her teacher caught her waitin' for a bus on lunch hour—*off of the school grounds*—and she admitted she was headin' downtown to meet her boyfriend! That's you! I bet you was surprised when she didn't show up, wasn't you? Wasn't you? Don't lie to me, you hear? You hear me?"

"Yes, ma'am, I hear you. But there must be some mistake, because I don't have any idea what this is all about."

"*Liar!*"

"Unless she has a boyfriend I don't know about. Maybe the teacher misunderstood her. Maybe the teacher thought she said that and what she really said was that she *wasn't* going to meet her boyfriend."

"The teacher went straight to the phone and called me, and that is what she said she said! Her boyfriend! And you're the only boyfriend she's got, more's the pity, having to go to the movies with a scrawny, bucktooth heathen son of one of those—those—well, I speak no evil. I'm a God-fearing person, and my daughter is going to be married in white, do you understand? She is going to marry a God-fearing man and bring him her virginity to the altar, do you hear me? Do you? Answer me!"

"Yes, ma'am."

"Now, young man, you are already in dutch with me, but I am going to give you one more chance to have my Christian forgiveness. Where was she going to meet you?"

"Ma'am, I swear on the Bible, if she was going to meet me, I didn't know anything about it."

"I gave you a chance to tell the truth, but you're too much of a Judas!"

"Ma'am, I can tell you where I was all afternoon, and you can check up on me, if you don't believe me."

She was so furious she looked like she wanted to bite herself, so I knew I had her. I even knew she was lying, because if Joy had confessed, she wouldn't need my confirmation so badly. "I went to the basement library at Rice to study after class, then after I finished studying I went to Heights Library, and the librarian helped me find a book and—"

"What's her name, the librarian?"

"Miz Hicks, ma'am."

She stared at me real hard for a few seconds, then she grabbed up the phone book and flipped through it, and got a number and dialed it. "We'll just see about that," she said. I could hear the phone ringing on the other end, then somebody answered, and Mrs. Hurt's voice got as sweet as Karo syrup. "May I speak with the librarian, Mrs. Hicks, please? Oh, good. This is a friend of Woodrow Johnson. He asked me to . . . Woodrow. Yes. His friends call him Bud—"

"Dub," I said.

"I mean Dub. Dub asked me to call and see if he left a book on the table there this afternoon. He said you'd know, because you helped him find a—oh, you did? Well, that was nice of you. Well, if you do find a book with his name in it—a schoolbook—hold it for him, please. Thank you." She hung up and glared at me, angry at being wrong again. "There's monkey business going on here. You cain't fool me."

"Excuse me, ma'am. Did you—you personally—ask Joy?"

"She's a bigger liar than you are! She claims she was goin' to see her brother! Wherever she was goin', she was playin' hookey, and when kids play hookey they're up to no good."

"I know she loves her brother an awful lot, Mrs. Hurt—"

"Don't you come around here with your mealymouth sweet talk and try to pull the wool over my eyes, young man! I don't trust you! Not one bit! So stay away from me and my daughter! If Joy walks out with a young man from now on, it's gonna be somebody she met in church! And let me warn you. Don't try to sneak around behind my back. I may look like a defenseless woman to you but I have got loyal friends and relations who will defend my honor and my daughter's honor at the drop of a hat! Let me remind you that Joy is sixteen, under age—*underage*, if you catch my meaning—and she has a big brother who would be only too happy to avenge any type of liberty any man would take with her chastity. And *I* have a brother! Joy's Uncle Phil is our human shield and buckler on this earth!"

119

Uncle Phil.

"He loves Joy more than his own daughters. And—you better listen to me close now, boy—my brother Phil is a Deppity in the Harris County sheriff's office! If any man dared to touch a hair on Joy's head, that man would wait a long time—believe me, with the friends in high places he's got, judges and such—a long time to see the light of day. Are you listening to me? Do you hear me? *Do you?*"

"Yes, ma'am."

"Well, you better, for your own gizzard. And just to put the icing on the cake I have got a friend, a former next-door neighbor, who is a professional prizefighter. And a good one. Maybe you heard of 'im— Eddie Suggs?" My eyes must've widened because she didn't wait for me to answer. "You did, sure you did. Well, lemme just put this to you straight: Eddie is a nice young man, even invited Joy and her brother to watch 'im fight one time, and his mother is one of the sweetest women God ever put on this earth, and Eddie has many a time said to me, 'Mrs. Hurt, if you ever need anybody to do your light fightin', or even the heavy stuff, call on ole Eddie and it would be my pleasure and privilege.' Do I make myself crystal clear? I am a Christian woman, and I wish no physical harm on nobody, but there are times on this earth when even the Holy Bible says punish the wicked. Do I make myself crystal clear, young man?"

"Yes, ma'am."

"Fine. Then go on home, now, and you and your mama pray to your statue of Mary Baker Eddy, or whatever you do, to keep you out of trouble."

"Yes, ma'am. Thank you, Mrs. Hurt." I got up to go, and I didn't have to put on my chastised look or do any kind of awshucks shamble around the table, because she had made me feel like a criminal and I had trouble even straightening myself up to my full height. I headed for the front door, working on being respectful and getting back my dignity at the same time. I wondered why I was starting to feel good about what had happened, and then it came to me: This mean lady was setting me free and saving me from—who knows what?

Mom and Jenny and I had a happy evening. I had a growing sense of liberation, of good fortune I didn't deserve, like being under a tree next to the one that is blasted by lightning. Still, I had the feeling that something bad was hovering around. I put it out of my mind, and after Jenny went to bed and Mom went in her room, I installed myself in my usual spot in the living room on the wicker sofa by the radio, to study. My mind was clear because my two big distractions, Joy and the fight, had been eliminated, one by Mrs. Hurt and the other by my decision to take Mr. Hugo's advice and not show up. I didn't feel bad about deserting Mr. Diamond. He was a flimflammer and he deserved it.

At about eleven o'clock Chester called with a tale of two sisters and a lot of bizarre details. He'd been out with them almost all night the night before, and he was in a honkytonk with them now, and he had told them all about his old pal Dub, and they wanted me to come and join them. "They will take you to countries you didn't know was on the map," Chester said, "and you might not never want to leave."

I begged off, but I told him it sure did sound fine, and I wished I didn't have such important courses in the morning. About the time I hung up Mom came out with her *Science and Health* closed over her finger and kissed me goodnight and told me not to stay up too late—everything she always did the same way she always did it, like one of those unicycle acts in a vaudeville show—and then went back in her room and closed the door. It was comforting. Everything was the way it ought to be.

I had a new adage in my head that seemed to me to describe the events of the day perfectly: It is sometimes wrong for things to go right, and right for things to go wrong. I was about to go in my room and write it in my book and get ready for bed when I heard something on the screen behind my head. Bugs had been bouncing off that screen all evening, attracted by my light, but this sound was different—it continued in a rhythmic way till I turned around. Joy had her face up close to the window, panting and fluttering with excitement. She looked like a giant moth. She whispered, "Mama's asleep. I snuck out. I'll be there tomorrow. I'm meeting Mr. Diamond at the gym." Then she darted away into the darkness. I pressed my face to the screen and watched her, barefoot and wearing only a white nightgown, fly through the night toward home.

God is love.

THIRTEEN

THE APPARITION at the window left me as wide-awake as I was that time I came out of the chute riding backwards on a black mule at Tom Sloan's rodeo in Matagorda County, dressed in a clown hat and with my nose painted red. That's one way for a thirteen-year-old boy who had breakfasted on pancakes made of wheat shorts swiped from the cows' feed barrel to make two dollars in about ten seconds and give a crowd a laugh at the same time. It's also a moment of aliveness and nowness you will forever measure other moments by. This new one was the first in the four years since then that could be measured against it. I knew I wasn't going to sleep. I knew I was trapped on the back of the biggest black mule yet, and when he finally threw me I wasn't going to land on soft rodeo dirt.

Why hadn't she waited at the window at least long enough for me to tell her I was canceling Mr. Diamond? But that would've caused an exchange, and Mom, who had the ears of a fox, would've discovered us. Should I have run after her and caught her in the street and told her? No, not with her hotheaded enough to argue with me at the top of her voice.

Could I just not be there tomorrow at 12:30, and hide someplace, and let her and Mr. Diamond figure out I'd betrayed them? No. Joy, with no discretion, would go to my classroom and look for me, inquire after me, and finally call Mom to see if I was sick, spilling the beans all over town. Then, having anguished a record amount of time (for her), she would make a decision, prompted by her constantly erupting, uncontrollable libido. What would this decision be? Would she give up her ride in the Roadmaster and the excitement of the fights and her naked time at the Main Motel just because I, the unpremeditated successor (by virtue of proximity and availability) to Uncle Phil and Eddie Suggs and probably unnamed others, was missing? Would Mr. Diamond encourage her to do so? I'd caught him savoring her flesh with his eyes. With his greasy tie and baggy suit and clacky store-bought teeth he made me think of a less-than-honorable past, a past maybe including little girls and little boys and time in county jails and quick boardings of rolling boxcars out of town. Everything a person is is in their face if we can only read it. (Even facing backwards on this new black mule I made a note to refine this for my collection). So when Joy made her inevitable decision to take the Roadmaster ride, the lecherous bastard was sure to encourage her, and away they'd go to the ranch.

Between the two of them they would have no trouble finding a surrogate or surrogates to perform the functions they'd assigned to me.

And after that? Would she get drunk and end up in a gang-bang? Would she be found somewhere, exhausted and smudged, tossed away like a used paper napkin in a drive-in parking lot? Something bad would happen. When she got in high gear she didn't give a damn for red lights and stop signs. And it'd be partly my fault, so I had to save her from herself.

Stop the bullshit, W. W. You're scared the whole thing is going to blow up in your face, and you're desperate to defuse it.

Joy's mother would leave for work at eight tomorrow morning. Joy would be alone. Should I sneak over there and explain to her that the fight was off? No. I'd never escape her succubus mouth. She'd inhale me, devour me again.

There was only one way to avoid some kind of a catastrophe. I had to be there at the front gate of Rice when they arrived and then insist that Joy get out of the car and stay with me, because I'd decided once and for all not to go through with the fight. I would even confess my inadequacy as a man of combat, and refer to the kind advice of Mr. Hugo to just not show up; and I wouldn't allow the blandishments of Mr. Diamond, nor my thirst for ten dollars, nor the sensual entreaties of Joy to change my mind. I would finally be strong. Strength of will, commitment to a correct path, no matter how difficult, were hallmarks of manhood, true maturity. I would have the courage and the strength to change my course, and Joy's too.

I'd have to be careful not to let Mrs. Hurt know we had met at all. She'd never believe I was working toward a righteous result.

I lay awake all night reviewing this decision, trying to improve it or find a better one. I didn't succeed.

Mom always remembered what time I had to leave in the morning, and she was sure to be in the kitchen when I came in for breakfast, with some kind of a treat for me to send me off into the world in a positive state of mind. One day it would be shredded wheat with strawberries and a sliced ripe banana. Another day it was pancakes light enough to take flight (The days of chasing the rats out of the cows' barrel and stealing feed to make batter were gone, now that Mom and Dad shared a roof again), with Log Cabin syrup and plenty of margarine (now that we had no cows) colored by a little packet of yellow powder kneaded through it to make it look like butter. What we ate depended on how close to payday we were. On this morning I smelled bacon long before I got to the kitchen. In spite of not having slept, I didn't feel tired; I felt lightheaded.

I tried to act bouncy and optimistic, but Mom saw right away that I was faking it. She wanted to know what was wrong. I explained that I was trying to read Jane Austen and it was like walking through deep mud in loose boots, and it was depressing to think that I was unable to appreciate a great writer like her because of something lacking in me. Mom hugged me in her comforting way and told me she was proud of me for being generous enough to blame it on myself instead of on the writer. This got me past the subject of what was wrong and even made me bigger in Mom's eyes, but it did not show me a way out of the wilderness. I wanted to talk to her. I was convinced that she was wise, wiser than I at least, and that with all the details frankly delivered to her, she'd be able to help me. But no. The details— underage sex, illegal fights, a thicket of lies—would do nothing but destroy the illusion of me she cherished most, her noble scholar-poet. Is that not the cruellest thing a son can do to his mother—tell her the truth about himself?

So I didn't bring my troubles into the breakfast talk. I told her I doubted anybody in the whole world made huevos rancheros like she did, which I truly believed, and that she fried bacon better than anybody else in the world, which I also believed. She fried it slowly till all the fat dripped out, leaving a crisp and tender tissue where the fat had been, yet with the lean part not burnt.

Jenny came in rubbing her eyes and sat on my lap and helped me eat my bacon, and by the sheer force of her sweetness made me forget my crisis for a while.

Being convinced—or almost convinced—that I was right about what I was going to do gave me strength during my two classes Saturday morning. I was a man of decision. The decision was made. The matter was closed. There would be no discussion, no argument, no appeal. After class I hung around Sallyport for a while, listening to a passionate but modulated speaker pleading for able-bodied men who cared about freedom to join an international brigade to go and help the Loyalists defeat the Nationalists in Spain. I didn't know which side I ought to be on, and neither did most of my friends. The baby-faced and bespectacled speaker, who, I was told by one of my classmates, had a Jewish name (I didn't know how he could tell), proclaimed that the only people outside Spain who were helping the Loyalists against overwhelming forces supported by the Nazis of Germany and the Fascists of Italy were the Russians. He was immediately branded a Communist by a couple of students who seemed to have mysterious sources of knowledge about these matters. I was pretty sure the Nazis and the Fascists were bad (the president of IBM had just accepted a medal from Hitler, and one of our biggest heroes, "Lucky Lindy" Lindbergh, seemed to think the Nazis were okay, so it was confusing—to me, at least), but I had no idea what a Communist was. When you're immersed in Lope de Vega, and Molière, and Shakespeare, and Ibsen, and Jane Austen, and strangling on trigonometry, and preoccupied with sex every moment, asleep or awake, struggles for power halfway around the world have a mythic, unreal quality. Still, somehow I knew from the young speaker's zeal that I was going to be forced to acknowledge the importance of these things whether I wanted to or not. He seemed only a year or two older than I, and I wondered how he'd become so enlightened, and so dedicated, and so focused, in such a short time. I was envious. I had walked out of Spanish class proud of my scholarship; five minutes later, I was ashamed of my ignorance.

I wanted to stay and listen, even to question him, but I was almost due at the main gate. Most of the kids walked past him with only a superior glance ("another nut . . . a Red"), a few paused and listened for a couple of seconds, then shrugged and moved on. We were a smug lot, safe in our peaceful academe, where for a few hours even the Depression couldn't touch us. The zeal of the speaker seemed out of place, unseemly, dangerous, maybe even un-American.

One of those who had stopped to listen was Olivia. She saw that I was fascinated, guessed that I was untaught, and offered me a Chesterfield from her little pack of ten, a special flat box that was cheap and easy to hide from parents. Olivia was the only truly beautiful girl on campus—not pretty, not cute, but beautiful—and so smart that any boy who knew her would never be caught saying "She's real smart—for a girl" again. She was so perceptive I felt vaguely guilty in her presence. It was well known that she was going steady, and I regretted not having the nerve to try to beat out her boyfriend, who was handsome and intellectual and sophisticated (he listened to Wagner and was on the debate team), and not, like me, penniless. I accepted the Chesterfield, a welcome change from Bull Durham, and told her I wished I could stay to hear more, but I couldn't. She gave me the exact time from her pretty wristwatch, and I hurried off down the long pebbled drive to the main gate.

The timing was exact. As I arrived I saw a white convertible Buick Roadmaster approaching from downtown, with Mr. Diamond at the wheel and Joy beside him in the front seat, and three people in the back seat. Joy had already moved close to Mr. Diamond to make room for me in the front seat, which struck me as a little premature but didn't surprise me. She saw me from half a block away and was waving to me and bouncing up and down as Mr. Diamond swung up into the wide delta outside the gate, throwing pebbles and skidding to a stop beside me. Joy was so excited she couldn't contain herself.

"Dubby! Look!" She held up boxing shoes. "Danny got you shoes! Elevens! Ain't that your size? Eleven? I knew it! See, Danny, I told you! Get in, Dubby! Hurry! We're stopping at Prince's for hamburgers! Get in!"

"Joy—Mr. Diamond—I gotta talk—"

She leaned over and opened the door, swinging it at me so fast it almost hit me. "We can talk on the road! *Git in*, Dubby! You're first up! Come on! Don't you want a hamburger? You're first up!"

I stepped close to the seat with the door open behind me. "Can we just—?"

"Tex, I'm buying you a cheeseburger and french fries and Coke," Mr. Diamond said with rare brevity. "We can discuss on the way."

Joy reached out and grabbed my arm, and yanked astonishingly hard for such a small-boned girl. I fell forward onto the seat. I dropped my books on the floor. "Dubby—Tex! We got to hurry! You know what else Danny got you? Your own mouthpiece! Look!" She held up the mouthpiece. "Brand spankin' new!"

During this she had gathered up my books. Her dress was halfway up to her crotch. I found myself sitting in the front seat, a brainless robot. She stacked my books on my lap.

"Shut the door," Mr. Diamond was saying. "You're first up."

I shut the door. Joy gave me a kiss, pulling my head to hers and holding it there till I heard tittering from the back seat. Then she pulled away with a deliberate smacking sound for the benefit of the three in back, and snuggled back down in her place close to me, leg to leg, all a-flutter. "Ain't this about the most elegant chariot you ever seen?" she panted, caressing the dashboard. "Danny promised he's gonna let me drive it one of these days."

"One of these days," Mr. Diamond sighed. The way he said it made it sound like the time was a long way off.

"Well," I said, "you're too big to sit on anybody's lap to drive."

She gave me an elbow. "I don't need to sit on anybody's lap to drive. I'm a fine driver. I started when I was twelve."

"Started what?" I said, feeling combative.

"Driving, you nasty man!" she giggled. "And I got taught by the best! A genuine deputy sheriff, in a genuine highway patrol car!"

Este muchacho es Tex," Mr. Diamond said to the titterers in the rear. "And Tex, these boys are Manolito, Pablo, and Gaucho—fly-weight, featherweight, and bantamweight." Gaucho wore a flat-top black hat like the bolo gauchos of South America.

I glanced back at them. They were still grinning from the show Joy had put on. In traffic, headed for Prince's drive-in, Mr. Diamond said something to Joy out of the corner of his mouth, which neither of us could hear. The wind was whipping her long yellow mane and through the sideview mirror (Mr. Diamond's car had one on each side, a novelty) I saw Gaucho holding his black hat on his head. Joy said "What?" and Mr. Diamond repeated himself loud enough for her, but not for me, to hear. Immediately Joy opened her purse, which was wedged between her legs against her pudenda. She pulled out a small piece of folded notepaper and handed it to me at waist level, apparently so that the passengers in the back seat wouldn't see. I unfolded it. It said, in Joy's schoolgirl handwriting, *Mr. Diamond says don't mention ten dollars. They only get five.* I nodded and gave it back to her. She stuck it quickly into her purse, which she then resumed squeezing rhythmically between her legs.

The three Mexicans ate chili dogs and drank Lone Star beer and smoked. Joy and I had cheeseburgers and Cokes. Joy gave me half her cheeseburger. Mr. Diamond didn't eat. He preferred to talk: "Tex, I notice you didn't bring your shorts. And I liked that hat and them boots. They create the correct impressionistics for a puncher named Tex. Next time, I sure do hope you won't forget 'em."

Next time?

"Well, Mr. Diamond, I couldn't hardly bring my stuff, because like I told you, I sure wouldn't want to have to explain to my mother what I was going to do. She'd disapprove strongly. This isn't going to get in the paper, is it? I don't want to be called by my right name out there."

"Oh, no, this don't go to the papers. The ranch strives to maintain the atmospherics of fun and unofficiality. It's like a big celebration-type thing, just for special friends and acquaintances of the ranch, that way we don't have any kind of obligatoriness where licenses and regulations are concerned. Mr. Harkins called me last night and asked me what name you wanted to employ, so he could put it on the card, and what kind of a record you had, so I told him you hailed from Laredo, Texas, and you've had eighteen fights, all along the frontier there, in small towns, and you won 'em all, seventeen by knockout. You're twenny years old, one hunderd and fifty-eight pounds, and at six foot three and a half you're the tallest middleweight in the U.S. of A. Stuff like that. They go fer lotsa picturesquitude, you know? You'll like it out there. They're good people. Lotsa camaraderyship."

"I still don't know why I have to fight middleweight. I'm a hundred forty-four."

"Mr. Harkins needs a middleweight. What difference does it make? Look how big you are."

"Who am I going to fight?"

"A Cajun boy. Any gringos, they always throw 'em in with a Meskin or a Cajun or maybe a Creole. You won't never see no pretty white-skinned, blue-eyed boy like you in with another blue-eyed boy. They like dissimilaritude. Make it more exciting."

Then Joy asked the question I'd dreaded to ask. "What name did you tell 'em to call 'im by, Danny?"

"Well, due to his fistic encounters being accomplished along the frontier, I thought Tex Frontier would be a nice moniker."

"Tex Frontier!" Joy shouted, so loud the carhop headed for the car, thinking we were finished. "Yeaaay! Deeeeeelovely!" She raised up in the seat and kissed me with a piece of lettuce stuck to her lip. She continued singing low, through a mouthful of cheeseburger, "It's delicious, it's delightful, it's delovely." Her inflection made sure the words weren't referring to mere romance.

As soon as I finished eating, Mr. Diamond opened a little jar of powder that came with my mouthpiece and mixed it with a little bit of water on a saucer and folded it over and over with a knife until it became a thick paste. Then he rolled it into a ball and mashed it down in the top of my mouthpiece and told me to put it in and shove it up tight against the top of my mouth, and be sure my teeth went all the way to the bottom, and hold it still. It almost made me gag. Some of the extra paste squashed to the back of my palate. After a while he said okay, and I opened my mouth and he took ahold of the front of the mouthpiece with his shaky fingers and pulled straight down and it popped out. He trimmed off the excess paste with his knife and told me to hold it on top of my books, wet side up, and it'd be fine by the time we got there. There was a caraway seed from my bun stuck in it, but I didn't dare try to pick it out.

Mr. Diamond had a gold pocket watch on a chain. He lifted it to his eyes, checked the time, swung it back and forth so we could see it shine, and said, "Time to roll." He dealt a couple of bills off of a thick deck of greenbacks as the carhop unhooked the trays from the side of the car. She swiveled her tight red shorts in appreciation of the tip. "Y'all sure do know how to give a pore girl goose bumps, Mr. Di'mon'. See you nex' Sa'dy."

I had never ridden in as grand a car as Mr. Diamond's white Roadmaster convertible, but I wasn't as thrilled as Joy. I wondered how a man like him latched onto so much money. He was still wearing the same greasy tie he had on that night at Heights Park and the same droopy suit. You'd think that a man with enough money to buy a Roadmaster would dress neater. And have teeth that fit.

On the highway he divided his attention between the road and the purse Joy was rhythmically pressing and releasing between her legs. I didn't want to look and I didn't want to think about it. The Intruder was already trying to lift my books off of my lap. The three Mexicans were silent, leaning down once in a while to use the seatbacks as windbreaks to light cigarettes, which they puffed behind cupped hands.

I didn't want to be where I was and I didn't want to go where I was going and I didn't want to do what I was about to do, and I didn't want to think about my opinion of myself. I shut my eyes. We were heading east into swampland, oil country, cattle country, crawdad country, Cajun country. Mr. Diamond had Cajun music on his radio. I could feel Joy wiggling to it. I couldn't let myself watch her. I concentrated on smells and sounds. For the first few miles the stench of the Pasadena paper mill dominated everything, then diesel exhaust, stale beer, honky-tonk music, burnt rubber, blood (only a whiff—not certain), manure, rotting fish, sour swampland, tobacco smoke (swirled in from the back seat), sulphur, garlic, cayenne, a skunk (probably dead-on-road), raw oysters, sweat, salt air (with a change of sound and pressure—the bridge over the Trinity River), ammonia (a barnyard? No, coming up on a truckload of bawling cattle, passing them), an unrecognizable odor, sweet and musty, herbal, dank, heavy, overwhelming all others, along with a change of light—shadows on my eyelids. I was forced to look—at thick-trunked oaks hung with Spanish moss. Mr. Diamond had left the main highway and was heading south toward the salt bayous on a narrow crushed-oyster-shell road. I guessed we had been on the road about an hour.

Two cowboys with spurs on their rubber boots splashed alongside the road, trying to cut a rank steer back toward a herd grazing in hock-deep water to our right. Ahead of us a mud-splattered pickup truck loaded with about a half-dozen small coops pulled out of a shell road to the east. It bore Louisiana license plates. It was slower than Mr. Diamond's Buick. As we came up behind it I saw that the two rear coops contained only one chicken each, both roosters.

"Ole Jean Peyre from Opelousas," Mr. Diamond chuckled. "He don't usually come so late." He tooted a greeting on his horn and the truck tooted back.

The rooster in one of the rear crates, a broad-shouldered combless bird, black and gray, became aware of us and flew against the wire mesh of his cage, ripping at it with his beak. I never had seen such an unfriendly chicken.

Mr. Diamond was pleased. "That's a good un!"

Now we were rolling over a built-up roadbed with deep swamp on both sides of us. A bearded man in a pirogue piled high with muskrat carcasses waved to us.

Joy crossed her legs, locking her purse tight against her crotch.

The Intruder, held down by books, throbbed and ached. How would I get him to bend enough to go into the protective cup Mr. Diamond had promised to borrow for me?

Up ahead I saw more moss-bearded oaks, dry land, and a man seated on a chair elevated about ten feet above the ground. He wore a wide hat and had binoculars slung around his neck. He was looking back along the road we'd traveled and didn't give us so much as a glance as we passed.

We heard music and laughter and shouting up ahead, beyond the woods. After about a minute more on the winding road we came to a wide gate and a barbed-wire fence. The gate was being swung open. It was guarded by two cowboys on horseback with what looked like .44 Winchester rifles in plain view in saddle holsters. They waved friendly greetings to Mr. Peyre's truck as it rolled through, and then to us.

"Only friends of Mr. Harkins are invited to the ranch," Mr. Diamond said, "and he exercises the strictest selectivitude in choosing his friends."

I didn't feel flattered somehow at having been selected as a friend of Mr. Harkins without having even met him, but the excitement in the air as we drew closer to the music and food smells just beyond the trees overwhelmed all the other feelings trying to get my attention. And suddenly the scene burst on us: a clearing with a long, low ranch house and a bunkhouse and a couple of corrals and big barns and a parking lot with at least two hundred cars and trucks and trailers, from banged-up, rusted-out junkers to a polished black Duesenberg, a couple of Lincolns, a one-seater with a long engine compartment that I found out later was a BMW, and even a white Cord convertible that made Mr. Diamond's Roadmaster look like a poor country cousin.

There was a crowd of boisterous, festive people—big-bellied men, young bucks strutting with pretty girls, tacky old women carrying drinks and fans—every possible make and model of human being, in a variety of colors. There was a small Cajun group on a platform, playing an accordion, a fiddle, and a washboard. A dance floor was laid out on the ground—sections of oak flooring hooked together—and several couples, beers or drinks in hand, were dancing, some as close together as they could get, even though it was only two-thirty in the afternoon. There was a line of booths where you could fire .22 rifles at targets, throw baseballs at wooden milk bottles, throw darts at balloons, or play blackjack against a beautiful black Creole who dealt with the speed of a prestidigitator. There was a refreshment stand with two pretty bartenders in short dresses and low-cut blouses making planter's punches and Sazeracs and Tom Collinses, and another stand with Coca-Cola and Dr. Pepper and Orange Crush and Jax beer and Lone Star beer and a dozen other brands of everything, all in tubs full of ice; and next to this a third one advertising hot gumbo and spareribs and chili dogs and hush puppies and catfish filets and tacos and hamhocks and collard greens and corn chips and crawdads.

Joy announced she was hungry again, and I felt sharp remorse at having eaten drive-in cheeseburgers instead of crawdad gumbo and hush puppies.

"We don't have time fer no lingeration out chere," Mr. Diamond said, as we walked past the cars toward one of the barns where a lot of noise was being created. "I wanted you boys to eat back yonder so's you wouldn't have to perform on full bellies." The three Mexicans followed silently as Mr. Diamond set the pace. They'd been here before. They had little bags with their gear in them. I was beginning to get stage fright, and possibly other brands of fright besides. The good news was that I wasn't going to have any problem getting the Intruder into a protective cup. He was scareder than I was, if possible.

"Gaucho's gonna lend you his cup," Mr. Diamond said as we got closer to the barn. "Now I got to try to rustle you up some shorts. You can't perform in them creased Sunday school pants."

"I kinda figured I would," I drawled, happy that, even without my hat and boots to help me, I was able to summon the gunslinger. "You said they liked picturesque stuff. I'll bet you don't get many fighters in the ring in creased trousers." There was no way I was going to let a raucous bunch of strangers get a look at my skinny legs.

"That's fer sure," Mr. Diamond said. "And maybe we can make something out of it. I'll hannel it."

Joy, drawn to the ferocious sound of the crowd in the barn, ran ahead of us, then stopped and called out: "Hey! C'mere! Quick! Hurry! Look!" As we came around the corner toward the entrance, a cardboard sign at least five feet square blocked our way. It was tacked to a permanent wooden frame. In vivid poster paints, in block letters, it said:

TODAY'S MATCHES!

3:00 P.M.
TEX FRONTERE 158 (18–0)
VS.   PURSE $2.00
GOOBER "BYE BYE" LETELLIER 160 (13–3)

3:20 P.M.
MANOLITO "TORO" GONZALES 112 (21–3)
VS.   PURSE $2.00
LUKE "BONGO" WASHINGTON 110 (9–0)

There were six other matches listed but I couldn't see anything except "Frontere."

Joy was jumping up and down. "Ain't that cute?" she squealed. "You are at the very tiptop of the whole shebang!"

"Look how they spelled my name."

"What's wrong with it?" she asked.

"Nothing. It's fine." The wrong spelling made it look more like a real name, but it sure did hurt my eyeballs.

"What does that mean, 'Purse two dollars'?" Joy asked.

"Just a little lagniappe there I thought I'd save fer a surprise. Winner gets two dollars."

Joy squealed. "On top of the ten? Dubby, we are rich!"

The crowd inside was screaming bloody murder. Joy hurried to the door ahead of us. A dark man wearing a money apron barred her way. "It's one dollar, mamselle," he crooned with a heavy Cajun accent. Then he leaned a little closer and whispered, "Even for sech a pretty girl."

Joy was both flattered and flustered, not having a dollar. She turned to wait for us.

Mr. Diamond said, "Good afternoon, Claude. This young lady is my guest."

"Oh, Mr. Diamon', *bon*."

"And this is Tex Frontere, top o' the card today."

He offered me his hand, but didn't stop looking at Joy. He was about forty, smelled of brandy or some other fumy drink, and had a strong handshake. "Pleasure to make you' acquaintance, Tex."

"And you know the rest of my boys," Mr. Diamond said, herding us through the door. Claude stepped aside with a sort of automatic smile on his face, watching Joy walk. I stopped watching him watching her. I already knew that came with the territory, and as long as I was in the territory I might as well learn to live with it.

The outside door opened onto a little anteroom, which was dimly lit. The main door to the barn from whence all the noise was coming was in front of us, guarded by an elderly man. To our left was another door, which Mr. Diamond pointed out to me. "That's where the fighters change, Tex."

The elderly man, who wore a straw western sombrero almost as big as he was, waited for a high sign from Claude, then swung open the door to the interior of the barn, and the sound exploded on us. We were looking along a narrow aisle at what appeared to be a boxing ring at floor level, with four strands of rope, except that the floor of the ring was obscured by wooden panels about three feet high that went from ring post to ring post on all four sides, secured by hooks over the second rope from the bottom. Two men in overalls were squatting on opposite sides of the ring, their eyes fixed on something I couldn't see on the floor. Around the ring were wooden stands, bare benches row on row, rising almost to the eaves. Three hundred people, I guessed at first glance, all focused with avid intensity on something on the floor between the two men, many of them screaming at the top of their lungs.

"Come on, Bear! You got 'im, Bear! Strike, Red, strike! He done fer! Hit 'im!" And so on.

Joy darted forward down the aisle and hiked up her ruffled party dress and dropped to her knees at the edge of the nearest panel just as two roosters flew up breast to breast, pecking and striking at each other with shiny metal spurs, feathers flying, and then fell back out of sight in undignified disarray as though hit with shotgun pellets.

"Come on," Mr. Diamond said, pulling at my arm, "we got front row."

Half a front bench was empty for the fighters and other participants. Mr. Diamond lifted Joy to her feet and showed her the bench. She didn't take her eyes off the cocks as she slid in ahead of him. I sat down next, with him between Joy and me, and then came Manolito and Pablo and Gaucho.

The cockpit was the most stomach-turning sight I had ever seen in my life, including the gored horse walking around the bullring with his guts hanging down to the ground in Monterrey two years ago. Feathers and chicken shit and blood were all over the clay floor. One of the cocks, Red, was flapping sideways, dragging a broken wing. Bear, whose feathers ranged from rusty yellow to black, was staggering and dripping blood from his open beak. His blank eyes seemed about to close. His head drooped. He had his back turned to Red, apparently not knowing where he was or what he was doing.

The partisans of the two birds screamed for them to finish each other off. The voice closest to me yelled shrilly, "Red! Red! You got 'im on the ropes! Kill 'im, baby! Kill 'im, Red!" The voice was Joy's. She was bouncing up and down, gripping her crotch with both hands.

Bear's handler, on his knees in the blood and dung, his overalls plastered with bloody feathers, grabbed up his bird and took its entire head in his mouth and sucked the blood out of its throat and spat it on the clay with the rest of the filth. Immediately Bear walked straighter. He had been choking on blood. His handler took a mouthful of water from a bottle and sprayed it on Bear's head, then blew on his face and tossed him halfway to Red. Red tried to fly but fell on his side. The revived Bear leapt on him with both spurs flashing, ripping open his neck and craw. In ten seconds Red was quivering in death. The handlers grabbed up both birds, Red's man quickly leaving the ring, Bear's man holding up his bird triumphantly as the fans moaned and cheered according to their allegiances.

135

A small mustachioed man in a battered top hat and a checked jacket stepped into the ring, leading the applause. He had a very white face and a carnival barker's attitude. "Great fight, huh, folks! Great battle! Two great birds! That completes the first main. Mr. Robechaux's Biloxi Blacks win four of the six fights, so he is the winner of the five-hundred-dollar purse for the first main. I would say Mr. Robechaux got to know just a leetle bit 'bout gamecocks ef he gone drive all the way from Miss'ssippi, let us watch them Blacks o' his strut they stuff!"

This got a kind of an insider laugh. Mr. Diamond said, "Tex, run in there an' put on yer shoes and stuff while they're fixing the ring up. Gaucho . . ." Gaucho produced a protective cup from his bag and handed it to me. "There's an ole boy in there to tape yer hands, lace yer cup."

"My mouthpiece."

"Oh," Joy said, and got it out of her purse.

I noticed there were two other fighters—or boys scheduled to fight —across the ring on another bench. They were already dressed for the ring: shorts, shoes, even taped hands. Manolito, I realized for the first time, already had his ring shoes on, and so did Pablo and Gaucho.

The announcer was continuing his spiel: "The next main is for four and a half pounds and under. All birds to be weighed, no more than two ounces apart for matches, unless mutually agreed. You got an hour for weighing, fixing gaffs, exercising, and bragging. I want to remind you that there will be no—" Here he assumed a comical, sanctimonious tone—"absolutely no wagering." Everybody smiled or chuckled at this absurdity. "Wagering on sporting events is unlawful and won't be tolerated if we notice it." This got a bigger laugh. "Next main starts about four o'clock, maybe four-ten. Purse for the next main is one thousand dollars. Oh, one other thing—no slasher gaffs. All gaffs will be inspected. Slashers will be disqualified, entrance fees not refundable."

"Don't these boys need to get their hands wrapped?" I asked. I sounded plaintive. I regretted opening my big mouth.

"They know how to wrap their own hands," Mr. Diamond said. "Run on now, Tex. I got to talk to the ring announcer 'bout you."

When I got up Joy jumped up and stepped one leg over Mr. Diamond's legs to get near enough to kiss me. Her mons veneris was in his face, but he didn't seem offended. She gave me a tonguey kiss and said, "Oh, honey, kick the livin' shit out of 'im for me!" The crowd cheered the kiss. Then she swung her leg back and sat down close to Mr. Diamond.

As I left, the announcer had stepped out of the ring and two men were removing the sides of the cockpit, and two other men were stretching a canvas tight over the dirty clay, attaching it to hooks in the bottom of the ring posts.

Under the stands on the other side, a hoarse voice was shouting, "Bring on the birds, the birds! Official weights! Ole Time she is a-wastin'!" Most of the people were leaving the stands, some going toward the voice, others in the direction of food and drink. I was the only one heading for the fighters' dressing room.

FOURTEEN

"E IGHTEEN FIGHTS, HUH?" Doc Arnold mused, like a man talking
to himself. He was wrapping my hands slowly, thoughtfully.
He seemed to know what he was doing, but it was strange to
see a man ponder over my hands as though they were of so complex a
structure that he had to make important decisions about the direction
the wrap ought to go and the tension of it. He was about my height,
over six feet two or three inches, and he had to weigh at least three
hundred pounds. Maybe that accounted for it. A person that heavy
would be sort of laconic by nature, just from putting that much bulk
in motion all the time. "You must be a ring-tail tooter, boy. Eighteen
fights, and nary a skid mark on your physiognomy."

"I dodge pretty good," I drawled. My grammar automatically
downshifted. I didn't want to sound like a college boy.

"Emerged victorious every time."

"Yep."

"Unmarked."

"Yep."

"Always fight in creased pants?"

"Yep."

"Some kind of a good-luck charm, I reckon."

"I figger with my nice trousers on, I cain't afford to hit the canvas."

"Makes sense. I'm kinda superstitious myself. There we go." He
had finished my hands. "Le's strap on this anti-ballbuster, now." He
put the cup on over my trousers and laced it in back. "You got the

same sized waist as little ole Gaucho. Listen, eighteen wins, no losses, how come you fighting out here for peanuts?"

"Just a one-shot deal."

"And how come you don't even know how to wrap your own hands? How many fights you really had, Tex?"

He had me cold.

"Amateur, one. Pro, none."

He grinned at me and nodded like he knew it all along. "Listen, boy, I'm not any kind of a real doctor, either. I went to pre-med school for a while, and my friends started calling me Doc. I dropped out but the name stuck. Be careful out there. Most of these boys don't get too severe, but don't trust this Goober. If it goes three, he wins. Local Cajun. Ref's the sole arbiter. Just protect yourself. You get hurt, you're on your own. Anything bad happen, we run you up to Beaumont, the clinic, claim you got drunk and sassed a Brahma bull. So don't git too rambunctious. We just part of the cover."

"The cover?"

"You see them boys out there with their hands taped, in the front row? They got shoes on, cups on, shorts on, ready to put gloves on. If somehow the sheriff makes a run at us, that fella in the high chair down yonder on the road sounds the alarm, and them chickens are gone and the canvas is down, and two boys are punching away in the ring in one minute flat. Not only that but the birds are all in their little coops, the coops on trucks and the trucks in the woods. So we just fill-ins for the ladies and ole folks that stay in the stands while the cockers get ready for the next main."

"We? You fight?"

"If you wanna call it that. I cain't fight for shit. But I know how to keep 'em offa my face. They can pound my blubber all they want. You got anybody with you?"

"Girlfriend."

"No second? Nobody?"

"Mr. Diamond."

"Mr. Diamond!" Somehow, shaking his jowls, he conveyed maximum contempt. "He don't give a damn. All these boys fight fer him, including me. So he don't show partiality by being in anybody's corner. He just furnishes the meat. No second, huh? I gotta laugh at us fools. The cocks got handlers, we got nobody. They weigh the cocks but not the fighters. It's legal for two boys to kill each other in there, but not for birds. Fills a man with admiration for the human race, don't it?"

I didn't have a smart answer. He was finishing lacing up my gloves. They were dry inside, one advantage of being up first.

The door opened a crack. A voice said: "They want you in the ring, Tex."

Doc said in a low voice, "Stick and run, Tex. Old Goober likes to showboat for the home crowd. And Tex—if he puts too much hurt on you, go down and stay down. Be smart."

Inside my creased brown school pants my legs were shaking. They refused to lift my feet. They threatened to let me fall ignominiously to the floor of the fighters' dressing room mumbling, "Mom, tell 'em it's a mistake. Tell 'em I have to study." Then I heard a voice, not mine, the voice of the lone gunslinger, drawling from a long way off, "Thanks, Doc. See you later." What I did next probably could not be explained, even by Dr. Freud. I took my comb out of my left hind pocket and combed my two-bit haircut straight back, neat as could be. Then my feet came unstuck and propelled me out the door.

Why does one condemned man walk on his own to the electric chair, with a calm, almost defiant look on his face, while another one collapses and has to be dragged? Another question for Dr. Freud.

There were less than fifty people in the stands, including Joy and Mr. Diamond. Even the three Mexicans had wandered off. Joy pointed to my protective cup and said, "Oooh, that thing looks sexy! Kill 'im, baby!"

I crawled into the ring in one of the corners where there was a stool. I was in there alone for about ten seconds, which seemed like an hour, and then the announcer appeared in his checked jacket, which was loose over his narrow shoulders and flared over his big buttocks. He had abundant brown hair that looked like a wig, very white skin, and wet lips. He came to me and leaned down and said, "I'll intro you first, Tex. Set on your stool and don't get up till I finish my spiel, then jump up and hop around a little bit and take a bow, okay?" I nodded obediently and sat down. Some of the people in the crowd started chanting "Goo-bair! Goo-bair!" and calling out affectionate messages in Cajun French. I was one of the stars of my French class, treated almost like a *copain* by Monsieur Bourgeois, but I didn't have any idea what these fans of Goober were saying to him. I may as well have been a Georgia cracker trying to understand Cock-

ney. It made me feel lonelier than ever, friendless. I glanced over at
Joy. She was talking animatedly with Mr. Diamond, then tipping a
bottle of Lone Star beer to her lips in the middle of a laugh. The
small crowd began to cheer. Goober was coming. The cheer brought
a few people in from outside, carrying hush puppies and drumsticks
and drinks. Then Goober appeared. He was accompanied by a heavy-
bosomed, big-bottomed girl with black hair. He wore an army cap
with GOOBER stitched expertly into both sides in red thread. His white
cotton jacket had GOOBER on it in the same thread. His white trunks
announced his nickname, also in red. He crawled through the ropes,
not deigning to look at me, dancing and turning and pounding his
gloves together. His lady friend lifted his white jacket off his impressive broad shoulders. He was muscled. His legs were thick and
knotty. His chest was deep. He looked heavier than 160. His belly
was flat and his ribs didn't show. He waved confidently to all his well-
wishers, bowing to the four points of the compass. His friend took his
cap and folded the jacket over her arm and sat down in the front row,
surrounded by pals and allies. He sat on his stool and put his mouthpiece in, still looking at the black-haired girl. I had forgotten my
mouthpiece. It was in the pocket of my trousers. I had to stand
halfway up to dig it out. It had lint on it, and the caraway seed was
going to forever mar the creamy whiteness of the palate side. I put it
in my mouth and bit down. It was comforting, a perfect fit. Suddenly
I felt like a fighter, or I felt that I looked like a fighter. I looked at my
feet and kept my eyes down, imitating a bored fighter who had been
there so many times he just wanted to relax till time to do his job. I
let my arms dangle and leaned back against the corner ropes. I didn't
even look up when the bell was rung to demand attention and the
announcer started his routine.

"Ladies and gentlemen! Your attention, please!" There
couldn't've been more than seventy-five people scattered in the
stands, most of them talking and eating and drinking, but he seemed
oblivious to this, as he gave the moment all the importance he could
muster. "We have got a special treat for you today, in bout number
one. This young man comes to us from the Rio Grande Valley, where
he has compiled a brilliant record of eighteen wins, seventeen by
knockout, and one decision. One of those knockouts was a first-
rounder against the unfortunate fellow who had dared go the distance
with this natural puncher in his third professional fight. This young

man has an interesting background. He became a pro when he attended a fight in Nuevo Laredo, Mexico, and volunteered to sub for a fighter who came down with a high fever and had to withdraw at the last minute. This young man, barefoot, with a borrowed mouthpiece, got into the ring and—using his experience gained in thirty amateur fights, and wearing his Sunday-go-to-meeting trousers—scored a first round kayo of Nuevo Laredo's top middleweight. The long pants have since become his trademark. In his last fight, in Brownsville, Texas, this walking stick of dynamite scored a one-punch knockout. Ladies and gentlemen, let's give a big welcome to—" He motioned me to rise. *"Tex 'The Dapper Destroyer' Frontere!"*

I rose lazily. I didn't bounce or gyrate or bang my gloves together. I turned slowly and gave a perfunctory, stern-faced nod to the spectators on each side of the ring, arriving at Joy last. There was polite applause, except from Joy, who was standing, lifting her Lone Star to me, and screaming, "Yeah, Tex! Take his head off, Tex baby!" The crowd laughed at the absurdity of this. I had the feeling that everybody knew my introduction was a fiction, including Goober. I made the mistake of glancing at him. He winked and grinned.

Goober was introduced as "Fifteen victories, ten by kayo, the ever-popular, always colorful, our own Goober 'Bye Bye' Letellier from Port Arthur, Texas!" The little crowd seemed bigger suddenly, stomping and whistling and calling his name. He not only leapt to his feet, he went about four feet in the air, and landed skipping and dancing and spinning, whizzing past me so fast he created a breeze, and finally doing a series of backward flips in the air to arrive back in his corner. The crowd was vastly impressed and amused. They rose to their feet, applauding and cheering. Even Joy was impressed, and tried to clap with her beer in her hand, causing it to foam over.

The referee was introduced, and the timekeeper, "counting for knockdowns at the bell." The ref, a trim little man wearing a dark blue beret, motioned us to the center of the ring, told us to break when he said break, not to hit below the belt, to shake hands and come out fighting at the bell. I looked down the whole time, but I could tell that Goober was grinning at me. I hunched my shoulders forward to make them look broader, even though I knew it made my chest look caved in to the people at the side.

The bell. I moved out warily. So did he. Maybe he did believe my phony record. As he got close, almost close enough for my light, probing jab, he bent over at the waist so that his torso was horizontal and his face was only about waist-high to me. He put his gloves on either side of his head and left me nothing to punch but the top of his head, his back and shoulders, or his gloves. I expected him to get close and suddenly leap up swinging, the way Choopy did at Ben Hugo's gym, so I backed away, zigzagging. He followed, trying to cut off the ring. When I was cornered he dove in and grabbed me around the waist with one arm and raised up straight, inside my punches, almost as though he was going to lead me in a waltz. He tapped me a few punches lightly in the ribs, then put a glove behind my head, pulled me down to him and whispered: "Ey, Tex, make 'er look good, ey? Not too hard, nobody git hurt, ey, like dis." Then he threw several punches to the belly and the ribs, all looking like big efforts, but pulled at the last split second so I hardly felt them. Then he danced back, snarling for the benefit of the crowd.

My God, he believed that fable. Fine by me. I stuck out some long light jabs, following his bobbing head. He put both gloves beside his face so that only I could see his eyes, and winked at me. Then he did a few fancy footwork moves and ducked under my jab and slammed a left to my ribs so hard I thought he'd caved them in, broken them, and maybe my back, too. Hot pains shot through my side, my back, my neck. I staggered sideways. His right, in a full roundhouse swing, connected with my ribs on the left side, even harder. I thought I heard them crack. My breath flew out of my open mouth, along with my mouthpiece.

The crowd cheered.

Don't trust this Goober . . .

I grabbed him with both arms under his arms, imitating a real fighter, lifting his arms, taking away his punching power as I tried to get my breath.

He butted me under the chin. Purple and yellow lights twinkled in my head. My teeth felt loose. Maybe they were all going to fall on the canvas too, like my mouthpiece.

Mom, Mom, forgive me they'll bring me home all broken maybe dead maybe crippled brain-damaged please forgive me lied deceived betrayed dishonored you Mom you don't deserve a nogood houndog son like—

"Leggo me, you fuckin' sissy fairy college boy!"

The crowd sounded bigger. They were booing.

143

I hung on. My breath was coming back. My ribs weren't broken; I could take deep breaths.

Joy's voice: "Kill 'im, baby! He's just a grandstander! Kill 'im!"

I put both hands on his chest. My weight had him leaning backwards. I shoved. He reeled across the ring against the ropes. The crowd booed. He did a few showoff dance steps and made faces at me, even stuck out his tongue. The crowd adored him. They laughed and cheered.

So he knew. College boy. They knew. Big joke.

Where would the fly be? Not top of his head, not his back. Where? Not his face. Can't get low enough to kill a fly on his face. Where? Here he comes, nothing but top of head back gloves shoulders. Gloves open cover both sides of face. Glove. Fly on glove make him take notice make him feel something quit grinning open up for fly somewhere else. Glove. Think it there think it there there it is big bluebottle back of glove.

He was having fun, waddling in, all covered, ready to jump in and slam me wherever he wanted.

Think it there think it there *be there!* My right landed on the back of the glove covering the left side of his face so hard it caught him in the middle of a silly soft-shoe showoff shuffle and sent him careening. Even through the glove the impact, unexpected, made his eyes bulge in amazement and pain and embarrassment and his mouthpiece came halfway out of his mouth sideways, stopped there by his reflexively clamped teeth. His feet crossed over each other several times as he went sideways into the ropes, grabbing with his right glove to steady himself, and, an instinctive real fighter, to get himself squared toward me so he could charge and punish me for my impudence. I knew the next fly was going to be on the left eyebrow he had cocked toward me as he came almost on the run half-upright with his right hand drawn back for a haymaker.

Which way did the book say move to avoid a right? The opposite of what seemed logical—left. My feet did it. The right went past my right cheek. I stepped back right and saw the fly on the bulge above his left eyebrow. Be there! My right landed dead on the bulge. It peeled down, a flap over his eye. Blood gushed. His nose and the left side of his face were instantly half a red mask. He howled. Seventy-five people gasped at once. I heard a scream from the front row. He spun away with both gloves over his face, blood running down his arms. The crowd was silent. The referee stepped between us, restraining me who needed no restraining, astonished as I was at what I had done.

Goober's black-haired sweetheart was in the ring screaming, "He's hurt! He's hurt! We got to git 'im to Beaumont! Look at all the blood! He gotta get stitched up!"

Doc Arnold, a kindly mountain, appeared beside them, pulled Goober's glove away, lifted up the flap and held it in place. "I'll tape it," he said calmly. "Then they'll sew it." Goober was crying. I didn't want to look. As I turned away Joy flew into my arms.

"Oh, baby! Oh, baby!" She kissed me, then she whispered, "I want you! I'm hot!" She started dragging me out of the ring.

The announcer stood beside the ring and told the shocked spectators, "The winner by TKO, Tex Frontere! Don't worry, folks, Goober gone be okay, good as new, few stitches is all." The crowd applauded mechanically, without enthusiasm.

Mr. Diamond took off my gloves. Gaucho was there to get his cup. "Nice shot," Mr. Diamond said, trying to be polite but not seeming too pleased. I remembered Doc saying all the fighters worked for Mr. Diamond. That explained it. Joy was impatient. She stood first on one foot, then the other.

I got my shirt and changed my shoes in the dressing room where Doc was putting a mound of tape on Goober's brow to keep the flap in place. Goober's girl stared white-faced and damp-eyed at me, silently accusing me of attempted murder. I got out as soon as I could, asking Mr. Diamond to take care of my shoes, and my mouthpiece, which he had retrieved from the ring curtain. They had made Joy wait outside the door, unlike Goober's girl, who was local and had pull.

Joy grabbed me and said, "Let's go, baby, Mr. Diamond gave me money for you, seven dollars. He took out three for the shoes and the mouthpiece. He'll get your two-dollar purse and have it for us next week."

"He took out—?"

"Three, for the mouthpiece and shoes. But look—seven dollars! And they rent rooms at the bunkhouse, fifty cents an hour! We can stay there till time to leave at six! Hurry! I had two beers and I got to pee bad and I am going to go off like a barrel of black powder."

She didn't even ask me if Goober hurt my ribs.

The room in the bunkhouse was only big enough for a single bed and room to walk beside it. There was nothing else. There was a bathroom down the hall that served all ten rooms. We could hear people on either side of us. As I lay on my back letting Joy do all the work—which she loved doing, being in control—I got to thinking about Goober's brow. He was going to have a big scar for the rest of his life, and I was the one who gave it to him. It was a sickening sight, the flap with the hairy brow on it, hanging down, and the red-splashed white bone above. Well, he ought not to have lied to me and tricked me. In a case like that, a man has got to get out alive and in one piece, whatever it takes.

Three dollars for those beat-up old shoes that some other fighter gave up on and a mouthpiece that I was only going to use one time, that larcenous old son of a bitch. And I'd get my two-dollar purse next week. In a pig's eye.

Joy shivered and shook and scrubbed and pounded till she was ready to pass out and couldn't wait another second to run down the hall to the bathroom. When she came back she lay there panting and smiling and making happy sounds.

I decided it was time to bring up something that was bothering me. "How are you going to explain to your mother where you were all day?"

She giggled. "Oh, easy. I was with Erna."

"Erna?"

"My sister-in-law."

"She'll cover for you?"

She giggled again. "She'll do anything I tell 'er to, 'cause I got the goods on 'er. See, my Uncle Phil—well, I was pretty mad at him, 'cause he kinda dropped me. I mean, he did drop me. He used to come by during the day sometimes in his car and pick me up and let me suck 'im off, which I just love to do, you know? But it just stopped all of a sudden. And then I noticed he was best man at my brother's wedding, and always hanging around Erna and even volunteering to drive her to the store and stuff when Roy was working, so I just put two and two together. So this morning, as soon as Mama left, I went and got the bus downtown and called Erna from the drugstore by their apartment, and told her to make some excuse to Roy and meet me at the drugstore 'cause I needed to talk to her real bad. So she give him some kind of a cock-and-bull story and come over there and we had a Coke in a booth, and—I had seen her nekkid once when she didn't know it, sleeping on her back with her nightgown pulled up, so I knew how she looked—all of a sudden I said 'Erna, Uncle Phil says you have got the biggest blackest pussybush he ever laid eyes on, and he just loves to push his face down in it.' And she just about dropped her teeth! She commenced to crying like a baby! 'Oh, why did he have to tell? Oh, that is so *mean!* Men are the meanest critters in the universe! Oh, please don't tell Roy! Oh, my God!' And on and on, just blubbering all over the place, using up all the paper napkins in the booth to blow her nose. Folks in the drugstore thought somebody died! So I promised I wouldn't tell nobody ever if she'd always tell Mama I was with her when I asked her to. And she promised. So I have been with Erna all day. Don't you think I'm smart?" Without waiting for me to answer, she reached over and grabbed me by the ignition switch.

At around six o'clock Mr. Diamond knocked on the door as he had promised Joy he would, to let us know it was time to go. It burned me up that Joy had confided her plans to this wet-lipped, clacky-toothed old man, but I didn't say anything. I was just glad she hadn't tried to do it to me on the dance floor outside in front of everybody. I wouldn't've put it past her.

There were only three of us—Mr. Diamond, Joy, and me—in the Roadmaster for the trip back to Houston. Manolito and Pablo and Gaucho had all won their fights and were staying for the *fais dodo,* which Mr. Diamond said was a dance where everybody was mostly drunk and raising hell till all hours of the morning. Joy said she sure did wish we could stay for that, and maybe one of these days when she ran away from home we would.

Mr. Diamond put the top up and Joy got in the back seat and stretched out and went to sleep. Mr. Diamond told me the crowd thought I was a real exciting fighter and they couldn't wait for me to come back next week, if he could find me a suitable opponent. It was hard to get decent middleweights, especially now that word would be out that I had split Goober's head open. But he had promised Mr. Harkins that he'd find somebody to send to the slaughterhouse, meaning me, so he could count on having Tex Frontere on the card next Saturday and having a bigger crowd for the fights. There was always a big crowd for the cockfights, but mostly the people who watched the prizefights were just friends or relatives of the cockers, up to now. But now there would sure as hell be people come from Port Arthur and Beaumont and Lake Charles and suchlike to watch ole Tex Frontere. "Tell you fer sure," he said, "there'll be something in the Beaumont paper about that barbarianistic one-punch destroyer, Tex Frontere."

"The paper?" My voice tweedled.

"Mr. Harkins knows a good thing when he sees it."

"But you said nobody would find out—"

"Nobody gonna put your picture in the paper! And nobody knows who Tex Frontere really is anyways, so don't worry about yer mama finding out. Mr. Harkins had to go up to Beaumont to see they took care of Goober, but he told me he wanted to meet you in person next Saturday, and he deputized me to tell you you're getting twelve dollars from now on, and the purse for next Saturday's bout will be three dollars. I bet you never figgered—I mean, twelve and three, that's fifteen—I bet you never figgered—you, going to school, pore as a church mouse—I bet you never figgered you was going to land with both feet in that kind of fantastical renumerationism in yer wildest dreams, huh? Huh? Did you?"

"No, I never did." Who said that? I did. Is there nothing to me, nothing at all? No. I guess not.

FIFTEEN

MR. DIAMOND DROPPED Joy off at the Rice Hotel so she could call Erna and get their stories straight about how much fun they had at Herrman Park Zoo all afternoon, and then catch a bus to the Swingatorium. I rode with him as far as the corner of Washington Avenue and Waugh Drive, where I could get a bus home. He asked me if I knew of a Mexican middleweight that might like to pick up five bucks. "It's hard getting fighters sometimes," he said. "Specially to match up with a blond-headed white boy. I could go down Niggertown, plenty nigger boys take you on for three dollars, but Mr. Harkins gimme strict orders, no big lips, no lips that pooch out past their nose. Creoles okay, Creoles look more like black white folks. Maybe I go to Lake Charles, get a Creole boy if I don't find a Meskin."

I wanted to say something, but I couldn't think of anything worth saying. Finally I said, "Does Mr. Harkins just think big lips are ugly? Or what?"

"You ain't old enough to unnerstan', Tex. Them pooched-out lips *signify*. You won't read about it. It ain't in schoolbooks. It's in years. You git a few years on you, be real observatory, and you'll commence a whole process of deep comprehensionism. You'll just *know*."

He believed that time had endowed him with an intellectual dimension beyond the reach of a beardless puppy like me. In other words, there comes a time in life when, just because you hung around so long, you're right. And you know it.

On spiritual matters Mom had often said to me that she didn't *think* she was right, she *knew* she was right. And now Mr. Diamond, who was even older and therefore, by definition, wiser than Mom, was telling me the same thing about anthropology, a word he probably didn't know. Or was this phrenology? Whatever it was, it was a deeper mystery than even the Spanish Civil War. I didn't challenge him. My chance to strike a blow for enlightenment had come and gone, due to my own lack of enlightenment. Or courage. I looked forward to being dry enough behind the ears to be sure I was right, even when I was wrong.

When I got home Jenny ran at me as hard as she could and jumped into my sore ribs, and I groaned so loud Mom asked me what happened. I told her I'd played basketball in gym after class and caught an elbow in the ribs, and it wasn't going to interfere with me going to church in the morning. This confirmed the onset of spirituality in me that she had been noticing, and it reminded me that although I wasn't dwelling on the existence of the Angel night and day she was still hovering just over the rim of my mind waiting to dart in as Sunday drew near. I was going to keep going to church at least until I saw the bottom half of the vision, and depending on that, maybe even after. No doubt closer inspection would dispel my self-induced mythification and I would return to my lame excuses for sleeping in on Sundays. The Angel would need to be all that my imagination had conjured up in human perfection, plus show reasonable promise of eventual accessibility, to make me continue to expose my incurable houndoggery to the guilt-slinging unattainable holiness of that hour. But Mom, in her innocence, perceived none of this.

"Oh, Dubby, I'm so proud when you sit with me in church."

Jenny thought this was disgusting. "I wish I didn't have to go to Sunday school," she said. "Sunday school is dumb."

Mom and I, both wise adults, laughed.

That evening was a rare one. We had guests. Mr. and Mrs. Hale Tamplee arrived half an hour after I got home. Mom had prepared a macaroni and creamed tuna casserole, and red beans, and salad with lettuce and tomatoes and radishes and chopped celery and a home-made dressing, and a sweet potato pie for dessert. She had charged some of the stuff at Mr. Schultz's store, which she hated to do. This made me feel very guilty, because I had four dollars and fifty cents in my pocket (I'd given a dollar to Joy to buy herself a present), and I hadn't decided how to explain it, so I couldn't give it to Mom.

150

Mr. and Mrs. Tamplee recited clichés. They had no more sense of humor than moldy bread. Mr. Tamplee kept his blue tie knotted at the very top the entire two hours they were with us. The skin of his neck hung out over the top of his starched white collar. Mrs. Tamplee put very small bites into her mouth and chewed slowly, but managed to speak by opening her lips ever so slightly. "Well, they elected a Catholic mayor of New York, I guessed you noticed, Letty."

"They've got enough Catholics in New York to do that, I guess," Mom said.

"And enough Eyetalians," Mr. Tamplee added. "Did you ever hear of such a name? Fiorello La Guardia. You'd think if he's a real American he'd change a name like that."

"One—" Mrs. Tamplee stopped her speech. She was unable to speak because of the amount of food in her mouth, so she held up her hand to keep the floor till she could swallow. "One of these days —we'll have—mark my words—a Catholic president."

"Oh, no," Mom said.

"You just mark my words, Letty."

"Of course," Mr. Tamplee said, "he won't admit it till after he's been elected."

"Oh, my," Mom said, a note of awe entering her voice, "do you think it's actually possible that such a thing could happen?"

"Well," Mr. Tamplee said, "we already have a Jew in the White House, if some of the information coming to me is correct."

"I do not believe that," Mom said. "Absolutely. Even if my own party did put out that pamphlet. I'm a Republican, of course."

"Oh, naturally," Mrs. Tamplee said, and Mr. Tamplee nodded. It was clear they wouldn't've been honoring us with their presence if they'd had even a slight suspicion that Mom might be a Roosevelt Democrat.

"The pamphlet did state, absolutely," Mom continued, "that Mr. Roosevelt was a Jew, but without offering any proof. It's my understanding that the Roosevelt family has been traced back—"

"There is a large body of evidence," Mr. Tamplee said, "that the family changed their name from Rosenveldt several generations back. Of course, I have not seen the evidence personally."

"Well," Mrs. Tamplee said, "he sure does act like one, trying to turn this into a Commonist country. Hale and I are convinced there's a dangerous conspiracy, aren't we, darlin'? Well, let's not frighten the

151

children." Mrs. Tamplee smiled widely at Jenny and me in turn, but with her lips pressed tightly together. "Now, a more pleasant subject. Letty, this macaroni and tuna casserole is a goremay treat, as they say in Paris, France. And let me congratulate you on your children, too. Hale and I have been to homes where the children prattled at the table and the grownups could not get a word in edgewise."

"I certainly do appreciate the compliment, Madge. My husband and I have tried, we absolutely have, and we have gotten mighty lucky, I think. They are no trouble atall. They mind and they study and they listen to learn. What else can a mother ask? Dubby—that's our nickname for Woodrow in the family—was involved in a collision today in college, got hit so hard in the ribs with an elbow during basketball that he still had considerable pain when he got home, but I did a little work on it right away, and I daresay he doesn't feel any pain atall anymore, do you, honey?"

"No, ma'am." If I bent to the right from the waist up, the pain was excruciating, but who could admit such a thing in answer to such a question at such a time?

Mr. Tamplee fixed me with a long, appraising stare, and finally said in an authoritative tone, "That means there's a lot of harmony already there. Your mother tells me, Woodrow, that you are already a freshman in college and you're only seventeen."

"He skipped a grade!" Jenny piped.

Mom put a restraining hand on Jenny to remind her she wasn't old enough to join in grownup conversations.

"Yes, sir," I said, "but I'll be eighteen next month."

"I like to see a boy who applies himself to his schoolwork. I hope you're equally diligent in your study of Science."

"Almost the first thing he did when he got home today," Mom put in quickly, "was remind me he was going to church with me in the morning. Not that it's a rare thing, but Saturday night's usually his one dating night, so some Sunday mornings I just sneak off to church without him so he can sleep."

Mrs. Tamplee seemed impatient to be part of the conversation. "If there's anything you want to know, any question you'd like to ask while Mr. Tamplee and me are here, we'd be happy to oblige."

I thought that was generous, but I didn't quite know what I should ask. Mom saw me hesitate, so she said, "Dubby, don't be bashful."

"Well," I said, "I don't understand the Spanish Civil War."

"Oh!" Mrs. Tamplee exclaimed. "Of course I meant questions about Christian Science."

"Mr. Tamplee is a practitioner, Dubby," Mom said.

"Oh, no, that's all right," Mr. Tamplee said, looking on me again with what I thought might be suspicion. "College students are sometimes naturally curious about these things, and how can a young man learn if he doesn't ask questions? To put it as simply as possible, Woodrow, the Commonists are trying to take over Spain the way they took over Russia, and General Franco's army is not going to let them do it. You know what a Commonist is, don't you?"

"Well, I'm not sure."

"Let me put it this way. In Russia, now that the Commonists run things, everything is owned by the state, and the people don't have any say in anything. They're just slaves. We don't want that to happen in Spain, do we?"

"No, sir."

"Because if it happens there, they have a foothold in Europe. They'd start subverting other countries. Do you know what 'subvert' means?"

"Yes, sir."

"The boy is very studious," Mrs. Tamplee said.

"And they'd keep on taking over countries till they got strong enough to take us over, too. Mr. Roosevelt and plenty of other people are already working from the inside to prepare us for that. But these things are too complicated for young minds. How did you get interested in this subject, Woodrow?"

"Well, sir, there was this speaker at school, and he said—I think he said—that the government General Franco was trying to overthrow was the elected government, and—"

"I thought so!" Mr. Tamplee almost shouted, then stopped a second to control himself. "One of those Red speakers! And on the campus, was he?"

"Yes, sir, he—"

"That ought not to be allowed! They ought not to allow these subversive speakers, pushing for Commonism, on these campuses, poisoning young minds, trying to recruit young American boys to go over there and give their lives to help the Commonists take over Spain. Letty, you ought to speak to the president of Rice about this. This is dangerous."

"I agree with you, Hale, absolutely. But I'm sure Dubby is too smart to be taken in by the Reds."

I didn't know who was right, but I hoped the baby-faced speaker in Sallyport was, because I liked him better than Mr. and Mrs. Tamplee.

That night, after the Tamplees left, I studied hard, waiting up for Chester. When he finally called, I was ready for him. Instead of listening to him relive devoutly his every in and out of every copulation since our last conversation, I pounced on him with the entire history of my life with Joy. The only thing I changed was her name. I started at the beginning and troweled on the details. By the time I got to the present Saturday afternoon at the bunkhouse, an hour into our talk, he was trying to stop me. "Dub, Dub, Dubby-boy! The bunkhouse, was it any different? I mean, did you just do the same ole thing?"

"Well, sure."

"Well, okay, I git the picture. I got to go. I'm at the Swingatorium and there's people waitin' fer this phone and Susie and Hilda done give up on me and are out there dancin' together."

Joy was probably bus-girling right in front of them, and I had come within an eyelash of telling Chester her name.

Shortly after I hung up Mom glided in, with her finger marking her place in *Science and Health,* and leaned down as always to kiss me goodnight. (Was it lavender or jasmine, that odor, or several flowers? For some reason I didn't want to ask her. Whatever it was, it suited her, and it was always the same. It was her scent. And it had to be cheap, but it didn't smell cheap.) She said, "I was proud of you tonight, honey, as always. Don't study too late."

Before I went to bed I wrote in my notebook, "Good luck is not always getting what you deserve."

I couldn't've been in bed two minutes before I jumped up and got my notebook out again and wrote, "It is impossible to live without lying." Then I went back to bed, but my head had hardly hit the pillow before I bounced up to hide my four dollars and fifty cents. What if Mom decided to send those pants to the cleaners and found that money? I didn't have any idea how to explain having so much cash. Usually lies came to me like water out of a faucet, but I had discarded every one that popped into my head as being weak or flimsy or incriminating. I finally rolled up the four one-dollar bills and shoved them down in a finger of my old baseball glove and stuck the two quarters in after them. Then I wrote in my notebook again: "Tainted wealth is a heavier burden than poverty," and went back to bed. After about ten seconds I realized all three of my entries for the night were pretty lame, but I decided to wait till morning to erase them.

SIXTEEN

THE TWO WORST THINGS about attending church with Mom were the trip there and the trip home. Mom insisted on being the driver, and if there was anything that everyone who knew her agreed upon unanimously, it was that riding in the car with her was torture. One reason was, she never stopped talking and turning her head to make eye contact with the passengers, including those in the back seat. There was something about being in a moving vehicle which exaggerated her natural garrulity. It was always cheery and enthusiastic, her monologue, but her captive audience couldn't fail to notice that in order to complete her narration without colliding with another vehicle or even a stationary object, she drove very slowly, well below the speed limit. If a car was trapped behind her and couldn't pass, it would sometimes honk politely, then insistently, then furiously, always without making a dent in Mom's imperturbability. If forced to interrupt her story, she might say something like, "That is a rude person behind us." Or if someone ventured that she was going twenty miles an hour in a thirty-five-mile zone, she would say, "The limit is the limit, not the ordained speed. We should never drive the limit. There should always be a safe yet satisfactory choice below the limit. Remember, I've never had a wreck." I was always tempted to ask how many she may have caused, but she was, after all, my mother, and I had to weigh these annoyances against all the great sacrifices she had made in life and the suffering she had endured.

Still, when she arrived at an intersection and stopped, and looked both ways, and failed to cross because a car was coming a block away, and waited till it had passed, and then turned to emphasize a point in her story to a person in the back seat, only to face front again and look both ways again, and discover that another car was coming too near for her to venture across the intersection, and when this procedure was repeated three or four times while behind us a bedlam of honks, raced engines, and stuttering tires grew and grew—cars having apoplectic fits—her passengers, no matter how much they loved her, were tempted to get out and walk.

This Sunday morning, the seventh of November, a dirty black pickup truck with no fenders and a driver who honked, yelled, and shook his fist at our old Dodge while it waited for car after car finally pulled up beside us and stopped on the wrong side of the street so that the driver could look Mom right in the eye.

"What air ye, dead?" he yelled. He needed a shave, his hair was matted, and his eyes were red. "Ef ye done died, how come ye don't lay back down in yer hotdern coffin, lady?" He gunned his engine and spun his back wheels and darted into the intersection directly in the path of an oncoming truck with a high load of baled hay. Both trucks swerved, but the big truck clipped the rear end of the pickup, spinning it around, and then tipped over, strewing baled hay for fifty yards along the street. Both drivers jumped out, unhurt, and started roaring oaths at each other.

Mom put her car in gear and, with everything at a halt around us, proceeded calmly across the intersection. "People who cannot control their emotions," she said tartly, "have no business being allowed to drive."

Ordinarily this would've been our excitement for the day, but it was nothing compared to what was about to happen to me in church.

When we arrived everything seemed normal: polite, cool, unemotional, contemplative, scientific yet inspirational. We even bumped into Mr. and Mrs. Tamplee at the door. They exchanged greetings with Mom. My having listened for a few minutes to the speaker in Sallyport had somehow tainted me for them, I guess, because they barely acknowledged my presence. Inside the plain rectangular building the individuals in their subdued finery were hushed and attentive as the First Reader began the routine of reading Mary Baker Eddy's Note, which begins, "Friends, the Bible and the Christian Science textbook are our only preachers." Jenny was down in the basement in Sunday school, and Mom and I were seated near the back because we had arrived at the last minute, as usual. As the First Reader continued I became aware that latecomers were right behind us, politely waiting in the door till the Note was completed. I only had to turn my head an inch and cut my eyes all the way right to see that the Angel, with a halo, was silhouetted in the door.

The moment the reading of the Note ended, a motherly, olive-skinned woman with short brown hair and no makeup appeared at my side, and slipped into a seat one row closer to the front and across the aisle from Mom and me. She was followed by a small, swarthy man in a dark brown suit. He waited in the aisle for the Angel to slide in beside the person I assumed to be her mother, then seated himself in the last remaining seat in the row, on the aisle. I had finally seen the Angel from her head to her toes! I was lifted. Nothing touched me. I floated. Is this what Dante felt when he first saw Beatrice at the age of nine? Did it come to him then that out of the infinite space of His universe God had selected this place at this moment for his eyes to look upon her form? That is what came to me.

I studied her profile. I had seen it before somewhere in a painting by a Renaissance master, of angels hovering over human beings. The fact that she was wearing a small straw hat with a narrow brim that had glowed in the backlight of the door to make a halo did not diminish her spirituality. The halo remained. Her skin, like her mother's, was olive-tinted, with a light shining through from within. Her eyes, which did not wander brazenly all about her as Joy's would have done but remained chastely down, were large and liquid, ready to weep for mankind. She wore no makeup. Her naturally red full lips seemed slightly pursed. Her hair, coiled in a pretty knot in back under the brim of her saucy little katy, was black with glints of copper. If there was a human element at all, even a hint of something lower than spirituality, it was the odor of Ivory soap, the faintest whiff of it as she passed. It probably was coming from one of her earthly companions.

Mom was not aware of them. She had handed me the open hymnal and I was mouthing words and pretending to sing along. The Angel had risen with her companions at the beginning of the hymn and was singing in a soft, sweet, seraphic voice.

In all my nearly eighteen years on earth I had never been this close to so much purity and beauty and flawlessness. It is a tribute to my limitless talent for deception that I stared at her head and the nape of her neck and her smartly woollen-clad delicate shoulders for the entire service, fantasizing a thousand things, none of them sexual, all of them high-minded, while giving Mom the impression that I was hypnotized by what was being dispensed by the First and Second Readers. Toward the end, during the reading of the Scientific Statement of Being, words came to my ears that seemed so linked to her that I heard them as part of my obsession: "Spirit is God, and man is His image and likeness. Therefore man is not material; he is spiritual."

The moment the service closed, the father, the mother, and the Angel rose as one, stepped into the aisle, and without a glance at anyone, with eyes straight ahead, walked briskly out the door. I shot to my feet, anxious to follow. Mom looked up at me as though some wild spirit had possessed me. I sat again, embarrassed, and then rose with Mom, who liked to take her time and chat with friends as she moved slowly outside to become part of a little group on the lawn for a few minutes of conversation. This was about the sum of Mom's social life most weeks, so on the rare occasions I was with her I tried to hide my impatience. Today I feigned being squeezed forward by the exiting crowd, and found myself outside alone, looking for the Angel. She was gone. Mom would be pleased to know that I was planning to be a regular churchgoer from now on, unless it turned out that the Angel, briefly visiting relatives, had come to dust our lives with celestial light and then move on.

I didn't mention the Angel to Mom. Who would believe what had happened to me? It couldn't've been love at first sight; I wasn't sure what love was. This was instantaneous adoration. Can an apparently sane boy, almost eighteen years old, explain such a thing to a person with a sore place in her mouth from ill-fitting dentures and not enough money to pay a dentist to adjust them? And why defile the Angel with gross, inadequate explanations inspiring doubt and ridicule? Dreams have to be private, or they crash. And they have to be limitless, or they're not worth dreaming. (Both of these conclusions, shared with Robert Browning and many others, went directly into "The Maxims of W. W. Johnson.") Down with lust! Up with spiritual adoration! If my own moral weakness could not keep me from wallowing in perpetual lubricity, Mrs. Hurt's alertness would. And the influence of the Angel would finally make me strong. I would be purified. I would meet her. I would do everything in my power to prove worthy of her company. I would get her parents' permission to invite her to dinner at a respectable restaurant. If she was a human angel, which I had to conclude she was, having human parents, she must eat like human beings, though certainly with more delicacy and restraint than most. No. Not the restaurant first. First, church. I'd ask her if, with her parents' permission, we could sit together in church. After that, dinner for two. The money! I would make enough from my secret fights. I'd horde it. Then I'd confess the truth to Mom—that I'd done it for love, for by then I was sure I'd know it was love, and I'd've risen above the curse of my duplicity. And once I knew love, reciprocal love with the Angel, this lustful aberration with Joy would wash away like dust in spring rain.

That would be the end of my fighting. By then she would know our true circumstances, our poverty, even the imperfections of our family relationships and, being an angel, would understand and forgive. Then money would be secondary, almost unimportant. Mom would invite her to come for chicken and dumplings, or red beans, or chili and rice and salad. It'd be homey, unpretentious, perfectly seasoned with love.

I would no longer coarsen my spirit by listening to the base carnality of Chester's phone calls.

I would stay late at Rice each day to get my studying done, so that by the time I got home, Mrs. Hurt would be home to restrain her daughter's compulsions.

I would help Mom in the kitchen in the evening, having done my lessons at school. I'd spend more time with Jenny, being her big brother. I'd even go over the Lesson of the Week with Mom. I'd go to bed early, and get up early, and insist on getting my own breakfast so Mom could stay in bed. I'd quit stealing my father's Bull Durham. I'd quit smoking. Or, if I didn't manage to quit entirely, immediately, I'd cut down drastically, and I'd use some of my boxing money to buy an occasional small pack of Chesterfields while I was strengthening my character.

Another good thing was happening, too. Whereas Saturday evening the ribs on my left side had hurt almost unbearably when I bent a certain way, making it difficult to speak without groaning, even while I was lying to protect Mom in front of the Tamplees, leading me to conclude that the cartilage between my ribs—if there was such a thing—had been torn, since leaving church I had felt only an occasional faint twinge to remind me of Goober's treacherous punches.

By Monday I was almost free of pain. I studied hard in the basement library, then went to Autry House and played ping-pong till time to catch my bus. I felt the stirrings of the new, virtuous me, and a mysterious elation.

On Mondays I always waited for Dad to come home from his long weekend and find his way to bed with his various noises and odors and fall into his sleep of exhaustion before I ventured into our bedroom. His snoring didn't bother me any more than nightbirds singing or cars passing or airplanes overhead. On this Monday he got home about eleven and wove his way through the kitchen and dining room and into our bedroom with a jovial, "How you hangin', Cowboy? G'night," in passing. I wanted to love him, did love him, I was almost sure, but I wondered if I'd ever know him.

Mom, too, always waited till he was safely in bed and snoring, and then she'd float silently through the living room in her raggedy robe to give me my kiss. But tonight, before this could happen, there was a scratching on the screen near my head. It was Joy, crooking her finger for me to come outside. I was sure Mom was going to come out of her room at that very second. My ears rang as though they'd been slapped. I pantomimed to Joy that she should be quiet, that I was coming out. Then I went quickly to the door of Mom's room and tapped. She said, "Come in, honey." I went in and kissed her and told her I'd gone to bed so early last night I wasn't sleepy, and I thought I'd take a walk before going to bed.

"That's a nice idea. You'll sleep better."

I went out. Dad was snoring when I passed through the living room and out the front door. Joy, in her nightgown, barefoot, was in the shadows by the porch. She grabbed my hand and whispered, "I know a place!" She tugged and ran. I followed, with all the self-will of a pull-toy on a string, across the street, into the schoolyard, to the back of the dun-brick building. There, concealed by plantings on either side, were the stone steps down to the basement, shielded from even the moonlight.

She was the same as ever, and so was I.

SEVENTEEN

JOY ALWAYS GOT HOME from school by four-thirty, and her mother didn't get there till around six. It pained Joy to waste that hour and almost a half that we could be alone in her house, so she kept after me to sneak over there in the afternoon. I made all kinds of excuses, but she called Rice and got my schedule and found out that I finished my last class at noon on Thursdays, and confronted me with this information, so I didn't have any better excuse than that I was too scared to try to do anything at her house in such a short time for fear her mother would come home early. Then she said I should borrow Mom's car and wait for her a block from school and she'd jump in and we could go do it in the car someplace. She'd heard Heights Cliffs was a good spot. That's what all the kids at school told her, anyhow.

I was finally out of excuses, so by four-fifteen on Thursday she was in the car with me and we were on our way to Heights Cliffs. This was an area of woods and thicket on the outskirts of the north side of Houston where erosion had carved a deep gulley in the clay, making it into a sort of a romantic spot, a lovers' lane, though using the word *cliffs* for such a modest height above such a trickle of a stream was sort of like calling a yearling colt a stud. Sure enough, when we got there there were already two cars parked, and one couple was necking up a storm, and the other couple were facing each other in the front seat, so engrossed in their activities that they didn't even glance up at the sound of another car; the world could go hang. I had read in Uncle Billy's Whizzbang that couples in London did it on the grass in

162

Hyde Park in broad daylight, but I didn't believe it till now. Joy was excited at the prospect of doing it in daylight, in public. "Oh, look!" she squealed, when she caught sight of the girl riding the boy's lap. "Oh, park here so's I can watch while we do it!" She had her panties off before I had the car stopped, and she hiked up her skirt and turned facing aft so I just had to slide over past the gearshift and get my pants pulled down, and she was astraddle me and off to the races. She didn't want to waste time on foreplay; that took place in her mind on the way over. And she sure didn't want to waste time getting into the back seat: rocking-chair-style didn't take much room.

After what I calculated as about an hour, I was ready to leave. I think I was lonely. I had the feeling that what I was supplying could be supplied by any number of other people. I was anonymous. Joy scrubbed away and watched the nearest car. "Oh, my God," she groaned, "she's outasight! She's down!" This information, and the image it furnished her, stirred her to feverish activity and another quick orgasm. I just leaned back and remained available and viable. It was almost boring. I could see her being another Hilda in a couple of years, with her interest in the other fornicators: sex as a team sport. When she collapsed against me to catch her breath, I told her it was late and we'd better hit the road. She wanted to stop at a Gulf station and neaten up, and, of course, she wanted to be home before her mother, which meant I had to let her out around a corner in time for her to walk home from the direction of Reagan before six. As soon as she came out of the ladies' restroom looking like the cat that swallowed the canary, she skipped around to the driver's side and said, "It's only five-forty by that clock in the window there, so we got time to let me show you how good I can drive."

"No way," I said.

"How come?"

"It's not my car."

"You think I'm gonna hurt your mama's dumb ole car? I'm as good a driver as you, any day."

"Can't do it, Joy."

She leaned in and kissed me and grabbed my crotch. "After how nice I been to you?" she purred. "After how nice I'm gonna be to you any time you want me to be, anywhere, do you mean to tell me you gonna be too chicken to let me just drive your mom's little ole car a couple blocks, just to show you how good I can do it?"

"Aw, hell, Joy."

"Come on, sweet meat. Just a teensy-weensy bit."

"Jesus." I slid over. She got in. She put the car in gear without a grinding noise. She put out her hand to show she was turning left out of the station and started us rolling smooth as pie, without any jerky motion at all, and we went along through traffic as though she was a licensed chauffeur to the queen of England. Then she turned right up Fifteenth Street toward the wasteland area of Heights Cliffs. "Where you headed?" I asked.

"This is just neighborhood, up thisaway," she said. "I want to let 'er out a little, see what she can do."

"You drove enough, Joy. I see you know how."

She jammed down on the gas and the sedate old Dodge did her ladylike best to act like she had power, accelerating faster than I'd ever made her do.

"Goddammit, Joy!"

"Wheee! Wisht we had a sireeen!"

Forty-five, fifty, fifty-five, sixty, right through an intersection. These little neighborhood streets, the dirt ones, didn't have stop signs. You were supposed to slow down and check out the crossroad to be sure you didn't have two cars arriving at the same place at the same time. But not Joy. Right through another intersection, doing sixty-five, with the sound of a horn in our ears. Joy didn't know Fifteenth Street like I did. The houses got ramshackle and farther apart, and then the road petered out into a garbage dump.

"Brake! Brake, Joy! End of the road!"

She braked. We skidded on the dirt surface, spinning, skidding backwards, backing to a stop right into the edge of a trash heap of old mattresses, bottles, rusty buckets, cardboard boxes, and busy rats. The rats loped off in all directions. A couple of them stopped and stared at us like we were crazy. Joy was laughing like she was flat-out insane. "Wow," she finally gasped, "this is a goin' Jessie! She ain't no patrol car, but she takes off!"

"Get out," I said. "Get out and come around here and get in, or I'm gonna throw you out and let you walk home." I knew I'd never punch a woman, but in a flash I understood how it could happen.

"Don't take everything so serious," she grumbled. "Sometimes I think you're about as straitlaced as ole Roy."

She got out, pouting, and came around the other side and got in.

We didn't say another word. I drove back across Heights Boulevard and stopped. She got out and slammed the door in a huff and stalked off toward home. I was just grateful Mom's car wasn't damaged. I didn't know how I was going to explain the coating of red dust that had settled on it when we spun to a stop at the dump, so I drove to Earl Bentler's gas pumps about a half a mile away and bought a dollar's worth of gas. Mr. Bentler was a little hangdog-looking man. He and Dad were beer buddies, so I figured I could ask him a favor. He was happy to let me borrow his hose and chamois skin. I washed Mom's car and chamoised it till it looked almost new.

She was impressed. "Not many people have the gumption to take such good care of borrowed things, Dubby," she said. "Sometimes when I look at you and realize you're my son, I swell up till I just about bust my buttons."

She sure did know how to make a person feel guilty.

EIGHTEEN

THE FIGHT MR. DIAMOND ARRANGED for me the following Saturday turned out to be a joke. When he and Joy picked me up at
the front gate of Rice there was only one fighter in the back
seat. I could hardly see him because his hat was pulled over his eyes.
He was fingering a rosary. He didn't look up when I got in the car. It
was a blustery day and Mr. Diamond had the top up. Joy gave me her
usual lingering kiss, the kind you don't feel like you ought to be
doing in front of other people.

"I guess you got a middleweight for me?" After only one fight I
felt like a pro, especially in front of other people. I was developing a
puncher's cockiness. Maybe it was my gunslinger, speaking with another voice. I was surprised at the way I said it.

"Him," Mr. Diamond said, with no enthusiasm, stabbing a thumb
toward the back seat. "Gaucho's cousin. He don't speak English.
Gaucho and the other two boys are off this week. I got some boys
from Port Arthur and yonderways."

I looked back at the man behind Mr. Diamond. He had shaggy
black hair and a wide, flat Aztec face with a small chin. He wiped his
eyes with his sleeve. He was crying and fumbling with prayer beads.

Crying? A grown man?

Matagorda County, 1932: "Hey, boy, ye ain' cryin', air ye?"
I can't answer. Breath knocked out of me.
Dad says: "Hell no, he ain't cryin'. My boy don't cry. Take more'n gittin'
pitched offa ole nag to make my boy cry, right, Dub?"

I nod, gasping for air. Nobody asks if I'm okay.

" 'Pears like to me a leetle bit o' juice runnin' outa them eyes o' his'n, Bill."

"Hey," Dad says, chuckling, "landin' on yer back like that bound to jar a little bit o' juice loose, but Dub sure as hell ain't cryin', are you, Dub?"

"No, sir."

"Well, Bill, I'm shore glad yer boy ain't cryin', 'cause I shore woutten want yer boy to be no sissy. Only sissies cry, boy. You ever hear about Green Witch Village, boy?"

"No, sir."

"Well, yer paw'll tell you this is the God's truth, Green Witch Village is a place up in Noo Yark City where the sissies live. Any boy in Texas turns out to be a sissy, he ends up gittin' run outa town and livin' up in Green Witch Village with the rest of the sissies, right, Bill?"

"That's what I hear tell, ole hoss, but don't you worry 'bout my boy Dub. My boy don't cry." . . .

Mr. Diamond slammed on his brakes and swerved the car, barely missing a steer that had bolted out of a small herd right up onto the highway.

After a minute or two I glanced back at Gaucho's cousin just as he was blowing his nose on his shirttail.

"What's he crying for?" I asked.

Joy giggled. "He's scared shitless."

"He figgers you might kill 'im," Mr. Diamond said, "but he needs the five dollars bad."

When we got to the ranch the parking lot was crowded. Mr. Diamond said it was because of something in the paper. He hadn't read it, but he'd heard it really bragged about Tex Frontere. I couldn't wait to see it.

The beautiful blackjack dealer had a copy of it and waved to us as soon as we got out of the car. M'sieu Claude, the doorman at the barn, had torn it out of the paper and left it with her. She didn't know which paper, the one from Beaumont or Port Arthur, or maybe even Lake Charles.

"Read it out loud," Mr. Diamond said to Joy, "so's we can all get the benefaction of it."

"It's real short," Joy said. Then she read: "Local fight fans have got a treat in store, if they manage to see Tex Frontere in action while

167

he's in these parts. Frontere, a middleweight, hails from the Laredo area, where he compiled a record of quick kayos. Last Saturday afternoon at a local fightery he just about tore off the eyebrow of local favorite, Goober "Bye Bye" Letellier, with one punch. Goober says it was the hardest he has ever been hit, but he hopes to get a rematch with the Dapper Destroyer before he returns to the Laredo area. Frontere got the—" She stumbled over a word. "The sob—what's this word?" She shoved the paper at Mr. Diamond.

He avoided it, turning away like a wasp was buzzing him, and started ripping the top off of a pack of Camels. "Ask Tex, he's the college boy."

She showed it to me. I said, as though I used the word every day, "Sobriquet. Means nickname."

There was screaming and cheering coming from the barn. "My God, the cockfights are still on!" Joy said. "I wanta see 'em!"

"Finish the article," Mr. Diamond said, pushing up a Camel.

Joy read quickly. "Sober—whatchamacallit—'Dapper Destroyer' not only because of his one-punch knockouts, but the fact that he fights in long creased pants, like a lawyer on his way to court." She handed the scrap of paper to the beautiful blackjack dealer and ran for the barn.

"M'sieu Claude will let her in," the dealer said, with a smile at Mr. Diamond. "She don' need no money."

I was not at the top of the card, so I went back to the car to try to slog my way through a few pages of *Mansfield Park*. When they called me for my fight I went in to see Doc Arnold and he showed me how to wrap my own hands. He told me Mr. Diamond spent all his time rounding up fresh meat for the fights, which I had already figured out, and that he got fifty dollars a head for finding them and transporting them, and everything he didn't have to pay out was his, so no wonder he could afford a Buick Roadmaster. "Not bad for a runaway orphan boy that can't read or write."

"He can't?"

"Not a lick. Oh, maybe road signs. Went to work in a New Orleans whorehouse, age nine, shining shoes and carrying towels. Tol' me he had fourteen mamas, never went to school a day in his life."

That made me look at Mr. Diamond with different eyes. He was still a con artist, but it wasn't as though it was his decision. It was like being a coyote. You're born to it.

Before I went on, Mr. Diamond introduced me to Mr. Harkins, Mr. Eliazar Beauchamp Harkins, who was a dangerous-looking man, taller than I, dark-skinned, black-eyed, dressed all in black, wide at the shoulders and straight but very slender when I looked at him sideways. He wore a black flamenco-dancer-type hat and he didn't smile when Mr. Diamond said our names but just nodded and shook hands with me, his hand slender and bony and not as strong as I expected. I said, "I'm very pleased to meet you, sir," but he didn't seem to hear me.

"Well, got to get the boy ready," Mr. Diamond said, leading me away. When we had gone a few yards he whispered, "He likes you, Tex. I can tell."

Goober was at ringside with his girl, his left brow puffed way out and red with iodine or something, with big crude stitches holding it all together. They both waved to me and smiled, no hard feelings, all in a day's work.

At the bell, Gaucho's cousin came out crouched over with his head so low to the canvas that I had no place to hit him except the top of his head, which he covered with his gloves, and his back. I was wary of him after the way Goober had faked me out and then tried to break my ribs, so I just stabbed and stabbed lightly at the top of his head till everybody started to boo and laugh and yell insults, none of which he understood, until Goober started yelling, *"Maricón!"* and mincing back and forth at ringside with one hand on his hip and the other limp-wristed out in front of him, like a sissy. The crowd decided they were stuck with a farce instead of a fight and they might as well laugh. Gaucho's cousin reacted to this by straightening up and leaping backwards out of range and swinging wildly, missing me by two feet, then going into his shell again. It was like a Chaplin film. I added to the fun by putting my glove on the back of his head and pushing down, at which point he fell flat on his face and took a count of eight before getting up and taking the same stance. I shoved him down two more times, and finally he stayed down for the count of ten and out. The crowd counted along with the referee. It was so ridiculous that in his corner, crying, he joined in the laughter. Then he fled to the privacy of the back seat of Mr. Diamond's Buick and stayed there the rest of the day.

Joy and I spent the afternoon in the bunkhouse. Most of the time I was thinking of the Angel, of her purity and my need to deserve it, but that didn't alter my activities with Joy.

On the drive back to Houston, Joy slept in the back seat. Gaucho's cousin, disgraced but five dollars richer and alive, sat up front with Mr. Diamond and me, his hat over his eyes. In the long silence I dreamed of tomorrow and the bliss of seeing the Angel in church.

All that night the dream-images continued. Most of the time I was flying with the Angel, holding her hand. There were no clouds, no background, nothing but the Angel holding my hand and smiling at me, totally trusting and dependent. Her hand was as cool and soft as Jenny's. We weren't going anywhere. We were already there: together.

When I woke up I started being nervous about church. I looked hard in the bathroom mirror. There was nothing I could do about my weak chin and my buckteeth and my stooped shoulders, but there were two other things that upset me. One was my hair. It was very fine, almost without body. I'd washed it Saturday night and it was flying all over the place like those dustballs that flutter up when you sweep a room after a long time. The other thing was the fuzz on my face. I still didn't shave because—at least this was what Mom had told me—my Cherokee blood made me real late in getting a beard. Most Indians had no whiskers or hardly any at all. A lot of my friends were already shaving almost every day, so I had begun to think maybe something was wrong with me. If I left the fuzz on and the Angel saw it, she'd know I didn't shave yet. Would that put me in an unacceptable category? I stared long and hard at Dad's razor. Such was my respect for—or fear of—my elders that I had never even considered moving this powerful symbol of adult manhood from one place on the shelf in the bathroom to another place a few inches away. This morning I considered it. I even picked it up and hefted it and made a few fake passes at my cheek but then put it down exactly where I'd found it. The only thing to do was take my mind off my fuzz and act as though it didn't exist and turn my attention to my hair. At least that was something I could do something about. I had a scented preparation called Rose Oil which would give it body and make it stay in place. I poured some in the palm of my hand from the greasy bottle. It made a little rose-pink puddle. I was overdue for a haircut. It was hard to tell because I combed it straight back without a part, and when it stayed in place it didn't look too bad, just fuzzy at the sideburns, but when it got wild it fell down in long, ugly, sandy strings over my ears and almost to my shoulders. I added a little more oil to the puddle in my hand and worked it into my hair. Then I combed it back. It stuck to my scalp. My scalp showed through. I looked almost bald in spots, and older, my hair darker. But at least it smelled good.

As soon as Mom and Jenny saw me, Jenny went, "Ooook! What's that stink?" and Mom said, "What on earth did you do to your hair?"

She took me in the bathroom and wiped my head with a towel, leaving the towel pink with the oil, but my hair still stuck to my head. It was late. We had to leave. So Mom, making the best of things, said, "I think it looks real nice now, don't you, Jen?"

"It looks oooky," Jenny said.

I wore my suit, Mom wore a flowered hat with a wide brim, and Jenny wore her Sunday school dress. As usual, we got there just as the service was about to start, and had to sit in the back row. The Angel and her parents were several rows in front of us and off to the side, so I got to stare at her quarter profile from the rear for the entire lesson-sermon. She turned several times to smile at her mother. No move that she made was less than perfect grace. There was no ungainliness, no crudeness, nothing earthly or flawed in any gesture. Yet something in this second vision told me that although she was an angel, she was a human one, as I'd been hoping to confirm. I'd made no progress in the past week in rising to a level worthy of her, but I'd kept the ambition to do so intact, a hopeful sign.

After about a half hour of fantasies, I felt something crawling on my neck. I reached around to find out what it was. It was Rose Oil, a few drops Mom's towel had missed on the back of my head.

When we filed out afterwards, I said, "Mom, why don't I go get the car and pick you up right here at the curb?" That way, the Angel would see me driving.

"Then you'd want to drive home. And you speed. I don't like it."

"I don't speed, Mom."

We were outside now, and Mom wanted to join her friends but not during a contentious discussion, so she hung back, smiling as though we were speaking of something pleasant. "You go the limit, honey. That's speeding."

"It's not speeding, Mom."

"The limit means exactly what it says, the limit. If a person is capable of eating a quart of ice cream at a sitting, if that's his limit absolutely, is he supposed to eat a quart of ice cream every time? No, he's supposed to eat below his limit, isn't he? What about a person drinking alcoholic beverages? Is he supposed to drink his limit? Many do, and with unfortunate results, honey, absolutely. So we're supposed to drive below the limit. Someday you'll realize that." She smiled sweetly and stepped away toward a small group.

I moved sideways and bumped into something light and soft. It was the Angel. I almost bowled her over. "Oh, 'scuse me, 'scuse me," I stammered, with no more presence or wit than Truck Ganney.

Unflustered, the Angel shot one glance directly into my eyes, crimped a quick smile of forgiveness, and looked away, taking her father's arm. Then, with all the aplomb of a clown trying not to fall off a slack wire, I added, "Good thing I don't drive like I walk, huh? I'd run over my own mother." This caused her to put a hand over her mouth—to cover a smile, I hoped. Her father and mother were already smiling—at Mom.

"Mrs. Johnson, nice to see you," the man said. And the mother said, "I love your hat."

"Oh, thank you," Mom said. She reached over the broad brim to touch the artificial flowers, which had fallen off once in the past, leaving her forever unsure of them. "It's so nice to see you-all. Dubby, I want—Woodrow, I want you to meet my friends Mr. and Mrs. Deutsch. This is my son Woodrow. He goes to Rice."

Mr. Deutsch shook hands with me. His hand was small but strong. Mrs. Deutsch gave me a sweet smile.

"And this must be that wonderful daughter you told me about!" Mom exclaimed.

"Yes," Mrs. Deutsch said, "this is our little Phoebe."

Mom maneuvered the Deutsches around to meet her other friends. Phoebe and I were left alone. She was indeed "little Phoebe," a foot shorter than I, and still an angel, though a lot of holiness falls away from angels when you're face to face with them. I groped for something to say.

She was quicker. "Do you like college?" A faun's eyes could not have been more ingenuous.

I didn't have time to answer. Jenny, coming up out of the base-

172

ment Sunday school, burst in between us and hugged me posses-
sively. "He has a girlfriend," she squeaked, "and she's blond, and
her name is Joy, and I hate her."

Phoebe laughed. The sound was musical. "Well, then I guess I
hate her too!"

Jenny smiled at Phoebe. "You're nice!" She ran to take Mom's
hand.

I shook my head. "Little sisters."

"She's cute. What's her name?"

"Jenny. Do you—uh—go to school around here?"

"I go to school in Philadelphia. At least I did."

"Philadelphia." That didn't sound promising. "What are you ma-
joring in?"

"Art."

"Oh, that's great. Art."

"Uh-huh. I'll go back in January. Probably."

"That's funny. I was going to go to the art museum this afternoon."

"The art museum?"

"Yeah. I go a lot. It's not far from Rice, so on my way home—say,
you wouldn't like to join me, would you? I mean, if your folks
wouldn't mind."

"Oh, I'd like to do that, Woodrow."

"Everybody calls me Dub." I told her why.

Her eyes swept over me in an unangelic appraisal. "Dub? That's—
it's kind of—"

"Ridiculous?" It was, and I wanted her to know I knew it.

"No! Oh, no! I was going to say it was a nice name, informal, but
kind of funny. It suits you."

"Well, I'm stuck with it, whatever it is. I sure don't want people
going around calling me Woodrow Wilson Johnson."

We made a date for two o'clock.

I hadn't asked Mom if I could borrow her car, but I figured from
the way she treated the Deutsches, and especially Phoebe, that she
would never put me in the position of having to call her and cancel a
date.

In the car, Mom talked about the beautiful thoughts in the service.

I waited till we got home, then I said: "The Deutsches sure do seem like nice people."

"They are lovely people."

I told her I'd like to take Phoebe to the art museum, if I could borrow her car this afternoon. She was delighted. Phoebe was a thoroughbred, she said. Her parents had credentials. Both were Christian Scientists, both educated, and—this was most important—both had suffered financial ruination because of the Depression, just as we had. It gave people a bond, like soldiers who share foxholes. "You remember Deutsch Cleaners and Dyers, don't you, Dubby, out on South Main, that burned down? Well, you know, the Depression just gnawed away at his business there till he just couldn't make all the payments on things, I don't know whatall. The Depression is over, they say, but the debts remain. They had this beautiful home out South MacGregor. I used to see them at First Church sometimes when I went out there. Such a beautiful church, absolutely, honey, you have to go there with me sometime, now that you've started church. Anyhow, Mr. Deutsch didn't tell me this, he has too much dignity to tell his personal miseries, but a close friend of mine who swore me to secrecy told me that they mortgaged their home to try to save the business, then they got down to where to make the mortgage payments they had to drop the insurance on the business, and then, about September I guess it was, that whole row of buildings there on South Main, where their dry cleaners was, burned down, and they lost everything. Absolutely everything. Nothing insured. Nothing. He not only didn't have his business anymore, he was out of work. Couldn't pay the mortgage on their lovely home, which, as I said, I never saw, but people who did see it said it was pretty much of a mansion, absolutely, and suddenly last month that was foreclosed. Foreclosed! And that girl, that pretty little thing, Phoebe, there she was up in art school in Philadelphia, and they tried everything they could to keep their tragedy from affecting her life, but finally they had to call her and tell her she had to come home—or rather back to Houston, not home, they didn't have their home anymore! From a mansion on the bayou to a rented two-bedroom place in a run-down neighborhood! From owner of a dry cleaning establishment to working as a presser in a shop owned by somebody else, and glad to get it! But they stand tall and look the world in the face, sustained by their faith. These are genteel people, honey. Genteel. Absolutely." She paused to stir her weak tea. Strong tea is a stimulant. Weak tea is still a sin but a lesser one. "If I have any criticism of these people at all, and it's a small one, compared to their overall fine character . . ." She took a sip of her tea. "Maybe I shouldn't say it at all. Maybe I should just keep it to myself." Another sip. "This green tea is so gentle. It has less caffeine than the black. Almost none at all. Well, honey, I may as well say it. I hear they're Roosevelt Democrats."

"There must be a lot of Scientists who are Democrats, Mom."

She thought about this for several moments. Then she said: " 'Tis a long road that knows no turning."

I picked up Phoebe at two o'clock, and we drove straight to the art museum, almost without conversation. Her perfection and purity were frightening. Her smile was warm, very human, but I was so afraid of doing or saying the wrong thing that I was almost frozen. As we arrived at the museum, and I was looking for a parking place, she said, "It's a beautiful day."

Ordinarily that would be something that somebody said because they couldn't think of anything else to say, but in the context of going to the museum, and the wistful tone in which she said it, it took on deeper meanings. Still, I parked and turned off the engine before I gathered the courage to ask, "Would you rather go to the park?"

"What would you rather do?"

If any other pretty girl in the world had asked me that question in that way, I'd've considered it an opening, but of course it wasn't meant to be; she was being polite. "Well, as cool and sunny as it is, maybe nature's art would be as nice to look at as paintings."

I had my cache of thirteen dollars and fifty cents in the fingers of my baseball glove, but I couldn't admit it, so I had accepted a dollar from Mom to buy treats. I got fresh roasted peanuts and Dr. Peppers and we stopped by the lake in Herrman Park where I had spent so many hours hot-necking with Betty and steaming up the windows on Saturday nights. We just sat there in the car for several minutes, looking at the lake, not touching. I was afraid to touch her, and either she was afraid to touch me or, God forbid, didn't want to. Finally I got out and went around and opened the door for her and we walked, looking at the trees and flowers and shelling peanuts and making conversation that was somewhere south of trivial. Finally she casually took my arm, and it was almost as much of a shock to my system as when Joy started sucking my thumb that first night. We walked like that for a few minutes, and then she let go of my arm and went to break off a few stems with oval leaves and little yellow flowers from a bush in the woods. I couldn't take my eyes off her delicate ankles. When she was beside me again she offered me a smell of the flowers and a crushed leaf. "Witch hazel," she said, excited by her find. Her empty hand was close to my hand, brushing it. I took her hand in mine and she held it tight and swung it happily and smiled up at me. The Angel melted away and in her place was a goddess, Phoebe the Moon Goddess. I was so much taller than she that once in a while, in spite of myself, my elbow bumped her breast. I tried not to let this happen, because I was sure that there was a point, a point that was very close, beyond which, if I went even accidentally, she would suddenly lose faith in my gentlemanliness and maybe even ask me to take her home. Still, I was emboldened by her apparent acceptance of these haphazard contacts. She was smaller than Joy, but her breasts were fuller. I tried not to stare at them. She told me about her art-school classes in Philadelphia, and how she'd made some nice friends there, and how she really missed them, but she was sure she'd have a good time in Houston too, and she was really happy she'd met me, and she hoped we'd be good friends.

She had an easy way of saying things, relaxed, simple, to the point, without even a hint of mindless rambling.

When we got back to the car a couple of hours later and I opened the door on her side, I was convinced she was the most beautiful, most interesting, most mysterious girl I'd ever met or ever would meet, and probably the sweetest too, and the most inaccessible in a carnal way. I didn't start the car immediately. We just sat in silence, looking out over the lake. There were things I wanted to say—though I didn't know what they were—and plans I wanted to make together, but I didn't want to be presumptuous. I was sure she liked me, though certainly not as much as I liked her. How could she?

It was time to take her home. I blurted, "Would you like to go to a movie tonight?"

She turned her sweet gaze on me for several seconds. Then she said, "If you want to."

At last I knew what love was. It was exaltation, spiritual levitation, and the transformation of the world into heaven, where nothing bad could happen.

When I got home, Mom said Joy had called four times and wanted me to call her back right away.

"She's probably failing Spanish," I said. "She probably wants me to tutor her."

NINETEEN

"MAMA'S AT A CHURCH PICNIC," Joy said on the phone. "I told her I was too sick to go. You got to git over here fast." Her voice sounded like she'd been crying.

"Joy's a sweet girl," Mom said. "I'm sorry she's sick. Don't stay over there too long. You don't want to be late for your date with Phoebe."

I trotted to Joy's house, wanting to get there and find out what she had to say and get away before her mother got home and started accusing me of statutory rape again. Even though I was guilty, I was still innocent till *proven* guilty. Whatever happened to the presumption of innocence? I practiced my look of young chastity and insulted honor, just in case I bumped into Mrs. Hurt.

I went down the alley to be as inconspicuous as possible. Joy met me at the back door. Her face was a storm. She was shaking all over with fury. It scared me. As soon as I got in the kitchen she let fly a stream of profanities and obscenities that would've taught my friend Chester a couple of things, all directed at her brother Roy. According to Joy, her brother was the lowest scum that ever got scraped off of a chamber pot, and she had a good mind to kill him before she ran away.

It was closing in on six o'clock, the time when most church picnics I'd ever heard of would have broken up, so I was nervous. "Tell me, quick, what happened," I said, "before your mother gets home."

She realized I had a point. She started talking fast, hesitating every once in a while to sob a couple of times or to blow her nose, or try to clear the hoarseness out of her throat. "Something bad happened last night. I got fired. See, there's this Meskin busboy, Ruben, he's real nice, and cute, and I like 'im a lot, not like you, I mean, we never did it or anything, but he always helps me in my section if there's a lot of tables to bus, if I get behind, because he's real strong and can carry a lot of stuff on one tray an' stuff, and when it's late his job is to get the garbage together and take it out and stuff, so I go down to the cellar to help 'im when it's kinda slow, and every Saturday for I don't know how long when we get a couple of minutes down there I suck 'im off, real quick-like, it only takes a minute, he comes real quick, you know, just to make 'im feel good, for helpin' me an' stuff, you know how I love to do that and make people feel good, and it's no big deal, so—"

"Can you tell me in the living room so I can watch for your mother?"

I went toward the living room and she followed me and kept on talking. "—I just do it nice for 'im and nobody's hurt, and everybody's happy, and we go on about our business, you know, and it's real nice, I just love doin' it for people I like, like you. Anyhow, last night the cook, Mitch, that son of a bitch and bastard, ugly oinkypig sweaty ole turd, I wish people could see him they'd never eat a bite of food in the Swingatorium, even if they was starving to death and got it free, he come down the cellar steps somehow without making a sound, and here I am on my knees with my eyes closed just bobbin' away happy as a clam, and Ruben's standing there kinda hummin' like it feels so good, and all of a sudden this mean filthy son of a bitch Mitch commences to yellin' at us from right beside us, and Ruben screams and pulls his dick away so sudden he like to broke my jaw, and runs out the cellar door to outside, and Mitch yells, 'You're fired, you whore! Wait'll I tell yer brother!' And he runs back up the steps to the kitchen and I'm thinking well, my brother'll stand up for me, no matter what, 'cause family sticks up for family, so I just walked up the stairs into the kitchen, big as Ike, ready to hear my brother tell ole Mitch that what I do ain't none of his business, and here's Roy standing there staring at me white as a sheet and stammering, 'Is it true? Did you—do—that?' And I said, 'If he said I was suckin' off a friend of mine, yes, it's true, so what?' And Roy kind of staggered and said, 'Wait in the car!' And when I didn't move fast enough he grabbed me and shoved me out the door like a complete stranger, and said, 'I said wait at the car!' And it was right at quitting time, and Roy come out almost right behind me, and he was so shook he could hardly talk, and he opened the car door and shoved me in and got in hisself, and he was white and tremblin' and all and I felt sorry for 'im and I said 'Roy—' and he screamed at me, 'Bitch! Whore! Slut! You disgust me! My own sister! Doing that! *That!*' And he said it like 'that' meant eatin' shit or somethin', you know. And I said, 'Roy, I know I oughtn't to do it at work, but there's not anythin' wrong with suckin' people off, I mean it's just a nice thing to do to make people feel good. Didn't Erna—?' And he slapped me! He said, 'Don't you speak my wife's name with your filthy mouth. My wife would never do such a filthy thing! I'd never kiss a woman that done such a filthy thing!' And I was so surprised I said, 'Roy, you mean to tell me you never got sucked off in your whole entire life? You're missin' somethin' so sweet and nice. Let me do it to you and you'll—' That's when he slammed me up side the head so hard I just about passed out, and he screamed at me that I wasn't his sister no more, that I was insane, that I was a bitchdog, and a I-don't-know-what-all, and I wasn't never to come near him or his sweet wife again, and if I did he was gonna tell Mama on me and she would have me put in a institution for crazy girls! And he drove me home and dumped me out and said he didn't never want to hear my name again!"

She was sobbing hard now. I put my arm around her. Roy was wrong. She wasn't crazy. Not crazy crazy, anyhow. I knew that for sure by now. Crazy's just a word people like Roy nail you with when you don't go by their rules. So what if she had different ideas about what was right and wrong, and seemed to run out of control sometimes? At other times, like now, when she was just a helpless little girl who didn't know what was happening to her or why, she felt weak under my arm, almost brittle, like I could yank on her and break her in two. All I could think of to say was "Jesus."

She cried for a little while longer, and then she said, "And my monthly is late."

"Jesus. Oh, no, sweet Jesus."

"I'm runnin' away. Erna and me won't be able to lie for each other no more, so I can't come out to the ranch with you no more and then come home, so I'm runnin' away. Saturday, when we go out to the ranch, I'm gonna have a bag with my stuff, and I'm just gonna keep on goin'."

"Going? Where?"

"New Orleans."

"New Orleans?"

"I called Mr. Diamond. I told 'im what happened—"

"You told Mr. Diamond what you told me?"

"Well, sure. He's my friend. And he told me he knew some people in New Orleans I could stay with—"

"Jesus." Then I saw Mrs. Hurt coming up the walk, all sunburned and wagging a picnic basket, and waving to somebody in a car that had dropped her off. "Oh, Jesus Christ! There's your mom!" I ran out of the living room and through the kitchen and out the back door. I pushed the door shut as quietly as I could just as I heard Mrs. Hurt say, "Why ain't you in bed? You look like somethin' the cat drug in." Then, running for the alley, stooped over, I heard Joy scream, *"Leave me alone!"* and a door slam hard enough to shake the house.

It was the time of day when a lot of people were moving about. Somebody had to see me. I straightened up as soon as I got to the alley and walked like I had a right to be where I was and to be going where I was going. My ole gunslinger came sauntering along the alley and joined up with me, and I knew that together we could handle whatever needed handling for the time being, but the future sure did look bleak.

I told Mom that Joy was just sick and feeling sorry for herself. I couldn't taste my dinner. Mom was as excited about me having a date with a pretty girl raised in Christian Science as I was. She made sure I didn't put Rose Oil on my hair, and she neatened up my sideburns and the fuzz on my neck a little bit.

I took Phoebe straight to the movies. We saw Charlie Chaplin in *Modern Times*, and I laughed so hard I embarrassed us both. I guess it was just my tension. The ole gunslinger went right out the window and here was this helpless person laughing like a fool while the pretty young lady whose hand he was holding kept glancing at him with concern. I was glad I could make an ass of myself and not have to talk. I drove Phoebe straight home afterwards, without going for a Coke or anything, just blathering on about how great Chaplin was and throwing in that I had an exam tomorrow. Maybe if I'd tried to talk to her, to hold a serious conversation, I'd've started crying. I felt like it. I hadn't cried since I was about ten. I had an automatic tear switch-off device built in, but tonight I couldn't hear anything in my head except "My monthly is late," and I was almost sure that if given the chance my tears would bypass the cut-off switch. I walked Phoebe up to her door and, feeling reckless, surprised her—and me —maybe mostly me—by kissing her. She kissed me back—with reserve.

I told her I really enjoyed it and I'd call her, and I hurried back to Mom's car.

I don't think I had ever been closer to wanting to jump off of a high building in my life, not only because of Joy's being late, but because I thought maybe Phoebe would be convinced now that I was a real drip and wouldn't want to ever go out with me again—even if I wasn't in jail or standing at the altar with a shotgun between my shoulder blades.

Monday was a good day. School went well. Joy didn't call. I talked to Phoebe on the phone and she was warm and intimate-sounding and friendly, as though she hadn't noticed I'd acted like a sap Sunday night. And Dad came home early and fairly sober, and sat around the living room with me for half an hour talking about wrestling greats. He was a big wrestling fan. He talked about Rudy Dusek and Dick Shikat and Strangler Lewis with reverence, men of agility and muscle and toughness. Toughness meant a lot. With the life he'd led, coming out of North Dakota blizzard country where he had to walk to school in below-zero weather, toughness was a big thing.

Mom even came in and spoke to him with civility almost bordering on affection, and asked him if she could make him anything to eat. He said no thanks, and she said well goodnight, and smiled wanly and went to her room.

Tuesday afternoon when I came home late deliberately, as usual, to be sure Joy's mother was home and she couldn't entice me to come over, I was happy when Mom said nobody had called. Maybe the late monthly was a false alarm. I started studying. All of a sudden I heard footsteps on the porch. I looked through the front window and almost had heart failure. It was Mrs. Hurt. Before she had time to knock I hurried to the front door and opened it, on the off chance I could keep her away from Mom.

"Mrs. Hurt."

"Maybe I could talk to your mother." She didn't smile.

"Oh, sure. Heck, yes. Come on in, Mrs. Hurt. How's Joy?"

She came in, looking around in that rude way some people have of checking if your house is clean, or your furniture is nice, or whatever their reason is. Mom had heard us talking, and appeared from the kitchen, drying her hands. "Mrs. Hurt! What a nice surprise!"

"I won't be a minute, Miz Johnson. It's about your boy. He talks Spanish. Joy is home sick and she's failing Spanish in school. I thought maybe if it was all right with you and didn't interfere with his college studies, your boy could come over and tutor Joy with her Spanish. He seems to be a steady kind of a boy, serious and all. I wouldn't want him to do it for nothing. I'd give 'im a quarter every time, if that's satisfactory."

"Oh, that's wonderful! Absolutely wonderful! I mean, if it's all right with Dub. Is it all right with you, honey?"

"Oh, yes'm. That'd be fine."

So with all the other turmoil in my life, I found myself sitting across the kitchen table from Joy again, acting like we barely knew each other, with her mother riding herd on us from a few feet away, knitting and listening to every inflection. The only thing she said was, "Joy's lazy. She could make good grades if she wasn't so lazy. She even got fired from her Saturday night job for flat-out goofin' off. Her own brother's disgusted with 'er." Joy was sick and hoarse and grumpy, but she still managed to arrange her mouth and tongue into tantalizing formations just to torment me while trying to repeat the sounds I was teaching her. We wanted to talk but it wasn't possible. After an hour I said I had to go, and Mrs. Hurt handed me a quarter.

Wednesday afternoon I called Joy from school. She still didn't have her monthly, she said, but maybe it was from being sick. I told her not to come to the ranch on Saturday. She started screaming at me on the phone as best she could with her bad throat, telling me hell, no, she was coming with her bag packed and going on to New Orleans from there, and nobody could stop her. Then she hung up on me.

There was no way I was going to let Joy run off to New Orleans and stay with friends of Mr. Diamond. I knew what that meant. She might be wild but she didn't belong in a whorehouse. I called her back and told her I needed to talk to her about running away. She hung up on me again. I was at Autry House, and people were playing ping-pong and laughing and yelling just a few feet away, but I called her back again and said I needed Mr. Diamond's phone number. "So you can make 'im change his mind?" she screeched, her voice high and barely audible. She hung up again. I called Mr. Hugo at his gym and told him I had to get in touch with Mr. Diamond about Saturday, and it was real important, and he gave me the number. I called and Mr. Diamond answered.

"Mr. Diamond," I said calmly, man to man, "I've decided not to fight anymore, so Joy and I won't be going out to the ranch with you next Saturday."

There was a short silence on the other end, and then Mr. Diamond came back at me as easygoing and affable as a man could be. "Well, Tex, that's a doggone shame. The folks out there love yer style. They been talkin' you up somethin' fierce. Some more stuff in the paper, I hear tell. The place is going to be downright pandemonious, and with all them extra paying customers I been authorizationed to pay you—this is a secret, now, don't want to make them other boys jealous—I'll give you twenty-five dollars."

"Twenty-five?" My voice falsettoed. It was embarrassing.

"Cash money, American."

"Well, in that case—but I don't want Joy to go. She's sick. And she's talking about running away to New Orleans. She's only sixteen, and I don't think that'd be a good thing for her to do. She comes from a religious family."

"Well, Tex, I'll leave that up to you and her. Whatever you young lovers figgers out is jake with me. So—we got a deal for Saturday?"

"For twenty-five?"

"Twenty-five smackeroos on the barrelhead."

"Plus the three-dollar purse for winning?"

"For winning. Sure. Three-dollar purse. I don't even have a boy yet. They're all ascairt of you. But I'll have somebody by Saturday. Deal?"

"I'll be there at the gate at twelve-thirty." We hung up. I was stunned. Twenty-five dollars. Some newspaper reporters didn't make any more than that for working all week. I was going to have this one more fight, take the money, add it to my cache, confess to Mom, and quit forever. No amount of money was worth taking the chance of ending up like Truck Ganney, slobbering and sweeping floors at Ben Hugo's gym.

TWENTY

I TOLD MOM my studying wasn't going well, and I had to beg off tutoring Joy for a few days, so she called Mrs. Hurt and explained to her. I expected something terrible to happen any minute, any second. If the phone rang I jumped. If somebody knocked on the door I wanted to hide. I hadn't lied to Mom about my studies—I couldn't concentrate. I couldn't sleep. I lay awake listening to Dad breathing in the next bed. Lately he'd been drinking less than usual. When he came home really tanked up he snored like a plane flying low with a sputtering engine, but recently he'd hardly snored at all. He sighed a lot in his sleep. Around one or two o'clock sometimes he'd get up and take a few deep breaths, like he had painful heartburn. Then he'd go in the kitchen and I'd hear him get the baking soda out of the cabinet and I'd hear a spoon clink in a glass, then water running in the glass while he stirred. Then I pictured him drinking and heard him put the glass and spoon on the drainboard and belch. Then he'd come back into our bedroom and let himself down on the bed and sigh again, and pretty soon he'd be asleep. I didn't let him know I was awake. I was afraid he'd ask what my problem was, and I might tell him. There's something comforting about having a parent as imperfect as Dad. I had the feeling I could tell him all about Joy and me and he wouldn't blink. In fact he'd've enjoyed it, and gone off and told his buddies on the job. Lying there thinking, I realized there was a lot of Chester in Dad, something I wasn't too proud of. Mom, on the other hand, if she found out what

185

was going on in my life, would go to bed with a sick headache and throw up green bile in a slop jar.

So I couldn't talk to her, and I couldn't talk to Dad either, because whatever advice he'd give me, if any, would be conditioned by his laissez-faire temperament, which at the moment wouldn't've suited a person like me, about to break into pieces like a shot clay pigeon.

I called Phoebe to tell her about my overload of studies. We got cozy on the phone. I think we touched more on the phone than in person. We made a date for Saturday night. I figured even if I didn't fight till five I could still pick her up by seven, which would give us plenty of time to grab a couple of cheeseburgers (now that I knew that her folks were just as poor as mine I no longer felt embarrassed to ask her to dine at a drive-in), and catch a movie.

She said seven was fine, but could we not decide on a movie right away unless there was one we really wanted to see? She liked movies a lot, she said, but she hated sitting through bad ones.

I was impressed by her independence of mind. She was smart and discriminating as well as beautiful and pure.

When I left home for school Saturday morning, Mom reminded me that I had to take good care of my pants because my other pair was at the cleaners and she couldn't get them out till she got some money, so I had to wear these same pants on my date with Phoebe tonight. I left for school with a bundle of guilt on my back. I wanted to give her my money from the ranch, but in spite of my proven talent for lying I still hadn't come up with a suitable explanation of how I got it.

When Mr. Diamond arrived at the gate to pick me up, he had Joy with him, and Manolito and Pablo and Gaucho in the back seat. She had makeup on, which didn't hide her puffy eyes and red nose. She had a fancy comb in her hair. All this said she had left home for good.

I surprised myself. Instead of being my usual bastion of unimpeachable moral cowardice, I erupted. "Where the hell do you think you're going?" I yelled at her as I walked toward the car.

"Where I pissy well please!" she managed to croak. "I got my bag in the trunk."

"You ain't got brains enough to pound sand in a rat hole, Joy!"

The three Mexicans were grinning in the back seat. This was more fun than they expected.

"We got to git going, Tex," Mr. Diamond said calmly, as though I hadn't even raised my voice.

"I'm not going!" I yelled. "If she's going, I'm not going!"

"I got a big fight for you, Tex."

"Then let her do the fighting! If she's heading for New Orleans she can use the money!" I walked away. Half of what I was doing was some kind of long-dormant, unsuspected, vestigial decency, I guess, and the other half was looking for an excuse to get out of going to the ranch. I already had thirteen dollars and fifty cents hidden away. Why be greedy? I kept walking toward the gate, toward the wide driveway up to Sallyport. Mr. Diamond got out of the car and ran after me and grabbed me.

"Tex! You cain't do this to me! Ain't I been square with you? You leave me hanging out on a limb, ridiculed, in front of my friends and associates!"

"Tell her get out of the car."

"I cain't control her."

I ran back to the car and yelled at her as I jerked the door open and got hold of her arm and started yanking her out of the front seat. "You crazy galoot! He's sending you to a whorehouse!"

Her eyes got wide open. She obviously hadn't figured this out. But she still resisted.

I got her out of the front seat, onto the pebbles of the entrance. People were passing, driving by us, leaving Rice and entering, slowing to see what the commotion was. Some of them—most of them—knew me, but I was only half-aware of them. "Mr. Diamond, get her bag out of the trunk, goddammit, if you want me to go to the ranch!"

He scurried to get the bag and set it down beside her. She was crying now. "I cain't go home. I'm gonna have a baby."

"Well, you don't want to have it in a whorehouse, do you?" There was a voice inside me saying *Let 'er go, let 'er go, God bless 'er*, and *You're the one that's crazy, Dub*, but I wasn't listening to other voices, even if they were right. I said, "Joy, we'll figure something out. Go across the road and get a bus home. Unpack and go to bed and pray. Your Mom won't even know you left. We'll figure out what to do later. You're sick. Go home." I kissed her on the cheek and put a dollar in her hand. "Take the bus, Joy. Go home."

She looked like a cat-chewed mouse, with her head slumped down and the suitcase making her slender body tilt as she staggered across the southbound lane and the esplanade and then the northbound lane to the curb without looking back. We were all watching her, Mr. Diamond and I and the three Mexicans. Everybody was still, almost reverent. When she got to the bus stop she put her bag down and looked up and gave us a little wave. Her face was just a white-and-red blotch framed in yellow hair.

"We got to hurry," Mr. Diamond said. We got in the car and drove off. After a couple of minutes Mr. Diamond looked at me accusingly and said, "You ought not to of said that about the whorehouse, Tex."

I never felt stronger in my life. I looked at him and waited till he took his eyes off the road and faced me for a couple of seconds, then I said, "The truth is the truth, you son of a bitch."

There was not another word said the whole trip to the ranch. The three boys in the back seat seemed to know that something serious had taken place. They had their church faces on. They didn't talk to each other, or sing, or smile. They just smoked. I could get glimpses of them in the sideview mirror. They just stared straight ahead as though they were remembering dead relatives or something.

As for me, I was halfway wishing I'd had enough Chester in me, or Dad, to listen to that voice that was telling me to let 'er go. I felt strong and scared at the same time, and I didn't have any idea what was going to win out. I remembered hearing people at school talk about a senior engineering student who had committed suicide during the summer, and nobody who knew him could understand why. I didn't know him at all, but for a minute or two I thought I was beginning to get a glimpse of what he might've been going through to make him do it.

The parking lot at the ranch was full. Some cars were even double-parked. I knew it was all because of me, the one-punch kayo man. I even heard a father say to his little boy as we made our way through the crowd, "There he is, that's Tex Frontere." I may have been a welterweight masquerading as a middleweight, but I was feeling like a heavyweight.

The big cardboard sign in front of the barn had me listed as the feature attraction of the day, the main event, and last on the card. My opponent, it said, was Willy "Sailorman" Jones, 161 pounds, no pro record, amateur record 53–29. As soon as I knew I was last on the card I headed back for the food stands. I had forgotten to eat lunch. The big blowup at the gate had Mr. Diamond so mad at me he hadn't offered to spring for his usual cheeseburgers. This time I was glad. I'd have plenty of time to eat all the hush puppies and gumbo I wanted, or anything else. They even had armadillo roasted on a spit like a shoat. It smelled pretty musky, but I tried a slice anyhow.

"This'll grow hair on your chest," the pretty blackjack dealer said when she saw what I was eating. Her smile was different now that Joy wasn't with me. She had three articles from the local papers she'd saved. They touted today's fight, saying almost nothing about Sailorman Jones but exaggerating my power and my style and mentioning my eccentricity of fighting in long creased pants. She wanted me to autograph each article for her scrapbook. I did, almost spelling my last name "Frontier" before I caught myself. She asked why I fought in long pants and I told her, "Just to be different." I didn't tell her nobody would ever believe I was a 158-pound middleweight if they saw my matchstick legs. Nobody was at her booth for the moment, so I decided to let her deal me a couple of hands. I won two dollars. This was my lucky day. She said, "Come back and see us, Tex."

I went to Mr. Diamond's car to study till they called me for my fight. I wished I could get all the way out of earshot of the cockfight crowd, because when they were screaming for the blood of some poor dumb bird they made me even more ashamed of the human race than when they were yelling for two more or less cognizant human beings to kill each other.

"Watch yerself in there, Tex," Doc said, as he laced Gaucho's cup over my trousers. "I don't like the looks of the Sailorman fella. I don't know where Danny dug 'im up, but seems like to me there's something fishy about 'im."

I was in my gunslinger mode, which didn't allow me to ask questions about the Sailorman. That would make me seem anxious. I just said, "Thanks, Doc, see you later," and went out to the ring.

There was not an empty seat in the barn. My opponent was nowhere in sight. I stepped into the ring and sat on my stool. Goober and his girlfriend were in the front row. They waved to me. Goober's brow was still discolored and swollen, jutting out over his left eye like an old storm-damaged balcony. The stitches had been taken out, but the stitchmarks were still glaring. The crowd applauded me and a few voices even yelled "Go git 'im, Tex!" and "You're our boy, Tex!" and "Hope this guy ain't a rabbit like the last one!"

Then I saw the crowd looking at something behind me and I turned around to see what was going on. A bald-headed man in a bathrobe with split sleeves, wearing boxing gloves, was coming down the aisle. He was accompanied by a woman in her forties with short bleached blond hair and about the widest hips I ever saw on a skinny woman. As the man got close I saw that he was in his forties, too, and he had a beer-belly. He climbed into the ring. Under the lights I got a clear look at him and I didn't believe what I saw. He had a cigar in his mouth, a stump of one, and it was lit. He was struggling out of his robe, and the woman was helping him. His face was a round, pumpkinlike thing covered with blotches and bumps and calluses and scars. He had a flat nose, a narrow mouth with chewed-up purple lips, and eyes invisible in dark holes surrounded by scar-puffed brows and cheekbones. His short arms were tattooed with snakes and skull-and-crossbone designs, among other things. There was a woman's face surrounded by glorious raven hair on his belly. It had probably been beautiful when it was put there in his young days, but now the keglike protuberance had stretched it into a ghoulish leer. There were black pistols on each shoulder and his chest featured a three-masted schooner under full sail. As far as I could tell he hadn't looked at me, wasn't interested.

My God, he's older than Dad. How can I hit an old gent like this?

The wide-hipped woman with the flat chest and the short hair that was several shades of blond with black roots reached over and took the cigar out of his mouth. It was chewed into a spatula shape. She put it between her own teeth, and held her hand for him to spit out his dentures, both upper and lower, which she put in her pocket. Then she put his mouthpiece into his outstretched glove, and he slipped it into his mouth.

The crowd wanted action. They began to clap rhythmically, and to stomp. Mr. Crabtree, the announcer, hurried down an aisle and into the ring. He wore the same checked jacket, polka-dot bow tie, patent leather shoes, and brown wig I'd seen on previous Saturdays. He started introducing Sailorman Jones. Jones' record was all lies, I knew, just like mine was, but Mr. Crabtree had an interesting fiction devised for him. He was an old boatswain's mate, fought in navy amateur tournaments all over the world, enjoyed the sport of fisti-cuffs, and, though retired from both the navy and the ring combat, had volunteered to share the ring with his opponent tonight when, because of his opponent's reputation as a dangerous puncher, a worthy challenger had proved difficult to find.

While this was going on, Doc Arnold came to my corner and leaned close to my ear and whispered, "This ain't no amatoor, Tex. This is a mean ole pug from somewhere trying to pick up a couple bucks under a phony name. If we knew his real name we'd prolly reconnize it. Stick and run, and keep yer ass in one piece." Then he walked away and took a seat in the front row, next to Manolito, Pablo, and Gaucho. I didn't see Mr. Diamond.

Armand Baptiste, the lithe little referee, was apparently a permanent employee. He poked the front of his beret with his fingers in a salute of recognition to me as he jumped into the ring. He moved like a dancer. I wondered how impartial he could be in rendering decisions after he'd worked enough fights with one boy to get to know him well. When he called Sailorman and me to the middle of the ring, Sailorman rolled out there on his bowed legs quickly, eagerly, pounding his gloves together. For the first time I got a glimpse of the eyes hiding back in those little caves of skin, just a brief glint of pink-white as he tilted his head up at me before facing Mr. Baptiste. I don't know how I knew, or thought I knew, that Mr. Baptiste and Sailorman knew each other. Maybe it was because Mr. Baptiste hesitated as though he were about to say another name when he said "Okay—Sailorman and Tex, you know the rules," before explaining them again as though we didn't. Or maybe it was some of the intuition I inherited from Mom. Or maybe I was wrong. The main thing I noticed about Sailorman as he stood there with what he wanted me to think was impatience to get the slugfest going was that he reeked of cheap cigars, as though his pores were saturated with smoke and juice from both inside and outside. I realized right away my instinct to be respectful of age could get me into big trouble, so I clung to what Doc had said about sticking and running. I couldn't afford to get in a big punching contest and end up landing on the seat of my best trousers. How long could an old geezer like this fight, anyhow? How soon would he be out of breath and just hanging on and faking it? If I kept him on the move chasing me, wouldn't he start panting and slow down and allow me to just pile up points with my left? I certainly wasn't going to see a fly on that big battered face and think my right hand there and maybe give him a cerebral hemorrhage. I didn't need death on my hands along with my prospects for charges of statutory rape and impending fatherhood.

When the bell rang Sailorman scuttled fast across the ring, right through my weak left jabs as though they weren't there. He had his head down so they landed on his bald pate with no more force than a tap.

This must be the way all short guys fight tall guys.

He was watching my feet. He kept me in front of him till I was in a corner, then he bulled right through and grabbed me around the waist with his left arm and pounded me in the left kidney over and over again, using the bottom of his right fist as a hammer. This was the classic kidney punch I'd read about, but Mr. Baptiste didn't seem to notice. I was trying to shove him off, trying to punch, but my arms were trapped outside and up and could only flail. Then his head came up under my chin like a battering ram. Lights in my skull. Blue and orange. Neckstretch toothrootpain Burmese ladiesnecksbrassrings two hands in front of me gloves in my face laces scrubbing mouthnose eyes elbow connects jaw mouthpiecemouthpiecegripit keepit hangonhangonhangoncan't go downongoodpants tohellthis sonofabitch seeflythinkitthere the chin thethethetheanything gripmouthpiece keepitinsaveteeth don'tgodownhangonpunchfly yourribsonbellychestanywherethinkit therethinkitthere be there . . .

I heard the crowd screamingstompingclappingcrazy. I was walking alone. No, someone with me. Crowd wild. Sound tearing down barn. BarnI'minbarn. Doc beside mehasmyarm. ComeonkidcomeonTexlemmeget them glovesyougonna be okaytheylove youloveyouloveyoulistenhearthecrowdthatsaysitallTex."

"Is it over?"

"Over? You don't know it's over? Yeah, it's over." He was taking off my cup as we went.

"Who? Who won?"

"You don't know? You didn't win, Tex, but you didn't lose, not really, kid. Great fight. Great fight. Listen."

The crowd, sure enough, was still cheering and clapping. I looked down at my trousers. The crease was still in the front. They looked clean. But what about the seat? "Are my pants okay?"

"Your pants?"

"Yeah. I didn't go down, did I?"

"No, you didn't go down. God knows you shoulda. But somehow —Jesus, Tex, you took one hell of a shellacking from that old sonofabitch. He got so tired he couldn't lift his arms. You just stood there waiting for 'im to hit you again, and finally he would, and you'd fall into the ropes, but somehow—here, wipe yer face."

We're in the fighters' changing room. Doc has my gloves in his hand. He puts them down and gives me an old towel. I wipe my face. Blood. I look in the mirror. My face, a red smear. Trickle of red from my nose, my lower lip, my ear, my brow. My nose—my nose sideways. Busted! I grab it with my thumb and two fingers, pull it straight. I snort to get the blood out of my nostrils. It starts flowing again. I stuff the towel under it, against my mouth. Pain. My buckteeth have gone through under my lower lip. The cut is swollen, clotted, numb. Touching it makes it bleed again. Mouthpiece? Gone. Won't need it anymore. Ever.

Doc said: "I better run you over to Beaumont, to the clinic."

"No. I'm fine. I got a date. Gotta get home." Home. The secret is unkeepable now.

Doc gave me twenty-five dollars. "Danny said give you this. He had to leave."

"He left? My books are in his car."

"You'll have to get 'em later. You sure you're okay?"

"He left? Left? How do I get home? I gotta date."

"Danny arranged a ride for you. You ready?"

"Gotta take a leak." I went into the toilet. My head was on a string, floating ten feet above me, like a balloon. I had trouble with the buttons on my pants. I swayed when I stood up to the urinal. What came out almost made me scream, almost but not quite, cry. Blood. Urine and blood, red urine. Jesus. Something was busted. I started to tell Doc, but I couldn't. He'd take me to the doctor for sure. What would Mom think? She'd forgive me for fighting, for getting banged up, but what about for going to the doctor? That would be unforgivable, a betrayal.

I hurried back out to Doc. For a second I saw two of him. "I gotta get home, Doc—fast."

"Button yer fly. Okay, your ride's waiting for you."

I finally managed to button my fly. Doc watched me, worried. We started walking. I stumbled. Doc steadied me. "What about him?" I asked. "What about Sailorman?"

"Oh, you landed some good shots. You punished 'im, you shook 'im. God. That rubber face of his. He wouldn't go down. You wouldn't go down. Both crazy. Trying to kill each other for a couple bucks. Crazy. They had to help 'im to his car. His wife's drivin' him to the clinic. He was havin' trouble breathin'."

My ride was a cocker with an old pickup truck. His birds had lost. He was sour and half drunk. "You ready?" he growled, as I came up to him with Doc.

"Yeah."

"Good luck, Tex," Doc said.

"Listen, Doc, my shoes. They're yours. Maybe you can get a couple bucks for 'em."

"You not comin' back? They gonna offer you a pisspot full o' dough. They gonna be after you."

"Not comin' back."

"Good move, Tex."

I grinned at him, glad to be able to, though it hurt my face. One of my front teeth was loose. "See you, Doc. Thanks for everything."

Tex Frontere was dead.

"Le's vamoose," the cocker said.

I shook hands with Doc and got in the pickup. The cocker got it started. It shook. It was hitting on about four out of six.

Now that I was seated, and in daylight, I saw that there was blood all over the front of my brown pants.

"I tol' Di'mon' I'd drop you off fer two bucks. You got two bucks, right?"

"Right."

I didn't ask his name and we didn't speak all the way to Heights Boulevard and Seventeenth Street. He stopped there and let me out. "Runnin' late," he said. "Two bucks."

I gave him the money and got out. I hurt all over. He didn't wait for me to slam the door. As soon as I hit the curb he reached over and slammed the door and drove off. I wondered if I could walk all the way home without falling down.

TWENTY-ONE

W HEN I WALKED through the back door into the kitchen, Mom called out, "Dubby, it's six-thirty! You had me worried. You'll have to hurry or—" In the door, she gasped. "Dubby? What —what in—what in heaven's name? *Honey!*"

"I was in a fight. I got beat up." I collapsed into a chair. "I'm okay, Mom." She was staring at me, white and horrified. I got up again. I had to go to the bathroom. "I'll be right back." I walked out of the kitchen, trying not to move like a windup toy or a ninety-nine-year-old man.

My urine was still deep red. I flushed the toilet twice to be sure there was no trace of pink left to be seen in the bowl.

Oh, God, I can't worry Mom.

I took a good look at my face in the mirror. My nose was the scariest part. It was pretty straight, but I couldn't get much air through it. The bridge was puffed out wider than the bottom. It was colored an ugly mix of blue and green and black and yellow, like an old box turtle's head. I also had two black eyes, two bruised cheekbones, a lacerated left eyebrow, a loose front tooth, and an ugly cut the width of two teeth under my lower lip. I probably had a concussion, too, because there was a slow throbbing in my skull, and every few seconds things kind of swam in front of my eyes, and time went by without me being always aware of it.

I washed my face and combed my hair and went back into the kitchen. Mom wasn't there. I saw her in the living room, with the

195

phone in her hand. I hurried to her. "Mom, not Mr. Tamplee, please."

"I'm calling Mrs. Gullman. Mr. Tamplee—well, he's a fine man, but he's not our type, is he, honey? I felt the inharmony."

Mrs. Gullman answered, and Mom started telling her she wanted her to work for me. I was glad. Mrs. Gullman was a sweet-faced woman with gray hair who to me radiated some kind of goodness you wouldn't expect from a person who had been as stomped on by life as she had. I hoped she was a good practitioner. I sure needed one.

When Mom finished her phone call she made tea and we sat in the kitchen. Her expression asked what happened. I had decided to tell her the truth about the ranch, except for the Joy part. I knew enough from hearing Mom talk about her religion that living a lie is living with poison in your system, and at this moment I needed to give myself every advantage over the many illusions of sin, sickness, and injury trying to claim me. She listened with a shock-pallor on her face. To leave Joy out of it I had to say I was lured into the fights for money alone, because I thought I might be able to help pay the bills. This brought tears to her eyes. Everything I did, according to her, had a noble motivation, and in this case, at least, she was partially right, because I was trying to tell as much truth with as little lying as possible and spare her the pain of the Joy connection. To prove my motive, I handed her the entire $34.25 I had left. She handed it back to me, powerfully affected, and said, "No, honey, you earned it. It's yours." Then she said, "Oh! Phoebe! Your date! It's seven o'clock! I'll call and explain you have to cancel. They'll understand." She hurried into the living room and started looking for the number. I gave it to her and she smiled. "Know it by heart already, huh?"

Mrs. Deutsch answered the phone, and Mom apologized and told her I'd been attacked by a gang of rowdies on Washington and Waugh Drive where I had to change buses on the way home, and they'd beaten me something awful, and she was going to run me a bath and put me to bed, and she'd already called a practitioner, and I'd be fine in a couple of days, and she hoped Phoebe would understand, and I'd call her tomorrow myself, and I was really disappointed because I was so looking forward to my date with her.

I was dumbfounded. My mother was lying. But then as I listened I realized that she wasn't really lying, she was "telling a harmless fabrication for the sake of family privacy," as she had explained it to me before in reference to her relationship with Dad. I was glad she'd done it, because I didn't know how the parents of the Angel would react to the truth about me and the ranch. It would make me look like one of those ruffians who were supposed to have attacked me, not the kind of person parents would want their daughter to go out with.

We agreed I'd tell Dad the same ruffian story. We didn't discuss it. We both knew Dad would've loved the Tex Frontere stuff and would've told all his friends, "My kid's a fighter, fights under the name Tex Frontere." He'd've been a lot more excited about that than the one-plus I got in Spanish.

The one thing I'd dreaded most didn't happen. As I was telling Mom the bowdlerized truth about my short boxing career, I kept watching for her to rub her temples, or brush her forehead with the tips of her fingers, or swallow hard, or take deep breaths, all signs I had learned to associate with her coming down with a sick headache. Far from this, she seemed to become more and more relieved, and energized, and finally downright elated. The past few weeks had been pushing down hard on her, she said. She had known something was wrong, something bad, something she couldn't fathom. But now that it was out in the open, and finished, the air was clean and pure again. The Divine Mind was in control.

She felt like dancing. She cranked up the Victrola and put on her scratched recording of her beloved *Carmen*, which she always called "the opera *Carmen*," and conducted the sprightly overture as she whirled around the living room. She got so carried away it embarrassed me. Something about my confession, edited though it was, had liberated her, made her soar into another time, a time I wonder if Dad even knew about. She was, for a few seconds, a young woman again, young and with tears in her eyes.

I went into the bathroom and threw up, fearful of seeing more blood. There was none. I urinated again, red as ever.

Was I going to die?

Mom made some hot soup. I ate it even though I didn't want it, to please her. Then I soaked in a hot tub and went to bed.

As I was drifting off a maxim came to me. It seemed important. I got up and wrote it in my notebook: "Where truth shines its light there are no shadows." Then I went to sleep.

When I woke up I remembered hearing something, or dreaming

I'd heard something, in front of the house in the night. I looked out the front window and saw my books in a neat stack on the front porch, tied together with a cord. Mr. Diamond was a pimp, a fraud, an illiterate phony, but he had respect for books.

My mind felt clear. My head was no longer throbbing. It was still painful to walk or bend. I yawned, and groaned in agony because of the gash under my lower lip. How would it heal? Would it seal itself? Practitioners don't do stitches. I'd have to remember not to yawn again and to chew carefully, give it a chance to come together on its own.

I dreaded going to the bathroom, but I went. The news was heartening: pink, not red. Thank you God. Or Mrs. Gullman. Or Mom. Everybody.

I was dizzy again. I went back to bed, and fell asleep.

Mom woke me up with a tray of bacon and eggs and blackberry jelly and toast and hot cocoa. She was chipper. "I see you don't look any better, but I'm sure you feel better, don't you, honey?"

She was right. I did. There was something about Mom that always, even in my deepest despair, as now, made me feel like everything was going to be all right, at least for a while. It took me a long time to eat. It was hard to open my mouth to bite the toast, and hard to chew, so I dunked the toast in my hot chocolate till it was soft. My jaw teeth were very sensitive, and my loose front tooth hurt when it came down on something, but I did feel myself improving physically moment by moment. Mom sat on the side of the bed and read pertinent passages from *Science and Health* as I ate, and I didn't resent it as I usually would've but welcomed it as one more thing that didn't cost a nickel and might be worth a million. If it could only ward off the demons in Joy a block away, her craziness, her fecundity, I'd gladly listen to a recitation of the entire book at one sitting. I almost made a silent commitment to go to church the rest of my life if my troubles would go away, but I caught myself in time to stop short of that, realizing there was probably still time to find a cheaper way out.

Jenny came in and almost made me pass out with the enthusiasm of her sympathy, throwing herself on me and banging a kiss against my throbbing lip cut. I was happy when Mom hauled her off to Sunday school. I went back to sleep.

The phone woke me up. I got up and started to go to the living room, but I was suddenly dizzy again, and I had shooting pains in my temples. I turned around and staggered back to bed and let it ring.

Mom and I decided I should stay home on Monday. The pressure of not knowing when I was going to be forced to deal with Joy made me jumpier and jumpier. About four-thirty she called. Mom answered the phone. She came to the bedroom and asked if I felt like coming to the phone for Joy. I didn't, but I did. Joy could barely speak. She needed somebody to drive her to the doctor for her appointment for her strep throat. She had thought she'd be able to go on the bus, but she had a high fever and couldn't. She didn't ask about me, either because she knew or because in spite of her craziness she was aware that I couldn't talk in front of Mom. I told her I was sick and couldn't drive her, but—and here I had an idea that proved I had suffered no real brain damage, and that my powers of imagination and manipulation had not been in any way impaired—I could call a friend of mine who ought to be getting home from work about now, and he'd be honored to come and get her and drive her anywhere she needed to go, because we were very close friends. I told her his name was Chester, she'd heard me mention him, and I was sure they'd get along.

Chester had just come in when I called. Five minutes later and I'd've missed him. He was in a hurry. I explained quickly.

"Joy?" he said. "Who the hell is Joy? I got a date with a tongue, a bung, and a wild ride at high tide, podner. Now, call me sometime when that there Marie you been tellin' me about needs to get took somewheres, and I'll come a-runnin'. Meanwhile, ole buddy, I got to keep my harem pacified."

"This is Marie."

"Whattaya mean? You said Joy."

"Joy is Marie."

"Joy is Marie?"

"I kinda lied to you about Joy's name. I said it was Marie. But it's Joy."

"You mean Joy is that constantly eruptin' volcano you been tellin' me about? Her true name's Joy?"

"That's right. And she's the one needs a ride to the doctor."

199

"Listen, Dub, ole buddy, what're buddies for, anyhow? Your gal Joy needs to get took to the doctor, I'm yer boy. I'll be there in three shakes. Gimme the address."

I gave it to him. It was painful to grin, but I couldn't stop myself. I crawled back in bed feeling euphoric.

Phoebe called about six to ask how I was. I felt loved. There was nothing between us, nothing but fantasies on my part and who-knows-what-if-anything on her part, but between my ongoing bliss and her demonstration of caring enough to call, I felt my wounds healing faster. We were full of innocent double entendres, not sexy ones, nothing suggestive, but romantic ones given meaning by tone of voice. She volunteered to come see me and bring me some cookies, but I said I didn't want her to see me so banged up. She said she wouldn't mind. She'd bet I looked handsome like that. I said, well, give me a couple more days till my lip is better. "Oh," she said—what a voice out of dreams she had!—"why are you so concerned about your lip?" We were like nestlings peeking over the edge of our twig-house aerie, teetering there, looking a thousand feet down into the valley, then falling clumsily back into security. We weren't ready to call each other affectionate names yet, or we were but didn't dare, so we made our true names, by tone and inflection, sound like endearments. My lip wound made it hard to inflect words, or even to whisper, but the pain was worth it. I could've been bleeding and not noticed. When we finally hung up after forty-five minutes, I took a deep breath of elation and was letting it slowly out when the phone rang. I waited a couple of rings, to control and savor my love, not wanting to vilify it with Chester's obscenities or Joy's lust.

A scratchy female voice was on the other end, saying, "Mr. W. W. Johnson, please."

"W. W.? Oh, this is W. W."

"This is Nurse McClain, Mr. Johnson." Her voice gave me a bad feeling in my stomach. She paused, as though she was reading something from a pad. "I believe you're friends with a young lady named Joy Hurt?"

"Uh-huh. That's right."

"She's been in a car wreck. We have her here at Dahlken Clinic on North Shepherd Drive. She gave your name to the ambulance driver and asked us to call you. Do you know where our clinic is?"

"Is she— Is she—?"

"We don't have any prognosis yet. She's in emergency. Do you know how to get here?"

"Yes, ma'am."

I hung up, and there was Mom, standing right beside me. She said, "Something's wrong." As soon as I managed to stammer out the essential facts, she interrupted me and said, "Honey, do you feel good enough to go over there?"

"Yes, ma'am."

"Then get dressed. I'll call Mrs. Hurt to be sure they've reached her. She can ride over there with you. Or if you don't feel like driving, I'll drive."

"I feel fine, Mom." I was emphatic, because Dahlken Clinic was only about fifteen minutes away, but if Mom drove it would be half an hour. I was in my underwear, but it didn't take me a minute to get into pants and shirt and tennis shoes with no socks. I was shaking. This was one occasion on which my lone gunslinger didn't seem to want to have anything to do with me.

Dahlken Clinic was famous in the area because some of the big hospitals had been trying to get it shut down, and the papers had been full of charges and denials and threatened lawsuits. A lot of people claimed Dr. Dahlken was a quack and a crook, but he was a civic leader and a big political contributor, and somehow, even when bigger and better-equipped facilities were closer to the scene of the accident, the ambulances ended up delivering enough maimed victims to Dahlken Clinic to keep it in a profitable condition. It was a long, low, ugly frame building with peeling white paint and an asphalt parking lot in front, and anybody looking at it would say that people would have to be helpless before they'd allow themselves to be carried in there.

A Harris County sheriff's office patrol car was in the lot, and a city squad car, plus four other cars, none of them very new or expensive except for the shiny black Cadillac in the spot marked "RESERVED DOCTOR DAHLKEN" nearest the front entrance.

I forced myself to walk in the front door, wishing I'd taken time to put on socks. What could've happened to Joy in the few seconds I'd've used to put on socks? And now if I sat down and crossed my legs, everybody would see that I didn't have any on.

The waiting room was small and tacky, with a low ceiling and some wooden benches. The first thing I saw was Mrs. Hurt, walking unsteadily across the floor, crying. A deputy sheriff in uniform was walking with her with his arm around her, looking grave. He was about forty, with hair almost as blond as Joy's, cut short. His uniform was fitted tight to his frame, showing off his big shoulders and his flat belly and his trim butt. He had ladies' man written all over him. He resembled Mrs. Hurt in his facial features except that hers were puffy and sour and his were lean and kind of self-satisfied. He was Uncle Phil, to a T. There was a woman who looked like both Uncle Phil and Mrs. Hurt sitting on a bench. She was dabbing at her eyes with a soggy, balled-up handkerchief. Mrs. Hurt and Uncle Phil didn't see me. I crossed to the desk, where there was a middle-aged nurse. Before I could say anything, she said, "You'll have to set down over there and wait awhile, boy. The doctor won't be able to see you for a while. We got a couple of emergencies. Here, fill this out." She shoved a form at me.

"I'm not a patient, ma'am. I—"

She stared at me, and I realized how bad I looked, how beat-up. "You're not a patient? Well, you look like you oughta be."

"My name is W. W. Johnson. Somebody called me—"

"Oh, you're the boy I talked to. Well, the girl's in the operating room, and the fella's getting bandaged up. He oughta be out in a while."

"Is she going to be okay?"

"Cut up a little. Prolly be fine. Set down over there." I started to go to a bench, but she stopped me. "Boy, hold it. C'mere." I crossed dutifully back to the desk. She was looking at me sternly. Finally she said, "Do you realize I tried to call you for almost an hour, and your phone was busy all that time. Do you realize that?"

"No, ma'am."

"Well, I did. And it was. Do you think all we got to do around here is dial the same number over and over for an hour?"

"No, ma'am."

"I'll bet my bottom dollar you're not paying the phone bill at your house, are you?"

"No, ma'am."

"I didn't think so. I ought to call your mama and tell her what happened. I just might, too, when I get time. Okay. Set down over there."

Mrs. Hurt and Uncle Phil were still pacing. They looked at me, but Mrs. Hurt acted like she didn't know me, or maybe I wasn't there, or it didn't matter if I was or wasn't. The other lady just kept dabbing her eyes. She didn't seem to see anybody.

I sat on a bench as far from them as I could get. Nurse McClain lit a cigarette and went out the back of her little office and disappeared.

After a couple of minutes some double doors right across from me swung open and a short round cop with a gun and a billy club and other equipment sticking out all over him, making him look like an overfed warthog on his hind legs, waddled through, brandishing a clipboard. He was followed by Chester, who had a bandage on his head, a black eye, and his right arm in a sling. Otherwise he seemed all right. He even threw me a grin and stalked over and sat down beside me, looking hard at my face. "What the hell wreck was *you* in?"

"I'll tell you later," I whispered. He was going to get the same story Mom made up.

The cop with the clipboard said, "Hiya, Phil," and crossed over to him, the handcuffs on his belt clicking together. They shook hands. "This must be that nice sister o' yours you tol' me about, the mother of the young lady," he said. "I sure am sorry, ma'am. But they say she's gonna be okay. I got a statement from the driver yonder. Dumb bastard, showing off fer the girl, rolled his whoopee. Both of 'em got bounced around pretty good."

"She was already sick," Mrs. Hurt said. "Strep throat."

"This'll prolly cure that, Ruby," Uncle Phil said. He and the cop grinned at each other.

"Well, nice seein' y'all," the cop said. "I got to go write this up." He headed for the door, a walking law-enforcement supply department.

"I oughta kick the bastard's ass," Phil said, "but I'll wait till he's in better shape, so's he can git the full benefit." He continued to walk back and forth with Mrs. Hurt, whispering comfortingly to her.

Chester leaned close to me. I'd never noticed before how old he looked for his age. With the big bandage covering up his black hair, there was nothing but his doggy brown eyes and his kind of saggy face. His skin looked yellow under his dark tan. He didn't want anybody to hear him. "Got a smoke, Dub?" I shook my head. "My smokes come outa my pocket," he whispered. "Must be in the wreck." He became agitated. "Sheee-it! My fuckin' Pontiac is

203

fuckin' defuckinmolished! It ain't even good junk!" He was still whispering, close to my ear, groaning the words out. Nurse McClain was back at her desk, with a cigarette sticking out of one corner of her mouth. Chester shot to his feet and shambled over to her. " 'Scuse me, ma'am," he said, bowing slightly in what he considered to be a gentlemanly way but what looked more to me like a convict talking to a warden. "Would it be possible fer me to borry the loan of a smoke, if you don't mind, please, ma'am?" Nurse McClain flipped up a cigarette, pulled it out of her pack, and handed it to him without a word. He patted his pocket, looking for a match. "Thank ye, ma'am." She handed him a table match and turned her back on him. With his right arm in a sling, he managed to strike it, after several fast swipes, on the seat of his dungarees, and light up. Then he came back and sat down close to me, looking conspiratorial. Phil and Mrs. Hurt had decided to sit with their sister for a while. Phil lit a cigarillo, and he and the two ladies just sat there staring into space, waiting.

"She was driving," Chester said, out of the side of his mouth.

"Joy?" I said, too loud.

He shushed me, took another drag on his cigarette, and continued: "You got a tiger by the tail there, boy. Don't take it unkind of me if I say she ain't exactly yer easygoin' gal-next-door."

"Never said she was, did I?"

"Naw, cain't say you did." He puffed away hungrily for a few seconds. "You ain't aimin' on marryin' 'er, or anythin' like that, are you?"

"Hell, no."

"I mean, you ain't in love with 'er, are you?"

"Hell, no. Oh, I like 'er, but—"

"Not too much, I hope. Can I talk turkey to you?"

"Shoot."

"I took 'er to the doc, okay? She didn't say boo the whole way, jus set there lookin' miserable. She was in there maybe fifteen minutes. I set there in the waiting room reading a ole Field and Stream the doc had there in his rack. Pretty soon she come sashayin' out, lookin' fit as a fiddle, with a big grin. She says, "Hi, Chester, thanks a bunch." Her voice was just about like nothin' ever happened. "He painted my throat and gimme some pills and I'm just about as good as new," she says. So we goes out to my pussy wagon and she says she sure does admire it. We git in and take off and she turns on the radio and they got that "Begin the Beguine" on there and she commences kinda swaying to it, and—you sure I can lay it on the line to you, Dub?"

"Why not?"

"You ain't gonna get sore at me? It might not go down too good."

"Come on, Chester, spit it out."

"Well, okay. She's swaying to the music, and kinda staring at me with this funny smile on her face and pretty soon she slides over close to me and reaches over and gets ahold of my hand and pulls it offa the steering wheel and shoves my thumb in her mouth and commences to suck it." He waited for me to react, but I didn't. I was way ahead of 'im. "Maybe you don't believe me—"

"I believe you."

"Well, it's the God's truth. And natcherly I git a rod on, like who wutten, huh? And she slips my thumb outa her mouth and says, 'I love this big ole Pontiac! Can I drive a little bit?' And I says, 'How come?' and she says—"

"So you let 'er drive."

"Yeah."

"That was a mistake."

"No shit." He dragged on his cigarette and shook his head in wonderment. "She headed out toward the Katy Road, got up to about seventy, and straightened out a curve. We rolled across the shoulder and down the embankment and up against a bob-wire fence. When we come to a stop my pussy wagon was upside down and Joy was on top of me. I felt like the cat that fell in the concrete mixer. Neither one of us was knocked out, but we was bleedin' pretty good, and kinda woozy. We cutten open the doors to git out. Joy says, 'You got insurance?' and I says, 'Yeah.' And she says, 'Good, 'cause I don't got no driver's license."

"So you figgered if a unlicensed driver wrecked your car your insurance wouldn't be no good." Anytime I spent a few minutes with Chester, I started talking like him. It was another character weakness of mine.

"So we had time to git our stories straight before the highway patrol come along and spotted us. I was startin' to git a little bit worried about 'er, cause her belly was hurtin' somethin' fierce, and—"

The swinging doors across from us banged open and here came a rolling stretcher-bed with Joy on it, and a nurse and a doctor pushing it. I jumped up and got to her side before anybody else had a chance to move. She had a neck brace on and her eyes were shiny and kind of foggy, but she had most of her wits about her. She hollered, "Dubby!" as soon as she saw me, and then started wailing loud enough to be heard in the next block, "I lost our baby, Dubby! I lost our baby! Our baby's gone! Our baby!"

I was trying to keep up with the rolling stretcher, but my legs almost gave way under me. Mrs. Hurt started screaming, right beside me, almost in my ear. "*Baby?* Did she say *baby?* What did she say? Did she say *baby?*" She grabbed me by the throat and started shaking me. "Did she say you and her was gonna have a—? Oh, my God! My God! My little girl! You raped her! Rape! Phil! He raped my little girl!" She started kicking me, kneeing me, shaking me, trying to punch my face. I managed to pull loose and keep my hands up so she didn't land any punches, but the shaking caused my whole head, especially my cut lip, to throb into pain. "Phil! Arrest him! Arrest this heathen! He raped my daughter! Sixteen years old! I want him in jail!"

Phil pulled her back from attacking me. "Ruby, Ruby, hold yer horses, sis. Come on, now. We're in a hospital here. Jus' get ahold of yerself. We got plenty time to arrest the boy. He ain't goin' nowhere. Le's go in and see how Joy's doin'. That's the main thing. But le's try to keep our voices down in the hospital here."

Mrs. Hurt was glaring at me, her eyes red, her face contorted. She growled, "Godless heathen, immoral trash, you'll suffer for this, you'll rot in jail, rot! As God is my witness." Her sister came and put her arm around her, and Mrs. Hurt responded with sobs. "Oh, Pearl, Pearl, Pearlie, honey, how could God let this happen to me? My little girl! Ruined! He ruined my little girl! Oh, God! God!"

A doctor who needed a shave was waiting to speak. He looked like he had a hangover, and he wasn't very happy. He said to nobody in particular, "When y'all get back in your mind I'll talk to you about the girl." Then he walked away. I must've been the only one who heard him or noticed him.

The stretcher with Joy on it had been rolled out of sight, and now Nurse McClain came down the hall and said, "Which one of y'all is Duppy?"

"Duppy?" Uncle Phil said.

"Yeah. The girl is asking for Duppy to come in."

"Duppy?" I asked. "Or Dubby? I'm Dubby."

"Close enough. She wants to see you."

I started to follow Nurse McClain, and Mrs. Hurt struggled loose from Pearl and Phil and ran after me. "He ain't seeing her alone! Not on your tintype he ain't! He ruined 'er! He ain't gonna never touch 'er agin! Never!" Phil and Pearl caught up with her and restrained her.

"We got to quiet down, Ruby," he said. "We're in a hospital here, sis."

"I'll leave it up to you, Depitty Beggs, to hannel these ladies," Nurse McClain said.

"Ever'thing's under control, ma'am. Ruby, honey, you heard what the lady said."

"I heard. I heard," Mrs. Hurt said, holding her voice down. "But he ain't gonna be alone in the same room with my little girl."

I followed the nurse to the room, and right behind me were Uncle Phil and his two sisters.

Joy was sitting up in bed. Her face was fine, only slightly bruised, but she had tears in her eyes. She held out her arms to me. "Dubby, you look like you been in a worse wreck than me." I went to kiss her but I was grabbed from behind by Mrs. Hurt.

"Don't you touch her! No! Keep your filthy hands to yourself!"

"Yall cain't stay but fi' minutes," Nurse McClain said. "She's full of painkiller, gonna go to sleep."

"Joy," Mrs. Hurt said, "Joy, honey, he forced you, ditten 'e? You never let 'im do nasty things to you of your own free will! I know you never done that. He's goin' to jail!"

"Mama, shut your stupid face," Joy said. "He's not going to any jail on account of me."

"Statutory rape!" Mrs. Hurt said. "Carnal knowledge of a minor chile! He's going to jail!"

"Him and a few others, Mama."

"What do you mean?"

Uncle Phil jumped in. "Ruby, the child's been in a wreck. She's hurt. Le's not make trouble at a time like this. We got plenty of time to straighten this out, Ruby."

Mrs. Hurt didn't hear a word he said. She was staring like a mad-woman at Joy. "What do you mean—*a few others?*"

207

"Mama, if you wasn't so dumb, you'd understand. Dubby wasn't the first, and he wasn't the second, and he wasn't the third, and—"

"You're lyin'. You're lyin'. You hate me and you're tryin' to hurt me. This boy ruined you, he ruined a virgin, underage! He's gonna pay."

"Bullshit, Mama."

"Ruby," Uncle Phil said very softly, "don't hurt yerself like this. She's all doped up. She don't know what she's sayin'. Le's get outa here and—"

"I know what I'm sayin', Uncle Phil, and you know what I'm sayin', too."

Phil was tugging on Mrs. Hurt's arm. "Le's git outa here, Ruby. Come on."

Mrs. Hurt said, cold and hard as dry ice, "He ruined you, and he put you in a family way, and he's gonna pay. He's gonna marry you."

"You crazy ole bitch," Joy said. "You think I'd marry somebody you wanted me to marry?"

"I'm gonna call his mama. I'm gonna tell the world what he done!"

"If you tell the world, Mama, I'll tell the world. An' I got more to tell the world than you got, by a country mile. Ain't that right, Uncle Phil?"

Phil was white as a brand-new cue ball. He acted as though he didn't hear Joy. He was trained to stay cool in emergencies. "Listen, Ruby, whatever mighta happened, one thing is sure, screaming it out to the world is not gonna help you or Joy or anybody. If these kids made a mistake, it ain't the end of the world. She's only sixteen. She's a nice girl, one of the nicest girls I ever met, and—"

"Bullshit," Joy said.

"—and she can graduate high school and meet a nice young man and go about her biness and nobody's the wiser. She can grow up and have a nice family. Le's not jump outa the fryin pan and into the fire, Ruby. Le's calm down and take it easy here. Okay, Ruby?"

Mrs. Hurt's eyes burned into Joy. There was a lot of hatred flying through the air. Finally she said, real low, like a growl, "Okay, I'll listen to my brother, fer now. We got time. But I'll tell you this for sure. He ain't gittin away with what he done. I'm calling his mama and telling her what a low-down skunk of a boy she's got. She thinks the sun rises and sets on her darlin' boy. Well, she's gonna find out different."

"Mama," Joy said, with a scary smile, "you ain't gonna do no such of a thing."

"You just wait and see, little lady."

"Dubby is a real smart boy, Mama. He's gonna be something someday. I wisht I coulda had his baby. I'da been proud. So don't do nothing to mess 'im up, you hear? Or I'll make you sorry for the rest of your life."

"You can't hurt me any more than you already did."

"Oh, yes, I can. Tell 'er I can, Uncle Phil."

Phil said, sort of stiffly: "Ruby, when people start hurtin each other and trying to hurt each other back, there's not any way it can lead to anything good."

Joy yawned while he was saying it. Then she said slowly, almost yawning in the middle of her sentence, "Mama, I'd just as soon take a butcher knife and cut your throat, anyhow. Yall get outa here so I can sleep. Dubby, gimme a kiss."

I went to her and kissed her lightly on the lips. Nobody tried to stop me. She whispered, "You're sweet, Dubby." Then she yawned again and closed her eyes.

We all went out together, nobody speaking. Chester was still waiting in the lobby. He said, "Dubby, you think maybe you could gimme a lift?"

TWENTY-TWO

CHESTER AND I WALKED out to Mom's car right behind Uncle Phil and his two sisters. Nobody said anything, but I could feel Mrs. Hurt's hatred and Uncle Phil's fear stronger than my own pains. After they got in his patrol car and slammed their doors, Chester said, "I know why I'm limping, but why the hell are you limping?"

I told him about the gang beating me up over on Waugh Drive. "And besides, my tennis shoes are rubbing a blister on my foot."

"They don't look new," Chester said.

"They're not new. I didn't put on any socks."

"I never put on any socks," Chester said. "And I don't get blisters."

"That's why." As we drove along toward his roominghouse, he moved his legs up and down, and raised his good arm, and moved his head back and forth, and opened and closed his hands. After a while he said, "I got a date tonight, and I got no wheels, and I don't think I got a muscle in my whole body that don't ache. You wanta double date in this car?"

"I gotta study. And you oughta take a night off."

"Yeah, I reckon. I wonder how quick I can get my insurance money and get me another pussy wagon. Damn. How'm I gonna git out to the job in the morning? Hell, I cain't work anyhow, with this fuckin sprained shoulder, and I got to go see about my insurance, my car. Shee-it. Hey, Dub, you mind tellin your daddy 'bout my wreck, an' how I cain't git to work on account of my injuries and no car and stuff, so's he won't can me?"

"You working with my dad now?" Like I didn't have enough problems.

"Well, not *with* 'im. On the same job. He's the boss. I'm just another stiff sawin' boards. But he could fire my ass if I looked at 'im cross-eyed. So will you tell 'im?"

"Well, he won't be home till late, but—okay, I'll tell 'im."

"Thanks, Dub." He felt the top of his head through the bandage. "I got to go back and git this bandage changed, too. They shaved off some of my hair on account of a cut in my scalp. You know what I wonder, Dub? I wonder how come they call 'em tennis shoes. You play tennis?"

"No."

"Me neither. But I'm wearing tennis shoes. I never even seen nobody play tennis." I stopped in front of his roominghouse, and he got out, stiffly, groaning. "Jesus, I'm sore. No female gonna git the famous Chester's Last Stand tonight. Don't fergit to tell your daddy, huh?"

"I won't."

Mom was waiting in the door when I parked in back of the house. She spoke with great conviction: "Joy is all right."

"She's not too serious, I guess." I realized I really didn't know. "She's got on a neck brace, but her face is not cut or anything. I didn't get to hear what the doctor had to say. She was talking all right. She didn't seem to be in a lot of pain."

Mom had a funny look on her face. I knew right away that she knew that I was hiding something.

"I'll call and get the official diagnosis," I said. I hurried to the phone. "Chester was in the wreck too, and there was a lot of confusion, and—"

"Confusion?"

"Well, you know, people coming and going." I felt like I'd been caught committing a crime. I heard myself stammer a little, even though I hadn't really told a lie yet.

"How is your friend Chester?"

"Well, mostly bruises, and his arm in a sling from a shoulder sprain. But he's pretty much okay."

I called the clinic and Nurse McClain told me that Joy had a sprained platysma, a lacerated scalp, and abdominal bruises, and she'd have to wear the neck brace for a couple of weeks, and they were going to keep her a week to be sure she didn't have internal injuries. I started to explain this to Mom, but she said none of it had any reality and not to name things that didn't exist. I had trouble talking to her because of the strange, accusatory look on her face. She gave me a little smile and went back into her room and shut the door.

I waited up till Dad came home, pretending to study. He was pretty beered up. When I gave him Chester's message, he said, "Chester?"

"Carpenter's helper, dark hair, brown eyes, tattoo on his hand."

"Oh, yeah. Good worker. Screwing himself to death. Works with Red Mueller. Okay, Cowboy, Red likes 'im, so tell 'im we'll hold his spot. And tell 'im to leave some of that pussy for tomorrow. It'll still be there." He drifted out a little on the turn as he headed for the bedroom. "G'night, Cowboy."

Mom didn't come out of her room to tell me goodnight. I went to the bathroom and saw that my urine was still pink. I tapped on Mom's door.

"Come in, Dubby."

I went in and gave her a kiss on the cheek. She was reading *Science and Health*, but she didn't fold it over her finger. She just glanced up.

"Goodnight, Mom."

"Goodnight, honey." She lowered her eyes to her book. She had never dismissed me like that before. I hesitated, hoping there'd be at least a mitigating smile, but she was completely focused on her lesson. All of a sudden we seemed to hardly know each other, to be almost strangers. I shut her door slowly, hoping she'd call me back or at least say "sleep tight," but she seemed to have forgotten I was there.

At around five Dad got up and left, but I faked being asleep.

When I finally got up and went into the bathroom I saw that my urine was a deep yellow-rose color, much worse than before. Mom wasn't in the kitchen when I went in for breakfast. I ate shredded wheat. The coffee I made was weak. I realized I'd never made coffee in that percolator before, hadn't made coffee in anything, in fact, since Mom took the bus to Espada over a year ago to stay with ninety-one-year-old Widow Sarcey, who was on her deathbed and didn't want to die alone. Nobody liked Widow Sarcey but Mom. When Widow Sarcey walked the three miles into town to shop, nobody offered her a ride, and nobody offered to carry her groceries. Seeing her hobbling along the street alone, people enjoyed saying, "There goes Widow Sarcey and all her friends." The reason people hated her was that she didn't go to any church, and didn't believe in God, and said the whole idea of God and heaven was nonsense. They resented Mom being nice to her. The theory was that she and Mom got along because Mom didn't think the Bible meant what it said in so many words, and thought God was some kind of a spirit, and didn't believe in doctors at all, which was almost as bad as not believing in God.

I was hoping Mom would come out and suggest that maybe I should stay home from classes one more day, but she didn't. So I got dressed and ready to leave, and tapped on her door, and said, " 'Bye, Mom."

I heard the springs squeak as she got off her bed and I knew she was coming to her door. She opened it and handed me her keys. "Take the car, Dubby, so you can go by and see Joy on your way home from school. I know she'd appreciate that. You could even call that office where Mrs. Hurt works and see if maybe she needs a ride out there to the clinic." Her voice had a peculiar tone, a tone of— efficiency and impersonality, like she'd rented out a room and I was the roomer instead of her son.

"Oh, thanks, Mom. Oh, sure. I'll go see Joy. But Mrs. Hurt doesn't get off till maybe five-thirty, and she has her brother to take her to the clinic." She tried to hand me a dollar but I backed off. "I've got that thirty-four dollars," I said.

She put the dollar back in the pocket of her robe. "Don't forget to buy gas," she said, and shut the door.

I heard Jenny talking to her dolls in her little front bedroom. I usually went in and kidded around with her before I left, but today I sneaked out and got in the car and left. I didn't want her to see me so down in the dumps, and I didn't want to try to act like I wasn't.

At Rice, with a bandage over my left brow, and my swollen, discolored nose, and my puffed-up, lacerated lip, I was the object of much discussion. I told the story about the six thugs beating me up, and nobody seemed surprised. Everybody agreed that certain parts of town were getting dangerous. I went to the bathroom every chance I got, hoping to see some improvement in my condition, but nothing had changed. I felt something like Widow Sarcey must've felt when she thought the end was coming. With Mom sore at me, I felt alone, and if I was going to die I didn't want to be alone when it happened.

After classes, I went into the business district where the big stores were. I didn't want to die with thirty-four unspent dollars in my pocket and with Christmas coming on. In spite of all the things for sale, I couldn't find anything that seemed right for Joy. Everything either projected too much sentiment, or didn't seem to suit her, or would probably be thrown in the garbage by Mrs. Hurt.

Ruby. When her mama named her that she probably thought she was going to grow up to be a nice person.

I got a new robe, emerald green rayon, for Mom, and a gold-plated Elgin pocket watch for Dad, and for Jenny a large doll that said "Mama" when you tilted it a certain way. Well, if I suddenly collapsed from internal bleeding and died, they would at least have a nice Christmas. I didn't pick out anything for Phoebe, because I didn't feel I knew her well enough to select anything suitable yet.

I drove to Dahlken Clinic with a little bouquet for Joy, but Uncle Phil's patrol car was in the parking lot and I decided not to stop. I took the flowers home to Mom. She accepted them with the same kind of reserved distance she'd shown me that morning. "Why, thank you, Dubby, that is so nice. Did you see Joy?"

"No, ma'am. The lady at the desk said she was sleeping, so I figured I'd try again tomorrow."

"I'll put these in a vase. They're really pretty, and they smell good, too." She turned away from me and got busy at the sink. I felt a pain in my side. I went in the bathroom, scared to look. Sure enough, my urine was darker yellow than ever, so dark the pink was hardly visible. Not only that, but my sins and my lies and my whole false life were on my back pushing me down like a granite tombstone. I felt it, too heavy to lift off, too heavy to carry. I looked in the mirror and I thought I saw the end of the world in my eyes. I had trouble walking into the kitchen. Mom wasn't there. My flowers were in a little vase on the kitchen table. I tapped on Mom's door.

"Yes, Dubby?"

She didn't say come in.

"Could I talk to you a minute, Mom?"

"Of course, Dubby. Come on in."

I opened the door. She was propped up in bed in her ragged robe, studying her lesson. She had the Bible in her hand and *Science and Health* open on her lap. I suddenly felt like I didn't deserve to be in her presence.

"Come on in, honey." She put the Bible face-down beside her. I went in and got close to the bed, but I couldn't speak. "Sit down, honey." There was one straight chair in the room. I sat in it, not looking at her. "Come closer, and tell me." I got up and moved the chair close to her bed and sat down again, and looked at her. She smiled. "It's all right, honey."

"Mom—" Then something terrible happened to me. I knew I'd never forget it as long as I lived. I started to cry. I couldn't speak. I could only cry. I thought, if Dad saw me now he'd decide I was a sissy, and he'd never have anything to do with me again. But Mom reached out and took my hand. She didn't mind me crying, but I did, and I couldn't stop. She just held my hand and patted it, and smiled at me. I used up both of my handkerchiefs, my regular one and the clean one in my other pocket, the one Mom had always told me to carry extra, to offer to a lady in time of need. Here I was using it myself in time of need.

When I finally was able to speak, I told her everything, everything, holding nothing back, not lying about anything, not minimizing anything, even my fears about the blood I saw when I went to the bathroom. I didn't go into details about the sex, of course, because I believed that probably Mom wouldn't believe some of them, wouldn't believe some of the things happened to anybody outside of the most depraved house of ill repute in Paris, which for some reason was her idea of the world's leading city of sin. I didn't implicate Uncle Phil or anybody else, or tell anything outside of my own personal participation. I just droned on and on, about the pregnancy, the awful scene at the clinic, how Joy had protected me. I told about my deceptions, my lies, my manipulations, everything right down to my theft of Dad's Bull Durham. Mom's reaction was nothing like I expected. She didn't turn white or get sick. She listened as though she had known all along and was glad it was out in the open. When I finally staggered to a stop, feeling exhausted, empty, there was a long silence. She continued to pat and squeeze my hand. "I'm sorry,

Mom," I said, starting to cry again. "I know I'm a lot less than you thought I was."

"No, you're not. You're more. I've never been as proud of you as I am this minute." I got out of my chair and sat on the side of the bed, and we hugged each other for a long time. She said over and over, "Everything's all right, honey. Everything's all right."

And sure enough, the evening began to glow with a light that made the world look almost holy. Mom and Jenny and I had a wonderful dinner of Boston baked beans, which Mom made with a lot of Grandma's Molasses, and salad and home-cranked ice cream. Mom was a toucher. Every time we passed near each other she put her hand on my shoulder, or smoothed my hair, or something. It was like balm, a magic unguent to the soul.

I called Phoebe and we had another long talk about nothing in particular. She had gone to work at a five-and-dime for the holiday season, and she talked about a couple of funny customers, not in a cruel or demeaning way, just to describe their droll behavior. I was sure I was in love. I asked her for a date for Wednesday night, but she said that since it was only ten days till Christmas she had to work every night that week till nine o'clock, and her folks wanted her to come straight home, but she was sure it would be okay for Saturday night, if it was okay with me.

Wednesday afternoon I went by the clinic but Uncle Phil's car was there so I didn't stop. That evening I dropped in at the five-and-dime and surprised Phoebe and bought a can opener for Mom. Phoebe wrapped it with red Christmas paper and acted so possessive of me in front of the other girls that I was walking about a foot off the floor. That night I studied for my finals, and Thursday I bought another small bouquet and went by the clinic again and, not recognizing any of the cars in the parking lot, stopped in to visit Joy. Nurse McClain told me in no uncertain terms that she had strict orders not to let me go to Joy's room. I asked her to take the bouquet in to Joy and tell her it was from me, and she said she would. After that I went to the store to see Phoebe again, and while she was selling me a singing yo-yo for Jenny and wrapping it in silver paper with green holly leaves and red berries on it, she whispered to me that the other girls in the store were envious because she had a college boy coming in to visit her, and they thought I was handsome, even with my beat-up face. I thought it was lucky they didn't know I was probably dying

216

of some kind of ruptured internal organ, and then I realized I hadn't checked my urine the whole day because I'd followed Mom's advice to sit down to make water, and not even give it a glance, not think about it at all, so as to be able to deny the reality of the claim of imperfection. I went straight home and looked and sure enough, it was almost as clear as it had been before I ran into that tattooed buzzsaw named Sailorman Jones, with just the slightest hint of a rosy hue to remind me that I was almost, but not quite, as good as ever. I was happy to give Mom and Mrs. Gullman credit for this, although I knew other people might argue that Mom's timing had just been right, and my almost-eighteen-year-old body was healing itself.

I was just settling in to study for my French exam when the phone rang. Mom was in her room studying, so I answered and got a surprise that ranked right up there in magnitude with the others I'd had in the last few days. It was Dad. He wanted me to make some excuse to go out, and to borrow Mom's car, and to come meet him at Steve's beer joint on Eleventh Street. He sounded relaxed and jovial. I could hear whiny honky-tonk music in the background. He'd been off work since about four-thirty, and it was almost six-thirty, so it was easy to guess that he was getting a little tanked. I said I'd do it right away. I hated to stop studying, because I wanted to keep up my good record in French, and not let Mr. Bourgeois down, but when your father tells you to come meet him someplace, you don't say no. I was about to hang up when he said, urgently, "Oh, hey, Cowboy, don't tell your mother it's me, huh? See you here." He hung up before I could agree to the last stipulation, and since I didn't want to start developing a whole new collection of lies right after I got rid of the old ones, I went in and told her exactly what happened. Her response was, "Well, he's your father, honey." She was just as serene as you please. I couldn't help thinking she'd've been upset about it if I hadn't so recently volunteered my voluminous confession. I didn't feel like I was betraying Dad to tell Mom, and I didn't feel too sanctimonious about having a clean slate with Mom, because I'd already realized it wasn't going to take me long to load myself down with guilty secrets again. I knew I hadn't cured myself of my basic houndoggery. No matter how hard a boy tries to be honest, he can't tell his mother everything, which is no doubt lucky for her. These thoughts on my way to see Dad reminded me I hadn't written in "The Maxims of W. W. Johnson" lately. I'd stored up several things to put in there, but my life had heated up so much that I couldn't remember them. The only one I could think of now was "Animals are never naked," which had come to me that time Joy turned into an animal while she was scuttling around with no clothes on, grieving for the way her daddy had died. I made up my mind to write that one down.

Steve's Place was a one-story frame building that took up most of a weedy lot in the run-down part of East Eleventh. It looked more like a warehouse than a beer joint. On a scale of ugliness it was about equal to Dahlken Clinic. Inside, when you first came in, you couldn't see much. It smelled like it had been mopped with leftover beer every night for years, till the springy saggy floor was soaked and alcohol-cured. The second I stepped on it I could hear Dad saying, "Weak floor joists under this sumbitch." Buildings were living, breathing things to him, and his critical eye never let one get away with anything. "Jake-leg carpenter" was, to him, a worse thing to be than a bindlestiff or a gutterbum or a moocher or a drunk—but not quite worse than a Communist, and certainly not worse than a sissy. That was the lowest. The structural flaws in Steve's Place, however, were safe from Dad's scorn because the beer was cold and Steve was a friend of his, part of the womblike haven where, for a few hours, nothing bad can happen, men are men, women are glad of it, and the rest of the world can take a long walk off a short pier.

Dad was hunched over the bar with Red Mueller. Through the tobacco haze they looked like two fishermen in a fog. Red was easy to recognize, with his flaming disordered hair and his round shoulders and short neck, all part of a hulking fleshy structure that seemed clearly suited to hard work in the outdoors. Dad was straighter, more square and spare and visibly muscled, his black hair standing up like hog bristles, without a sign of gray at forty-five. Red spotted me first, said something to Dad, and both of them rose from their stools. "Hey, Cowboy," Dad said. "Le's set over here at a table." We moved across the dance floor where a shapeless woman in dirty white slacks, carrying her bottle of Jax beer, was dancing bouncily with a shorter man in greasy khakis. She had a blissful expression on her face, her eyes were closed, and it was easy to see that at that moment she was beautiful and young and would be that way till the voice of Wee Bonnie Baker sighing "Oh, Johnny, oh, Johnny, how you can love" expired on the jukebox.

We sat at a wobbly table with cigarette burns and moisture rings and carved initials. I realized that Red Mueller hadn't spoken to me, was just looking at me steadily with a big gap-toothed grin on his freckled face. The waitress, leathery skinned but habitually perky, came over quickly and swiped off the table with a gray rag and stood up against the back of Dad's chair with her hand on his shoulder and said, "What can I git you?"

"Want a beer, Cowboy?" Dad asked.

"No, thanks. I'll have a Coke."

"Yall okay?" the waitress asked, leaving.

"For now," Dad said. Then he looked at Red. "He don't want his mom to smell beer on 'im, right, Cowboy?"

No point in trying to lie out of it. "Well, yeah, that, and finals. First semester. I don't think too well when I have beer."

Red was shaking his head and grinning at me. He said, "You son of a gun, you."

"How've you been, Mr. Mueller? I haven't seen you since I water-boyed on that Pasadena job."

"Oh, I been fine, fine as frog's hair—Tex."

So that was it. I just waited.

Dad just waited, too. He wasn't the talkative type. I got my gab and my stooped shoulders from Mom's side.

"Ole Tex Frontere," Red said. "You son of a gun, you. You thought you could git away with that, huh?"

Dad said: "Your buddy Chester come out to the job today. He told Red that a young lady told him—a young lady from over on Sixteenth Street—a young lady that Chester says—well, you tell 'im, Red."

"Chester says you been humpin' this little split-tail from over on Sixteenth, got 'er knocked up. Right so far, Tex?"

I could hardly make my voice work. "Was," I said.

"Was? Was what? Oh, was knocked up, you mean, huh, Tex? Had to wreck Checky's car to git rid of it, huh? Lucky fer you. You end up marryin' a little split-tail like that, you wish you was dead. Them kind o' roundheels, they kill a man. Look, Tex, your daddy jus' thought we ought to have a talk. He ain't sore at you, are ye, Bill?"

"No way." Dad had a satisfied smirk on his face, staring at his Lone Star beer bottle. I got the impression he not only wasn't mad at me, he was proud. Maybe even relieved.

"If you git tangled up with a woman, Tex," Red drawled—"we'll git to that Tex shit in a minute—be sure she's the best there is. Be

sure she's too good fer ye, 'cause regular, ordinary females, the kind
you bump into in everyday type o' life, if they didn't have pussies,
there'd be a bounty on 'em. Now, Tex, this li'l gal, she tells Checky
you been pickin' up extry money fightin' on Saddy afternoons at
some place over towards Beaumont, she went with you and she seen
it, and you done scored several one-punch knockouts. Is that right,
Tex, or is she full o' shit?"

"Well," I said, drawing it out a little, trying for as much gunslinger
cool as a boy can hope for in the presence of his own father, "I
wouldn't say several."

Dad was beaming like a lost man that finally found his way out of a
cave into the sunlight, but he still wasn't looking at either me or Red.
He fished his Bull Durham out of his pocket and started to roll a
cigarette but changed his mind and offered the pack to me.

"No, thanks."

Dad started to roll one for himself. "You know, Red, we got the
damnedest mice over at our place."

"Oh, yeah, you do?" Red said, the straight man. "What kind o'
mice is that, Bill?"

"They smoke."

"Steal yer Bull, do they?"

"Yep. Damnedest mice you ever seen. But that's okay. What the
hell. Mice gotta live too."

He still didn't look at me. He didn't need to. I didn't have anything on my face but a sheepish grin, and he knew it.

"So," Red said, "this little split-tail says to Checky that she didn't
git to go with you las' time, 'cause she was sick, an' then the fella that
hauled you out there called 'er up and says you got the shit kicked
outaya."

"And it wasn't six tough guys out on Waugh Drive," Dad said. He
licked his cigarette paper and caressed the little cylinder and twisted
the end and shoved it in his mouth. He was having a great time.

"But the fella says you didn't go down, and you didn't quit, and
you didn't cry, and the other fella had to spend the night in the
hospital, in an oxygen tent."

At least he didn't die, I thought, and neither did I. I concentrated
on drinking my Coke.

"Coke cold enough for you?" Dad asked.

"Oh, sure, it's fine."

"Ole Steve's got the coldest beer and Cokes in town," Dad said. "Listen, Cowboy—"

He thought a moment, hesitating.

"You mean Tex," Red said, chuckling.

"No," Dad said, "I think we better let ole Tex lie silent in his grave, don't you, Cowboy?"

"Yessir."

"Because I wouldn't want your mother to find out about this. Your mother is as fine a woman as ever drew breath, I hope you realize that. Do you?"

"Yessir, I do."

"Good. So I don't think any of this stuff would be good for her to know about. She don't deserve to have that kind of stuff in her life. She's got it tough enough as it is."

"Yessir."

"Well, Cowboy, I'm glad you come over. One of these days I want you to tell me the whole deal, okay? But for now I guess you want to git on back to your books, huh?"

"Well, pretty soon."

"Fine. You go right ahead."

I finished off my Coke and got up. "Nice seeing you again, Mr. Mueller," I said, and stuck out my hand. He shook it, and I started to leave.

"Oh, by the way, Tex—uh, Dub—yer dad says you been writing poetry, poems, says you kinda go for that kinda stuff."

"Yessir, I guess I do."

"Well, fine, why not, right, Bill?"

"Hell, yes. You go ahead and write all o' that kinda stuff you want to, Cowboy, and more power to you."

"Thanks, Dad." I hurried out past the bar.

"So long, Tex," Steve said, in a low voice as I went by. I didn't slow down or answer. I just got a glimpse of his baggy laughing eyes and his white-whiskered dewlaps shaking as I went out the door. Fame flares like fire in a haybarn. I hoped it would burn out just as fast.

TWENTY-THREE

MOM DIDN'T ASK what Dad wanted to see me about, and I didn't offer to discuss it. I studied with a mind released from all turmoil, at least for the time being. My exam the next morning went so well I handed it to the ebullient Monsieur Bourgeois in half the allotted time, eliciting a big smile and a "*Joyeux Noël*, Woodrow!"

Since I wasn't allowed to visit Joy in her room at the clinic, I used up my extra time playing ping-pong at Autry House, then took the bus home to study for my Spanish final Saturday morning. I knew that one was going to be a snap. It was Friday, and of course Dad was gone till the following Monday night, so Mom and Jenny and I found ways to dispel the gloom, with a dinner of fried chicken and mashed potatoes and gravy, and cole slaw, and tapioca pudding, and then songs with Mom at the piano, and popcorn dripping with a really special treat, sweet butter.

Saturday morning as Mom and I sat at the kitchen table, she having tea and toast and I devouring blindfolded eggs and country sausage and whole-wheat toast and blackberry jelly, there came a knock at the front door. It wasn't quite eight o'clock yet, so a knock on the door had a strangely unsettling effect on us. I started to go, but Mom quickly got up, saying, "I'll get it, you have to get ready for school," and pulled her raggedy robe around her and headed for the front door. I was wishing it was after Christmas so she'd be wearing her shiny new emerald green rayon job, enough to knock anybody's eye out. My back was to the door, but I heard her voice and then a male voice and another female voice, very low, and then Mom saying, "Please, come in," and then calling in a voice that had a slight quaver in it, "Dubby."

When I turned around and looked toward the living room, I saw Mrs. Hurt and a man in a nonstop collar. I wiped my mouth and hurried out to meet them, expecting the worst. Mom was saying, "Of course I remember you, Reverend Hollowitz. We worked together on the earthquake relief drive last year. How is that sweet wife of yours?"

Before he could answer, I was there, and Mrs. Hurt, whose face looked like it was made of that gray clay that sculptors push and pull and slice till they get a shape they want, was saying to me in a low, frightened voice, "I'm not here to make trouble, boy. I only came to ask you to tell me, if you know."

Reverend Hollowitz, a youngish man with a pleasant face and an easygoing, modest manner, offered me his hand. "I believe Mrs. Hurt told me you're known to your friends as Dub."

I shook hands with him. It was a strong hand with calluses, not at all what I expected from his mild face. "Yes, sir."

"Pleased to meet you. We have what appears to be an emergency here, Dub, and we hope you can help us."

"I'm not going to make trouble for you. I don't hold any ill feelings," Mrs. Hurt said pleadingly.

"Her daughter is missing," the Reverend said.

Mom and I said at the same time: "Missing?"

"The clinic called Mrs. Hurt this morning at five and said Joy was not in her room, and—"

"If you know where she went, boy, for God's sake, don't hold anything against me!" Mrs. Hurt blurted, and then started to cry.

Mom looked at me. I said, "Mrs. Hurt, honest, I don't know anything. This is the first I heard."

Mrs. Hurt wailed, "She still has her neck brace on! She hates me! I tried to be a good mother. I tried to be a good person. I just want my little girl back. I tried to obey God's laws and bring up my kids good. I don't know what happened. Oh, God help me! God help me!"

She began to tremble and fall. Reverend Hollowitz just managed to grab her to keep her from falling hard. He led her to the wicker sofa.

"Here," Mom said. "Over here. She can just lie down here. I'll make her some tea. Would you like some tea or coffee, Reverend?"

He deposited the almost-limp form of Mrs. Hurt on the creaky sofa. She lay back, taking deep breaths. "Coffee," Reverend Hollowitz said, "if it's not too much trouble, Mrs. Johnson."

"Not in the least," Mom said. Then: "Dubby, you go on, now, get your things together and get off to school. Go on. I'll handle this." Then, to the Reverend: "He's a freshman at Rice. He has a final in Spanish this morning."

"I'm sure he'll do fine," the Reverend said. "Don't be upset by this, Dub. We don't mean to intrude on your lives."

"I don't want to hurt anybody," Mrs. Hurt whispered. "I forgive everybody everything, whatever. I just want my girl. I want her home. I want her to learn to love me again. Please, God."

"Run on, honey," Mom said. "You can't be late. You didn't finish your breakfast. Finish eating, then get the keys off of my bedside table and take the car."

"Yes, ma'am."

Mrs. Hurt raised partway up and called weakly after me, "I don't blame you, boy. Not for anything atall. I don't hold a grudge against nobody. I just want, please God, my little girl back home again, safe and sound."

"Yes, ma'am." I hurried back into the kitchen and shut the door. I tried to finish my eggs but they stuck in my throat. Mom came in to make coffee. I kissed her and left. "Don't think about anything except your exam, honey," she called after me.

I tried, but I couldn't get Joy out of my mind, a crazy girl out there somewhere with a neck brace on. I took the full time to do my Spanish exam, which was a surprise to Mr. Battista, because he was used to seeing me finish first. I had no idea what I had written on the paper I handed in. As soon as I got home I asked Mom if she'd heard anything and she said no. Mrs. Hurt and the Reverend had stayed for an hour, till Mrs. Hurt's brother Phil came in his patrol car to take her to the clinic to question the people there and start an investigation. After that, the Reverend had stayed for another hour, chatting with Mom about the literal meaning of the Bible versus an interpretive reading of it, and she was proud to say that he agreed with her that one must spiritually interpret many things in the Good Book, because much of it was translated from translations, and some of the literal Greek and Hebrew meanings had been lost.

I was free of academic pressures until the new year, but I couldn't enjoy my freedom. Mom went in her room and studied her lesson, "knowing the truth" for Joy, and I listened to a football game on the radio, just waiting till we heard something or till it came time for my date with Phoebe at nine o'clock, when she got off.

Then, at about eight, Chester called. "Hey, Dubby, how's it goin?"

"I tried to call you at your roominghouse, Chester, a couple of times. Where've you been? Did you hear what happened to Joy?"

There was a short pause, then he said, "Naw, what happened to 'er?"

"She disappeared."

"No shit."

"This is not a joke, Chester. Joy has disappeared."

I could hear a strangling noise at the other end of the line, and he covered the phone with his hand. Finally he came back on and said, in a sort of organized tone, very flat, like a person minimizing big news: "Dubby, ole buddy, you are speaking with the person that disappeared 'er."

"What?"

Then I could hear him laughing and, in the background, Joy giggling. "That's right, ole buddy, I'm the criminal that disappeared the little gal. Guess where I'm calling from? Huntsville."

"Huntsville!"

"Lemme tell you, Dubby. I went to git my stitches out, and I went in to see Joy, and she says to me, 'Chet,' she says—she commenced to calling me Chet right off—she says, 'Chet, I want outa this place, and I wanta just take off somewheres, anywheres, 'cause I ain't gonna live with my mama no more—' "

"Call Mrs. Hurt. Call her. She's—"

"Hang on, ole buddy. Joy, she says to me that she hates her mama and if she hangs around her much longer she's gonna take a butcher knife and kill 'er. So I says did she want to ride up to Huntsville with me and see my Uncle Hank. So she says sure. So—"

"Chester! Dammit! Listen to me! Mrs. Hurt has put the police on this. She's having conniptions. You got to call 'er!"

"We'll git to that, ole buddy. Don't git your bowels in a uproar. So

Joy, she sneaks out of that dump around midnight, and I'm waiting for her in my new secondhand white convertible coupe DeSoto, clean as a whistle, good rubber, only twenny-eight thousand miles—" In the background Joy shouted, "It's a dreamboat!"

"Chester! Dammit! Can you put Joy on?"

"Here, Joy, talk to Dubby."

"Hi, Dub." Suddenly she was very subdued.

"Joy, whatever you may think of your mama, you can't treat her like this. You have to call her. It's common human decency."

"We did. Uncle Phil and her's on their way up here right now."

"They are?"

"Chet," Joy said, her voice a little frightened, "you tell 'im."

"Dubby, ole buddy," Chester said, coming back on the phone, "me and Joy, well, we got to know each other pretty good the last couple days, shacked up here with my Uncle Hank and Aunt Gert. My Uncle Hank's a guard at the pen, I tol' you that, I think, mentioned it, anyhow—he's got ten years in. He says to me, 'Chester, you want a job at the pen?' and I says, 'Hell, yes, beats swingin' a hammer,' and he says, 'You got it,' and he calls his boss and tells 'im he done filled the guard vacancy, and I start next week."

"Well, congratulations, Chester."

In the background I heard Joy say, "Chet, honey, tell 'im, for Pete's sake."

Chester took in a deep breath. He said, "Dubby, Joy and me's getting married tonight."

"Married?"

"Uh-huh. It just kind of hit us like that, whammo, you know? Like they say, love's like a water moccasin, she don't rattle, she just strikes. You ain't sore at me, are ye?"

"Hell, no, Chester. Congratulations."

"Thanks, ole podner. Hold on, here's Joy."

"Dubby," Joy says, her voice sort of high, "you gonna wish me happiness?"

"I sure am, Joy. Long life and happiness."

"Thanks, Dub. I called Mama, expecting to git chewed out, and instead she cried and said—" She was having trouble with her voice, choking up. "Mama said she loved me and wanted me to be happy. And her and Uncle Phil's on their way up here so she can sign the underage thing for the justice of the peace."

"I'm glad it's working out this way, Joy."

"Aw, Dubby, it's workin' out dreamy. 'Member one time I told you 'bout how I was gonna treat my husband if I ever got one?"

I remembered how lonesome she looked, maybe even a little scared, when she talked about that at her back door that day. I said, "I sure do, Joy."

"Well, me and Chet we talked about that a lot. It's real nifty to have somebody you can talk about stuff like that with, even when you're—you know—"

"Fuckin'!" Chester yelled into the phone.

"Hush up, you dirty thing!" Joy said, proud of him as she could be. "Dubby, him and me swore over and over agin how good we gonna be to each other. He's my king, my king, I mean it, Chester is my king and he can set on his easy chair and drink his beer and use my back for a footstool, and that's the God's truth. And he's gonna be good to me too, and we're gonna be true to each other. I'm gonna make him so happy he's gonna think he done died and went to heaven. I remember everything my daddy taught me about cookin', and I'm gonna feed my king, King Chet, like he was king of the world. I'm gonna fatten 'im up a little bit, put some meat on his bones, and we gonna have some babies and we gonna raise 'em up without no fightin', and no yellin', and no switchin'—nothing but hugs and kisses, mornin' noon and night!"

So she did notice my skinny legs, after all, and my ribs sticking out.

"An' I'm not just sayin' that on my own, Dubby. Him and me agreed on that, didn't we, honey?"

"We sure as hell did, baby!" Chester hollered.

"Dubby, he makes me feel like I'm flying up through the stars."

"Well, Joy, I can tell you this . . . I'm happy for you and Chester, both of you, and I know it's going to work out fine, just great."

"Thanks, Dubby. I hope you did good on your exams."

"I think I did okay. You just about over the accident?"

"Well, uh-huh." She giggled. "Except for this neck brace. It kinda —you know—" She giggled again.

Chester yelled, from behind her, "It'll take more 'n a damn neck brace to slow this sex machine down!"

"Filthy thing," Joy said. "I just love 'im to death, Dubby, I really do. And he's got a nice job and everything. I'm as happy as I can be."

"Stay that way, Joy, for about a hundred years."

Mom came out to remind me that I had to be somewhere important at nine. I got off the phone as quickly as I could and told her the
news. It made her happy. I think she was happier for Mrs. Hurt than
for anybody else.

I was happy for Joy, and for Chester, too, but the phone call left
me feeling sad. At first I couldn't figure it out, then I realized Joy had
been jabbering away like a little girl playing with dolls, inventing
castles and kings and things that were in short supply everywhere,
especially in those low, dusty hills around Huntsville, a prison town
with a kind of a grim air about it. All the stuff that she never had as a
little girl was popping up to the surface like bubbles. I could have
almost loved her myself if she hadn't been so reckless. And Chester
wasn't exactly the stuff kings are made of. Nobody had said anything
about him treating her like a queen. Well, maybe he would, anyhow.
And maybe marriage would calm her down.

I parked right in front of the store at five minutes of nine, and went
in to wait for Phoebe. As soon as she was finished she came over and
took my arm and told everybody goodnight and we marched out
together. I was about to explode with excitement. I knew that if I
didn't control my exuberance, Phoebe was going to conclude that I
was an unstable person, so I called on the lone gunslinger to try to
balance out my emotions. Even he had a hard time keeping me
under wraps.

As soon as we got in the car, Phoebe said, "Do you know about the
flares?"

"The flares?"

"A girl at work said they're beautiful."

The flares were several acres of tall pipes on the outskirts of town
where, for reasons nobody had ever explained to me, gas from an
underground deposit had been burning for years. It was considered a
very romantic spot. "Wanta see 'em?" I asked.

We didn't talk at all till we got there and parked facing the weird
field of flames. We still didn't talk for several minutes, just staring at
the kind of unearthly phenomenon. Then Phoebe said in a very small
voice, "Do you smoke?"

I was startled. It was the last thing I'd expected her to ask. If I
smoked her folks probably wouldn't want her to go out with me.

"Smoke? No. Oh, I did. I used to. I have smoked. I still do, some-times. But I'm planning to quit. I mean, give 'em up completely."

She was silent again. Then: "Would you like to smoke now?"

"Oh, I don't have any."

After another few seconds, she opened her purse and rummaged around and pulled out one of those Chesterfields ten-packs, the same kind Olivia had in her purse in Sallyport when we were listening to the recruiter talk about the Spanish Civil War. She offered me one.

We both stuck cigarettes into our mouths and lit up, staring at each other and grinning. Then we both started to laugh. I said, "Man alive, that's really rich! Both of us almost scared to admit we smoked!"

We rolled down our windows so we could blow the smoke out and the odor wouldn't stick to our clothes. We sat there staring at the flames, thinking and chuckling and puffing. I didn't know what she was thinking, but I was thinking the gas that's burning there comes from somewhere down in the belly of the world, from Hell, maybe, and look how close we are to it all.

Winter fog folded over us. It haloed the flames. It invited reverie. When we'd smoked our cigarettes about halfway down, Phoebe mur-mured something, very low, not looking at me.

"I'm sorry. What did you say?"

She brought her cigarette up to her lips again, holding it in a spe-cial way, very close to the ends of her index and middle fingers, which trembled. Then, instead of taking a puff, she said, barely louder than before:

"Are you a virgin?"

TWENTY-FOUR

PHOEBE'S ANGELHOOD, which even I knew I had invented, just as I had invented Mom's perfection, persisted in my mind for all the next week. Though she had brought the subject around to sex at the flares, still it was hard, even painful for me to imagine that she was interested in it as something to do rather than something to mention to the boy you were with as a test, to find out how experienced he was, how much danger you might be in, and to let it be known that you were a modern young woman to whom such words as *sex* and *virgin* were not taboo; indeed, you were capable of discussing them, within limits, on an adult level. I concluded that this was the case. I treasured the concept of her purity, modified as it was by her human concerns, her healthy female fascination with a process that one day would bring her a husband and children. More and more I hoped the husband would be me. With that in mind I treated her with the respect her virginity deserved. She became my girl, my steady, my o.a.o. By Christmas Eve we had progressed to hot necking. I began to wonder if I was fated to be in another Betty-type relationship, a life of nearlies, almosts, shame, and frustration. Phoebe trusted me. She let me lead. She was compliant. She didn't stop my hands. My hands stopped my hands—my what-I-believed-to-be sense of honor, of responsibility, stopped my hands. A fantasy struck me every time I made up my mind to go forward, to risk everything . . . If I moved another quarter of an inch toward my goal she would stiffen, freeze, shudder, begin to cry, whisper, "Take me home, please, I can't see you anymore . . ." I was so in love, so in the thrall of worship that I lived in dread of that imagined moment.

At Christmas my devious past was all forgiven when the presents were opened at home. Dad looked at his new Elgin and said, "Cowboy, this is as nice a present as I ever got." It was genuine, open emotion. I thought for a second he was going to hug me, something he had not done in my memory, but instead he offered me a strong man-to-man handshake.

Mom said nothing when she took her robe out of its fancy-wrapped box. She began to cry and ran out of the room. She returned a few minutes later, wearing it proudly, and gave me a hug.

Jenny did not put her new dolly down all day. It sat on her lap as she ate. She refused to take a bath because her dolly couldn't take a bath with her. Mom had to give her an extra pillow so her dolly could sleep like a person beside her. Santa Claus, who didn't have a lot of room in his sleigh that year, brought her a smaller dolly, which became the little sister of the one I'd given her. She named them Polly and Molly.

Santa Claus brought me my first-ever sports jacket, so that I could look properly festive when I took Phoebe dancing on New Year's Eve.

Phoebe and I, to prove our maturity and our intellectual intimacy, had talked about limiting our giving to each other and saving our money for other—unspecified—things. We knew each other admired the Brownings, so she gave me *The Poetical Works of Browning*, leather-bound, from Smith's Used Books, and I gave her *Sonnets from the Portuguese*.

New Year's Eve when I went to pick her up, her parents had already left for the evening. We were alone in her house. She wasn't quite ready. I got a glimpse of her in her slip as she darted from the bathroom to her bedroom. I walked to the open door. Her back was to me. I went in and put my arms around her from behind. She turned to face me and we kissed in a way we had never kissed before. She clung to me, pressed against me. The next thing I knew we were on the floor, on the rug by her bed, and it had happened, was happening.

Angelhood, and maidenhead, if there was one, were gone forever. I didn't know what you were supposed to feel when a maidenhead broke. I'd heard stories. Some girls lost them at play, I'd heard. At any rate I felt nothing give way except our will to chastity. Having no one but Mrs. Sandusky and Joy to use for comparison, I was shocked. Mrs. Sandusky, the fleshy, sweaty vulgarian, and Joy, the perfect, insatiable wood-nymph beyond all human inhibition, had not prepared me for this brief, sweet, ladylike gift of Phoebe's passion.

We declared our love. We settled into an orderly schedule of dating and making love in motels. There was none of the irrational and unpredictable behavior that had imperiled my academic success. There was none of the coarseness of Mrs. Sandusky, none of the reckless, mad lust of Joy. Once in a moment of intensity I found myself thinking of Joy, of the time we parked on a back road in broad daylight and she jumped on and scrubbed away like a maniac while cars passed us honking, the people laughing and yelling encouragement ("Go baby, go baby, *go!*"), and her waving and laughing and chanting at the top of her voice "I don't care if I do die *do die do die do!*" and me feeling somehow mortified and dumb like the time I rode the black mule backwards but loving it anyhow, scared as I was. I was sorry I thought of Joy at a time like that but told myself there are times when our minds don't mind us, and besides, Phoebe and I soared on the diaphanous see-through wings of love, and that was the rarest, finest thing of all.

It was beginning to look like 1938 was going to be a great year, at least for me. I was going to make all the honor rolls Mom could wish for, and I had a stable and happy love-life, enthusiastically endorsed by both mothers—except, of course for the sexual encounters, which, if known, would have been bigger tragedies to each of them than the deaths of two hundred civilians in the recent rebel bombing of Barcelona.

Joy and Chester called from Huntsville to give me the great news that Joy was probably pregnant. It would be another month before they could be sure, but they were keeping their fingers crossed. In the meantime, Chester said, he was going to keep giving her booster shots every night. Joy asked me if I'd heard the Joe Louis–Nate Mann fight on the radio. It had taken Louis almost three rounds to knock out Mann, and Joy said she was sure ole Tex Frontere coulda done it with one punch in the first. She was serious, which reminded me of her problems with reality. The next day, just reliving a few things, I walked past the house on Sixteenth Street. Mrs. Hurt had moved away, and the yard was growing up in weeds again.

I went by the Potters' to see if they would like for me to keep the grass mowed over on Sixteenth till the place was rented again. Mrs. Potter answered the door and told me that Mr. Potter was in the hospital again, and they were going to leave the property like it was, as his medical bills were very high. She had heard that Joy had got married and was very happy. "Probably what Mr. Potter heard about her was just vicious gossip," she said, "as it usually is, that sort of thing." I told her I was sure that was the truth of the matter.

My world got dark all of a sudden when Phoebe told me her daddy had got a job in Philadelphia through some Christian Science friends, and they were moving up there right away so she could start back to art school. We had a tearful—on her part—farewell date. We declared our love over and over again, made plans for the future, swore to write daily and to save up our money so we could visit each other, in Philadelphia or Houston, when schools were out in June.

And then suddenly she was gone.

I went to church with Mom that Sunday, half-hoping I'd been in a dream and I'd see Phoebe there. Instead I saw the Tamplees, who seemed all too happy to talk to me out front on the lawn after services, because Franco's forces in Spain had trapped the Lincoln–Washington Battalion in the south at Tortosa and destroyed it, leaving few survivors. "They got what was coming to 'em," Mr. Tamplee said. "God does not love the godless. They were Commonists, Reds, looking to bring godless Commonism to Amurrica. I say good riddance to bad rubbish."

The following week I got a long, beautiful letter from Phoebe. It and my mushy letter to her had crossed in the mail.

Joy called me from Huntsville one afternoon while Chester was still at the prison. She was crying. She said she had gone to the doctor with her slight bleeding problem—spotting, she called it—and he had said that the baby was in danger because of her car wreck, and she had to be very careful from now on, no sex, and Chester was really upset about it. I sympathized with her and told her the baby came first, and Chester would just have to make do with her other

233

talents. She laughed, but she sounded like reality was starting to intrude pretty rudely into her life.

I scribbled out a letter of some kind to Phoebe almost every day, but hers started slacking off, and finally they stopped. She had been gone only a little over a month. Rereading her last few letters, I realized she had been telling me between the lines that we were sliding away from each other. I discussed it with Mom and she said it was likely that Phoebe had a boyfriend up there before, and they'd gotten back together. I was bitter for a while, but not as bitter as I thought I would be. When I reflected back on how many times I'd missed Joy while Phoebe and I had been having sort of pale sex, I realized what had happened was the best thing for both of us.

Mr. Potter died. We hardly knew the Potters, but because he had always been so nice to me, treating me like a person instead of something that would someday with luck become a person, which was the usual way boys my age were treated, I felt a sense of loss. Mom cried. She went to the funeral. She said nobody she had ever had any dealings with had ever been nicer to her. She had been late with the mortgage payments so often I think she felt like she had lost a protector, too.

One Saturday while I was listening to the Kentucky Derby on the radio, Chester called. It was just at the wrong time. The horses were coming down the stretch and Eddie Arcaro was about to win, on a horse named Lawrin. I had a nickel bet with Mom, so she was listening with me. I told Chester to hold on. Lawrin won, I won the nickel, and Mom went in her room to get it, and I explained to Chester why I had done something unheard of—made somebody hang on when they were calling long distance. He said no, that was okay, he was in Houston.

"Is Joy with you?"

"Naw, she's layin' down. She cain't be on her feet much these days, cain't do much of anything." He sounded a little drunk, and grouchy.

"So how come you're down here in Houston?"

"Aw, I had the day off so I come down to see a couple friends of mine. Why don't you haul yer ass over here to Steve's Place and have a beer with us? You might git some enjoys out of it that would make yer eyes bug out."

I heard female giggles behind him. Then Mom was back, handing me a nickel with great ceremony. "Well, thanks, Chester, but I can't make it. Y'all have a ball, huh, and say hi to Joy."

That phone call really put me down in the dumps. Everything seemed to be going wrong at once in the world. The war news in Europe was getting worse, or sounding worse to me, although I was the first to admit I didn't know how to evaluate it. Not only was Hitler down in Rome reviewing Mussolini's troops, but British Prime Minister Neville Chamberlain was telling everybody what a nice guy Il Duce was, and the Pope was agreeing with him. A lot of people were speaking out against Hitler, and Mussolini, and Franco, and a lot of other people were hinting that the ones speaking out might be Communists or at least sympathizers, pinkos. Pretty soon the House of Representatives showed how serious they thought the situation was getting by forming a committee called the House Un-American Activities Committee, whose sole purpose was to root out and destroy un-Americanism. Nobody seemed to be quite sure where the dividing line was between being American and not quite being purely American. People started being more careful what they said, because the committee, HUAC, had started calling people before them and grilling them on what they believed and what organizations they belonged to. One of the things that made you un-American was being in the slightest degree pinko, or seeming to be, even if you weren't sure what that meant. When I went to mow the Widow Potter's grass I asked her about it, because I didn't dare ask my professors at Rice for fear that asking about it might be a little bit subversive, like listening to that speaker in Sallyport trying to get volunteers to go to Spain to fight against Franco. Or they might not want to talk about it for fear of putting their jobs in jeopardy. So I just casually, almost jokingly brought the subject up when she came to the front door after I knocked to ask her if it was okay with her to cut the grass that day. I said I wondered if any of our friends were going to get called up to Washington by that Un-American Activities Committee, and I asked her how they found out people were subversive unless they did something to hurt the country. I could feel her staring through the screen at me, wondering if I was a good one to talk to. Finally she opened the screen door and said, "You interested in talking about it, Dubby?"

I was shocked at how much she had changed since Mr. Potter died. She seemed even smaller than before, and thinner. Her face was paler and she was more wrinkled, or seemed to be, and she had bags under her eyes. She was wearing a simple straight-cut black dress and what looked like ballet slippers on her little feet, which made her look even shorter. She was smoking a cigarette in a long holder. Her hair was cut short, almost like a man's, and it looked thinner and whiter than before. I said, "Well, I don't know much about it."

"Come on in and have a cup of coffee with me. Forget about the mowing for now."

I was a little awed by her, and by being invited into her house for a serious conversation. I knew she had been to a couple of European universities, so I figured I was out of my league intellectually.

Her house was dark and crowded with old-fashioned furniture and bric-a-brac, and the floors were covered with antique oriental rugs which looked pretty worn. I had the feeling that the Potters had been well off in the past, and that something bad had happened to them during the Depression, or before.

Mrs. Potter served some strong coffee and some little sticky buns in her kitchen, and we sat at the kitchen table. When she was sitting in a straight chair at the table she didn't look any taller than Jenny. She was like a very old little girl, except that her voice was deep and husky. She took a long drag on her cigarette holder, eyeing me with a steady, calculating look. She didn't seem unfriendly, just serious. "Well, Dubby," she said, "what do you think about it?"

"Well, ma'am, I don't know what to think about it. I haven't really discussed it with anybody, anybody with any, you know, uh, let's say background."

"Background. Yes, I do have some background. I'm glad you came to me about it. I'm proud. It means you think I'll give you a straight answer. Well, I will. A lot of people you know won't agree with this, or they'll say they agree with it, but they won't try to live with it, but in my opinion when a country founded on the idea of freedom starts investigating people for what they believe and what they say, then the investigators ought to be investigated. I'm not being too blunt for you, am I, Dubby?" She said it all with a gentle hoarse voice and a nice smile, almost apologetically nice.

236

"Too blunt? No, ma'am." It would've been too blunt for Mom, I thought. When she'd heard about HUAC she'd said, "It's about time."

Mrs. Potter and I talked for about an hour. She told me about life in Russia when she was a girl, and how she and Mr. Potter fled the pogroms against Jews more than forty years ago, ending up first in England, then in Italy, then in France, and finally in the United States, almost thirty years ago. "We became Americans," she said, "citizens. And I truly believe that no one every understood better than Mr. Potter and me what it means to be a United States citizen, what a privilege, what a blessing it is. And yet, even here . . ." Her voice trailed off, and for a little while she was silent and seemed deeply saddened. Then she perked up and fitted another cigarette into her holder. "Would you like one, Dubby?" I hesitated, then took a cigarette. "I'm sure your mother would not approve of my offering you that," she said with a little laugh. "But if you smoke, why be dishonest about it?"

"Yes, ma'am, I guess it is dishonest to hide it, but I just don't want to hurt her feelings, somehow."

"I understand. Listen, Dubby, the one thing I want to be sure you give a lot of thought to is this: When the government intimidates people into not saying what they think, the people lose their power to express ideas. If we lose freedom of ideas, what have we really lost?"

The question scared me. I had expected her to tell me, not ask me. I wanted to impress her, to make her realize I'd been listening, that I understood. I thought hard for a few seconds, realizing that the longer I had to think to get the answer, the stupider she probably was going to think I was. Finally, I took a deep breath and said, "Freedom."

"Bravo," she said, in that scratchy whisper of hers. "Freedom. Which is to say everything. So let me tell you what I think of Mr. Martin Dies and his little band of inquisitors. They ought to be renamed the Un-American House Activities Committee, and if they were ever to call me before them, which they'll never do because I'm not important enough, I'll be only too happy to tell them so. But you, Dubby, don't spread your wings too soon. If you have an idea that you want to speak out, by all means do so, but try not to infuriate the

237

authorities who have direct power over your academic career. I hope you'll be able to finish college before we're pulled into this war."

"You really think that's going to happen?"

"I hate to say it, and I pray I'm wrong, but—yes."

This sounded pretty farfetched to me. I put it down to her being depressed because of Mr. Potter's death and seeing only the dark side of things. She tried to give me fifty cents when I left because, she said, she'd used up my lawn-mowing time and kept me from earning it, but I insisted she keep it as partial payment for her frank insights and clarifications. She said most of my professors at Rice would have told me the same things if I had known which ones were willing to discuss the subject.

It was exciting to go home custodian of such dangerous concepts as every person having the right to say what they think without fear of government reprisal. I was tempted to throw caution to the winds and challenge Mom. I felt superior. I was in the know. Then, as usual, I started rationalizing, making excuses for her illiberal mind-set. Hadn't she spent her young girlhood in a bookless world with a Cherokee mother and a truck-gardening, storekeeping father? Hadn't she lost her mother young and been presented with a stepmother and five stepbrothers within a few months of having become the fifteen-year-old lady of the house? Hadn't she and her younger sister lived in terror while their lawless stepbrothers beat them and threatened them with death and almost succeeded in raping them, till driven away by their father at the point of a Colt .45? Hadn't she run away from home the day after receiving her high school diploma? Married to a frequently out-of-work carpenter, living from hand to mouth, trying to raise a family, boiling water in a pot over a woodfire to wash clothes, struggling with no running water, no plumbing, no electricity, and often no money to keep body and soul together? What possible chance was there ever for her to go to a university and have her mind opened to the vasty reaches of learning?

Like what's happened to your mind, you hope, Woodrow Wilson Johnson, with her help and sacrifices, you ungrateful, arrogant whelp.

I found myself ashamed of my unearned privilege and the advantage I had over Mom. But wasn't she proud of what her vision had helped me accomplish? She was, but that didn't give me the right to lord it over her, to use it to gain ascendancy, to threaten her authority.

I decided the mature thing to do would be to hide my special awareness of the way HUAC was mocking our Constitution.

Fool, self-satisfied whippersnapper, this is your mother, the reason for you, the cause of you. You're eighteen, her pride and joy. Share your thoughts with her, be closer to her. It'll do you both good to avoid your usual games of intellectual dodge-'em, even if it ends with her standard line: "Honey, you *think* you're right, but I *know* I'm right."

Mom was ready to go out when I got home at about a quarter of five. She was dressed for church, and she was excited; it was a meeting to select a new reader. I suspected the excitement was because for years she had yearned to be selected as a reader—an honor she would decline because of her apparently incurable panic when called upon to speak in public. She had tried once to speak at a PTA meeting, and had found herself tongue-tied. But to be asked would have thrilled her. As she bustled around doing last-minute things I said, "Mom, I've been wondering about this Un-American Activities Committee. What are they going to do to people?"

"Well, honey, if the people turn out to be Communists, let's say, they'll probably put them in jail."

"Even if they haven't done anything?"

"But if they're Communists they *have* done something."

"What've they done?"

"They've adopted ideas, and sometimes tried to spread those ideas, that aren't in the best interest of our democratic society."

"But I thought our democracy was based on freedom of speech, freedom of thought."

"It absolutely is, honey, but everything is relative. You have your finals coming up. You ought to be thinking about trigonometry, not the House of Representatives. Let our elected congressmen handle these things, honey. Thank God we have the House and the Senate to keep Franklin D. Roosevelt from going hog-wild. Dubby, honey, I'm in a hurry right now, but let me just say this: Don't listen to leftist propaganda. Remember the Pledge of Allegiance. And someday you'll understand."

She hurried out to her car, breathless and aflutter with anticipation. She had actually said to me that someday I'd understand. I tried not to think about the last time somebody had said that to me—Danny

Diamond in his Roadmaster, on the subject of pooched-out lips. It made me feel very alone in the world.

Jenny came out of her room with her ball and jacks, wanting me to play with her. Mom had waited for me to get home before leaving for church.

"Mom said you was gonna be home in time for her not to be late, and you done it," she said.

"Did it."

"That's what I said. Come on, play jacks, Dubby."

We started playing on the front porch and immediately I was on a run. I got onesies, twosies, threesies, foursies. Then the phone rang. "You answer it, Jenny. I'm going for fivesies."

"You might cheat."

"I'm not going to cheat! Answer the phone!" I made fivesies and went for sixies. The phone kept right on ringing. Jenny reluctantly stopped watching me and went in to answer it.

"I'm watching through the window! Don't cheat! Hello . . . what?"

I made sixies. That was all the jacks. I threw them out again and went for sevensies. I heard Jenny saying, "What? I cain't hear you. Who?" I missed sevensies and went in the house. Jenny handed me the phone. She had a disgusted, puzzled look on her face.

I said, "Hello, this is Dub. Who's this?"

On the other end I couldn't hear anything except sounds like somebody strangling or sobbing. Finally I made out a muffled, jerky gurgle that could've been "W. W.", but I couldn't be sure. Nobody called me W. W. but Mrs. Hurt, and it sounded like her voice, like it could be her voice. She pronounced it "Dubyadubya."

"Is this Miz Hurt? Is that you, Miz Hurt? What's the matter? Is something the matter?" The line was empty for a few seconds, but I heard sounds in the background.

Jenny said, "Come on, Dubby."

"Hold your horses."

"What'd you git up to?"

"Sevensies."

"You didn't do sixies!"

"Yes, I did." Somebody was talking to me, a new voice. I said to Jenny, "Hush!"

The voice, a male one, said, "Is this W. W. Johnson?"

"Yes. Yes, sir." The voice sounded like it ought to be called "sir."

"This is Dr. Guest, at Heights Hospital."

Oh, God, Mom's been in a wreck. No, she hasn't been gone long enough.

"I'm calling for Mrs. Hurt. Her daughter's been in an accident. She's been asking for—"

"Is it serious?"

"Could you come to the hospital?"

"How bad is it?"

"I can't give you a prognosis at this time, Mr. Johnson. Are you available to come to the hospital?"

"Yes. Yes sir, Doctor. I'll be right there." I hung up. What would I do with Jenny? Mom never left her alone.

"Come on, Dubby."

"Jenny, honey, I gotta go to the hospital."

"You sick?"

"No, something's happened. A friend of mine. Joy. She's been in a wreck."

"Is she dead?"

"No. I don't know. No, she's not. Look, I'll drop you at Rosey's house. You can play with her till I get back."

Jenny objected, saying that Rosey always beat her at jacks, but I reminded her that she always won at hopscotch, and by then we were there and Jenny was yelling, "Le's play hopscotch!"

I ran all the way to Heights Hospital. It was only three and a half short blocks and I made it in record time. Mrs. Hurt was in the little lobby, sort of collapsed on a bench, with a nurse beside her. There was a man leaning against the wall, looking down at the floor. He looked like Chester, only younger.

Mrs. Hurt looked up at me when I came in, but her mouth just went open and shut without words coming out. The nurse got up and met me halfway across the lobby.

"Are you W. W.?"

"Yes, ma'am. Where's Joy?"

"She's in emergency. You won't be able to see her now. Emergency was occupied with a gunshot victim when she got here, and she was calling for you, but—"

"Is she gonna be okay?"

"You'll have to talk to the doctors about that."

241

"Naw, she ain't!" The man who looked like Chester had been staring at me and had finally strode toward me. He was very agitated. "Naw! That's the answer! You don't need no doctor to tell you! I see 'er! She's all cut up! You're Dubby, ain't you? I'm Check's brother! He ain't gonna be all right, nuther! He's—he's—" He started sobbing. The nurse tried to put her arm around him. He pulled away. "His spinal cord—the doc tol' me—he went through the winshiel'! It's cut! Cut! You git it? Git the pitcher? Ain't never gonna move nothin' south of his belly button agin! I heard the doctor! Heard 'im say it!" He fell to his knees on the floor, crying. A square-built doctor came through a door and grabbed him and jerked him to his feet, shaking him.

"You be quiet! Quiet, you hear me? Your brother doesn't know anything about his condition, and you're not the one to tell him! If you don't be quiet I'm going to put you out on the street!"

"I'm sorry," Chester's brother whimpered, barely audible. He staggered to an empty bench and collapsed onto it, his head in his hands.

I sat beside him, in the only available spot on the two short benches. Heights Hospital was small. No wonder the doctor was angry at Chester's brother. A person with a loud voice could be heard probably in the farthest corner. We sat in silence. All I could hear was Mrs. Hurt's strange low moan-wail sound. Then I heard a scream from somewhere in the building, and silence again. Then the doctor came out and motioned to the nurse, who was still consoling Mrs. Hurt. The nurse went to him and they conferred in whispers for about a minute, then the nurse went to Chester's brother and said, "If you think you can behave yourself you can go in and see your brother for a few minutes. But if you tell him anything the doctor will have you arrested, do you hear? You don't know anything. Not anything. You understand?"

"Yes, ma'am. I swear."

"Come on. I'm going in with you." She started to lead him away.

"Ma'am," I said, "could I maybe see 'im after his brother's through? He's my friend."

"We'll see."

They went out. Mrs. Hurt continued making her strange sounds. After about five minutes Chester's brother came out with the nurse. His face was white and his eyes were starey and set in the distance.

He was like a blind man. He walked to the bench under some kind
of a spell, then he saw me and stared at me like I had suddenly
appeared out of nowhere. "She done it," he said. "She done it."

"What did she do?"

He screamed like a man hit with a red-hot branding iron, which I
had seen happen one time in a fight down on the Circle J. There's
not any sound like it. "SHE DONE IT A-PURPOSE! SHE
STEERED A-PURPOSE HEAD-ON INTO THE CONCRETE
PILLAR DOIN' NINETY MILE A HOUR! A-PURPOSE!"

Mrs. Hurt was staring at him. "That's a lie," she growled.

"HE TOL' ME! HE SAID IT! SHE DONE IT A-PURPOSE!
TO KILL 'EM BOTH!"

The doctor charged into the lobby and threw a body block into
him and knocked him up against the front door. Then he grabbed
him in a choke hold to shut him up and twisted one arm behind him
and shoved him out the door. The whole thing took only a few
seconds. Then he shut the door and bolted it from the inside. "That
kind of activity is not allowed in this hospital," he said, panting just a
little, but unruffled otherwise. He stuck his head in a side door.
"Mrs. Dudley," he said, to an unseen person, "get the cops over here
to take care of that fellow." Then he went into the interior of the
hospital through another door.

Mrs. Hurt was on her feet, swaying. The nurse steadied her. "He's
lyin'," she said. "That's a lie, what he said there. Joy wouldn' do
that."

"You just set down and try to calm yourself, Miz Hurt," the nurse
said, and Mrs. Hurt obeyed.

"Joy would never do a thing like that."

"I know. Of course not."

"She wouldn't. She just wouldn't."

The nurse turned to me. "If you want to go in, it's upstairs in
three-oh-one. I got to stay here. You'll behave yerself, okay? You
don't know a doggone thing. There's a nurse on the floor. She'll give
you five minutes. Cheer 'im up a little, but don't git rambunctious.
Jus' keep 'im calm. The elevator's through those double doors."

"Yes, ma'am." I went through the doors she indicated and took the
elevator to the third floor. Chester was in some kind of a contraption
that covered everything but his head. His bed was butted up against
the wall between two windows. When I walked around to the head of

his bed I found myself looking out the window down on the goldfish pond and the bench where Joy showed me a couple of things that night after my fight in the park. I thought I might be looking out the same window that old man was standing at to watch us. That picture was in my mind ahead of Chester's wasted face. "Man alive, you'll do anything to keep from having to go to work," I said.

"She tried to kill us," Chester said, before I had sat down in the chair beside his bed.

"Oh, she wouldn't—"

"Done 'er damnedest. Bitch. Plumb loco."

"She's just a bum driver, Chester. She's crazy about you. She wouldn't do that. She's always dreaming about you and her and babies—a nice family, nice home—"

"Takes ever'thang too serious." He spoke slowly, his voice a tired monotone. "Dad-blamed duck in the oven changed her back into a virgin agin. Cut off my supply of poontang."

"The doctor told her she couldn't—"

"Dubby, buddy, you cain't cut off a man's daily supply of poontang. I ditten mean no harm. It wasn't like cheatin' or anythang. She takes everythang too serious."

"What do you mean?"

"I went out to git serviced a couple times, like a man gotta do. No big deal. She th'owed a fit like ten cats tied in a tow sack. Then she tells me she got to go to the doctor so she gotta keep the car, drop me at the pen, then pick me up later. Fine. Then she calls the warden's office an' says can I git off early, she got to go to Houston to a specialist, can I go with 'er. Fine. She come by, says she wants to drive. Fine. We take off down Forty-five South. I'm tryna ask 'er how she's doin', what the doctor said, stuff like that, she don't say diddly. I see she's pickin' up speed. She got wet cheeks, tears rollin' the way women do to git their way. Passin' Willis she's hittin' 'bout sixty. I says, 'Joy, honey, watch yer foot there, gittin' heavy, highway patrol prowling down here.' She keeps on pushin' down. Conroe goes by 'bout like eighty. Then I hear that fuckin' si-reen. I say, 'Joy, goddammit, now you got a bull on our tail. Pull over an' sweet-talk 'im.' 'Like you done me?' she says, an' floorboards the sonofabitch. We're comin' up on the San Jacinto River Bridge. I'm yellin' at 'er to slow down. We're hittin' ninety on the speedometer of that pretty white DeSoto o' mine—oh, my God, my pretty car, pore thang—Anyhow, she was like to take off an' join the clouds, leavin' that damn highway patrol in the dust, but I could still hear that si-reen. I see the San Jacinto River Bridge comin' at us. I'm yellin' at 'er slow down, an' she's yellin' right back at me, 'King Chet! Queen Joy! An' our little ole prince in my belly! Here we come, God! Here we come, heaven!' An' she headed dead-on fer that goddamn concrete thing, that pillar-type deal right there as you git to the bridge. I grabbed 'er arm an' tried to straighten 'er up but . . ." He trailed off, his face all twisted up. "Jesus," he said. "Jesus, I wisht I had me a smoke. Jesus." He was crying. A gray-headed nurse stopped in the door and said I had to go. I stood up. "When I git outa here, Dubby, you an' me's gonna have some fun. I'm done bein' married. I ain't goin' back. Her an' me's done-fer. She's too loco fer my blood. Hey, Dubby, they prolly gonna keep me here a few days. You gonna come see me, huh? Sneak me a smoke in here, huh? Come see me."

"Okay, Chester, I will. Take care of yourself." I went out. I knew I had lied. I wasn't coming to see him. I wasn't going to have any more friends like Chester, not if I could help it.

Coming down in the elevator I heard screaming in the lobby. Hysteria. I knew. I don't know how I knew, but I knew. When I pushed through the swinging doors into the lobby Mrs. Hurt was out of control. The doctor and the nurse were trying to restrain her. She was yelling "NO!NO!NO!NO!NO!NO!NO! NOT MY BABY! NOT MY BABY! NO!"

Her brother Phil came through the front door and saw what was happening and jumped in to help hold her. I stood there like a cedar post for a few seconds. I figured if I was ever going to cry, this was a good time, but my training was too strong. I couldn't cry. Any time I was supposed to, something was there to shut it off. The only exception since I was a little boy was when I had that long confessional with Mom. That time it just happened when I didn't want it to. This time I felt I ought to, but nothing happened. I left. Nobody seemed to notice.

Mom lent me her car so I could leave my French final exam and drive straight to the funeral. I didn't know what I wrote on the exam. I didn't remember any of it as I parked at the church and hurried in. I wore my suit and a new conservative tie Mom bought for the occasion. The casket wasn't open. The undertaker had not been able to fix her up so people could look. Not many people were there. I saw Phil and a couple I took to be Joy's brother Roy and his wife Erna in the front row with Mrs. Hurt.

The Reverend Hollowitz, the same preacher who had come with Mrs. Hurt to see me and Mom when Joy ran away from the clinic with Chester, said a lot of nice things about Joy, all or most of which were lies, but he spoke them with a lot of conviction, which I guess is part of a preacher's training. I couldn't help thinking that Joy might've been even better than he made her out to be if she'd had half a chance in this world from the start, instead of having her soul and spirit kicked and punched out of shape from the opening bell, till she was so full of hate and pain she didn't care whether school kept or not, and finally tried to kill her latest source of pain and busted dreams and look for happiness in the arms of God. If she had a way of knowing Chester was going to spend the rest of his life in a wheel-chair, useless to women instead of being dead, she probably would think it had worked out just fine.

The graveyard they were going to put her in was different from the one where her daddy was buried. I knew that if Joy could've had her wish she'd've been put down next to her daddy. I had heard people claim that when you depart this world you can link up with the people you loved in life, but as far as I knew nobody had ever proved it one way or the other. I hoped it was true, but I doubted it.

I didn't follow the short procession of cars with their lights on out to the cemetery because I knew what they were going to do when they got there. They were going to put her at the bottom of a dark hole and throw dirt on her. That was something I did not want to watch.